DUKES, ROGUES & VILLAINS

A DARK HISTORICAL COLLECTION

JOANNA SHUPE

MY DIRTY DUKE

Violet knows that her father's best friend, the Duke of Ravensthorpe, is the most powerful man in all of London with a reputation for sin.

But nothing can stop Violet from wanting to shed her wallflower ways and fulfill her darkest, most forbidden desires…even if it means seducing a man twice her age.

CHAPTER
ONE

IT WAS the social event of the year and Violet was squandering it. She should have been dancing or chatting with friends. Instead, she was propped against the wall, hiding in plain sight, staring at him.

She could not stop staring at him.

The ballroom was filled with titled lords and ladies, but she was always able to find him. He was tall, nearly the tallest man in any room. Elegantly dressed. Starkly handsome, without frills to pretty up his visage. His features were strong, harsh like a Roman warrior, with dark hair, and eyes like twin pools of midnight. If she could photograph him right now, the caption would read, "Feared by most, revered by the rest."

Once upon a time he spoke to her with kind words, during her parents' dinner parties when she was deemed old enough to attend. That was before finishing school. Before her debut. Violet fell in love with him then, this intelligent and beautiful man who commanded every room.

At the time, she hadn't a clue as to why her stomach dipped and swirled in his presence. Now, at eighteen, she understood. She'd read books and seen racy photographs. Moreover, she'd overheard the maids talking about their beaus. So, Violet knew why her breathing quickened around him, knew the reason for the slickness between her thighs when she thought about being alone with him. Why she possessed this mad desire to have him smile at her again.

He never looked at her, though. Not once. Nor did he visit her father, his closest friend, at their home any longer. Since Violet's debut, he'd not asked her to dance, though most of her father's friends had indulged her at least once. He hadn't even spoken to her during her season. It was as if she were beneath his notice.

But then, most of London was beneath him. He was a duke.

And not merely any duke. His was one of the wealthiest and oldest of the titled families, the Duke of Ravensthorpe, Maximilian Thomas William Bradley III. She once looked his lineage up in Debrett's and learned that the very first Ravensthorpe received the title after thwarting an assassination attempt against Charles II.

"Why are you not dancing?" Her friend Charlotte appeared, her gaze studying Violet's face. "You are forever on the outskirts, observing. You should be having fun."

"I am taking a break."

"Who were you watching?" Charlotte's head swung about, searching. "Was it that newly widowed viscount everyone is talking about? He is scrumptious—and under thirty years of age."

"There is a newly widowed viscount?"

"Have you not heard? Honestly, Violet. What do you do with your time at these things?"

Stare at Ravensthorpe, obviously. "Why should I exert myself to learn all the latest gossip when I have you to do that for me?"

Charlotte laughed. "Fair enough. Tell me, at whom are you staring? Perhaps I can help you get his attention."

"Do not be silly. There is no one here for me. Just a bunch of old dukes and boring dandies."

"The dandies are quite nice to look at, however. Better than the stodgy dukes."

Not all dukes are stodgy, Violet wanted to say. Some were quite glorious.

"I wish I had my camera," she told her friend. "Then I could prove to you how not boring it is to watch."

Her father had gifted her with a camera two years ago and Violet had been taking photographs ever since. She'd converted a space in their attic into a developing room and had been studying photography at London Polytechnic for the last six months. She liked the challenge of photography, of achieving the perfect image. One of her dreams was to someday photograph Ravensthorpe, to capture the harsh angles and pretty features of his face. The cool stare and the haughty lift of his brow. Then she could have the image forever.

Such was the advantage of photographs. They were a way to record an instant, preserve a memory that might otherwise have been forgotten to the sands of time. Who knew what sorts of discoveries were ahead as cameras grew more advanced?

Violet continued to watch Ravensthorpe out of the corner of her eye so as not to alarm Charlotte. Her friend would try to dissuade Violet from her singular purpose this season, which was to somehow get Ravensthorpe to notice her. Again.

Suddenly, a woman walked behind Ravensthorpe and lightly touched his shoulder. The edge of the duke's mouth hitched and he leaned to whisper in the woman's ear. She was a countess, wife to the Earl of Underhill. Whatever the duke said must have satisfied her because she nodded once, and then slipped through the terrace doors.

An assignation?

Envy spiked in Violet's blood, violent and sharp, like she had poked herself with an embroidery needle. Charlotte kept talking, not taking notice of Violet's discomfort, and Violet was glad for it. She needed to gain control over her emotions.

Perhaps Ravensthorpe would not go. He would reconsider and decide—

Her stomach sank as he excused himself and followed the countess out the terrace doors. Definitely an assignation. She could hardly catch her breath; jealousy lodged in her lungs. She longed to beckon him to the gardens where she could touch and kiss him, explore that generous mouth and bask in his stern gaze . . .

Violet fanned herself vigorously as she burned with curiosity. What would Ravensthorpe and the countess do in the gardens, kiss? Fellatio? Sexual congress?

There was so much more she needed to know. For example, was Ravensthorpe a bold and demanding lover? Selfish? Or was he eager to please, as many of the erotic photographs she'd seen depicted? Perhaps if she learned more about what he liked, then she stood a better chance of getting him to notice her.

Charlotte must have perceived that Violet's attention had wandered. "Violet? One minute you are flushed and the next, pale as flour. What is wrong with you?"

She had to go. She had to see what was about to happen in the gardens. There wasn't a moment to lose.

Gripping Charlotte's arm, she kissed her friend's cheek. "I apologize. I'm not feeling well. I think I shall tell my father I'd like to go home."

Charlotte nodded, her expression brimming with affection and concern. "Excellent idea. Go on, then. Rest. I'll call on you tomorrow."

Violet bid Charlotte good night, then wove through the crowd, pretending to search for her father. In reality, her goal was to lose Charlotte and blend into the crush. With a final check to ensure no one was watching, she slipped through the French doors and onto the terrace.

The night smelled of lilacs and fresh dirt. Only a sliver of moon added to the soft torchlight along the edge of the garden path. Lifting her skirts, she moved carefully, desperate to not make any noise. She had been to this house before and knew the garden was designed as a large square, with a fountain at the far end. Tall hedges surrounded the path, high enough to offer cover to any couple. Her guess was that Ravensthorpe and the countess would meet near the fountain, farthest from the house.

She found a break in the bushes large enough to slip through and continued along the outside of the hedges bordering the lawn. Likely her slippers were ruined but she could not stop, not when she was close to discovering more about the duke. Sartorial sacrifices were necessary in the pursuit of all things Ravensthorpe.

Silent, she made her way along, allowing the hedge to be her guide in the dark. Near the final corner, she heard a lady's light laughter and a deep chuckle.

Ravensthorpe.

She crept closer, hardly daring to breathe. She needed to hear and see it all, so she bent and peered through the branches. After some maneuvering, she finally located the perfect vantage spot. Two figures were locked in an embrace, one of them clearly the duke.

Light from the house provided enough illumination to see that Ravensthorpe was kissing the countess, her body pressed tightly to his long frame. He clutched her waist with one hand while his other hand massaged her clothed breast. Violet's own nipples stiffened to peaks under her corset, the crisp air a delicious torture on her hot skin. The couple was ravenous, their mouths attacking one another between gasps of air.

In a flash, Ravensthorpe spun the countess so her back rested against his front, with both of them now facing Violet. He wrapped one set of his long fingers around the woman's throat as he shoved his other hand into her bodice. He lifted her breast out of her dress and undergarments, exposing it before caressing the plump flesh. His mouth slid along her cheek as the countess's lids fell shut, her lips parted with her rapid breathing.

"Look at you," he said, his voice like smooth silk. "A dirty girl with your gorgeous tit out. Ask me nicely and maybe I'll play with you."

"Please, Ravensthorpe," the countess whispered on a groan. "Oh, please."

Violet swallowed, her throat clogged with desire. Could they hear her heart pounding inside her chest? She would give anything to trade places with the older woman. Had the countess any idea of her good fortune?

"How pretty you are when you beg, Louisa."

Using the pads of his fingers, he stroked the taut bud at the tip of the countess's breast, pulling and pinching it. Louisa writhed, rubbing her body along his as he continued to work her, his other hand never leaving her throat.

Blood pooled between Violet's legs, her quim pulsing in time with her heartbeat. He was beautiful and compelling, an angel of sin and lust. Light reflected off the threads of silver at his temples, the effect like a match to her insides. She had never wanted anything or anyone more in all her eighteen years.

"If I lift your skirts, will I find you wet?" he asked.

Yes, Violet wanted to answer. *So very wet.*

The countess panted. "Oh, God. You . . ."

"Yes?"

"I cannot think. Please, do not stop."

"Do you need my cock, Louisa? Shall I place you over the end of that bench there and fuck you?"

Violet pressed her thighs together to ease her aching flesh. Sweet mother of mercy, he was potent. The angles of his face were harsh and unforgiving, his mouth almost cruel in its lasciviousness. Again she longed for her camera, wishing she could capture him in this stolen moment.

The countess shuddered at his words. "I cannot. As much as I crave you, I must return."

"What is another moment when I can make you come so hard?"

"Oh, you devil." She drew in a deep breath and covered his hand to stop his movements. "Unfortunately, I need to get back. I've been away too long. My husband will be wondering where I've gone."

"Hmm." Shifting her clothing, he tucked her breast away. Then he released her. "I suppose we will need to pick this up later, then."

The countess turned and bit his jaw, then drew her fingertip along the heavy ridge in his trousers. Ravensthorpe sucked in a breath, and she smiled. "Tonight, Ravensthorpe. Leave your side door unlatched. We'll play one of our naughty games."

Without waiting for his agreement, the countess hurried along the path toward the house. Ravensthorpe stood unmoving for a long moment, his chest rising and lowering in his evening clothes. A lock of dark hair had fallen over his forehead, a stripe of ink slashing his perfect skin. Violet could not look away, completely entranced.

He finally raised his head—only to pin her with a dark stare. "You may come out now, little mouse."

————

Violet froze.

Little mouse?

Was he talking to her? She had been so quiet, completely concealed by the hedges. Heavens, she was standing on the lawn. He couldn't possibly know she was there.

Cold terror filled her lungs as he walked directly toward her. She considered running, but where would she go? He'd see her for certain the instant she took off.

Bending, he came eye to eye with her from the other side of the hedge. "Come out of there, Violet. Now."

The tone was decidedly ducal, one used to being obeyed, and dread and embarrassment washed over her entire body. Violet prayed for the ground to open up and swallow her whole. She'd wanted him to notice her, but not like this. Never like this. She'd only wished to watch him with the countess like a voyeur hidden in the dark.

The hedges parted thanks to Ravensthorpe's arm, and there was soon enough room for her to slip through the branches. She tugged her skirts free, no doubt ripping the delicate silk. Clothing, however, was the least of her concerns.

Ravensthorpe's eyes were like frozen ice, a winter storm that chilled her to the bone. He put some distance between them, and his mouth was set in a flat, unhappy line when he whirled around. "What in hell do you think you are playing at?"

Her mind blanked in the face of his anger. "I went out for a walk."

"A lie. No lady walks on the lawn and risks her slippers." He pointed to her now-ruined footwear. "Again, what are you doing here?"

What happened if she admitted the truth? Would he finally see her as an adult, not some silly child he'd ignored for the past two years? She hated that he no longer talked to her. He acted as if she didn't exist, instead spending time with women who were married to other men, like the countess. What was so wrong with Violet?

"You are trying my patience, little mouse."

The truth fell from her lips. "I followed you."

"That is obvious," he said, the words like icicles, sharp and brittle. "What I cannot fathom is why."

"I was curious as to the type of woman who attracted you." She winced, but there was no taking it back now.

"Again, why?"

God above, was it not obvious? Was he actually going to make her speak it aloud?

You have nothing to lose. You have already embarrassed yourself.

"Because I wished to take her place, Your Grace."

Ravensthorpe dragged a hand down his face. Turning, he went to the iron bench near the fountain and sat, his long legs spread out before him. Violet wrapped her arms around herself, feeling like the world's biggest fool.

"Violet, you must return to the house and forget this ever happened. You must forget *me*. There are dozens of men in there tonight who would gladly share a tryst with you."

"But they are not you," she whispered.

He winced as if struck. "I am far too old for you."

Old? She paused, blinking at him. He was not old. He was male perfection wrapped in a cloak of confidence and swagger. She'd seen plenty of decrepit men and Ravensthorpe was far from that group. Besides, it was nothing for a lord his age to wed a debutante. Such matches happened every season. "You are forty-one. Hardly old."

"No, but I am too old *for you*. I am your father's friend. I've known you since you were born, for God's sake."

"You are two years younger than my father, if memory serves."

He gave a dry laugh. "Christ, Violet. Are you trying to say two years makes a difference?"

"I don't care how old you are." There. She'd said it.

"You should. It would be far better for you to find a man your own age. Or close to it."

She cared little for the men her age. Foppish fools who worried more about appearances than anything else. During dances, they merely stared at her bosom and stepped on her toes.

Besides, how could she ever be interested in anyone other than Ravensthorpe? He'd starred in her dreams for so long there wasn't room for anyone else in her head. "I don't want a man my age." *I want you.*

"You are eighteen. You have a lifetime ahead of you. Find someone to share that life with, someone who makes you happy."

He appeared less angry at the moment and more like the kind man she remembered, so she decided to present him with a reasonable argument. "Many girls my age marry older men. It's common amongst the ton."

"Are you . . . Is this about becoming a duchess?" He sounded horrified. "Even if we were closer in age, I am not interested in marriage, ever. I will never take another wife."

She hadn't known his feelings on marriage, but she didn't care about titles. She wanted the man, end of story. If that was outside of marriage, so be it. "I am not proposing marriage, Your Grace."

"Christ, do not use my honorific in that tone of voice."

Why? She'd called him "Your Grace" hundreds of times. "I apologize, duke." It was a more personal form of address, one he would reserve for intimate members of his circle. She hoped to one day join that inner circle, whispering in his ear whilst they were in bed.

"Fuck, that is worse." Standing, he put his hands on his hips, an imposing tower of disapproval. Something about his scowl made her want to bow and scrape for his admiration. She nearly licked her lips. He said, "You are the daughter of my closest friend. This is inappropriate and needs to end, Violet."

She would not back down, not without answers. "Is that why you stopped talking to me? Why you won't even look at me anymore?"

He glanced away, not meeting her eyes. "I have no idea what you are talking about. I do not interact with children."

"You did. With me. For years and years. And then you stopped like I'd contracted smallpox."

"That was before. When it was harmless."

"What does that mean? Have I hurt you in some manner?" She didn't understand. He was speaking in riddles. She had made her position clear, yet could he not do the same?

A muscle jumped in his jaw. "Before you developed breasts and hips. Not to mention an arse I'd like to sink my teeth into. Have you no looking glass? Your body is made for sin and your face would make angels weep." He dragged a hand through his hair. "You have every man panting after you the second you walk into a bloody room."

Violet's knees wobbled. The air left her lungs and she feared she might faint. This was what Ravensthorpe thought of her? Lord above. She was rounder than most girls her age, with their tiny waists and bosoms that barely peeked out from their gowns. Indeed, she was what her mother called "robust."

But Ravensthorpe liked the way she looked. He said she had every man panting when she walked into a room. Did that mean him as well?

Was this why he no longer talked to her?

Men were so confusing.

"I don't understand," she said. "If you like the way I look, then why ignore me?"

Something dangerous flashed in his gaze. "You must stay away from me, Violet."

"Why? I am not pressuring you for marriage. I merely want . . ."

Heavy, angry footsteps brought him directly in front of her. "To fuck me. Is that it, little mouse? Do you need me to put my cock inside you and make you scream?"

Lust rushed through her veins, heavy and thick, and her lips parted as she exhaled. Lord, she wanted that so badly. To experience all she'd seen in those erotic photographs with the man standing in front of her.

He read the answer on her face. "Have you ever been fucked, Violet? Had a man's fingers inside your tight pussy? Or maybe a thick cock?" When she said nothing, he barked, "Answer me."

"No." She hadn't considered even trying with anyone other than the man standing in front of her.

"Do you even know what it's like to make yourself come? Do you stroke your clitoris under the covers at night, or perhaps in the bath?"

Her mouth dried out, speech impossible. Triumph lit his eyes, as if he'd succeeded in exposing her as inexperienced and unsuitable. "Stay away from me. Do not follow me again. Forget you even know me."

Ravensthorpe stepped around her, his footsteps crunching on the gravel path as he stormed away. She sagged against the prickly hedge behind her, more aroused than she'd ever dreamed possible.

Do you stroke your clitoris?

Was that the place between her legs that she rubbed in order to climax? She might not have learned the proper names, but she had explored her own body. She wasn't nearly as innocent as he thought.

And someday, now that she knew their attraction was reciprocated, she would prove it to him.

CHAPTER
TWO

I AM DESTINED FOR HELL.

Not that Max was a religious man, but the Devil himself was certain to come collect him for the dirty thoughts he harbored for Lady Violet Littleton.

He *burned* for her. So badly he could hardly stand to be in the same room with her. And she was wrong—he *always* noticed her. Since the moment she'd developed into a woman, Max hadn't been able to take his eyes off her. If they were anywhere in close proximity, his body remained in a permanent state of readiness, arousal simmering beneath the surface.

That was precisely how he'd known she was behind the hedge, watching him with Louisa. And then he, God forgive him, put on a prurient show meant to scare Violet away.

Yet he hadn't scared her.

Worse, she'd called him *Your Grace* in the high-pitched, breathy tone used by yielding lovers, those who adored nothing more than getting on their knees and taking whatever he was willing to give them.

Fuck.

He straightened his clothing and tried to compose himself. He was forty-one years old. Far too advanced to feel this twisted giddiness, this dark lust for a girl less than half his age. Hell, he had a son who was two years younger than Violet. Max was positively decrepit in comparison.

Not to mention that he'd fucked plenty of women since losing his virginity at the age of fifteen. Even more after his wife died while delivering their son. He had enjoyed a lifetime of debauchery and pleasure, hardly any of which he regretted. Moreover, he had no plans to give it up, not even for a fresh-faced virgin begging to ride his cock.

Jesus, her father would skin Max alive if he knew.

Max would need to adjust his social schedule for the remainder of the season to ensure Violet and he never attended the same event. It was for the best. She was far too tempting, especially now that she'd admitted her feelings for him.

Because I wished to take her place, Your Grace.

The statement had made him instantly, painfully hard, and it had been followed by a deep sense of shame. The girl was eighteen. A virgin. His friend's only daughter.

What the hell was wrong with him?

Max stepped inside the ballroom, not bothering to close the terrace doors. Charles Littleton, Lord Mayhew and Violet's father, grabbed Max's arm. "Ravensthorpe, have you seen my daughter?"

Charles was one of Max's close friends, a man he'd met shortly after arriving at school, long before he'd become Ravensthorpe. They had crossed cities and continents together, growing up in luxury, as many entitled aristocrats did. They knew each other's darkest secrets —well, all save one.

He forced his expression to remain blank. "No." Max held Charles's gaze like the competent liar he was, thanks to years in Parliament. "I was, ah, outside with Louisa." Not a lie.

Charles chuckled. "Of course you were, you bounder. Never one to pass up the opportunity for quality quim, are you?"

Uneasiness slid through Max. He reminded himself he'd done nothing untoward out there, at least not with Violet. "Cannot seem to help myself."

"I've an appointment myself tonight. Going to a little place on

Holywell Street, one where they all wear masks. Perhaps you'd like to tag along?"

"I thought you said you were scaling back on your nocturnal activities after the missus discovered that you fathered a bastard."

"Well, what she doesn't know won't hurt anyone. So, what do you say?"

"Afraid I have plans, Mayhew. Have a pleasant time. If you'll excuse me."

Max had to get out of here. His skin was crawling with hunger for a girl he could not have. A woman, he supposed, but barely.

Violet was the type of gorgeous woman oblivious to her appeal, which in turn made her all the more appealing. An angel's face with a siren's body. Lush tits barely contained by any neckline, a round arse that beckoned with every stride. A woman built like a mistress, not a wife. In other words, utterly fuckable.

However, he was no green lad lacking in self-control. He could not pursue her. Even if the age difference did not bother him, there was the issue of his friendship with her father. While Max may have been a scoundrel, he was a loyal one. God knew he would not want his profligate friends anywhere near a daughter, if he had one.

No, Charles knew too much of Max's sordid history. Charles would reach for his pistol the instant after hearing word of his daughter in Max's bed. And Max wouldn't even bother to defend against such an egregious breach in friendship. He would deserve a bullet or two for defiling her.

Do you even know what it's like to make yourself come?

No idea why he'd asked such a crude question, other than to frighten her away, but it was clear by her reaction that she had touched herself. In the bath, perhaps? Or, had her seeking fingers drifted beneath the covers at night to stroke and circle her clitoris?

Blast. He had to stop or else he'd grow hard in the middle of this godforsaken ballroom.

Tonight, he would see Louisa and do all manner of wicked things to her. Moreover, he would forget about the blond beauty that haunted his dreams.

"Ravensthorpe."

Max stopped and found Louisa's husband, the Earl of Underhill, at his elbow. Hellfire and damnation. Was he conjuring these men through his illicit thoughts of the women in their lives? "Evening, Underhill."

Underhill wasn't a bad sort, actually. Louisa had been a penniless third cousin to a viscount before Underhill married her twelve years ago. More to the point, he was aware of Max's sexual relationship with his wife. Underhill might even have been relieved over it, seeing as how the Underhills had stopped screwing eons ago.

And, as much as Max loathed it, his mistresses enjoyed an elevated social status during their time together. It had nothing to do with him and everything to do with his title. Still, husbands had been known to leverage that status a time or two, including Underhill.

Sodding aristocracy.

"Need a favor, Ravensthorpe."

Indeed, here came the leverage. "Oh?"

The skin above Underhill's cravat flushed, and he cleared his throat. "I suppose it is unusual considering the circumstances, but I, uh . . ."

Out of the corner of Max's eye he saw Violet slip into the ballroom. Awareness skated over every inch of him, his flesh hot and itchy under his clothes. He had to leave. Piercing the man across from him with a harsh glare, he barked, "Spit it out, Underhill."

The other man leaned in. "I need you to stop seeing Louisa. Just for a time. I'd like to start trying again for a son and, well, you understand."

He couldn't risk raising a duke's bastard. "Have you spoken to her about this?"

"No, but it is her duty to provide me with an heir."

Max smothered a sigh. He was disappointed, but probably not for the reason Underhill assumed. He needed the diversion of a woman closer in age, one who did not make him randy at every turn. Losing Louisa meant he needed to find another woman, fast. "Of course. There were plans for tonight, so . . .?"

"I'll take care of that. Appreciate it, Ravensthorpe."

"I wish you luck. She is a remarkable woman."

They parted and Max wanted to punch the wall in frustration. All he could do was pray his hand would suffice for tonight.

———

Violet's father found her almost the instant she slipped back into the ballroom. Papa was protective of her, especially in settings such as this. Perhaps it was because he was a rogue himself and knew the dangers that lurked during these night events. In fact, Mama frowned every time he left the house after dinner, as if she knew the illicitness he would seek out in those evening hours.

Violet and her parents had never been close. She'd never understood her father's philandering. Mama would yell and carry on, demand he stop seeing other women, and he would settle down for a few months. But the cycle soon repeated itself, her father incapable of remaining faithful, apparently. He never cared about the harm he caused, or the burden on his wife in enduring it.

For her part, Mama seemed unhappy, angry with everyone. Withdrawn. She refused to attend large social gatherings, even during Violet's debut, so Papa escorted Violet about instead.

"There you are," her father said. "You had me scared half to death. Where were you?"

Violet caught Ravensthorpe's tall form across the room where he was speaking with Louisa's husband. The duke appeared uncomfortable, his shoulders stiff and straight, looking nothing like the man who spoke seductive filth in secluded gardens.

You have every man panting after you the second you walk into a room.

"Violet," Papa snapped. "I asked you a question."

"I required fresh air. I went out on the terrace for a moment."

"It is unsafe for you to be there alone. Did you . . . see anyone?"

"No," she lied. "Not a soul."

Her father visibly relaxed. Had he known Ravensthorpe was outside?

"Good. Shall we leave, then?"

Ravensthorpe headed to the door, most likely leaving the ball. With the duke gone, there was no reason to stay. "Of course. I've had my fill of heated ballrooms."

"You are looking flushed. Are you all right?"

"I am?" She patted her cheeks. Was Papa able to see the lust on her face?

Lord Patton suddenly appeared at Papa's elbow. Patton bowed to Violet, his gaze lingering on her bosom in a manner that had her longing for a shawl. She'd never liked the man. He stood too close when speaking with her and found excuses to brush against her whenever possible. It made her skin crawl.

"The lovely Lady Violet." Patton reached for her hand, taking it before she could blink, and brought it to his lips. "Good evening to you, miss."

"My lord," she offered with a curtsy.

"Do you mind if I steal your father away for a moment?" Patton asked. "Then perhaps you'll honor me with a dance?"

She said the first thing that came to mind. "We were just on our way out."

Her father nodded. "We were leaving, but I'll only be a moment, Violet. Meet me by the front entrance, won't you?"

She excused herself and sighed in relief over evading Patton. Perhaps a stop in the ladies' retiring room was in order. At least there she could splash water on her face in an attempt to cool herself after the encounter with Ravensthorpe. The man possessed an uncanny ability to send her up in flames at the snap of his fingers.

The retiring room was empty. She took a moment to relieve herself and clean her hands. When she cracked the door, she discovered Louisa and her husband, Lord Underhill, behind a plant in the corridor, embroiled in what appeared to be a heated exchange. Had Lady Underhill's husband discovered her affair with Ravensthorpe?

Violet slowly retreated into the retiring room while keeping the door cracked ever so slightly for sound. Terrible of her to eavesdrop, but how could she help herself? This conversation could provide her with additional insight into Ravensthorpe.

"You will do what I say, Louisa," Underhill said, his voice low and sharp. "You will not see him again—not until I have an heir."

Violet sucked in a breath, then covered her mouth with a hand. So, Underhill knew of the affair and was forcing Louisa to call it off.

"Absolutely not," Louisa hissed. "You have no right to ask me to do so."

"As your husband, I do, actually."

"We've tried for a child twice without success. I have no desire to try again. It's exhausting."

"Understandable, as it's no picnic on my end, but that does not change the fact that we must do it. I've looked the other way on your affairs for years. This is the least you can do. Otherwise I'll be forced to move you out to the country. Try meeting your paramour way up there."

"You wouldn't dare."

"I'll have your bags packed tomorrow if you don't agree."

Violet's eyes widened. Between her parents and this couple, marriage seemed like a nightmare for wives. No fidelity or trust. Just threats and tantrums each way one turned.

"But I may return to him once I give you an heir?"

"Of course." Underhill actually sounded accommodating, as if he were doing her a favor. "Not that Ravensthorpe will wait for you."

"We have a bond you could not understand," she said—and Violet's stomach sank. Were there legitimate feelings between Ravensthorpe and Louisa? The possibility made Violet nauseous.

Underhill chuckled, but not with humor. "No doubt his wife thought the same before he caused her death. Besides, the man has screwed his way through the ton for years. You don't believe you are special to him, do you?"

"Again, you would not understand. I have kept his interest longer than most."

"Even still, do not find yourself surprised when he moves on."

"We have plans tonight. When I see him, I'll inform him that—"

"No need," Underhill interrupted. "I took care of it earlier when I spoke to him."

Violet leaned closer to the door, surprised. Lord Underhill had canceled the assignation with Ravensthorpe. Was that why the duke had appeared so uncomfortable on his way out?

Louisa gasped. "You had no right!"

"I beg to differ. I plan on getting started immediately, Louisa. And no doubt Ravensthorpe is wallowing in a Covent Garden bordello by now."

Was that where Ravensthorpe had gone? Out to visit a bawdy house? Violet's throat tightened, choking on the possibility that she might never be alone with him again.

"He despises those types of establishments," Louisa said. "Which is why I know he'll wait for me."

A group of women came laughing and chatting around the corner, likely headed for the retiring room. To avoid being caught eavesdropping, Violet pushed open the door and walked into the corridor. Lady Underhill brushed by as if headed for the ballroom, while her husband had already turned away, drifting deeper into the house. Violet's mind spun with possibility as she nodded at the blur of young ladies as they passed, not really noticing them.

Would Ravensthorpe return to sit in his house, alone? Or would he find feminine companionship elsewhere?

If he were at home . . . would the side door be unlocked, even with his cancelled plans?

No, she couldn't.

Could she?

He would never allow Violet inside . . . but what if she didn't ask? What if she surprised him? He was attracted to her—he'd admitted it outside—and she might convince him to act on it, if they were alone together. Isolated, where no one would find them.

The moment felt fortuitous. Momentous. Everything she wanted— a chance with Ravensthorpe—was dangling right in front of her like a sweet treat. She merely had to be bold enough to take it.

Was she content to wait around and hope he noticed her again?

Your body is made for sin and your face would make angels weep.

One thing was perfectly clear: he would never come to her. He had ordered her to stay away from him, had pushed her to find a man her age. She would need to take matters into her own hands.

Did she dare?

MAX LOUNGED in the darkness of his study, legs angled toward the fire as he sipped the most expensive brandy his vast amounts of money could buy. He'd long lost track of the time, the chime of the clock forgettable since he arrived home. His plans for the evening were ruined, and he hadn't been able to do much of anything except sit and brood.

I could be fucking her right now.

He shouldn't think it, shouldn't even let the hint of it cross his mind. He should imagine screwing Louisa instead, with her bold caresses and wicked tongue—not a girl barely out of the schoolroom.

And yet.

The brandy lowered his defenses, and Violet crept into his mind like a vine that burrowed under his skin to hold and drag him down. He couldn't resist wondering and speculating, his mind storing a mental list of all the depraved things he'd do to her glorious body if but given the chance.

This had to stop. Lusting after her like this caused him to feel like a filthy old man. Many dukes in their twilight years married young girls, but Max had secretly sneered at those pathetic louts. Yes, they all needed heirs—Max had already scaled that particular mountain—but there were plenty of seasoned women who could bear children. One need not marry a girl barely more than a child herself.

His eyes drifted to the mound of paperwork on his desk. His nights with Louisa were necessary diversions, an escape from the responsibilities of his life. To pleasure and be pleasured in return, to let his mind focus on something other than numbers.

You're lonely.

He snarled at the fire, as if the voice had come from the flames. The idea was ludicrous. He was invited everywhere, had his pick of bed partners, and there was Will, his sixteen-year-old son and heir. Will was away at school, off to Eton as all young aristocratic males did at his age.

Will had been the center of Max's world for so long. Since the boy's birth, Max had kept his son close and made certain to spend time with him, to show Will how much his father loved him. Then perhaps Will would not hate him when he came to learn the circumstances of what happened to his mother. How Max had utterly failed as a husband.

He didn't want another wife or any more children. Ever. He had an heir and, thanks to Max's proficiency on the Exchange, Will would inherit more money than God when Max died, not to mention a dukedom. Ducal duty had been fulfilled. Max never needed to go through that again.

He did, however, need another mistress. This required an immediate search, though there were some options. Such as the viscountess who had propositioned him at the opera last month, or the Spanish princess he'd flirted with at the palace dinner weeks ago. As well, his former mistress, Georgina, had written recently in the hopes of reestablishing their association.

None of them caused his blood to race, unfortunately.

That's because you want her.

Christ, this had to stop. He downed the rest of the brandy in his snifter and debated pouring a fourth. He had a meeting with his estate manager in the morning and a hangover would only make the bloody business take longer.

The scrape of metal caught his attention. Someone was slowly opening his study door.

No servant would dare to enter without knocking. This could only be one person, and Max's mood picked up considerably.

Louisa. She'd found a way to sneak off from her husband after all. Fortunate that he'd unlocked the side door earlier, despite Underhill's warnings.

Relief flooded him. A distraction was exactly what he needed, and he should reward her a bit for coming. Louisa liked when he ignored her and she had to beg for his attentions. Max didn't mind. What man wouldn't want a beautiful woman begging him to fuck her?

Playing coy, he focused on the glass in his hands, twirling the empty crystal in the firelight. Slippers moved across the carpets, skirts rustling, and lust sparked in his belly as he contemplated what was to come. Louisa rarely wore drawers and kept the hair on her mound trimmed short. Was she already wet and eager for him?

The outline of a black cloak caught the corner of his eye. She'd come prepared like a thief in the night. Underhill wouldn't like this, but one last time as a way to say good-bye properly wouldn't hurt, would it? Max wasn't fully hard, but it wouldn't take much to excite him, not after his encounter with Violet.

Because I wished to take her place, Your Grace.

No, not now. He could not think of her *now.*

Louisa stopped just out of his reach, her face turned away from him, toward the fire. She trembled slightly, anticipating his touch, and he relished the reaction. It made him feel more powerful than any man on earth. "I see you escaped," he said, his voice a low rasp. "Are you here to play?"

The hood moved as she nodded.

"I like that you couldn't stay away from me. Needy little thing, aren't you?"

Another nod.

In deference to Underhill's request for an heir, Max said, "I cannot fuck you tonight, sadly, but I do plan to enjoy you in every other way possible."

She was quiet, but he could almost feel her vibrating with excitement. Normally, Louisa would break character about now with a giggle or urging him to hurry. She was showing incredible restraint . . .

and he meant to honor that effort by giving her unimaginable pleasure.

"Bend over that chair," he said, pointing to the plush armchair opposite his. "Fold yourself over the arm."

For a second, she hesitated. Then she walked over and draped her front over the side of the chair, arse in the air, with her face hidden.

"Such a good girl," he praised, unfolding from his seat and rising. "Now, lift your skirts."

She struggled awkwardly with her skirts, almost as if she were shy. Or innocent.

Lust unwound in Max's groin, a slow warmth that traveled along the backs of his legs and through his bollocks. He didn't care to question as to why her performance aroused him—he was terrified of the answer—so he just accepted that it did.

"Higher," he barked when she paused. "Show me."

Damn, it was as if they'd switched and were now catering to his fantasies. His cock lengthened, pushing against his underclothes. Her calves and the backs of her knees were already bared to his gaze, and he saw the lace of her drawers peeking out to tantalize him.

His skin hummed with a familiar sensation, one he'd experienced at the ball, but he forced it away. This was no time to let those thoughts intrude. That particular young woman wasn't here and he needed to focus on the woman in front of him, to continue their games until they were both exhausted and dripping with sweat. "I see you are a tempting little minx tonight," he growled, dragging a finger along her spine.

She moaned softly and he couldn't wait a second more. Dropping to his knees behind her, he shoved her skirts out of his way. "Spread your legs," he ordered, and hurriedly stripped off his waistcoat. Gripping her inner thighs, he pushed her open further. He couldn't see much in the dim firelight, but the lips of her quim glistened with arousal, causing his mouth to water. Leaning in, he dragged his tongue through her folds.

The heavenly taste, a sweet and musky flavor, exploded on his tongue just as bells went off in his head, a clamoring that something was very wrong. The feel of her body was different. The smell of her skin was not the usual vanilla and lavender, but rather lemon. The hair on her mound was longer. The drawers . . .

Bloody hell.

Shoving himself away from her, he fell back on his arse, skittering on his limbs like a bloody crab, desperate to put distance between them.

No, no, no. She hadn't. *He* hadn't. This could not have happened.

"Turn around," he choked out, dread pressing on his chest. "Turn the fuck around, right now."

Legs shaking, she slowly straightened and let her skirts fall. Then she faced him . . . and Max's stomach dropped.

Violet.

"You." Blood rushed in his ears as he stared up at her, unable to believe it. "What in God's name have you done?"

Red bloomed on her cheekbones and she stared at his shoes. "Is it not obvious?"

"Not to me. Spit it out, Violet. Why have you come here tonight, sneaking into my house and making me believe you were someone else?"

"I never said I was her." Her head snapped up and she straightened, almost defiant. "And I thought you saw my face."

Fury raced through his veins like a lit fuse, sending flames to every part of his body. He nurtured it, grateful to replace the other unwelcome emotions from a moment ago. "A lie if I've ever heard one. As far as you knew, Louisa was coming tonight and you tried to take her place."

"I knew she wasn't coming. I overheard her husband telling her that she could no longer see you."

"So you draped yourself in a cloak, thinking I wouldn't know the difference between you and her. One cunt is just as good as another, is it?"

She flinched, but he would not apologize. Just having her taste on his tongue, picturing her bent over his armchair, had him balancing on a precarious edge. He wanted her too badly for politeness.

"You were able to tell the difference just from . . . that?"

God save him from innocent virgins. "We men are simple creatures, but yes. Even we are capable of recognizing the woman we are currently fucking from behind."

"*Were* fucking," she corrected with a knowing smirk. "Seeing as how her husband has now forbidden it."

The little she-devil was entirely too pleased with herself, and he liked this brazen side of her. A lot. Which meant he had to distance himself from this young woman at all costs. "Get out, Violet. Before we both do something we will regret."

"Did I . . ." She took a deep breath and let it out in a rush. "Did I not taste acceptable to you?"

The conscience he'd long forgotten chose that moment to rear its ugly head. He could have cut her down with a few simple words, destroyed her newfound confidence and probably sent her from the room in tears. But he couldn't do it. Nor would he lie, not about this. "You tasted like the sweetest ambrosia. I could spend a week doing nothing but licking you to orgasm and not tire of it."

Desire darkened her eyes and she swayed on her feet, a tiny gasp escaping her lips. Goddamn, she was magnificently responsive. So easily affected by him. More blood pumped to his groin, his cock hardening further beneath his clothing. He wanted nothing more than to dive beneath her skirts once again, hear her cries of delight ringing in his ears.

She is Charles's daughter.

Only eighteen.

He will never forgive you.

You cannot marry her.

With her taste in his mouth and the image of her naked quim in his brain, the usual reasons why he should stay away from her weren't working. He resorted to pleading with her. "Please, Violet. You should—"

"Did I cause that?" She pointed to the obvious erection between his legs.

"Yes," he answered without thinking. "But you should not know of such things, little mouse."

"May I see it?"

Every muscle froze and all the moisture fled his mouth. *Oh, Christ.*

What was she trying to do to him? He'd end up in an asylum before the end of the night at this rate. Why was she not fleeing his house in terror?

Because she's far stronger than you've imagined, you dolt.

He swallowed. "If you cannot even say the word, then you are not ready to see it." His voice came out husky and teasing, not the biting tone he'd imagined in his head.

Violet must have sensed his weakness, because she took one step closer. "May I see your cock, Your Grace?"

His lips parted, his breath sawing out of his chest, short and swift. The question and the honorific uttered in her pliant, pleasing voice were his undoing. He'd tried so hard, but he wanted her too badly. Craving sizzled in his veins, like an addict denied his pipe, and Max could deny it no longer, whatever the consequences.

He let his lips curve into a sly smile full of wickedness. "You may, but you must take it out first."

VIOLET HAD NEVER BEEN SO scared in her whole life. But there was something underneath the trepidation, an emotion that emboldened her and turned her into a wanton creature worthy of Ravensthorpe. Perhaps it was longing or passion, or the ravenous desire he inspired in her. Whatever it was, he seemed to appreciate it.

Even while angry with her, Ravensthorpe made her feel safe. Protected. Like she could say or do anything and he'd not judge her harshly for it. Which was probably why, despite her inexperience, she wasn't afraid of whatever was happening between them.

He remained sprawled on the study floor, his long limbs akimbo as he studied her, the erection in his trousers enticing her to come and play. Firelight danced off the sharp angles of his face, the glow reflecting off the silver strands at his temples. He was irresistible and shameless, and the darkness only enhanced his appeal.

Ravensthorpe said nothing, his chest rising and falling with the force of his breaths. Though he was on the ground, he was clearly still in control of the room, like a jungle cat taking a momentary break to tease its prey, daring her to approach him.

Did he believe she wouldn't follow through?

Flicking open the clasp on her cloak, she shrugged off the heavy cloth and let it fall. Then she lifted her skirts and dropped to her knees, the carpet soft beneath her stockings. Without a word, he widened his legs, making room for her between them, so she shuffled forward, her heart pounding behind her corset.

When she reached his thighs, he growled, "Unfasten my trousers."

With trembling fingers, she reached to do as asked. Her nail traced the edge of the wide black button before slipping it through the hole. There were more buttons underneath, so she carefully undid each one around his bulging erection. Her fingers brushed his belly, the brief contact making him jump. She pressed her lips together to keep from grinning. *I affect this gorgeous man with a simple touch.*

"Now the braces."

He made no move to assist her, only held perfectly still as she slipped one brace over his shoulder, then the other. When she finished, she sat back on her knees and waited for him to continue with instructions.

"My shirt."

His collar and necktie had already been removed, so she leaned in once more and set to work on the small buttons on his chest. His lean muscles rippled beneath her fingers, the carefully leashed power betrayed by his rapid breathing.

When enough buttons were loosened, she dragged the expanse of fabric over his head, Ravensthorpe lifting his arms to help. The thin garment he wore underneath was of the finest cloth, and it outlined the thick muscle and sinew, the flat planes and elegant grace. Another wave of heat rolled through her, centering between her legs.

More.

She was greedy when it came to this man. Dark need buzzed beneath her skin, a yearning to see every bit of him.

When she stared too long, he said, "The undergarment, Violet."

Instead of unbuttoning the garment at his chest, she reached for his groin. After all, they both knew what she was after, considering she'd asked to see it.

Behind the opening in his trousers, she found small buttons and began working them open. He didn't speak but she could feel him watching, his intense gaze like a caress over her breasts, along her center. Would he lick her again? Because that one swipe of his tongue between her legs had felt like heaven.

Bare skin appeared as she continued, her first peek at the man underneath the polished exterior. She could hardly breathe for all the excitement coursing through her.

"That's it," he said, his voice a silky whisper, and her body shivered under his encouragement.

More.

She purposely paused, just so he would start talking again.

"Keep going. Just one or two more, my little mouse."

Oh. She pressed her thighs together, nearly groaning under the weight of her longing. She would do anything if he kept speaking to her like that and calling her his. Her hands moved faster now, following his direction as if she'd been born to do it.

Reclining onto his elbows, he lifted his hips slightly as she tugged his trousers low on his hips. Fabric shifted on his stomach, and his erection emerged from between the open sides of his undergarment. His penis sprouted proud and thick from a patch of dark, coarse hair, and she stared at it, fascinated by its reddish cap and smooth, tight skin.

Their breathing and the pop of the fire were the only sounds in the room. Was he assuming she'd run screaming from the house? Hardly. The sight of him made her mouth water. If only she had her photography equipment. . .

She licked her lips, uncertain but definitely eager. "What do I do?"

His dark eyes glittered from underneath his long lashes. "You worship it."

Yes, yes, yes. Indeed, that she could do.

He watched carefully, every bit of his attention on her, and she vowed not to disappoint him. She dipped to press a kiss to the head of his shaft, not looking away from his eyes. His lips parted and she heard him give a swift intake of breath. Emboldened, she touched her tongue to the same spot, and he hissed a very creative curse.

He reached down, gripped the base with his elegant fingers, and angled his cock toward her mouth. "Suck."

She wrapped her lips around the plump head and drew him in. His entire body tensed. "More. Take me deep."

Pressing down, she slid him as far back as she could manage. He tasted clean and musky, so firm and silky on her tongue. It was much better than she'd ever imagined. She repeated the journey, noticing how his cock jerked when her tongue glided over the skin underneath the head. The next pass was slower, with more attention paid to that sensitive spot. His muscles clenched, and the reaction felt like a victory.

She worked hard then, moving faster to show him without words how much she wanted to please him. He grunted and rocked his hips, lost in the moment, until he suddenly lifted her up and away from his erection. In a blink, she found herself on her back, Ravensthorpe leaning over her, pressing her into the floor an instant before he sealed his mouth to hers in a punishing kiss.

This was no sweet melding of lips as described by poets and schoolgirls. No, he devoured her, his mouth immediately opening to give her his tongue. She took it eagerly, widening to allow him in, reveling in the slick heat as his tongue twined with hers. This kiss was a battle, a test. He was showing her all the passion, all the lust inside him, and she had to prove that she could accept it. Prove that she wanted it.

Violet never could resist a challenge.

She kissed him back just as eagerly, with just as much fervor, their lips and teeth crashing into one another as their mouths worked. It was messy, almost angry, and she loved every minute of it. Ravensthorpe kissed as if he could bend the world to his will through this alone, and she wasn't entirely sure he couldn't.

Tearing his mouth away, he slid his lips down the column of her throat. "I might not ever recover from the sight of my cock between your lips, sweet girl."

Her back arched as he bit her skin, his teeth digging deep to mark her, and wetness pooled between her legs. She dug her nails into his back.

Without warning, he sat up. For a moment she worried they were done, but he let his gaze travel the length of her. "I want you naked," he growled. "Here in my study."

"Yes," she breathed, ready to give him almost anything if he'd just continue kissing her.

Relief flashed over his expression, as if he'd feared she would deny him. He made a motion with his hand. "Roll over."

————

Max helped Violet turn onto her stomach. He wouldn't take things far tonight, but whatever happened, he would damn well ensure that Violet enjoyed it. Nothing else mattered at the moment.

Quickly, he unfastened her bodice and unlaced her corset. Untied her bustle and skirts. He was no stranger to women's clothing, well familiar with the tapes and hooks, and the process took hardly any time at all. Violet remained on her stomach, lifting when he ordered, allowing him to disrobe her.

With the outer layers removed, she was down to a chemise, drawers, and stockings, all white with pink satin ribbons. Perfect skin glowed underneath, the shape of her tempting him, an outline of the curves he'd imagined for months. The tip of his cock leaked, his bollocks aching with the desire to pump inside her. To defile and pleasure her. To *ruin* her.

You cannot fuck her. You cannot marry her.

But he could do everything else.

"On your back."

She turned over, giving him the perfect view of her ample tits. Full and ripe, the creamy mounds spilled out over her chemise, the berry-tipped nipples jutting against the thin fabric. Her chest heaved with her excitement, thrusting her breasts higher, and Max's mouth went dry.

He clenched his fists and contemplated rending the flimsy fabric in half. "Take off your chemise."

She did as he asked, wriggling her hips and shoulders, revealing her bare torso to his greedy gaze. Fuck, she was perfect, with curves exactly where he liked them. His hands shook as he reached for her, his sanity slipping. "If I do something you don't like, tell me and I'll stop. All right?"

She nodded, but that wasn't enough. "The words, Violet. Tell me you understand."

"I understand, Your Grace."

She peeked at him through her lashes, shy but emphasizing his honorific, and he couldn't bring himself to care. He fell on her like a man possessed, kissing her hard and deep, needing her like he'd never needed anyone before in his life.

Before the weight of that thought could bring him down, he moved to take the tip of her breast into his mouth, drawing deep. His hand cupped the supple flesh as he licked and sucked, loving the little whimpers she gave before he moved to the other breast to give it the same attention. Her nipples were thick, each surrounded by a large areola, and he adored the way they felt on his tongue. When she was writhing under him, moaning loudly, he pulled back to admire her. The suction from his mouth had caused her nipples to puff even more.

Jesus, everything about this girl was so damn arousing.

"You are absolutely gorgeous," he muttered as his hands went to her drawers. "But you still have on far too much clothing."

In a flash, he divested her of her drawers and stockings, marveling that she hadn't yet shied from his touch or tried to cover herself. She seemed to want him every bit as much as he wanted her. Surely that wouldn't last. It couldn't.

It never did. His former duchess had proven that, hadn't she?

So he would enjoy this with Violet while he could.

When she was naked, he sat on his haunches, marveling at the picture before him. Lush breasts, smooth skin, generous hips that would cushion his own perfectly . . . and her mons with its delicate triangle of hair. No man had explored there, and while Max knew he didn't deserve to be the first, he was bastard enough not to refuse it.

"Spread your legs. Show me."

Those pale thighs parted, revealing her pussy, and he couldn't breathe. *Goddamn beautiful.* Arousal glistened on the petals, with more gathered around the entrance. He traced the soft flesh with a fingertip, relishing the slick her body produced for him. "Is all this for me?" She watched him with wide eyes as he brought the finger to his mouth and sucked the sweetness onto his tongue. "Oh, my darling girl. I fear I'll never get enough of your taste."

Dropping onto his stomach, he let his breath tease her until she started to squirm. Then he began licking her, gently at first, getting her used to the feel of a tongue between her legs. The taste was exquisite, tart and musky, and he felt like a fifteenth-century explorer on a voyage of discovery and delight into unchartered lands while she gasped and mewled beneath him. His cock leaked onto the carpet, the skin pulled so tight it hurt, and yet he somehow resisted the urge to hump the floor.

When his attentions focused directly on her clitoris, her entire body twitched. *"Your Grace!"*

He swirled his tongue over that swollen bud, loving it with his teeth and mouth, sucking and laving until she trembled. One of her hands found its way onto the back of his head, where she held him in place, fingers clutching his hair, and nothing made him prouder than his little mouse demanding her pleasure.

She was close, her body stretched like a bowstring, her chest pumping in a desperate plea for air. Max needed to feel her inexperienced walls clamp down, if not on his shaft, then on his finger. He carefully slid the tip of his smallest finger inside her cunt, and her slick walls sucked him inside as if starved. God, how he wished . . .

No. He could not even contemplate it.

Then it happened. Her thighs shook around his head, her cries ringing in his ears as she found her peak. The release went on and on, her body completely his in that moment, and the satisfaction he experienced as she climaxed on his tongue was incomparable.

When she relaxed, he removed his finger and continued to lick her, softer, relishing the additional wetness that now pooled at her entrance. So responsive, so delicious . . . he longed to do this until sunrise. But his bollocks were tight, almost painful, with the need for his own release. He feared he would spend on the carpets if he waited another moment.

Rising onto his knees, he took his cock in hand and stroked, admiring her luscious form the entire time. Christ, she was beautiful.

"Play with your breasts," he ordered, little electric shocks of lust shooting through his groin. "Pinch your nipples."

Her hands crept to her tits, cupping them as if offering them up to him. Then she squeezed the tips, her mouth rounding in surprise, as if she'd never touched them so intimately before. Her innocence—not to mention her willingness to do as he said without question—drove him positively wild. "More," he grunted, his hand moving faster along his shaft.

She watched his hand, seeming fascinated, as she rolled and tweaked her nipples, her tongue swiping across her lower lip. Was she thinking of sucking on him again? Swallowing his spend down her throat? God, the idea of it . . .

"Fuck," he gasped, sensation overtaking him, heat sizzling along nerve endings, and spend erupted from the top of his cock to land on her stomach. He clutched her thigh to steady himself, his tight fist milking all the pleasure from his body while his limbs jerked and twitched. "So good, so damn *good,*" he gritted through clenched teeth. He couldn't remember the last time he came this intensely, as if his entire body were being wrung inside out in pleasure.

Each blissful pulse washed over him, renewing and reenergizing, breathing new life into his old and tired brain. He never wanted this feeling to end.

Yet it soon did. His faculties returned slowly, and with them came the dawning horror as to how low he'd sunk.

I've debauched her. Touched her when I hadn't the right.

Taken another innocent girl and horrified her with my base ways, just like Rebecca.

He hung his head, unable to look at her. What had he done?

CHAPTER
FIVE

"THIS WAS A MISTAKE."

Ravensthorpe's words, combined with the remorse stamped on his features, had Violet's stomach churning. This had been the best night of her life. She could not allow him to destroy what had happened between them with recriminations.

Yes, she'd come here in the hopes of seducing him, but she hadn't meant to trick him. Not really, anyway. While she may have tried to keep quiet at first, she hadn't known the room would be so dark, that he wouldn't see her face until . . . well, until it was too late. He'd made it clear at the ball he desired her. She'd planned to come tonight and give him a small nudge, to talk to him in private and convince him to give them a chance.

Of course, she hadn't realized Ravensthorpe would begin orchestrating a seductive play the moment she walked through the door. Not that she was complaining. The man merely had to open his mouth and she was at the ready, waiting like a good little soldier to follow his instructions.

And he believed this was a mistake?

Coming up on her elbows, she said, "I don't regret any of it. I'd do it again, in fact."

The duke dragged a hand down his face. "Violet, you cannot possibly—"

"Stop. Do not dare tell me I cannot understand. I have much more to lose than you by being here, and I am well aware of the possible repercussions."

"I won't marry you."

She flinched. The reminder was meant to put distance between them, and it worked. Pushing aside the sudden ache surrounding her heart, she reached for her stockings and pulled them on. "I haven't asked for marriage, Your Grace."

He mumbled something under his breath.

"I beg your pardon?"

"I said to call me Max."

He was giving her leave to use his given name? That had to mean something, didn't it? "I haven't asked for marriage, Max."

Head down, he began putting his clothing back to rights. She ignored his unhappy expression and studied him instead, from his wide shoulders and strong arms, to the perfectly sculpted flat chest. Even partially dressed, he made her heart flutter.

If she ever saw him completely naked, she'd likely faint from lust.

She was tying her drawers when he moved to still her hand. His gaze was soft, but filled with resolution. "Let me help you."

Her body melted at his sudden tenderness, and she leaned back to let him proceed. When he'd finished tying the ribbons, he ran the silk through his fingertips. "Pink and delicate. I think you wore these to drive me mad."

Before she could ask what he meant, he righted her chemise and dropped it over her head. He smoothed the fabric down, taking extra care at her breasts. "A shame to cover these beauties." One finger traced her right nipple slowly, almost reverently, and the flesh quickly puckered under the attention.

"My God," he murmured. "I do love the way your body responds to me."

Because you are the only man I've ever wanted.

She didn't dare say it, however. Not while he considered tonight a mistake.

She knew otherwise. This evening had proven how much he desired her, how explosive they were together. Nothing about coming here had been a mistake.

They hardly spoke as he assisted her with the corset and bustle, the petticoats and dress. The emotional distance grew as more and more layers of clothing separated their bodies. After he handed her the black cloak, he gestured to the door. "I'll see you out."

The sentence held a note of finality, that this was the last time, and the possibility terrified her.

She dug in her heels. "When will I see you again?"

He sighed and shoved his hands in his trouser pockets. "You won't."

Pain ripped through her chest and settled behind her ribs. "Max—"

"Do not argue with me, Violet. We've satisfied our curiosity and that was that. This is not an affair."

"I am far from having my curiosity satisfied—and it could be an affair, if you'd but allow it."

"You ask the impossible," he said, his voice low and angry. "And one day you'll thank me for preventing it."

"Because you believe you're too old for me."

"I *know* I am too old for you. And your father would never—"

"My father hardly has a moral ground upon which to stand. You of all people probably know that better than most."

Max shifted and did not bother to deny it. She'd hit her mark, then. Indeed, Max was privy to her father's sins. "Nonetheless, he is your father and my friend. An affair between his daughter and me is impossible."

She hated how rational and calm he sounded, as if his mind were made up. What happened to the wild lover of moments ago, the one spewing filth from his mouth and clutching her as if he never wanted to let go? "Are you saying you've never slept with a woman more than twenty years your junior?"

His expression darkened at the reminder of their age difference. Stalking away, he grabbed the decanter on the side table and refilled an empty glass. After taking a large swallow of what had to be brandy, he said, "I haven't, actually. I make a habit of choosing experienced women who needn't be shown how to pleasure a man."

The wounded lion lashes out.

Violet was not fooled. This man had nearly fallen at her feet moments ago, dazed by her kisses and drunk on her taste. His body's reaction to her couldn't have been faked, so she knew her innocence hadn't bothered him. In fact, she would guess the opposite based on his rabid ardor—that he'd enjoyed instructing her.

Confidence surged through her like a great gust of air and filled her with newfound knowledge and purpose. She lifted her chin. "Perhaps I'll find a young buck to teach me, then. I'll return after some tutelage and you might reconsider."

His gaze, possessive and dark, narrowed on her. "Do not even contemplate it, Violet."

"Or?"

"Or I'll put a stop to it. And beat whomever you've convinced to help you within an inch of his miserable bloody life."

She bit her lip to hide her smile. Oh, yes. This was far from over between them.

"Stop looking so pleased with yourself," he snarled. "I will only destroy you and never marry you. Consequently, you should run from this house and never look back."

"And yet I cannot."

"I do not want you to return. Is that clear enough for you?"

The words were like spikes through her heart, tearing the tender flesh straight through, but she would remain strong. He was stubborn . . . yet so was she. "I think you're lying."

His lips flattened into a thin, angry line. "I've pummeled men for lesser insults than the one you just handed me."

"You won't hurt me. I've known you nearly all of my life."

"You know nothing about me."

Yes, I do. I see you. I've always seen you.

She had observed him carefully during her parents' dinner parties. Well read and intelligent, Max could speak to almost any topic, no matter how obscure. He was also kind and thoughtful. He made certain to escort elderly Aunt Harriet, who had difficulty walking unassisted, and he doted on his son, refusing to ship the heir off to boarding school when William was a young boy.

Now she'd discovered more about the allegedly wicked Duke of Ravensthorpe. His sweetness. His giving heart. His jealousy when she mentioned other men.

He believed he would destroy her, but that was impossible. Tonight she had discovered herself . . . and Max had helped her do it.

"We shall see," she said, cryptically.

"Goddamn it. You must listen to what I am saying."

Yes, she was listening, and one thing was perfectly clear—she could no longer chase him. She had to give Max space and let him come to her instead. Whatever was between them only worked if they were both amenable, both willing to take risks for the other. As it was, she had risked enough for him.

What if he moves on without you?

It was a gamble, certainly. No telling how many women were angling to get in his bed. And yet, everything inside her screamed this was the right choice.

"I'll see myself out," she said and turned to the door.

"You are not leaving until you agree never to return."

She paused and tried to remember this was for the best. Either way, win or lose, she couldn't pursue Max like a hound after a fox forever. "I won't return until you invite me."

Glancing over her shoulder, she gave him a heated look from under her lashes. "Because you will come looking for me, *Your Grace*. And when you do, I'll be waiting."

———

Fourteen days.

It had been fourteen days since the night in his study, the moment when Violet had turned his world upside down, and now Max worried he was losing his mind.

He couldn't stop thinking about her, couldn't stop remembering their night together, and somehow the girl had burrowed under his skin with her shy smiles and bawdy demands. So eager, so brave.

Looking up at him as if he were a good man, one capable of solving any problem on earth.

And he most definitely had gone mad, because he was currently circulating the social event of the evening whilst searching for a blond-haired she-devil.

This is a mistake.

Yes, entirely. He could readily admit it, yet he could not stop himself.

For a week he'd held out, staying busy with his accounts and clubs. By day nine he'd begun drinking heavily, fisting his cock as he relived the memories of her kiss and the feel of her skin.

Day eleven had found him at one of the city's high-end brothels, one he hadn't visited in ages. He'd turned around and left before even removing his coat. How could he fuck another woman with the taste of Violet still fresh in his brain?

By the end of day twelve, he was stalking his London home like a starved dog, snarling at anyone who dared bother him. He locked himself in, convinced that Violet was a fever in his blood, one he merely needed to ride out. Then she would be out of his system forever and he could get on with his life.

It hadn't worked.

Now he was broken, unable to concentrate. An utter mess of a human being. A man on the verge of hysteria.

Just once more, he'd promised himself earlier today. If he could touch and kiss her just once more, that would be enough to get her out of his head. Then he could set her free, where she could marry anyone she pleased.

He was doing her a favor, really. Most young women—his deceased wife included—came to the marriage bed completely ignorant and unprepared. Max would leave Violet a virgin but at least teach her about sex and her own pleasure.

God, you're pathetic. You're attempting to justify bedding an eighteen-year-old woman.

Yes, but he was too far gone. He'd beg if necessary. Everything about her had been too perfect, too right. It had been the most erotic night of his life, one he couldn't help but relive every time he closed his eyes.

She was confident for her age, self-assured in ways that had surprised him. When was the last time he'd been surprised? Perhaps his liaisons had becoming boring of late, more rote than exciting, but Violet had energized his existence. She made him feel ten years younger and more randy than a university lad in a bordello.

"Ravensthorpe."

Max froze at the sound of the familiar voice, making sure to wipe his expression clean. He'd avoided Violet's father since the night in his study, uncertain how he could face his friend after what had occurred. The only good part about seeing Mayhew meant that Violet was likely in the room, as well.

He cleared his throat and spun around. "Mayhew."

Charles slapped Max's shoulder. "Haven't seen you in ages. Where have you been keeping yourself?"

At home, dreaming of fucking your daughter.

Instead, he said, "Here and there."

"Heard Louisa gave you the shove-off, my friend. A shame, indeed. Have you already found someone new?"

Max suppressed a wince and adopted an easy smile. "Not as of yet, no."

Charles leaned in closer and lowered his voice. "In that case, I'll happily show you a new place I've discovered. It's in Cheapside and the women are willing to do anything for the right price. And I do mean *anything*."

After spending so many nights in Charles's company, Max had a good idea of what "anything" might include. "I believe I'm set for the moment, but I'll let you know. Are you here with your wife and daughter?"

"Just Violet. The missus is peeved with me again. Said I came home smelling like perfume too many nights this week."

My father hardly has a moral ground upon which to stand. You of all people probably know that better than most.

How much did Violet know about what went on between her parents?

Max frowned at his friend. "I hope you shelter your daughter from hearing such things. It could leave a damaging impression with her."

"Come now, she's a grown woman. I've got two suitors sniffing around her skirts, so best she learn how marriage works between a husband and a wife." Charles's brows lowered, his expression etched with disbelief. "Besides, you cannot tell me Will isn't aware of your mistresses."

Suitors? A dark cloud rolled through Max, his mood blackening at the thought of some repulsive masher pawing at that lovely girl. Scowling, he said, "Will is a man, not an impressionable young woman. And just who are these two suitors?"

"The young lords Wingfield and Sundridge. I had hoped Surrey would take an interest, but he seems enamored with the Gabriel chit's dowry."

"Wingfield undoubtedly has the pox and a bowl of porridge contains more intelligence than Sundridge. You cannot in good conscience encourage either of those fools."

"How on earth did you come by that information?"

His son, actually, who loved to gossip more than a maiden aunt, but Max didn't say as much. "Just know that I am right. She can do better, Charles."

Mayhew hooked his thumbs in his vest pockets. "Might not have much of a choice. The girl isn't exactly putting forth an effort. She stands against the wall and watches at every event. I never should have encouraged that photography habit of hers."

Photography? Violet was one of those Kodak Girls? He could almost picture her behind a camera, studying and observing. Laboring over her prints in a developing room. He hadn't much experience with photography himself, but he'd love to see her in action someday. "Perhaps you should put it off, let her experience this first season without pressuring her to marry. Then choose her a husband next year."

You are going to Hell, Max. Straight to Hell.

"Can't. I promised the missus we'd marry Violet off this year." Charles lifted a shoulder. "No idea why my lady is in such a rush, but I won't disappoint her—not on this."

Because he planned to disappoint his wife in other ways.

Max shifted on his feet and stifled the urge to say more. He had no right to interfere with Violet's future. After his own disastrous attempt at playing husband, he couldn't marry her—or anyone else—so he should just leave off, turn on his heel, and quit this bloody ball.

Yet he wouldn't. Because she was here, somewhere in this very room. And if he didn't find her soon, he might tear this ballroom apart with his bare hands.

Charles tipped his chin toward the dance floor. "Ah, I see Wingfield's claimed her for another dance. That's the second one tonight."

Max's head whipped toward the dancers, and he spotted her right away, her golden hair gleaming in the gaslight overhead. The breath locked in his lungs and he had to remind himself to breathe as he examined her. She was absolutely lovely in a cream silk evening gown with intricate beaded work covering the bodice. The delicate column of her throat was bare, begging for Max's mouth and hands.

That same sizzle whispered over his skin, like desire had commandeered his flesh, making him burn everywhere. *Once more. That's all I need.*

Wingfield's gaze drifted down to Violet's bosom, where it lingered far longer than was polite, and Max's hands curled into fists. Wingfield would need to be put in his place, it seemed.

"I'm headed to the card room," Charles was saying. "Care to join?"

"I'll pass. Excuse me," Max said, already drifting into the crowd. He moved to the edge of the dance floor, not bothering to hide as he caught Violet's eye. She stumbled when she spotted him—requiring Wingfield to steady her with a hand on her hip—and blinked.

Momentarily setting aside the need to pummel her dance partner, Max tilted his head toward the terrace. She nodded ever so slightly then looked away.

Excellent.

He ignored those who attempted to catch his attention as he strode through the crush. The whole world could wait, as far as he was concerned.

Now was time for play.

CHAPTER
SIX

HE WAS HERE.

Ravensthorpe was here and wished to see her. Violet could hardly believe it. Had her plan worked? It had been two weeks since their night together and she'd grown despondent, certain she'd erred in giving him space. So, she'd buried herself in her classes at the Polytechnic Institute and in her photographs. In fact, after so many hours in the developing room, the chemicals had begun to sting her lungs.

All that had been worth it, however, because the handsomest duke in London had arrived . . . and he'd motioned for her to meet him outside.

Her chest worked to draw in air, her corset growing tighter at the idea. Would he kiss her again? Goodness, she hoped so. She hadn't been able to stop thinking about their night together, the way he'd touched her, as if he already knew every part of her. As if they'd been together for years.

He thought he'd ruin her. Destroy her and toss her aside. Violet didn't believe it. She was safe with him, protected. Cared for. He'd pushed her away out of loyalty and an overblown sense of nobility, but perhaps he'd come to realize that he was safe with her, too.

Finally the music ended and Wingfield led her off the dance floor.

"Lady Violet," he said, and she noticed the beads of sweat on his upper lip. "Would you do me the honor of joining me—"

"No, thank you, my lord. I must find my father. You'll excuse me?"

Without waiting on a response, she curtsied and then darted into the throngs of lords and ladies as she made her way to the French doors.

To Ravensthorpe.

Giddiness ignited in her chest like flash powder—and then Charlotte appeared in her path, a questioning expression on her friend's face. Violet stopped before she careened into the other woman. "Hello, Charlotte."

"You never finished telling me about your new suitor during our shopping trip yesterday." Violet's expression must've reflected her sudden panic because Charlotte continued. "Calm down. I meant Wingfield."

"Right." Violet exhaled in relief. "Wingfield."

Charlotte's brows lowered. "Who did you think I meant?"

"No one. Just unaccustomed to having a suitor, I suppose."

Her friend drew closer. "I am so happy to see you dancing. Three times tonight! For once you're not standing against the wall, watching everyone else."

Violet had no desire to converse at the moment. She tried to gracefully edge around her friend. "I don't know what's come over me. Perhaps I should get some air."

"Oh, excellent idea. I'm due for a dance, so I'll find you after." Charlotte squeezed Violet's hand and then disappeared into the crowd.

Violet wasted no time in hurrying to the French doors. She slipped onto the terrace, where cool night air washed over her exposed skin like a caress, causing her to shiver. With no torches or lamps outside, darkness engulfed her.

Strong fingers wrapped around her arm and began pulling her deeper into the gloom, helping her down the stone steps. She didn't need to see his face to know it was Max. His presence surrounded her, a feeling of safety and danger, arousal and comfort all at the same time. She went willingly, eagerly, unconcerned with getting caught.

Once on the ground, he tugged her into an alcove hidden underneath the stairs. Before she could see his face, he was on her, the muscular length of him flush to her front, her back against the rough stone.

But he didn't kiss her.

He put his mouth near her ear, his warm breath coasting over her skin. "Happy, little mouse? For two weeks I've tried to forget you. A goddamn fortnight, yet here I am—all because I cannot get the taste of your pussy out of my head."

Her lips parted on an exhale, his words both thrilling and arousing. Wetness gathered between her thighs, her pulse hammering in every bit of her sex. "Very happy, Your Grace," she whispered and slid her hands along the rigid slope of his chest.

"Christ," he bit out, bending to rock his hips into her thigh, his erection large and hard against her. She melted, her limbs growing languid. "I want to fuck you right here," he growled. "Turn you around and toss your dress above your head, bare you and sink inside."

"Yes," she gasped, definitely ready for that. There was emptiness, a place in her soul earmarked just for him, and she needed him to fill it.

"Hold your skirts."

"What?"

But he didn't explain, merely sank to his knees and began pushing layers of silk out of his way. He looked . . . possessed. Wild, like a starving man at a buffet. She moved to help, gathering the skirts in her arms until cool air washed over her stocking-covered legs.

Finding the part in her drawers, he lunged, pressing his face toward her sex, disappearing underneath layers of cloth. Then she felt the bold swipe of his tongue along her seam, and her knees wobbled as sensation jolted through her. His hands cradled her buttocks and lifted her left leg to place it over his shoulder.

"You must remain quiet," he ordered and dove under her skirts.

He wasted no time, licking and sucking until she whimpered. She thrashed her head as he tended to every part of her, driving her higher and higher, and lust tightened her muscles. He feasted, softly grunting in response to her moans, his mouth and tongue unrelenting, unforgiving against her flesh.

Voices suddenly sounded above on the terrace, a few revelers out for a bit of fresh air, no doubt.

Though she was well hidden, she froze, her chest heaving, and stared down at Ravensthorpe. The light of the moon revealed Max's smirk as he appeared from under her skirts. "Quiet," he mouthed, then returned to his task.

Sweet heavens.

She trembled under the onslaught, but her mind was stuck on the fact that they weren't alone out here. What if they were discovered? She tried to dislodge his face from between her legs, but the duke wouldn't budge. In fact, he doubled his efforts with her clitoris, sucking on the bud, laving it with his tongue.

It was too much.

Her eyes closed, the pressure building as fear and arousal mixed to overwhelm her, and she shoved her forearm into her mouth to stifle her cries as she came apart. Her body spasmed as her walls convulsed, white light exploding behind her eyes. When she regained herself, he gently dipped and swirled his tongue at her entrance, like he was trying to soak up every last bit of her taste.

Finally, he shot to his feet, his dark eyes glazed and hot. Her wetness coated his face and chin, and he licked his lips as he brought her hands to his waistband. "Finish me, Violet. Right now."

Oh, yes. She wanted that desperately. "What about . . ." She pointed to the terrace.

"They left. Hurry."

Swiftly, she unfastened his trousers and moved his shirtfront out of the way. "So many clothes." He made no move to help, staying perfectly still except for the breath sawing out of his chest.

She unbuttoned his undergarment and reached in, taking his shaft in her hand. The soft skin was stretched tight, her fingers unable to meet around his girth.

He dropped his forehead against her temple. "Squeeze hard," he said, giving a little thrust of his hips. "Stroke me. Fast."

Obeying, she tightened her grip and pumped his erection. He sucked in air and placed his hands on the wall behind her head. "That's it, my little mouse. Precisely like that."

He was so beautiful with his chiseled jaw and the few silver threads at his temple, his skin taut with excitement. She reached her other hand down to his testicles, rolled them in her palm, and Max let out a drawn out, "Fuck."

Hot breath hit her cheek as he began to talk. "We haven't long. Your father is in the card room and he'll come looking for you when he's done. I have the taste of you in my mouth. Would you like the taste of me in your mouth, as well?"

Her nipples tightened inside her clothing, and she rubbed her thighs together in a desperate bid for friction. Goodness, yes. She most definitely wanted that.

She started to lower to her knees, but he held her upright. "Wait."

He tore off his evening coat, folded it over, and dropped the cloth to the ground. She lifted her skirts and kneeled on his coat as Max began working his cock, rougher than she had, focusing almost entirely on the head. "Now, Violet," he gritted out, so she pressed forward and opened her mouth. Steadying her with a hand on her crown, he slid the head past her lips and groaned when she sucked. It took one swirl of her tongue and he reached his peak, his fingertips trembling on her scalp as spend coated the inside of her mouth.

"Yes," he gasped and shuddered. "That's it. Take it all."

She did, gladly. Her body sang in self-congratulatory pleasure as he climaxed, and when he finally pulled out she swallowed him down. Resting a palm against the hard stone, he lifted her chin with his free hand. His thumb traced her lips. "I expected you to spit but you didn't, did you?" He helped her stand then pressed his forehead to hers. "My God, Violet. What have I ever done to deserve you?"

He touched his lips to hers, kissing her softly, sweetly, with so much tenderness that she wanted to bottle it and hold onto the emotion forever. "Max," she whispered into his kisses, clutching him tightly. *"Your Grace."*

When they broke apart, he breathed, "Thank you, sweet girl," before stepping back. He tucked and smoothed her hair instead of righting his clothing. "There. Now you may return inside."

"What about you?"

"I'll go around the side and find my carriage. I've no desire to stand around a stuffy ballroom this evening."

Did that mean . . .? Giddiness flooded her chest, her heart swelling to a ridiculous size. "Did you come just to see me?"

"Go back to the ball." He began redressing, his attention on his buttons.

She shifted on her slippers, the gravel crunching beneath her feet. "When will I—"

"Inside, Violet." His tone was sharp and authoritative, the one he no doubt used when the Duke of Ravensthorpe wished to get his way.

But he was not the duke with her, not any longer. He was Max. He would not push her aside, especially when she still had the taste of him in her mouth. "Not until you tell me when I will see you again."

"We cannot do this." He pushed his shirtfront into his trousers. "It's too risky."

"Then let me come to your home."

"Violet—"

"Max," she snapped. "If you do not tell me precisely when, then I'll show up and surprise you."

"I won't let you in. I'll have the doors and windows locked at all times."

Silly man. She slid her hand up his chest, tucking her body close to his. "No, I don't think you will. In fact, I don't believe you'll last even fourteen days this time."

"Do not try to play games with me. You will lose."

She nipped his jaw with her teeth—and he shivered in response. Moving away, she whispered, "We shall see, Your Grace. We shall see."

———

Most days, Max avoided visiting his clubs. They were a waste of time, the rooms filled with brash young men barely older than Will, laughing and joking as if they hadn't a care. They caused Max to feel a hundred years old. Had he ever been so carefree, so jovial?

Not since assuming the title at fourteen, certainly. After a decade of wrangling the ducal accounts into shape, including taking risks on the London Exchange to refill the empty bank accounts, he'd been ready to do his duty. His choice of bride, the daughter of a high-ranking earl, had seemed a good one at the time, but he and Rebecca had been a poor match.

From the start, there had been problems in the bedroom. She preferred he not undress, and refused to let him see her without clothing. She remained perfectly still during the act, not complaining, but not participating, either. Kisses were to remain chaste and he was to leave immediately upon finishing.

Unhappiness had gnawed at him until Rebecca started increasing. Then he'd taken a mistress, relieved to finally enjoy himself with an eager partner. It had been selfish of him, a decision he'd regretted when his wife found out. Hysterical over his infidelity, Rebecca had gone into early labor and died whilst delivering Will.

A year into his marriage, Max was left widowed with a young son. And guilt. Plenty of guilt.

And the guilt hadn't yet subsided, not even sixteen years later.

None of it had been Rebecca's fault. Max should have been more patient, more understanding. He should have tried harder to explain his needs and desires, instead of rushing off to another woman's bed. Young and stupid, he leaped into marriage with the belief that a wife was no different than the other highborn ladies he'd slept with, the lusty widows and bored society wives.

But Rebecca had been different. It was Max who hadn't bothered to adjust his behavior, and he'd caused her death. Not a day went by when he didn't chastise himself over what he'd done, and he would repeat his pledge never to marry again.

Some men were not cut out to be husbands.

Still, he had no choice but to protect Violet.

Brooks's was quiet at this time of morning. After handing his hat and cane to the attendant, Max found his quarry in the main room, nursing coffee. Only a handful of men were spread out amongst the furniture.

Wingfield frowned at Max's approach. "Why must I be here so early, Ravensthorpe?"

Max slid into the chair opposite. "Because I wish to speak with you. And you are at my service, not the other way around."

Wingfield scowled but said nothing as he took another sip of coffee.

After an attendant brought Max a cup, they were alone again. Max came right to the point. "You will cease your pursuit of Lady Violet."

The young man's mouth fell open. "You have no right to—"

"I have every right," Max said icily. "I am a close family friend and have known the girl since she was born. You are not good enough for her."

"Not good enough for her?" Wingfield's voice rose several octaves. "The girl is the unequivocal flop of the season. I am doing her a favor by paying her attention."

His little mouse, a flop? Outrage roared through Max's veins like cannon fire, yet he tamped it down, hiding his emotions behind a bored expression. "You are a drunk and a spendthrift. Also, I have it on good authority that you've had mercury treatments—multiple times, in fact. You are not marrying Lady Violet."

Twin spots of scarlet dotted Wingfield's cheeks. "How dare you? My father—"

Max sighed loudly. "Your father is in debt to the West London Bank for hundreds of thousands of pounds. Would you care to guess the identity of that bank's largest shareholder?"

Wingfield sputtered. "Are you . . . Is this a threat?"

Christ Almighty, how was the world to survive with men this stupid?

"Yes," Max admitted, and then downed the rest of his coffee. "I am threatening you in order to keep you away from Lady Violet. Is that clear enough for you, Wingfield? Shall I put it in writing so there are no misunderstandings?"

Wingfield swallowed hard. "No, I understand. I'll stay away from her."

"Good." He rose. "See that you do."

Wingfield mumbled, "She's a stupid cow, anyway."

Max's entire body clenched and he leaned close to the younger man's face. "What did you say?"

"Nothing."

Max's hand shot out and he jerked Wingfield up by his collar, lifting the younger man until his feet barely touched the floor. Conversation in the room died, every eye turned their way. No one would dare say a word to stop Max, one of the most powerful men in Britain, from doing whatever he liked with this piece of filth.

"How dare you insult her." He tightened his fist, cutting off Wingfield's air supply. "If I hear of you talking about her, I will feed you to the pigs on my estate. Are we clear? You don't breathe her name ever again. If you see her on the street, don't even offer a polite greeting. She no longer exists for you."

Wingfield gasped, his eyes bulging, but Max didn't let up until the other man nodded. He let Wingfield go and straightened his cuffs. "Glad we understand each other."

With that, Max collected his things and strolled onto St. James Street. Instead of taking a hansom home, he decided to walk and clear his head. Rage from the encounter with Wingfield continued to burn through him, and he still had no idea what to do about Violet.

Two days had passed since the night of the ball . . . and he was already weakening. The craving for her lurked his blood, always present and growing stronger every minute.

I don't believe you'll even last fourteen days this time.

How had she known?

She was so certain about him, about *them.* The folly of youth, he supposed, not to understand the whole picture. He was bad for her, too old and too . . . rough. She deserved better. Someone sweet and kind, closer in age. Hell, Max would be lucky to live another twenty years. She needed a man who could marry her, give her children, and make her laugh into her old age.

Max was not that man.

Yet he wasn't certain he could stay away from her. He thought of her nearly all the time, his cock currently chafed thanks to his hand and his memories. Like a teenaged boy, he'd stolen a small jar of oil from the larder to protect his skin while pleasuring himself.

It would be funny if it weren't so mortifying.

As he crossed Piccadilly, he spotted a camera shop in the middle of the block. He recalled Charles mentioning Violet's interest in photography. Did she frequent this establishment?

She'd always been a clever and curious child, asking him questions about Will, the ducal estates, and anything else that crossed her mind during the Mayhew dinner parties. Math and history had been her favorite subjects, as he recalled, but they'd even debated philosophy at one point. Those qualities, along with her current voyeuristic tendencies, likely made her a stellar photographer.

Charles hadn't seemed appreciative of Violet's photography habit, but it was important to nurture hobbies, even for women. Perhaps especially for women, as they were told so often what they could not do, rather than be allowed to express themselves. Max would hate to see any of Violet's creativity stifled.

He was walking toward the shop before he could think better of it.

A bell chimed over the door as he entered. A middle-aged man emerged from the back and his eyes widened at the sight of Max. "Good morning. How may I help your lordship?"

Max didn't bother to correct the form of address. "I am interested in purchasing some photography equipment for a friend. Is there anything new or something you'd recommend?"

"I'd be honored. Has your lordship an idea of this gentleman's level of experience with photography?"

"It is a she, and no."

"I see. Then allow me to recommend this latest Kodak box model, the number one. Most women find it lighter and much easier to operate. It also comes pre-loaded with a flexible roll of film." The clerk pointed to a camera in the glass case. "It is our best seller."

"I'll take that, then."

"Excellent." The clerk withdrew a box from a locked drawer under the case. "Shall I wrap it for your lordship?"

Max considered this while he studied the other items in the case.

Have them deliver the camera with a note saying you cannot see her again.

The black heart in his chest instantly rejected the idea. He needed to watch Violet's face as she unwrapped his gift, see the youthful exuberance that hadn't yet been snuffed out by this harsh life. Drink in her happiness as if it were his own.

He wasn't ready to give her up.

You'll regret this.

Pushing aside his conscience, he handed the clerk his card. "If you would, yes. Have it delivered here."

The man's brows shot up. "Your Grace. Forgive me, I hadn't known. I shall see to it personally."

"Thank you." Max placed his bowler atop his head and left the shop, feeling lighter than he had in two days.

Soon, my little mouse. Soon.

CHAPTER
SEVEN

VIOLET WAS in her dark room, developing photographs. She loved swirling the paper in the chemicals, watching the still image slowly take shape before her eyes, preserved forever. Memories that no one could take away, indisputable proof that someone had put their mark on this earth.

It required patience, which Violet had in abundance. After all, hadn't she waited years for Max to finally notice her? And now that he had, she'd never been happier.

What if I cannot change Max's mind about a relationship?

Then life would march forward. Women were more independent nowadays, at least outside of the ton. Perhaps she could convince her parents to let her live over her favorite camera shop in Chelsea in a set of small apartments. She could sell her photographs for money and support herself. Unless she could marry Max, there was no pressing need to find a husband.

I won't marry you.

If she couldn't change his mind, then she would suggest a long-time affair. Better to have Max in her life and suffer the social consequences than to live without him.

She removed the last photograph from the fixer bath and rinsed it in fresh water. Then she hung the paper on a line to dry along with the rest, taking a moment to appreciate it. This image might be her best yet. The light had hit the buildings perfectly, the women in the foreground sharp and clear. A perfectly captured London morning.

It took several minutes to clean up and remove her apron. Coming down the narrow attic stairs, she heard her parents arguing inside their bedchamber. She started to creep by, ensuring not to make a sound on the way to her room, when she heard her name.

". . . Violet's two suitors?" her mother shouted. "You are supposed to be hurrying them along."

Violet paused. Why were they discussing her marriage prospects?

"Only one now," her father said. "Wingfield's gone to Devonshire for the rest of the season."

Wingfield had left town?

"So marry her off to the other one. I need her settled, Charles. You promised me."

The other one? Violet had no idea who they were discussing.

"I don't know, Elsie. Sundridge seems a bit dim."

Violet put a hand over her mouth. Sundridge? He'd called her Victoria during their first two dances, even after she'd corrected him. He hadn't let her get a word in edgewise, either, talking about playing cricket each time she saw him. Her parents wished for her to *marry* him?

Her stomach turned over, her brain woozy. This could not be happening. And why was her mother so anxious to be rid of her?

Her father continued. "Perhaps we should let her finish this season and find her a husband next year."

"Absolutely not. I want her married as quickly as possible—and it hardly matters to whom. I will speak to Sundridge's father myself, if necessary."

"No, no," her father said. "I'll see it handled, though I cannot understand why you are in such a hurry."

"It's best for Violet. Prolonging a betrothal won't help her prospects. A second season will only make everyone wonder what's wrong with her."

"There's nothing wrong with her with the girl. A bit shy, is all."

"Because you've indulged her. Our duty is to see her married now that she is of age. You promised, Charles. Have a betrothal in place before the month is out."

Violet put a hand on the wall to steady herself. Before the month was out? That was little more than a week from now. Was her mother serious?

She hurried away, moving swiftly along the corridor, her ears ringing with impending disaster. She had no destination in mind, only the need to keep going, to put distance between herself and this information.

Her mother wanted Violet gone. Married off to whomever would have her.

What sort of mother had no regard for the match her daughter made? Charlotte's mother hovered at her daughter's side, ensuring Charlotte only spoke with bachelors from the very best families. Violet's mother, on the other hand, hadn't attended large social events in months and anticipated ridding herself of her only child.

Tears burned Violet's lids as she moved toward the front door, the desire to escape overwhelming her. Their butler appeared, and his brow lowered in concern when he saw her face. "Did you wish to go out, Lady Violet?"

"I'd like to take a walk and visit my friend Charlotte."

"Of course, my lady. Shall I send for your maid?"

"No need. I am not going anywhere but to Charlotte's and it's not far."

"Then allow me to fetch a groom—"

Instead of waiting, Violet opened the door and dashed down the front walk. When she was far enough from her house, she hailed a hansom to take her to the far side of Grosvenor Square.

To Ravensthorpe.

She needed him to comfort her, to tell her it would be all right.

Even if it was a lie.

Max's large home sat on the corner of the very public square. Considering it was the middle of the day, she could not pay a call on him. Instead, she instructed the driver to let her out a block over and she then snuck into the rear of Max's gardens.

Tears streamed down her face as she hurried along. Thankfully, the gardeners were on the far side of the property, their backs to the house. After slipping onto the terrace and through the French doors, Violet ran along the corridor, hoping to avoid detection by the staff on her way to Max's study, where she assumed he was working.

Not bothering to knock, she turned the knob on the study door and slid in. Max was seated behind his desk, a young man scribbling on paper in the chair across from him. The duke's head snapped up, dark blue eyes locking on her face—and his jaw dropped. She hadn't a clue as what to do now that she was here, so she waited, silent tears rolling down her cheeks.

Max recovered quickly, coming to his feet. "Webber, let's pick this up later. You have enough to get started."

The other man gathered his things and bowed. "Your Grace."

Violet moved aside to let the young man pass. When they were alone, she tried to catch her breath, but emotion clogged her throat. Max came toward her, concern etched on his handsome features. "Violet, what is it? What's happened?"

Without waiting another second, she threw herself at his solid chest. He caught her, his arms holding her tight to his frame, and she breathed in his now-familiar scent of orange and tobacco. He was strong and safe, a balm for her misery. After a few seconds, her tears dried on his necktie, her shudders ceasing. When he picked her up, she clutched at his shoulders and buried her face in his throat.

He lowered them into a chair near the empty grate. The moment stretched and he seemed in no hurry to make her talk. For some reason, his calm fortitude helped soothe her. Finally, she sighed. "I'm sorry. I shouldn't have burst into your home in the middle of the day."

"I don't mind, though I do hope you came in the back."

"I did. No one saw me except the man who was here a moment ago."

"Webber is discreet. His job depends on it. Now, are you ready to tell me what is wrong, or shall I give you a present?"

She leaned back to see his face. "You bought me a present?"

The duke appeared adorably embarrassed, with his cheeks turning pink. "Yes, I did," he said. "Shocking, but I am capable of simple kindness, Violet."

This was more than simple kindness. This was . . . monumental. He'd bought her a *gift*.

He cares for me.

Her spirits lifted immediately—a considerable feat, seeing as how she was to be betrothed by the end of the month.

Max slid out from underneath her and went to his desk. When he came back, he was holding a rectangle-shaped box wrapped in brown paper. "I hope you like it."

Was he serious? The box could contain rocks and she would treasure them always. She tore through the paper with all the restraint of a three-year-old on Boxing Day. She gasped. "You bought me a camera."

Max thrust his hands in his trouser pockets and gave her a half smile. "I did."

"I've wanted a box camera for months. How did you know?"

"I had no idea. The clerk at the store recommended it."

She stood and placed the camera on the chair, then wrapped her arms around his middle. "Thank you, Max. It's the perfect gift. I love it."

He squeezed her tighter. "You're welcome."

They stood there for a long moment, locked in an embrace, and Violet thought she'd died and gone to heaven. Her problems felt far away while in the warm security of Max's arms. "Why does my mother hate me?"

Max's lips touched the crown of her head. "Come sit." He led her to an empty chair and pulled her onto his lap once again. "Why do you believe your mother hates you?"

She relayed the conversation she'd overhead. "She wants me betrothed by the end of the month."

"Perhaps it is as she said, that she is worried a second season will harm your chances."

"Do you believe that to be the case?"

"No. However, I haven't any daughters and I only married to produce an heir, so I am hardly an expert."

He so rarely spoke of his late wife and his son. She was curious about them, about anything regarding his life. "Tell me about her."

"Who?"

"Your wife."

He started, his body jerking slightly. "Why?"

"Because I'd like to know her."

———

Max didn't know what to say. Part of him wished to refuse. He hated talking about Rebecca, and Will had long stopped asking about his mother. Those were memories best not stirred.

But perhaps Violet needed to understand. Marriages in their world were not for love or happiness. They were for progeny and legacy, to transfer wealth and property. Moreover, she needed to know of his past and why he'd never marry again.

He cleared his throat. "I decided to marry when I was twenty-four. I'd wrangled the accounts into some semblance of order and made several wise investments on the Exchange. There was no reason to wait."

He'd been the last of his friends to marry. Charles had settled down two years prior and Violet had already turned one. There was no need to mention it, however. Doing so would only make him feel like an old lecher, and this moment was about comforting her.

"Rebecca was pretty, the daughter of an earl. Her father had a large farm in Scotland with some sheep that I envied. He offered it as part of her dowry and I accepted." He'd sold the farm ages ago, as it had only served as a bitter reminder of his failure.

He stroked Violet's leg through her skirts. Thankfully, she'd stopped crying—a sight that had shredded his heart—and seemed to be breathing easier. He liked having her here, even during the day. Returning to his tale, he said, "I had thought we were a good match, that we'd muddle through together, but Rebecca was scared most all the time. Scared of acting improperly, scared of the staff gossiping. Scared of me."

"Scared of you?" She leaned back to see his face. "That is ridiculous. I've always thought you quite kind and generous."

He shook his head. Sweet girl. "I mean in the bedroom. She could not stand for me to touch her."

"Oh." Violet's nose wrinkled in the most adorable way. "I see."

"She knew her duty, of course. She allowed me to visit to her room at night, take her only under the covers and in the dark. Never undressed. I suspect she gritted her teeth through the whole business, despite my concerted efforts to ensure she enjoyed it. But the harder I tried, the more miserable she became."

"Perhaps she found the pleasure shameful."

It had crossed his mind, but he'd never learn the truth, unfortunately. "Perhaps. She wouldn't discuss it, though, and when she began increasing, I assumed we were both relieved." He had been so happy, so eager to be a father. To nurture and love a child as he hadn't been by his own father.

"Assumed? You mean she wasn't happy about carrying your child?"

"No, about sleeping with her. I assumed she'd gladly see me go elsewhere for my physical needs. That I could fuck whoever I wanted, seeing as how she didn't want me."

She frowned, her nose wrinkling. "A mistress."

He sighed, wishing he didn't have to tell Violet of his sordid past. *She'll never look at me the same.*

Perhaps it was for the best.

He carried on. "There was a woman from before my marriage. She was the wife of a viscount and we got on well together. I thought . . . I thought I was doing the right thing."

"It was insensitive of you, but you would not be the first married man in the ton to take a mistress."

"I realize as much, but as time went on I didn't try to hide it, either. Call it hubris or the idiocy of a twenty-five-year-old duke. I started staying away for longer stretches of time. Then I took my mistress to Rome—despite her husband's objections." He'd felt invincible, a man who had everything that mattered: wealth, a child on the way, and a beautiful woman at his side. He was cocksure and fearless, certain he knew best. "Rebecca was eight months along when the viscount wrote to her, informing her of what I'd done."

Violet began rubbing his chest, as if to soothe him—him, the man responsible for it all—and something inside Max shifted, unlocked. No one had comforted him in quite a while. He hadn't wanted it, frankly. But it was different with Violet. She eased his troubled soul, smoothed some of the jagged edges that scraped and cut inside him.

Clutching her tighter, he finished it. "There was no denying the viscount's claims, as I'd just returned days earlier. The news sent Rebecca into hysterics. She was inconsolable, crying and refusing to eat. She resented that I'd taken a mistress while she was carrying our child and considered it a betrayal of our marriage vows. Because of the unrest, the baby came early. I had the very best doctors at her side, but they couldn't save her."

"They were able to save the baby."

"Yes. Will was small, but he lived." His son had been so tiny, so fragile. But Will had fought to survive and Max had done everything in his power to see that his baby thrived. He had wet nurses around the clock and an army of nannies to keep a vigilant eye over the future duke. Max hardly left his son's side during that time.

"Max, you don't know whether she would have survived or not. Many happily married women die in childbirth."

He pressed his lips to her hair. "There's no need to lie. I was responsible for her death." That shame would follow him to his grave. "Which is why I will never marry again. I have no intention of subjecting another woman to that life."

"What life?"

"With me, failing at faithfulness."

"Max, you were so young."

"Older than you. Old enough to know better."

"Perhaps you wouldn't be unfaithful next time."

The hopeful note in her voice caused his tone to harden. "There will be no next time, Violet. I have no need to tie myself down when I already have an heir." He was not interested in ruining another woman he'd promised to honor and cherish. Max wouldn't risk it. A second dose of guilt would bury him.

"What about love? What about companionship?"

He hated to shatter her illusions, but it had to be said. "My dear, I've no need of the first and can find the second anytime I wish."

She was quiet after that, but he didn't take it back. Someone must give her the unvarnished truth. Someone must lower her expectations, both with regards to him and her future marriage.

A marriage not so far in the future, it seemed. Max hadn't a clue as to why Lady Mayhew was in a rush to marry Violet off, especially to a twit like Sundridge. Lady Mayhew hadn't ever seemed cruel, but perhaps the resentment in the Mayhew marriage had bled into her relationship with her daughter.

Still, Sundridge and Violet, married? Max's gut cramped at the thought. That fool did not deserve someone with Violet's spark or adventurous spirit. To hear her moans or capture her sighs with his mouth. To suck on her gorgeous tits or tongue her luscious cunt. It was out of the question.

"I'll have a word with Sundridge," he said curtly.

"Why?"

"Because you don't want to marry him."

"You say that as if they won't merely find someone else, another hapless soul to take Sundridge's place."

He didn't care much for that, either. "I won't let you marry just anyone. I'll use my influence to help you make the best possible match."

"Such as?"

"There's . . ." Every name that went through his head was instantly discarded. No man he knew was good enough for her. "Hmm."

She studied his face, observing his indecision like a hawk searching for prey. "Well?"

"I shall need to think on it."

She snuggled into his side and buried her nose in his neck. "I cannot see why I must marry at all. I could move into a small apartment in Chelsea above a camera shop, then maybe open my own photography studio."

And leave herself open to all sorts of mashers, charlatans, and miscreants? He sat straighter. "Absolutely not. That would hardly be safe."

"Perhaps, but I would be independent. I'd be willing to trade some peace of mind for that."

"I wouldn't."

"And I could still see you."

Satisfaction raced through him as he considered it—and he was instantly ashamed. Violet could not become his mistress. To do so would ruin her social standing and likely get Max shot by her father. "You do not want that life, darling. You deserve the protection and security of a proper marriage. To be pampered and provided for until you die."

"By a man like Sundridge? No, thank you." Clever fingers played along Max's jaw, stroking the skin above his collar. "Will you grant me a favor, Maximilian Thomas William Bradley III?"

His lips twisted into an affectionate smile. "Indeed, someone has been studying Debrett's."

"I used to write it on paper when I was younger."

Surprised, he leaned back to lock eyes with her. "You did?"

"Yes, and I drew little hearts around it, too."

He dropped his head onto the chair back. "Violet, my God. I should toss you in a carriage and send you home." But he wouldn't. Good sense had departed ages ago when it came to this woman. He couldn't get enough of her.

He'd never felt this connection with a lover before, this consuming need to not only touch and kiss her, but to just be with her, to talk about everything and nothing. Maybe it was because he'd known her for so long. Or perhaps it was merely Violet, this daring and intelligent woman who challenged him at every turn.

She playfully pushed his chest. "Stop talking nonsense. Will you grant me a favor or not?"

He tapped his fingers on the armrest, thinking. He didn't like agreeing without all the terms. However, this was Violet. History had shown that he had a difficult time telling her no, unless the topic was marriage.

He kissed her temple. "It depends."

"On?"

"On whether this request involves a lack of clothing and a flat surface."

"As a matter of fact, it does. Would you like to hear what I want?"

Blood gathered in his groin as he considered all the ways he planned to defile her this afternoon. "Of course. Name it and it's yours."

"May I photograph you?"

He blinked. "But I thought you said . . .?"

"Oh, I did." She cocked her head, her eyes dancing. "I want to photograph you without your clothes."

CHAPTER
EIGHT

WHEN MAX CHUCKLED, Violet did not join in. The request hadn't been a jest. Devastatingly handsome, the duke was a specimen of living, breathing art, and if he did not deserve to be photographed and preserved, then nothing did.

He angled to see her face, the light catching on the threads of silver in his ink-colored hair. Her lower half clenched at his beauty, so harsh and masculine it hurt to look at him. His dark gaze narrowed on her. "Why?"

"Why not?"

"That is hardly an answer."

She smoothed the fabric covering his chest, petting him. "Because you are so very pretty and I wish to try out my new camera."

"Violet . . ."

He sounded exasperated, so she explained. "It's not uncommon. Shops near the Strand sell all sorts of—"

"You should not know of those places," he said sharply.

"Everyone knows of those places, Max."

"Do not wander in there. If you wish to see those types of images, I'll purchase them for you."

"Why not pose for them instead?"

"Back to this, are we?" He shook his head. "Not the sort of portrait a duke poses for, darling."

The endearment warmed her insides, but she didn't stop pressing him. "Please? The light is gorgeous right now, with the perfect amount of afternoon sun. We'll lock the door and the photos will only be for me, I promise."

"Until you are angry with me and then copies are shipped off to my enemies."

That stung. "Do you honestly believe I would ever do such a thing?"

"No, but they could end up in the wrong hands. What if your mother or father discovered them?"

She sensed victory. "My darkroom is in the attic and they never go up there."

"And you'll lock them up?" He pinched the bridge of his nose with a thumb and forefinger. "I cannot believe I am contemplating this. My ducal ancestors are undoubtedly spinning in their collective graves."

"What if you turn your head, so the camera cannot clearly see your face?"

"That sounds better, but only if you allow me to take some of you as well."

"Nude photographs?"

"Yes."

She licked her lips and shifted on his lap. Did she dare? He would see all her imperfections and flaws, captured for eternity.

"Not so brave now, are you?"

The taunt hit home, making her feel foolish. "Fine. I will if you will."

He ran a hand along her side and cupped her breast. "As long as I am able to keep the photographs of you."

She arched her back, pushing into his palm. "What will you do with them?"

"Stare at them while I stroke my cock."

The place between her legs pulsed at the idea. "Perhaps I'll do the same with your photographs."

"You mean use them whilst you masturbate? Oh, my sweet girl, nothing would bring me more joy."

Before she melted into a pool of lust on his plush carpets, she got up and readied the box camera. Max locked the door and then disrobed garment by garment until he was naked, his long and powerful body making her mouth water. On display were wide shoulders and a strong chest dusted with dark hair that trailed south, toward his flat belly. His penis was half-erect, the crown peeking out from the foreskin, with dark veins running along the shaft. And his muscled thighs were—

"If you keep staring at me like that, we'll never get around to actually taking the photographs."

She shook herself and tried to adopt a more professional demeanor. "Let's move the divan to maximize the light."

He helped her arrange the furniture to her liking, and then she told him to lie down. "Stretch out so the camera sees all those glorious angles and ridges."

"I had no idea you were so enamored by my looks. You are embarrassingly good for my vanity."

Please. Every woman in London salivated over him, as he well knew. "Put your arm behind your head and lean back."

He did as she asked, taking direction as she arranged him the way she wished. Goodness, he was delicious, as perfect as any museum sculpture. The sun cast him in an otherworldly glow, though certainly not angelic. More like a sinful treat on a hot summer's day, wicked and irresistible. The path to ruin, one she would choose time and time again.

Crouching, she took the first photo from an upward angle, where she could see his body but not his face. "Good. Just breathe and hold still."

The box camera was easy to hold and manipulate, and she was able to get close on his bicep, his rib cage. The whiskers on his jaw. He was quiet, letting her work, the sound of the camera doing all her talking. She couldn't wait to develop the full-length photos, the ones with his face in shadow while the rest of him was on splendid display, including his rapidly hardening cock.

He was relaxed grace and banked power, and she struggled to breathe. Her skin was hot and itchy, the throb between her legs growing more insistent. A fine sheen of sweat broke out on her forehead, like a fever had taken up residence inside her veins and the only cure was to lick him from head to toe.

Ahem.

"Now roll the other way."

He cocked a brow. "You want a photograph of my bare arse, then?"

Her face flamed but she didn't shrink from the request. "Seems a shame to waste the opportunity."

Max presented her with his back, his muscles shifting as he settled. She quickly pressed the button to capture the shot and turned the key to advance the film, even before he finished moving. The impulse to save every bit of him, forever, burned through her. Who knew how long she'd have the privilege of seeing him unclothed? If her parents had their wish, she'd be betrothed to another man by the end of the month.

Ignoring the heaviness in her chest at the thought, she kept working to find the perfect image of him, her legs dipping and bending, stepping closer, then farther away, while the minutes advanced.

Finally, Max's hand drifted between his legs. "I cannot stand this any longer. The more you look at me the more I want you. Are you finished?"

She nodded, her mouth dry. He'd rendered her speechless.

"Violet?" He peeked over his shoulder. When she didn't speak, he offered up a smooth grin. "Oh, I see. Enjoying yourself, are you? Perhaps I might offer assistance."

The film had run out, so she carefully placed the camera on a side table. "Thank you for humoring me."

Now flat on his back, he continued to stroke his large erection. "Are you wet, my little mouse?"

She watched the slow movements of his hand, mesmerized as he pulled and dragged, the muscles in his forearms popping. "I wish I had more film," she murmured.

He chuckled. "Too bad you don't have a moving picture camera."

Oh, there was a fine idea. "Would you—?"

"Indeed, not. This is for your eyes only. Come here." She reached him in two steps, and he tilted his head to look at her, his stern expression full of lust. "Take off your clothes."

It took her longer to undress on her own than if she'd had his help, but soon she was down to her drawers, stockings, and shoes. Color stained Max's cheeks, his chest rising and falling rapidly with the force of his breaths as he stared. Deciding to tease him, she lifted her foot and placed it on his thigh, the heel of her boot digging into his flesh. He jerked, his pupils dilating until his irises were nearly black.

He grunted. "In the mood for a bit rough?"

She unbuckled her shoe and removed it. "Perhaps I wish to torture you."

"Then press harder," he said with a daring lift of his brow.

She brought her other foot up and leaned on him, slowly unfastening the buckle on her shoe. He sucked in a harsh breath, his body tensing. "Hurry with the rest of it and get up here."

She shed her stockings and drawers and started to stretch out next to him, but he grabbed her arm. "Sit on my thighs. Put your knees on either side of my legs."

Climbing up, she positioned herself, which left her sex completely exposed. It would have been mortifying if Max weren't focused on her like a starving man. "Like this?"

"Yes. Lean back and put your left hand on my shin, then use your right hand between your legs. Show me what you'll do when you develop the pictures you took this afternoon."

Oh.

He was ordering her to do . . . that. In front of him.

"Max . . ."

"You are gorgeous, Violet. Show me, please."

She bit her lip. He hadn't stopped pleasuring himself. Where was the harm if she did the same? No one would know except for him, and he wouldn't judge her. He never did.

"Go on," he urged, his voice a low rasp.

Arching, she steadied herself with a hand on his leg. The position thrust her breasts up, which Max must have enjoyed because his hand moved quicker. Emboldened, she slipped her fingers into her sex, dipping into the folds until she grazed her clitoris. Pleasure sizzled in her veins and she sucked in a sharp breath.

"Goddamn, that is beautiful. Keep going. Let me watch you."

Gathering her courage, she used the pads of her fingers to swirl and tease, the skin swollen and slippery, while the scent of arousal permeated the air. They observed one another, a shared and intimate experience with hardly any contact, and somehow that aroused her more. She tried to bedevil him, exaggerating her movements, thoroughly enjoying herself while her body climbed toward its peak. Max panted and cursed, his muscles straining as he pumped his fist, and his reaction spurred her on.

At some point, Max released his erection and placed his hands on her thighs, a light sheen of sweat coating his entire body. His penis was a dull red and fully engorged, resting on his stomach, waiting to be put to good use. And she wanted it. There was an emptiness inside her, an ache, and there would never be another man in her life like this one. Not like Max.

The time was right. She knew it in her bones.

"Max, I want another favor."

His gaze remained focused on the place between her legs. "Anything, darling."

"Will you be my first?"

He froze, his eyes locking with hers while his fingers dug into her thighs. "Your first time should be with your future husband. Not me. I cannot marry you."

Lord, she was tiring of hearing him say that.

She pressed harder on the taut bud and her eyes nearly rolled back in her head. "Why should I wait . . . to bestow this honor . . . on a nameless and faceless future husband?"

He licked his lips, his expression turning decidedly predatory. Like he was imagining all he wished to do to her. Streaks of white-hot pleasure rolled along her spine.

"You want me to ruin you." His voice was rough, with sharp edges and unyielding authority. He could command an army with that tone. God knew she'd do anything he asked when he spoke to her like that.

"Yes, I do." Then she landed a blow of her own. "Please, *Your Grace.*"

As if on cue, his right eye twitched. "You'll regret it."

Impossible. She'd dreamed of this for so long, and he had exceeded her imaginings, the elaborate fantasies she'd concocted in her head over the years. The real man was infinitely more alluring, more caring, and there was no reason to hold back. She wanted to drown in him, to lose herself in his breath and surrender to his caresses. "No, I won't."

"Stand up."

She crawled off his lap and stood on the floor. Max rose and towered over her. "You still wish to do this? You want me to fuck you?"

"Yes."

"You are going to be the death of me. Let's go." Not bothering with clothes, he took a hold of her wrist and led her to the back corner of the study. Where were they going?

He pushed a section of the wainscoting, and the wall popped open.

"A secret passage?" How thrilling.

"Go." He ushered her into the darkness, then flicked a switch that illuminated a single bulb. A set of stairs waited to the left. "Climb."

She ascended the stairs, Max right behind her. She could sense him, large and looming, and her skin crackled with awareness, every cell vibrating with readiness. Was this truly happening?

At the top of the stairs, he reached to open a latch, then pushed on the wood. Beyond, a bedchamber was revealed. *His bedchamber.*

Her heart pounded, a steady thrumming of disbelief that she was finally here after so many years of dreaming about it. It was like she'd been invited into Heaven—or more like Hell. This was Ravensthorpe, after all.

She walked inside, her wide gaze taking it all in. A huge dark walnut bed dominated the space, while an armoire, side table, and single leather chair comprised the remaining furniture. Sparse artwork on the walls. As decadence went, the space left quite a lot to be desired. Standing by the bed, she dragged her fingertips over his simple bedclothes. "Hmm."

"You sound disappointed." He closed the panel in the wall. "What were you expecting?"

"Velvet and gilding, I think. A list of men you're exacting revenge upon. Perhaps a special coitus chair, like the one the Prince of Wales supposedly owns in France."

He made a choking sound, his eyes bulging. "How on earth do you know about that chair?"

"Have you seen it?" His lips flattened, and she had her answer. "Tell me. I overheard ladies discussing it in Paris at a ball."

"I will not. And I'd rather discuss you than Bertie. Are you certain about this? You may change your mind at any time, you know."

Even though she was feeling shy and longing for a dressing gown, Violet had never been more certain of anything in her life. "I want this. I want *you.*"

He pulled her close with one arm and used his free hand to roll her nipple between his thumb and forefinger. "Have I told you how much I adore your breasts?"

"You do?"

"Very much so. I would love to pierce these gorgeous nipples with jewelry. Did you hear of that when you were in Paris?"

That was something people did? "No." She watched his hand, her breath stuttering as his thick fingers pulled and massaged the tip of her breast. Each movement sent spikes of pleasure straight between her legs.

"It's in fashion these days. Rings that hang from the breast, sparkling with gems. I could tug on them gently, give you a tiny bite of pain. Would that be rough enough for you?"

"I think I might like that," she said, feeling dazed, drunk on his presence. Yet his talk of the future penetrated the fog in her brain. "So, does this mean we'll continue to see each other?"

———

Clever girl. Max should have known she'd pick up on that. "For now, let's focus on your request, shall we?"

She reached to stroke his shaft. "Just tell me what to do."

Max groaned and struggled for composure. He knew this was a

mistake. He had no right to take her virginity, but he was past the point of talking her out of it. She was a grown woman and if this was what she wanted, then who was he to deny her?

His erection was so painful, he had to grit his teeth. Twice he'd nearly orgasmed while watching her pleasure herself and if he didn't spend soon, his balls might explode.

Still, he had to make this good for her.

He stilled her hand and gestured to the bed. "Lie back on the mattress."

The bed was the perfect height for him to feast on her cunt, and he wasted no time in doing so as soon as she was in position. He kissed and licked her, leaving no bit of skin untended between her legs. He even brushed his tongue over the puckered rose of her bottom, which caused her to gasp, and he made a mental note to return to that area someday soon. *Oh, the pleasures I will give you, my little mouse.*

"Max, please," she begged, her thighs trembling aside his head. "Your Grace. Oh, please."

He couldn't resist her when she begged in that tone, so he tongued her clitoris, suckling while sliding his index finger inside her. Her walls gripped his skin, reminding him of the narrow width of her opening. *You cannot hurt her.*

On his wedding night, he had tried to prepare Rebecca, but she'd wanted the whole business done quickly. Max had assumed his wife's reticence had been nerves during her first time, but it soon became clear Rebecca didn't enjoy their coupling. At all. No amount of preparation had pleased her.

He had to do better by Violet.

Her hips soon met the pumping of his hand, his finger slipping easily into her quim, so he added another. Violet's fingertips curled into the bedclothes, fabric bunching in her palms as she mewled in her throat, her body undulating toward its peak. "Oh, God."

By the time he used three fingers, she was drawn tight, shaking with need. Then the taut bud swelled and tightened in his mouth and she broke, her walls clenching around his fingers, milking them, and Max nearly came on the floor. Goddamn, he could not wait to be inside her.

Rising, he climbed onto the bed and slid between her thighs. "Lift your knees."

She obeyed without question, spreading herself open, her sex flushed from her orgasm, the skin glistening with her slickness. Had he ever seen anything more arousing in his life? Gripping the base of his cock, he lined up at her entrance then paused. His chest heaved as desire clawed inside him like a rabid beast, desperation a fever in his blood. "Are you certain?"

She widened her thighs even further and Max's brain turned to porridge. He pushed forward ever so slightly, working the head of his cock inside her tight sheath. The walls squeezed him like a fist, and he had to close his eyes, breathe deeply, to keep from rutting at her like an animal.

"Oh," Violet said.

He lifted his head and studied her. Violet's eyes were wide, as if she was surprised. "Are you in pain? Discomfort?" Rebecca had cried their first time, her tears soaking their bed. "Shall I stop?"

She shook her head. "Do not dare."

He exhaled, relief and affection settling in his chest, lightening his mood. Vowing to go slow, he moved carefully, steadily, watching her the entire time for signs of distress. She was breathing heavily, her skin flushed, as he slid into her body. It was bloody torture, with streaks of lust crackling along the backs of his thighs, his cock demanding friction.

When he bottomed out, he held there, motionless, sucking in air as he gave her time to adjust. Being inside her was heaven, a tight, wet paradise that he never wanted to leave. Violet was all he could see, all he could feel, and he wished he could stay right here, like this, for the rest of the day and into the night.

Soon he couldn't wait any longer. "All right?" he asked through clenched teeth.

"I expected to be torn in two. Instead I feel . . . full." She wriggled, causing him to shift inside her, and he screwed his eyes shut, struggling not to spend before they even got started. "I like it," she said.

Dear God.

Max gave a thrust of his hips, his shaft dragging along her sensitive tissues, and Violet purred. "Goodness, I like that even more."

He was done for.

Any civility he possessed disappeared and Max snapped, driving into her again and again. At some point she dropped her knees and clutched at him, pulling him closer as he fucked her like a man possessed. Her body slid higher on the mattress and he chased her, unwilling to let her get away even for a moment. A part of him knew he was being too rough, too barbaric for her first time. But she only moaned and scored his skin with her nails, telling him in breathy pants, "more" and "faster."

The woman would be his undoing.

He leaned over her, snarling in her ear as his hips worked, his cock plunging in and out of her channel. "You like this, my little mouse? You want more?"

"Oh, Max, yes. Please."

"You're going to let me fuck you whenever I want, aren't you?" He couldn't seem to stop talking, especially when her walls clenched every time he did. *She likes my dirty words.* "Your cunt was made for my cock. I've never had better."

It was the truth. But he knew it wasn't her body—it was *her.*

You're falling for her.

Unwilling to give credence to such ridiculousness, he shut off his brain and thrust hard. Then he used his thumb on her clitoris, stimulating the button until Violet's back began to bow, her breasts bouncing as continued to work himself in and out of her. Finally, she arched, crying out as her walls contracted around his cock. Flashes of heat streaked along Max's spine, through his bollocks, but he somehow held out while watching her orgasm, the sight more alluring than anything he'd ever witnessed.

As soon as she started to relax, it was tempting to let his body take over, surrender to the bliss that rocketed through his system. Yet he couldn't finish inside her. Quickly, he pulled out and crawled up her body, his knees astride her chest, and aimed the tip of his shaft at her mouth. "Open," he growled.

She parted her lips and he drove between them, groaning as her tongue swirled on the underside of his shaft as if coaxing his spend.

Then it happened. The orgasm roared through him, sensation shooting along his thighs and out the tip of his cock. It went on and on, wave after glorious wave of euphoria, his muscles trembling as he gave her everything he had.

He slumped, nearly falling over, weak as a kitten in the aftermath. Violet continued to lick his shaft, her mouth gentle, and stared up at him with such adoration and satisfaction that his lips twisted into a half grin. He hadn't smiled this much in . . . ages. But Violet had that effect on him. In the short time they'd been lovers, he found himself thinking of her at the oddest moments, with small comments he wished to tell her, as if she'd invaded his brain with her sweet and earnest nature.

Running his hand through her disheveled hair, he almost blurted out a very stupid sentence.

You cannot ruin this girl's life. Begging her to be your mistress is selfish, Max.

God, but he wanted her. Day and night. Ready at his disposal, with her easy smile and keen observations, not to mention her delectable body.

He dropped onto his back and tried to catch his breath. Violet rolled closer, snuggling into his side, and he wrapped his arm around her.

"You are very good at that," she said, her head resting on his shoulder. "No wonder your mistresses fight to keep you."

It had never been like this, but he didn't tell her that. "I am pleased you enjoyed yourself. I haven't much experience with virginity." Only his late wife, and no one would deem that a success.

"Max, it was perfect." She pressed a kiss to his skin. "Just as I knew it would be with you."

He shifted to cradle her cheek in his palm. "I should be reassuring you. Did I hurt you?"

"No." She bit her lip and wiggled slightly. "I am a bit sore, but I cannot wait to do that again."

A chuckle escaped Max's throat. "What am I to do with you, my sweet girl?"

"I am certain you'll think of something, Your Grace."

CHAPTER
NINE

VIOLET FORCED a smile at her dance partner. What on earth made her parents believe Lord Sundridge a good choice for a husband? While he wasn't particularly hard on the eyes, he talked nonstop. She'd stopped listening ages ago, instead memorizing three rote comments to interject whenever he paused for a reaction: "Indeed, I daresay you are right," "How clever of you," and "One can never know, I suppose."

Thus far, he hadn't seemed to notice that her mind was elsewhere. Or, rather on *someone.*

Max stood on the far side of the room, towering over the other men in his perfectly tailored evening clothes. His dark hair was expertly styled, his expression bored to the casual observer. Violet knew better, however.

The Duke of Ravensthorpe was watching her every move.

Oh, he might not have stared directly at her, but he observed carefully, keeping to her vicinity, and his keen gaze brushed over her person no matter where she was in the room.

She could swoon with the possessiveness of it. The duke, possessive of *her.* Her core squeezed in happiness, despite the soreness from yesterday. Though she and Max would never marry, she would never regret giving him her virginity. The experience had been utterly divine, satisfying in every way.

Which left her the problem of Sundridge. Her current dance partner was carrying on a one-sided conversation that seemed more like a lecture aimed at no one in particular. Above all else, she could not marry this man.

Had her father already spoken to Sundridge's father? Dread slithered over Violet's skin, turning her stomach. Why was her mother anxious to marry her off, even to a nincompoop? It made no sense.

Perhaps she should try and reason with Sundridge.

"My lord," she said, interrupting whatever he'd been saying.

Sundridge blinked at her. "Don't care for cricket, do you?"

Was that the topic on which he'd been rambling? "Our dance will end soon, and I wished to ask a question before we part."

"Oh. Has this to do with cricket?"

"No, actually." God help her. "It has to do with us. Are you . . . that is, our fathers . . ."

"Yes?" He had the nerve to sound impatient.

"Are you considering marriage? To me, I mean?" Two months ago, this conversation would have mortified her. Now, too much hung in the balance not to address it.

"I . . . yes. I thought my intent was quite clear."

"Why?"

"Why is it clear?"

"No, why me?"

He cleared his throat. "Well, why not?"

Hardly a statement of ever-loving devotion. "I cannot see that we have anything in common."

"You shall come to like cricket, Lady Violet, I swear."

"It's more than that. We hardly know one another." She lowered her voice. "Wouldn't you rather marry a girl with whom you are somewhat familiar?"

He gave her a look that suggested she belonged in an insane asylum. "You seem like a nice, quiet girl, docile. I think we'll get on just fine."

He made her sound like a cow. Her back straightened, anger

burning her throat. "I am hardly quiet. I have opinions and thoughts of my own, which I cannot verbalize because you never cease talking!"

Heads around them swiveled. The other dancers looked shocked at the outburst, and she pressed her lips together, chagrined . . . but not apologetic.

Indeed, this was not the time or place for such a conversation, though she did intend to dissuade him from offering for her. Soon.

"Excuse me, my lord." Offering a quick curtsy, she dashed off the dance floor and headed toward the terrace doors. She kept her head down and hoped Max wouldn't see her. She needed solitude at the moment, not Max's insistence that all marriages were miserable or— God forbid—another offer to help find her a husband. How would she survive it if the only man she'd ever wanted arranged to wed her off to someone else?

Violet would rather die.

And what happened if she could not get out of a marriage to Sundridge?

A light mist fell onto the empty terrace, the dreary type of precipitation London served in a never-ending supply. Violet didn't mind the water. It felt cool on her overheated skin, a balm for the rawness in her chest. Was this her destiny? To marry a man she didn't want and relive memories of Max for the rest of her life?

She tilted her face to the sky and let the rain mix with the tears building on her lashes.

What am I to do with you, my sweet girl?

His words haunted her, even hours later. *Love me,* she'd wanted to tell him. *Never let me go.* But she knew what he would have said in response . . . and it would have broken her heart.

Can I do this?

Could she love a man who would never claim her publicly? Who would rather keep her hidden away in the darkness? Violet had once thought it wouldn't bother her, that she would do anything the Duke of Ravensthorpe asked.

But it *hurt.* Far more than she'd ever expected. She didn't want to hide or pretend. She longed to be at his side, in the daylight. Bear his children. *Be his wife.*

That would never happen. He'd made it painfully clear from the start.

A sound near the door had her wiping her face. Was it Max? She didn't wish for him to find her crying out here.

"Lady Violet?"

Sundridge. Her shoulders sank.

Turning, she folded her arms and inclined her head. "My lord."

After casting an unhappy glance at the sky, he drew closer, stopping just within reach. His dark blond hair immediately lost its artful tousling thanks to the water droplets. "I sensed you were upset on the dance floor and I wanted to check on your welfare. And apologize, of course, for whatever I might have said to aid in your distress."

Perhaps Sundridge wasn't so bad after all. "Thank you. I shouldn't have raised the topic of marriage in such a public place, I suppose."

"I had assumed . . . Well, I assumed when I kept asking you to dance that you realized I was serious about courting you."

"Why me?"

"As I said, I've found nothing objectionable about you. I think we shall get on quite well together."

"Is it the dowry?" Violet was aware that her status as an heiress would entice nearly any man. *Save Max, of course.*

"We do need it," he said. "I cannot pretend otherwise. That is not my only reason for choosing you, however."

Do I not get a choice, as well? She wished to shout the question into the cool night air, but what good would it serve? The answer was obvious, and everyone knew it. Still, she had to try. "What if I told you my heart was promised to another?"

Sundridge lifted a bony shoulder. "I think we should focus on friendship and compatibility. A marriage is a partnership, sort of like a cricket team. You see—"

"What about happiness?"

"If you are asking if I'll tolerate pursuits outside of our marriage, I won't object. We'll need children, of course, but that's no hardship."

Violet wilted, unable to countenance what was happening. Her life was spinning out of control, her future full of nothing but misery and compromise.

Sundridge gripped her arm and moved closer. "May I call you Violet?" Without awaiting an answer, he said, "Violet, I realize how young girls romanticize these things, but this is a time for strategy. Like in cricket, you might give up something now to gain a run or two later."

What in God's name was he talking about? She tried to pull free, to no avail. "You aren't listening to me—"

A voice cracked through the night like the lash from a whip. *"Release her."*

The Duke of Ravensthorpe emerged from the gloom, looking like an avenging angel ready to lay waste to everything in his path. Violet's heart clenched as he stalked forward, his eyes burning into the younger man at her side. "I said to release her, Sundridge. *Now.*"

Sundridge held up his hands. "I—I didn't hurt her, I swear."

Max glanced at Violet. "Are you hurt, Lady Violet?"

"No, Your Grace." She didn't know what do. Why was Max here? Had he been worried about her? She bit her lip and tried to contain the urge to throw herself into his arms.

You're a secret. You'll always be just a secret.

Max rounded on the younger man. "You are lucky no one else caught you out here. Were you trying to ruin her reputation? I hadn't thought you such a bounder, Sundridge."

"I came to converse with her. That's all." Sundridge sidled away from Max, his skin going pale. "I never meant any disrespect."

Max advanced, his hands curling into fists. "I saw her try to pull away when you grabbed her. Are you telling me I am wrong?"

Sundridge's back met the balustrade. He was trapped. Max didn't stop, snatching Sundridge's throat in a strong hand and leaning in. The younger man pleaded, "Your Grace, I swear. It was innocent. We were only talking. Tell him, Lady Violet!"

"I know what I saw," Max snarled and shook Sundridge once. "I ought to punch you in the mouth for lying."

Sundridge's face started to turn purple and Violet panicked. She'd never seen Max this enraged, this out of control. Would he honestly harm Sundridge in the midst of a ball?

Rushing forward, she put her hand on Max's arm. "Max, stop. Let him go!"

Max released Sundridge's throat and the younger man began to cough in an effort to breathe. Not quite finished, Max jerked Sundridge by a lapel and tossed him in the direction of the terrace steps. "Go home, Sundridge. And if I ever see you near her again I'll make certain you regret it."

Sundridge didn't look back. He hurried down the stone steps and disappeared into the gardens, likely headed to the mews. Max smoothed his jacket and pulled on his cuffs. She frowned at him, shocked by his display of irrational behavior. "Have you lost your—"

"What in the bloody hell, Ravensthorpe?"

Spinning, she saw her father near the French doors—and he appeared livid.

———

The rage-induced fog began to recede from Max's brain, only to be replaced by dread. Violet's father stood on the terrace, his mouth flattened into a furious line. Just how much had Charles seen and heard?

Max decided to go with the easiest reaction, which was righteous imperviousness. "I was returning from the gardens, Mayhew, when I happened along Sundridge manhandling your daughter. I assumed you'd appreciate my lending her my protection to avoid a nasty scene."

Charles stalked forward, his dress shoes slapping on the wet stone. "You were not in the gardens, Ravensthorpe, because I saw you slip out the terrace doors a few moments ago. I followed because I wished to talk to you—and then I catch you nearly strangling a man to death and my daughter calling you Max." He pointed in Max's face. "So I'll ask again, what in the bloody hell is going on?"

Shit. Charles had seen and heard most all of it, apparently. Though his chest burned with regret, Max forced out a lie. "I am saving your daughter's reputation, obviously."

"Violet, return inside," Charles barked, not taking his eyes off Max.

"But Papa—"

"Now, Violet."

Max raised a brow, using calm logic to diffuse this disastrous situation. "She's soaked to the bone, Mayhew. You cannot order her inside the ballroom in her current state."

Charles's gaze, full of fury and resentment, narrowed on Max before shifting to his daughter. "Go around the side of the house and find our carriage. *Now.*"

Max had to bite his tongue to keep from admonishing his friend for the way he spoke to Violet, who had done absolutely nothing wrong in this instance. Instead, he clasped his hands behind his back and tried to wipe any trace of emotion off his face.

"No, Papa. If you are going to discuss me, then I have a right to stay."

"Absolutely not. Get to the carriage this instant, daughter." Charles did not waver and Violet licked her lips, uncertainty creeping into in her expression.

Finally, she addressed Max. "Thank you for coming when you did, Your Grace." Her voice wavered slightly, making him long to pick her up and hold her, but he merely nodded instead. In a swirl of wet silk, she disappeared down the terrace steps.

"I want to know what is going on between you and Violet," Charles snarled. "You will tell me this instant."

"Don't be ridiculous," Max drawled. "There is nothing going on."

Charles's lips twisted. "She called you Max. She put her hand on your arm. I saw the way she looked at you, unafraid and adoring. There is a familiarity there, one that hasn't existed before, and I want to know why, goddamn it."

Max clenched his jaw, his mind spinning on a plausible response . . . but came up empty.

"My God." With both hands, Charles shoved Max into the stone balustrade. Anger hardened his features into a mask of rage. "You bastard. Have you compromised my daughter?"

There was no hope for it. Charles had seen too much and they knew each other too well. Max braced himself. "Yell a little louder, Mayhew. I don't think they heard you in Cheapside."

"How could you? My *daughter.*"

Charles stripped off his right glove and pulled his arm back. Max knew it was coming, so he waited, holding perfectly still, aware that he deserved it. The fist connected with his jaw, driving him into the stone railing once more. *Bloody hell, that hurt.* Max bent over and dragged in a breath, struggling through the pain. "That's the only one you'll get, Mayhew."

"You goddamn arsehole. My only child and you had to defile her. What, are there not enough women in London already for you? No doubt you've given Violet the clap, you prick—"

Max grabbed Mayhew and reversed their positions, shoving the other man against the stone before leaning in. "I do not have the clap—and watch your mouth."

"She's not much older than your son. You've known her since she was a baby."

Stepping back, Max swept the water off his face. "She is not a child anymore. She is a grown woman. Nevertheless, I did not plan this. It just happened."

"I never thought . . ." Charles shook his head. "You've never gone for the young ones before. I thought she was safe with you around."

"She *is* safe with me around," Max growled. "I would never hurt her."

"She was an innocent, Ravensthorpe. By touching her, you've harmed her."

"I am discreet. No one knows of our association."

"Except for Sundridge. And now me." Charles raked Max with a look full of disgust. "All these years you've been coming to my home, eating dinner with my family, and you've been lusting after her. I ought to put a bullet in your rotten heart."

Anger swept through Max at the indecent implication. He pointed a finger in Charles's face. "I never lusted after her until recently. This all happened within the last month."

"Christ." For a moment, Charles appeared like he might cry. Then he drew himself up. "Is she carrying your child?"

"Absolutely not."

"Are you entirely certain?"

Max paused, because how could one ever be entirely certain? "I am fairly certain."

He'd taken precautions over the years never to subject another woman to childbirth. The possibility of death was too great a risk, and the idea of Violet writhing in agony, bleeding to death because of his lust, sent a bolt of cold fear through his veins.

Charles slapped the stone with his palm. "Goddamn you, Ravensthorpe."

"Even still, I won't marry her."

Charles's jaw fell. "You think I want my daughter married to *you*?" He gave a bitter laugh. "You killed your first wife. Do you actually believe I'd give my sweet and trusting daughter over to the likes of you?"

Max folded his arms across his chest and worked to remain calm. It wasn't anything he hadn't told himself, but it stung to hear it out of his friend's mouth. "No, I suppose not. Fortunately, no one knows of my association with her. Sundridge will assume my friendship with you to be the reason I intervened tonight. Her reputation remains pristine."

Charles acted as if he hadn't heard a word Max said. "Now the rumors about you and Wingfield make sense. I heard you accosted him at Brooks's, but I hadn't believed it. That was over Violet, wasn't it?"

"Do not make this into something it isn't, Mayhew."

Charles dragged a hand through his wet hair. "I cannot believe, after all our years of friendship, that you would do this. That you could care so little for my family. That you could be so callously cruel."

The moment stretched, the steady drizzle of rain continuing to soak them both, but neither moved. An awful sensation swept across Max's skin and burrowed into his chest like talons—a sensation he suspected was guilt. However, no promises had been hinted at between him and Violet. He hadn't lied—she'd known his intentions at every turn. He hadn't whispered pretty words merely to get under her skirt. He hadn't needed to.

Still, he didn't relish exposing the affair and hurting her. Damn Mayhew for forcing him to do it.

It's for the best. She was never meant for me, anyway.

The world believed him vicious and selfish. A monster who drove his first wife into the grave. It was past time to prove it.

Drawing himself up to his most menacing height, he drawled, "You are overreacting. I haven't hurt her or ruined her chances at marriage with Sundridge. 'Tis a lark between us. Nothing more."

"It had better be, because I'm betrothing her to Sundridge, if he'll still have her. As for you, I hope you rot in hell, Ravensthorpe."

Charles shoved Max out of the way and headed for the steps. "Oh, and Ravensthorpe?" He glared at Max. "If I ever see you in the vicinity of my daughter again, death sentence or not, I'll shoot you right between the eyes."

Then he disappeared and Max was alone, the sound of the raindrops his only company. He stared at his shoes and tried not to drown in his regrets.

I did the right thing.

There had been no choice but to tell Charles. Violet wouldn't agree, certainly, but she'd thank Max one day after she married some young lord and had a passel of children. A cantankerous, cynical duke such as himself had no right to a vivacious and optimistic young woman like Violet. She had years of joy and discovery ahead of her, while he had long crested that particular hill.

He rubbed the center of his chest, where a dull ache had set up residence. Yes, it was definitely for the best.

CHAPTER
TEN

VIOLET COULDN'T MOVE, her back stuck to the stone as rain slithered into her bodice and behind her neck. Her stupid heart oozed misery, as if it had been sliced open to bleed out on the grass.

A lark. He'd called her a *lark*. Dismissed and diminished her.

That is what you get for eavesdropping.

Yet how was she expected to leave when her father and Max were discussing her? Of course, she had stayed—though a big part of her now wished she hadn't.

Chest tight, she lifted her face toward the sky, longing to start over again, back before she'd romanticized thoughts of a dark-headed duke with eyes like midnight.

It's better to know how little you mean to him.

She would never be more than a secret, a diversion he used to the pass the time. He would never love her, not as she loved him.

Indeed, she'd thought she could handle an affair, that having a piece of him was better than nothing at all. What foolishness. What hubris. Turned out it hurt to settle for scraps. She wanted every bit of Max, his body and his heart. His soul.

'Tis a lark between us. Nothing more.

Goodness, she couldn't breathe. She tapped her sternum with her fist, reminding her lungs to function. It must have worked because she was still standing when her father came storming down the stairs.

When he spotted her, he stopped. "I see you heard." Grimacing, he closed his eyes. "I would have spared you that, but I suppose it's best you learn what type of man he is."

Your cunt was made for my cock, Violet. I've never had better.

Even if he'd been telling the truth, their intimate moments had meant nothing to him. *She* had meant nothing to him.

Swallowing, she faced her father. "I'd like to go home."

"Come." He took her arm and towed her along in the rain. "God, Violet. I would have wished any other man in the entire world for you. He is the very last one—"

"Not now, Papa."

There must have been something in her voice, something desperate and broken, because he clamped his lips shut. They ended up in front of the house, and the Mayhew carriage was soon brought around. With the evening still in full swing, the streets remained quiet at this hour. Violet was grateful for the rain, as it washed away the tears leaking from her eyes.

When they were settled inside, her father handed her a dry cloth. Violet wiped her face slowly. "I am sorry, Papa."

"Sorry it happened—or sorry you were caught?"

She couldn't answer. The wound was too raw, her body still sore from Max's attentions yesterday.

Papa exhaled and pushed the wet hair off his forehead. "I am trying to remain calm, but it is a struggle. How on earth did this happen?"

She forced the admission past the lump holding court in her throat. "You mustn't blame Ravensthorpe. I threw myself at him—more than once, I might add—and he tried to warn me off many times. Also, he told me that he would never marry me."

"Then, why?"

"Because I've loved him ever since I was a girl."

And I thought I could make him love me, too.

"Your mother was right. I allowed you far too much independence with your camera and your classes. We should have kept you limited to traditional pursuits at home with a governess."

On the dark street were the familiar houses that lined their perfect little world, a society where young girls had no control over their future. Where parents used their daughters like bargaining chips. There was a great fascinating city out there, one she'd never experience or explore because it had been deemed unsafe for girls like her.

"We'll marry you off to Sundridge and no one ever need know," her father was saying.

"Papa, he could barely bother to learn my name and all he talks of is cricket."

"You act as if you have options at the moment, Violet. Allow me to dissuade you of that notion. Sundridge is your only hope."

A sob worked its way out of her chest, but she pushed it down. There would be time enough for that later. "I do not want to marry him."

"You could be increasing," Papa hissed, his eyes full of disappointment and anger. "Have you thought of that?"

Max hadn't spent inside her, so she doubted a child would result. Those details were not something she wished to discuss with her father, however. "Nevertheless, that is no reason to rush into a miserable marriage."

Papa leaned in. "I will not have my daughter bear a child out of wedlock."

The absolute nerve . . . Her lips curved into a knowing sneer as she leaned in as well. "You mean like the child you fathered with a mistress two years ago?"

One could have heard a pin drop in the carriage. He stared at her as if she'd smacked him. "How . . . how do you know of that? Did he tell you?"

"Ravensthorpe and I never once discussed the particulars of your reprehensible behavior. I heard the maids talking about it. The woman came to the house when Mama and I were away, apparently."

He dragged a hand down his jaw. "You mustn't tell your mother. She'd . . . well, she has a weak heart and I'm afraid the news might kill her."

More like he feared Mama might kill *him* if she found out.

"Then you'll not marry me off to Sundridge."

"Are you—are you *blackmailing* me, Violet?"

She hadn't planned on it, but she wouldn't take the words back. Resolve hardened inside her, a small sense of satisfaction that eased her misery. "It appears I am."

"What happens if you find yourself with child?"

"Then I'll go away. No one will know."

"Absolutely not. It's too great a risk. You must marry quickly, Violet. For this . . . and other reasons."

Because her mother wanted her gone.

She turned toward the window. "I will choose my husband."

After a long silence, her father said, "He won't marry you, even if you're carrying his child."

As if she didn't know that already. Tonight, Max's position regarding her had been made abundantly clear. She fought to hold back the tears burning behind her lids. "I am aware. I want nothing more to do with the Duke of Ravensthorpe."

"Well, I'm relieved to hear it. He has promised discretion and I believe he means it. We'll find another suitor soon. Dowry's too large to ignore for most of these gents."

Violet didn't speak. She had no intention of entertaining another suitor, ever.

"Most importantly," Papa said, "I will ensure he keeps far away from you."

Max wouldn't chase her. Why would he? There were other larks, women who wouldn't hope for more. Women who wouldn't develop feelings for him. Sophisticated and smart women like Louisa, satisfied with stolen moments and the occasional tryst.

But that was not Violet, not any longer.

———

A letter. He'd sent her a letter.

A week had gone by—the most miserable seven days of Violet's life

—and now Max had sent her a letter. She stared at the paper warily, as if it might burst into flames at any moment.

Why had he bothered?

"Lady Violet? Are you all right?"

Shaking herself, Violet looked at the housemaid who had presented Max's secret communiqué. "Forgive me, Katie. You said a boy delivered this?"

Katie nodded. "Yes, milady. He appeared while I was picking herbs in the back. Told me to give it directly to you and no one else."

"Thank you. I trust I can rely on your discretion."

"Of course, milady. I promise not to tell a soul." Katie curtsied and departed, leaving Violet alone in her bedchamber.

She placed the missive on her bed and studied it. The letter was thin, just a single sheet of paper, with no writing on the outside. Max's familiar ducal signet ring had been pressed into the sealing wax.

Part of her wished to tear it open and devour every word.

The more rational side, however, feared additional heartbreak. Hadn't she suffered enough? Unless his letter contained words of undying devotion and a marriage proposal . . .

A bitter sound escaped her throat. Max? A marriage proposal? Ludicrous. He would never marry her and she would forever be his secret.

Her door flew open and Charlotte appeared. "Violet, you missed our appointment."

Violet lunged for the letter and tried to shove it under the pillow. Unfortunately, her friend wasn't fooled.

"Is that a letter you're trying to hide?"

"No," Violet lied. "We had an appointment today?"

"Shopping and tea, remember? I cannot believe you forgot." She pointed at the pillow. "Was that a letter from one of your suitors?"

"No, definitely not." The idea of Max courting her was laughable.

Charlotte folded her arms, a determined set to her chin. "Out with it. You forgot our outing, there are dark circles under your eyes, and now you have this letter. What is going on?"

Violet waivered. The strain of keeping all this heartbreak to herself for so many days weighed on her chest. Ever since the night of the ball, she'd swallowed her grief, pushed her misery down to where no one would notice, and it made her brittle. A fragile creature who might break at any moment.

Perhaps sharing a slice of her anguish might help.

"It is from a man, but not a suitor."

"The plot thickens." When Violet remained silent, Charlotte removed her hat and tossed it on the bed. "Are you planning to tell me who?"

Before she could reconsider the wisdom of a confession, Violet let the words out. "The Duke of Ravensthorpe."

Charlotte gasped and clutched a bedpost. "Ravensthorpe? Have you lost your mind?"

"Yes, apparently."

"But he's . . . old. Handsome, but old. And Violet," she dropped her voice, "they say he killed his first wife."

Though he'd broken her heart, Violet still felt the need to defend him. "He didn't. She died in childbirth."

Charlotte studied Violet's face carefully. "I cannot believe this. You care for him."

Unshed tears scalded the backs of Violet's eyelids, and she struggled to retain the tenuous hold she had on her composure. "I love him. I have loved him for a long time."

"And you never told me?"

Charlotte's mouth flattened, hurt lingering in her gaze, and Violet added guilt to the mountain of emotion dragging her down. "Forgive me. Things with Ravensthorpe progressed quickly, and he made it perfectly clear that it was temporary. That I was temporary—"

"That bastard." Charlotte stiffened, her fingers turning white on the walnut bedpost. "He seduced you and then refused to marry you."

"More like I seduced him, but yes."

"Even if you threw yourself at him, he should have told you no. I cannot believe he ruined you and then tossed you away!"

"That's not exactly what happened. Sit down and I'll tell you everything."

Stiffly, Charlotte moved to the bed and sat. Violet took a deep breath and launched into the entire tale, starting with watching Max with Lady Underhill and ending with the letter.

"Wait, he called you a *lark?*" Charlotte's brows went up, outrage clear in her tone. "We should storm into his house and put a bullet in his black heart."

That sounded a tad extreme. "He never lied to me. He never led me to believe it was more."

"You should hate him for how he treated you."

"I don't hate him." She swallowed and tried to keep her voice from shaking. "But while I still love him, I cannot be a secret. I deserve better."

"Indeed, you do." Charlotte reached forward and grasped Violet's hand. "So what will you do about his letter?"

"I haven't decided." She lifted the note with her free hand and tapped it against her thigh. "At best, it's an apology for telling my father. At worst, it's a formal ending to our . . . friendship."

"Do you think there is a chance he's come around on marriage?"

I won't marry you.

"No. Absolutely not." Time and time again Max had made this clear.

"There's always Sundridge. He's not so terrible."

Violet gave her friend a disbelieving look. "He's awful, Charlotte. I won't marry him."

"Then what will you do? You must marry, especially now."

Because Max had ruined her.

Violet didn't feel ruined, however. She felt tired and deeply sad. Fed up with both her parents and society. Ready to make her own decisions and escape any reminders of Max.

This was not the future she wanted, years of circling ballrooms and watching as Max ignored her. How long before he followed another woman out to the gardens? Perhaps he already had.

She pressed a fist into her stomach. Everything hurt and staying here wouldn't solve any of her problems. Her parents would only marry her off to some fop and Max would carry on with his paramours.

She didn't want that life—one that would tear her down, bit by bit, day after day until she was absolutely nothing at all. No, she wanted love and a large family, a place where she fit in, but on her terms, not with a man who cared only about her dowry.

It appeared she must find happiness all on her own.

"Violet, you're scaring me," Charlotte said when the silence stretched. "What can I do to help you?"

Plans began forming in Violet's mind, wisps of ideas that grew clearer, slowly revealing a path forward like an exposed image darkening in a developer bath. She could see it, a fate of her own choosing, even if the prospect seemed daunting at the moment.

Her heart pounded with renewed purpose and resolve. "Actually, there is something you may do. I need you to deliver a package for me."

———

Max stumbled toward the carriage, his legs shaking like jelly. The dockside buildings dipped and swirled, the midmorning sun causing the world to look like a kaleidoscope. Somehow, he put one foot in front of the other and managed to reach his conveyance.

A groom rushed to assist him, but he held up a hand. He deserved the punishment. "No need," he mumbled. "Just allow me to get inside."

Once on the seat, he collapsed like a newborn foal and closed his eyes. He'd been rowing on the Thames for three hours, as he'd been doing every morning for the last fortnight. He hadn't rowed this much since Eton, and his body did not appreciate the punishment. There were blisters on his fingers and palms, his back screamed in pain, and he thought he might have cracked a rib.

But he would not stop. The torture was necessary.

Many times, he'd considered departing London. After all, he had three estates and several townhouses to choose from, including a beautiful apartment in Paris. Yet he couldn't bring himself to go. He couldn't bring himself to leave her behind.

You're a fool. She is better off without you.

He gasped when they bounced over a particularly nasty hole in the road, the agony in his side like being stabbed with a dull knife. Moaning, he clutched the leather seat and tried not to vomit on the carriage floor.

"Apologies, Your Grace!" the coachman called.

Several calming breaths later, the spots receded from his eyes. "Fuck," he whispered.

You cannot do this much longer.

There was no choice. He couldn't sleep at night and this was the only way to exhaust himself enough to rest. When he returned home, he'd fall into bed and finally find a few hours' sleep. It was a neat little system he'd worked out, one that was keeping him sane.

Last week, he'd broken down and written to her, stupidly confessing how much he missed her and apologizing for telling her father. He'd also asked to see her, certain that they could smooth over their troubles if given a chance.

She sent the unopened letter back.

And that wasn't all she returned. She also returned the photographs of him, the ones without his clothes. As if she couldn't stand to look at him. That had hurt worse than the unopened letter.

She must hate him—and he couldn't blame her.

So he rowed. When he wasn't on the river, he was brooding by the fire, draining every bottle of brandy in the cellar. He was pathetic, a miserable husk of a man, yet he couldn't seem to bring himself out of this funk. Nothing mattered. Work piled on his desk; food went uneaten.

He missed her desperately, like a piece of his soul had been removed. This was nothing like when he'd lost his first wife. Losing Violet was a howling despair haunting his every waking moment. He'd found happiness, had tasted salvation, and then let it slip away through his foolishness and vanity.

I hope you rot in hell, Ravensthorpe.

Indeed, he was already there.

Another carriage sat outside his home, but Max couldn't bother with callers at the moment. Or ever. "Send them away," he told his butler as he stumbled over the threshold.

"Your Grace," his butler said, following. "Lady Mayhew is here to see you and insisted on waiting."

Max froze. "Did you say . . . Lady Mayhew?"

"Indeed. She is in the front drawing room."

Why was Charles's wife here? They'd never liked one another. In the early days of her marriage, she had blamed Max for corrupting Charles. Out of loyalty to Charles, Max hadn't denied it, though Charles required no help whatsoever when it came to corruption.

Still, this visit might have something to do with Violet. "I'll see her now."

A horrified look crossed his butler's face—likely because Max wasn't bothering to change before receiving a caller—but Max didn't care. This might concern Violet, and that was far more important than the sorry state of his person offending Lady Mayhew.

He slowly made his way to the drawing room, doing his best not to crumple onto the Italian marble floor.

"Lady Mayhew. This is a surprise."

"Ravensthorpe. I have to say, you've looked better." She was perched on the edge of the sofa, appearing ready to bolt at a moment's notice. She and her daughter had the same hair, a similar chin and bone structure. It sent a fresh wave of agony through him just to look at her.

He cleared his throat. "What may I do for you this morning?"

"I've come to seek a favor."

"A favor from me?" This was unexpected.

She nodded once. "You see, when a wife is saddled with a lying, philandering husband, she must develop a trusted and reliable source of informants. These are often servants, which is certainly the case in my household. And I've recently been given an interesting piece of news."

"Oh?"

"According to Violet's maid, you wrote a letter to my daughter, which she returned along with some other papers. More letters, perhaps?"

Max braced himself, saying nothing and allowing her to come to the point.

"Regardless, my husband confirmed that you and Violet had been involved for some time."

"Our involvement has ended."

"I assumed as much, based on the returning of your note. Not to mention that she's disappeared."

He blinked. "What do you mean, disappeared?"

"She is missing. She left the morning after sending back your letter."

Max strangled the armrests in a death grip, his fingertips digging into the wood. That had been a week ago. Why hadn't he been—?

Fuck. Of course, he hadn't been informed. Charles didn't want him in the same room as his daughter.

Max had to find her. He would tear this city apart with his bare hands, if necessary. A hundred terrible things could befall a sweet young woman such as Violet in this god-awful city. "I assume the police have been summoned and are currently searching for her."

"No. My husband thought it best if we kept this quiet. Family only, that sort of thing." She studied his face. "But it's plain you still care for her."

"I do." He swallowed, his chest pulling tight. "I beg your pardon, but I didn't plan for it to happen."

"You needn't apologize to me. In fact, this makes things easier."

He bounced his leg, anxious for the woman to take her leave so that he could begin searching for Violet. He had to make sure she was safe. "Easier, how?"

"I need her married, Ravensthorpe. As quickly as possible."

His lips twisted derisively. "Yes, she was aware. Hardly matters to whom, does it?"

"You judge me, of course. As a man, you wouldn't understand that all women are pushed into marriage, whether we want it or not. We are traded like cattle, treated little better than dirt."

"Yet you treat your daughter the same."

"Violet is smart. Independent. A thoroughly likable girl. I love her, I do—but I have put up with Charles for long enough. It's time to be free."

Max sat up sharply, ignoring the pain in his side. "Free? Are you saying . . .?"

"I plan to divorce him as soon as Violet is married. The solicitor is ready with the paperwork."

"Divorce?"

She gave him a brittle smile. "I am tired of being disrespected and lied to. You, perhaps better than most, understand what I've endured for the last twenty years. He's fathered two bastards that I know of, probably more. I won't allow him in my bed any longer. Do you want to know why?"

Max remained silent, almost dreading the answer.

She continued, "My husband is riddled with disease. He's had mercury treatments to try and cure it. Lord knows it would be a miracle if I were not infected as well. I cannot stand to look at him any longer. If I must endure the scandal of a divorce to be free of that man, then so be it."

The explanation made sense. If Violet had known, it would have eased her mind regarding her mother's motives. His heart ached for his little mouse. "You should tell your daughter. She believes you want rid of her."

"And I am sorry for that. When I have the chance, I will explain it to her. I had thought to wait until she was married, when she would better understand what happens in the marital bed." She cocked a brow. "But I see you've taken care of that."

"I . . ." For once, Max was at a loss for words. He had taken Violet's innocence against his better judgment.

"Go and find her, Ravensthorpe. Use your considerable influence to locate my daughter and convince her to forgive you. Then marry her, quickly. You, more than most, are immune from any scandal. Your name will shelter her from any . . . unpleasantness during the divorce proceedings."

Marry?

He hadn't wished to marry again, yet he was miserable without her. He couldn't let her go—he needed Violet in his life, in his bed. In his home, making him smile and taking photographs. Being with her was easy, fulfilling in a way he hadn't experienced with any other woman before.

Could he try again? He'd failed with Rebecca, but Violet was nothing like his late wife. Violet was a spark of optimism and light, a beacon of joy and happiness. Intelligent and lusty, she would never bore him or let him run roughshod over her. Moreover, he was different than the selfish man of twenty-five, who'd believed himself invincible. He would treat Violet as a wife should be treated.

Violet . . . *his wife*. He liked the sound of that. Quite a lot, actually.

Suddenly, he didn't care whether Charles disapproved or whether people sneered at the age difference. He had to have her. To love and hold her until he took his last breath.

He tapped his fingertips against his thigh. She had disappeared, but Max would find her. In fact, he had an inkling of where she might have gone. "I cannot promise she'll forgive me, but I will try."

"Good," Lady Mayhew said, rising. "She is headstrong, but Violet's been in love with you for years."

Her mother had noticed when Max hadn't? Of course, he'd been busy avoiding Violet since her debut, terrified of his feelings for her. That ended now. He was ready to admit he loved her and that he couldn't live without her.

He stood. "I am not the only one who must seek Violet's forgiveness. You've hurt her, you know."

She winced, her brow furrowed. "That was not my intention, but I suppose I have been so focused on my own happiness that I forgot about Violet's. I haven't been the best mother."

"Help her understand. Be there for her."

Lady Mayhew cocked her head, her lips pursed in thoughtfulness. "You really care for her, don't you?"

"More than anything else in the world."

"Make her happy, Ravensthorpe."

Resolve settled in his chest like a rock, and he nodded. "You may count on it, my lady."

CHAPTER
ELEVEN

VIOLET POURED hot water into the teapot and returned the kettle to the tiny stove. Then she placed the lid on the pot to allow the leaves to steep. The stove had been a challenge, but she'd grown proficient with it in the past week.

Heartache turned a person productive, it seemed.

Since leaving home, she'd taken photos and explored the city. Walked the streets and observed the inhabitants. She'd also met her new neighbors, three other young women living in apartments above the camera shop in Chelsea. The girls worked in department stores and offices, each a new kind of independent woman, one in control of her own life. Just like Violet.

She hadn't told them of her aristocratic upbringing, but they knew. It was in the way she spoke, the way she dressed. Even in the tea she drank, apparently. But they didn't judge her. Instead, they fondly called her "countess," which Violet didn't mind. She'd never had a nickname before.

Actually, she'd never had this many friends before, either.

She still missed Max, though. He was in her head, her heart . . . in her bones. Part of her regretted not reading his letter, but it wouldn't have said what she wished to hear. Max would never tell her sweet words of undying devotion, the things a husband said to a wife. After all, she was a lark to him. A woman to pass the time.

Goodness, that still hurt.

Pouring her tea, she gave thanks that at least she hadn't conceived a baby. That was one worry she needn't add to the pile, which now included finding employment to cover her rent and living expenses. And those particular problems grew more pressing by the day as her funds dwindled.

Had he thought about her at all? Or had he picked up with one of his many mistresses?

A knock sounded on her door. She placed her cup in the saucer and stood, smoothing her dress. It was probably one of her friends stopping by to have a chat.

Opening the door, she jerked in surprise.

The Duke of Ravensthorpe stood there. Max. Here. In Chelsea. How . . .?

Oh, yes. She'd once told him about her camera shop idea. How had he remembered?

Dark blue eyes burned from under the rim of his hat, his mouth set in a firm, determined line. Though his face was gaunt, he was unmistakably a duke, with his frame draped in expensive fabrics and the gold of his watch fob glinting in the daylight. She could hardly breathe due to the need to throw herself at him.

No, no more playing the fool.

Her friend Irene stood next to him. "I hope it's all right that I let him in. He said he knew you." Irene leaned in. "Is he really a duke?"

"It's fine, Irene. Thank you." Drawing in a deep breath, she said, "Would Your Grace care to come in?"

Max removed his bowler and stepped into her tiny apartment. Irene's eyes were as big as saucers when Violet whispered, "I'll tell you later," and shut the door.

He dominated the small room, a force of nature in her private space. Violet wasn't certain where to go or what to do. Why was he here?

He held his hat and cane in gloved hands and inspected his

surroundings. No doubt he found it lacking, but Violet certainly wouldn't apologize for where she lived. She loved this place.

Without prompting, she produced another cup and saucer, set it on the table, and poured tea for him. Then she retook her seat and calmly sipped her tea, waiting for him to break the silence.

After clearing his throat, he sat and removed his gloves. "Are you curious as to how I located you?" His voice was rough and cracked, like he hadn't used it in days.

"I once mentioned that I would rent a small apartment above a camera shop in Chelsea."

"Yes, and fortunate for me, there are just two camera shops in Chelsea, and this is the only one with apartments atop it."

She frowned, her brows lowering. "Why is that fortunate?"

"Because I needed to find you."

"Interested in a lark, were you?"

He winced. "I saw you leave with your father so it's obvious you overheard us, and I'm sorry I ever said anything as stupid as that. I didn't mean it."

"Why? It's true. That's all we were to one another."

"No, that wasn't all, not for me."

Bitterness welled up in her chest like a fog, its dismal fingers sinking into her heart to squeeze. "Forgive me if I have a hard time believing that, Max."

"Violet, I was trying to convince myself there was nothing between us. That I could go on living without you after you'd happily married your Sundridge or Wingfield. But I cannot do it. I am utterly miserable without you."

Hope fluttered in her stomach, but she beat it back with a ruthlessness that hadn't existed two weeks ago. "Because you need someone in your bed."

"Because I need *you* in my bed. In my life. With me, wherever I go. For however long I have left on this earth."

Her hands curled into fists, her skin burning with humiliation and anger. The gall of this man. "I see. You found me living here and assumed I would jump at the chance to become your mistress or whatever else you wanted. That I would be content to stay hidden and wait for your scraps. Well, you may return to Mayfair and shove that cane—"

"Wait." He reached into his coat pocket and produced a square box, which he sat on the tabletop. "I came here to ask you to be my wife."

The room spun, and Violet's mouth fell open. Was that . . .? No, it couldn't be. "But you said . . ."

"I know what I said, but that was before I tried to row myself to death in the Thames."

She shook her head, confused. "What?"

"Never mind. What's important is that I do not wish to exist in a world without you calling me 'Your Grace' in that breathy way of yours, or running your fingers through my hair. Or taking photographs of me, or talking of philosophy and history and all the other clever things in your head. I cannot do it. I need you."

"You want to marry me? Marry? Me?"

He sighed in that arrogant way of his, as if he hated repeating himself. The sound was so Ravensthorpe that she nearly grinned. "Yes, Violet. Please, marry me."

She bit her lip, not quite ready to give in, though her heart was nearly bursting with happiness. "I thought you were too old for me."

"I only care what you think. Do you think I am too old for you?"

"Of course not. What about my father?"

"I believe he'll soon be too busy with other matters to worry about us."

"Whatever does that mean?"

"Your mother came to see me. She plans to begin divorce proceedings. She was merely waiting until you were married off."

Divorce? Violet stared at the wall, her mind whirling. "Was that why she was so eager to see me settled?"

"Yes."

She paused, uncertain how to feel about this revelation. Looking back, the fights with Papa and the emotional distance from the family made a bit more sense. Mama clearly hadn't been happy, not for years, so if she needed to divorce Papa for her well-being then Violet would support the decision.

Yet why had Mama pushed for Violet to make an unhappy match, as well? If anyone knew the risks of marriage, it was her mother.

Mama should have tried to protect her, not sacrifice Violet for her own gain. Instead, her mother had washed her hands of Violet's future, practically pushing her out the door to any man who'd have her.

And why had Mama shared this information with Max, instead of her daughter?

Suspicion cast a shadow over the moment, and her stomach churned with emotion. "So this," she said, indicating the square box, "is your way of helping her?"

"No." Dipping elegantly onto one knee, he took out the ring and held it up in his fingers. "This is my way of keeping you all for myself. I'll never deserve you, not today. Not tomorrow. Never. You're beautiful and pure and I am the very Devil. But I love you, Violet Littleton, and I shall do absolutely everything in my power to ensure you never forget it, not for a moment."

She covered her mouth, her heart skipping in her chest. "You love me?"

"Indeed, in the very worst way."

She stared at his gold collar stud and voiced her deepest fear. "You won't hide me away? I'll be your wife in every sense of the word?"

With one finger, he lifted her chin to meet her gaze. A wrinkle had formed between his brows. "I'd be proud to have you by my side. I need you. Without you, I'm wrecked. You hold all my happiness in your dainty, camera-loving hands."

"I am not that powerful. After all, even you call me 'little mouse.'"

He stroked her jaw with the backs of his knuckles. "Violet, do you not remember the fable of the mouse and the lion? It is the mouse who shows great courage and bravery, saving the lion from a slow, painful death."

Oh, goodness. She hadn't considered that. Her belly dipped and swooped, as if she might actually swoon. "Are you saying I saved you?"

"Of course, you have, darling girl. You brought color and joy to a man who had lived in gray for so very long." He leaned in and pressed his forehead to hers. "You are the sunshine to my bleary dark soul."

"Max . . ."

"Is that a yes?"

Taking a deep breath, she steeled her voice into something more businesslike. "I have conditions."

The side of his mouth hitched, his expression soft as he rose to his full height. "Is that so?"

"I wish to keep this apartment. That way, I'll have a place just for me when I need to get away."

A muscle jumped his jaw, his dark gaze sparking as he studied her. "Is this about having a lover on the side? I won't share you, Violet. Not with anyone."

"I do not want another lover." She thought of his first wife. "And if we marry, I won't share you either."

"Agreed."

"That easily? Forgive my skepticism, considering your proclivity for lascivious behavior. Does the Duke of Ravensthorpe possess the ability for monogamy?"

"He does, if the woman in his life is you, with your clever brain and bold spirit. If you need to keep the apartment to retain a bit of your independence, then I'll not complain."

"Independence—and my photography. I'll use it as a portrait studio."

"As long as said portraits involve clothing."

She stood and closed the distance between them, using a fingertip to trace the edge of his collar. Goose bumps appeared on his skin and she smiled up at him. "You are the only one allowed to pose for my nude portraits, Your Grace."

A growl rumbled deep in his chest. "Yes to the apartment. What else?"

"I want to try for children."

His large body tensed. "No, Violet. I could not bear it if—"

"I am not your first wife." She stroked his lapel, soothing him. "I'll be fine. But I want a piece of you and a piece of me to live on, together, to make this world a better place."

"Goddamn it," he said and shifted his gaze to the wall. "What if you die?"

"Death stalks us every day. I could choke on a fishbone at dinner and die. But I've spent my entire life watching, observing, never fitting in while waiting for something to happen, and I am tired of waiting. I want excitement and laughter, little feet running through the halls. Most of all, I want to see your face in our children."

"Christ, Violet." He bent to kiss her hard on the lips. "I suppose I'll need to find the best doctors in this bloody country to watch over you, then."

"Does that mean you agree to my conditions?"

"I don't have a choice, do I? I will give you anything you want to get my ring on your finger."

She nearly swayed, the exhilaration almost too much to bear. "Anything I want? Oh, the heady power of having the Duke of Ravensthorpe at my feet."

"As long as you never leave me, I'll lie at your feet anytime you like."

The afternoon light played across the angles of his face and throat. Harsh and beautiful, he was hers, and she'd never tire of looking at him. "What about now? I like the idea of more nude portraits of you."

Taking her hand, he slipped his ring onto her finger. Then he reached into his coat pocket and withdrew a folded stack of photographs. She cocked her head. "Are those the pictures I took of you?"

"I thought I should return them to their rightful owner." When she moved to take them, he lifted the stack far above her head. "With one condition."

Crafty man. Of course he had his own condition. "Which is?"

"That you use them for their intended purpose while I watch."

He wanted her to do *that* in front of him? "Now?"

"Right now." His gaze burned with adoration and desire, but there was something else there, as well. Something new that was serious and far more meaningful.

He loves me.

Her skin could barely contain the joy coursing through her. Sliding her arms around his neck, she pulled him closer and put her lips near his ear. "Yes, Your Grace."

. . .

The End.

SOLD TO THE DUKE

Though she once lived a life of privilege, Lady Eliza is now destitute and desperate to care for her ill sister. She decides to sell the one thing of value she has left: her virginity.

At the auction, a shocked Duke of Blackwood recognizes Eliza and refuses to allow her to fall into the clutches of a depraved bidder. But his role of noble rescuer is upended when the proud beauty insists on giving him his money's worth...

CHAPTER
ONE

THE CHAPEL, LONDON, 1895

A STRANGER WAS ABOUT to bid on her body, for the right to take what should belong to a husband.

But Eliza had no husband, nor did she want one. What she wanted was money—a lot of it.

Most people didn't understand desperation. Not true desperation, the kind that sat in one's belly, rotten and relentless, dragging a person down into a pit of despair. Over the last year, as her sister grew sicker, Eliza had come to know desperation well. Too well, in fact. She was drowning in it, completely out of decent options.

Which left her with only indecent options.

The Chapel auctions were legendary in certain segments of London, whispered about on the streets, with women bragging of the money to be had and the chance to find a wealthy protector. After thinking on it for months, Eliza finally submitted her name, agreeing to auction herself off.

Please, let him be kind.

"Cor, you look bloody nervous." A woman sat next to Eliza. "Is this your first time, love? It won't be as bad as that."

Eliza swallowed and wrapped her arms around herself. They'd

given all the women a simple white shift to wear, the fabric nearly transparent. "Yes, it's my first auction." *My first everything.*

The woman's brows rose slightly at hearing Eliza's accent, which still held hints of Mayfair. "What's a fancy dove like you doing here?"

"Same as everyone else. I need the money."

The woman struck out her hand. "I'm Helen."

They shook hands. "Eliza."

"Nice to meet you, Eliza. This is my third time. You'll be fine. Just do as he asks for seven nights and then you'll go home with a fat purse full of coin."

Seven nights.

A cold prickle of fear snaked down Eliza's spine. For seven nights she would be at the mercy of a stranger with unlimited rights to her person.

This was your choice. You knew what you were agreeing to.

If there was any other option, she would take it. But she had a younger sister to consider, one who would die without treatment. This required money—and Eliza did not want to become a mistress, always at the mercy of a man's whims. Her current predicament notwithstanding, she wanted to keep her independence, which was why the auction was perfect. Seven nights, then she was free.

"Never heard of a cruel bidder," Helen was saying. "The Chapel's owner is particular about who he lets attend. It's why the women are so eager to get a spot each month." She patted Eliza's knee. "Stay bricky and you'll be fine."

Eliza drew in a deep breath. No matter what happened, she would be fine, wouldn't she? She'd survive this, as she had everything else.

She'd survived the death of her parents, as well as the death of her brother, Robert.

She'd survived being cast out with only a few possessions by the new earl, their second cousin and Robert's successor.

She and her sister had survived the streets, the uncertainty. The hunger. Demeaning jobs for meager wages.

Eliza would survive this, too.

It's only your body. No one can touch your heart or your mind.

For one week, she could do anything if it helped Fanny get better.

"Thank you," she murmured to Helen gratefully.

"You're welcome. Oh, and go see the midwife for some pennyroyal at the end of the week. The kind that prevents consequences."

"My neighbor suggested cotton root tea." Martha worked in a bordello, and she'd filled Eliza in on what to expect after the auction. According to Martha, intimacies with a man were generally pleasurable, if not downright addicting. Eliza figured it must be true, considering all the babies in the world.

In the last five years, Eliza had seen and heard quite a lot. Knife fights, opium addicts, pickpockets . . .and yes, sexual favors. The alleys were full of all kinds of grunts and groans, people desperate for physical release.

Most of Eliza's education, however, came from their former neighbors, who'd been loud and enthusiastic in their intimacies, not to mention very specific about what they liked. Thanks to thin walls, Eliza wasn't completely ignorant as to what would occur during these seven nights.

Truthfully, she was looking forward to ridding herself of her innocence. Eliza didn't have time for courting—those dreams died long ago, about the time she cleaned her first privy—but she would like to be held, to experience true pleasure, and to pleasure someone in return. Someone to fulfill these *urges* that haunted her at night, the physical cravings that had her reaching underneath the bedclothes to touch between her legs. . . .

Being a virgin was lonely and exhausting.

"Yes," Helen said, "cotton root tea works too, though I think the pennyroyal tastes better."

Before she could thank Helen again, the side door opened and the room fell silent. A woman holding a journal entered and began reading names. It was the same woman who'd signed Eliza up for the auction. Each auction participant answered when her name was called.

"Eliza," the woman said.

"Here," Eliza said in the loudest voice she could muster.

"Are you still a virgin, love?"

The air seemed to disappear out of the room as every head swung her way. "Yes."

The woman nodded once and closed her journal. "Ladies, we'll begin shortly."

Then she left, leaving the women alone, and Eliza's skin burned. Everyone here now knew she was innocent.

"A virgin," Helen said, her voice full of wonder, as if Eliza had declared herself a mermaid. "Bloomin' hell. You're going to fetch a fortune."

———

Hands were everywhere.

Lucien groaned, lust heavy in his blood, like a drug weighing down his veins. The carriage had stopped ages ago and he truly didn't wish to break up this lovely party . . .but he'd promised.

"My darlings," he said gently, trying to gain the attention of his distracted companions. Delicate fingers slid inside his trousers to stroke his hard cock through his underclothes, and he groaned. Ginny was sliding to her knees, a devilish twinkle in her eye, while Mollie pushed her bare breast deeper into Lucien's hand. He tweaked her nipple, unable to help himself.

"Your Grace needn't attend this auction," Ginny cooed as her fingers started on the buttons of his undergarment. "We are perfectly happy seeing to your needs."

How well he knew this. Ginny and Mollie were delightful in every way, the two actresses having been his regular bed partners for three months. Their time together had been a blur of orgasms and sensual spankings, but he'd promised Jasper, his closest friend, that he'd attend tonight.

"I'm not bidding on a girl." Reluctantly, he covered Mollie's abundant tits with her dress. "Nevertheless, my presence has been requested."

While Lucien avoided the auctions, preferring to get women through natural charm, Jasper attended often. Unfortunately, Jasper had terrible taste in people—hence their friendship—and was no stranger to getting fleeced by unscrupulous women. He'd begged for

Lucien's help in selecting a girl tonight, and Lucien hadn't been able to refuse.

Mollie's lips met the edge of his ear. "Wouldn't you rather fuck me up the bum instead?"

A rush of need surged inside him, his cock pulsing as if pleading for Lucien to follow through on the suggestion. *Damn it.*

Lucien closed his eyes and dug deep for control. Once he had a grip on himself, he helped Ginny up off the floor and began righting his clothing. The girls laughed as his fingers fumbled on the task, his haste and hunger making him clumsy.

He pressed a long, deep kiss to Mollie's mouth, then gave Ginny the same. "I won't be long, loves. You may wait here or the house in Cheapside. I'll find you after."

Before they could argue or tempt him further, he alighted from the carriage. The cool night air slapped his overheated skin and he willed his erection away. Aware of the rules for auction nights, he removed the domino from his coat pocket and slipped it over his face. Then he straightened his shoulders and walked toward the club, determined to get this over with as quickly as possible.

The smell of sweat and desperation hung heavy inside, the interior of the club crowded with men clad in evening suits and masks, each hoping to win a woman for seven nights. *Fools.*

"I was beginning to wonder if you were coming," said a voice behind him.

Annoyed, Lucien turned to his friend. "Have you any idea what you've interrupted? This had better not take long."

"Your mistresses, I know. Don't worry. You'll help me win a woman and then we shall all go our separate ways."

"Why do you keep bidding on these women if you can't trust them?"

"That's what I need you for. The last woman I won here stole two of my favorite paintings."

Christ, Jasper was too trusting by half. "You are hopeless."

"Yes, absolutely. But if anyone knows women, it's you. Please, you must help me, Luc." Jasper clapped him on the shoulder, pushing

Lucien through the doorway. "Just sit down. I'll have you out of here shortly."

Instead of arguing, Lucien continued into the room. An empty table along the side seemed as good as any, so Lucien sat and surveyed the crowd. The masks provided appallingly little anonymity, and he could identify most everyone here, the titled gents and rich industrialists who frequented all the same clubs and theaters.

He had to hand it to the owner. These auctions were quite the rage. To participate, a man required someone respectable to vouch for him, and any hint of violence in one's past was just cause for refusal. This meant women came willingly, eager to be auctioned, and they received every quid of the auction price paid. The owners knew the real money was in the exorbitant participation fee and the liquor sold when the room was packed.

Lucien ordered drinks for them both and relaxed. Within minutes, movement from behind the curtain caught his eye. The audience quieted, anticipation thick like fog in the room.

A large barrel-chested man stepped out onto the stage. "Owner of the Chapel," Jasper whispered to Lucien.

The owner, who looked like a dockside worker, gave a speech about how the auction would proceed, the rules for how the women were to be treated, and the consequences for those who disobeyed the rules. Lucien had little doubt that those consequences were doled out by the owner himself, whose hands could probably snap a smaller man in half.

The auction began. Woman after woman was paraded on the stage as men shouted their bids. Jasper settled on a cheeky-looking blond beauty somewhere along the way.

"May I leave now?" Lucien asked after Jasper was declared the winning bidder.

"No. You must meet her, just to see if she's going to give me trouble."

Though eager to bolt, Lucien sighed and forced himself to stay seated. Only for Jasper would Lucien postpone a night of glorious fucking and debauchery.

Bored by the auction proceedings, he studied the crowd. Odd, but several men here hadn't bid at all, their hawkish gazes never leaving the stage. Rathbone was one, a marquess who, according to Mollie, had sexual tastes that skewed toward the macabre. Something about cutting the insides of Mollie's friend's thighs before he fucked her—as she pretended to be a corpse. Has word not gotten around about Rathbone? Curious that he'd been allowed to participate tonight.

Lucien leaned over to Jasper. "I've heard some unsavory stories about Rathbone. Surprised to see him here."

"Unsavory? Rathbone? I've never heard any hint of that."

"Mollie has a friend, said he—"

"And now," the auctioneer said, "we have our final offering for the night. Gents, I give you, Lady E."

The curtains parted and a pale young woman slowly emerged. She was lovely, with golden blond hair piled atop her head, wisps surrounding her delicate face. Bright blue eyes surveyed the crowd nervously, her body shaking in a clear case of nerves. She couldn't have been more than nineteen or twenty.

The shift she wore did little to cover her. Dusky nipples, furled into hard points thanks to the cold air and lack of undergarments, poked the thin fabric, the small swell of her breasts evident. She had long bony legs, thin arms, and he could see a hint of dark hair covering her mound.

Something nagged in his brain at the sight of her. Why did she look vaguely familiar? The auctioneer took the girl's hand and led her around the stage, like a prized stallion at Tattersall's. Lucien couldn't tear his gaze away, knowing there was something about her. Something he couldn't finger. A puzzle he couldn't quite solve.

"Lady E is the Chapel's most special offering," the man crowed. "Genteel, mannered, and best of all . . .a virgin."

A collective gasp went through the room.

"That's right, gents. This lovely creature has never had a man between her thighs. Whoever wins her for seven nights will be her first."

Color suffused the girl's skin from head to toe, but she didn't run or pull away. Was she truly here willingly? Who would do such a thing for their first time? Bad enough to let a stranger take her innocence, but then keep her for a week? That seemed cruel.

"Now, where shall we start the bidding? I think two thousand pounds."

"Two thousand!" someone in the crowd shouted.

Jasper edged closer. "Why do I feel as if I recognize her?"

That feeling returned, the one that told Lucien the answer was staring him right in the face, like a maths problem he couldn't solve. He scowled as the bidding progressed, now above eight thousand pounds. "I feel as though I do, too. Who—?"

All of a sudden Lucien's body jerked. The puzzle clicked into place, the solution as plain as dirt. That golden hair and those big round eyes that used to stare at him like he was the most fascinating man on earth.

No. *No, no, no.*

Lady E. *Eliza.*

"No," he repeated. "I don't believe it."

"Who?"

"Goddamn it. Robert's sister. Lady Eliza." Her brother had been the Earl of Barnett before he died.

Sharp pain pushed under Lucien's sternum, the familiar guilt twisting him up inside. The memories rushed through him, of the three of them—Jasper, Robert and Lucien—and their steadfast friendship. Without siblings of his own, Lucien had considered the two men like brothers, and he'd spent quite a bit of time at Robert's home. That was back when everything was simpler. Back when Lucien actually gave a damn about being a duke and doing right by his responsibilities.

He remembered Eliza. She'd been a serious girl with a keen head for numbers, and Lucien used to give her maths problems to solve at the dinner table. Robert had tried to quiet her, saying it wasn't appropriate for a girl, but Lucien enjoyed the interactions with her. There had been something pure and innocent about her, a thirst for knowledge so sharp he could almost touch it.

The last time he saw her was at Robert's funeral, a sad-eyed fourteen-year-old girl gripping the hand of her younger sister. The two girls had been surrounded by family—or at least what he'd assumed to be family.

So why was she here, selling her body to a stranger?

"Fuck," Jasper said. "We have to help her, Luc—and I don't have the funds left to outbid them."

Eliza bit her lip and ducked her head, holding onto the auctioneer as if her legs wouldn't hold her without support. What had brought Robert's sister here, nothing more than skin and bones, willing to sell her innocence to the highest bidder? Where was her second cousin, the current earl? Why wasn't she married, with a husband taking care of her?

Robert wouldn't want this for her.

Rathbone called out a bid for fifteen thousand pounds, an outrageous sum of money.

Before Lucien could blink, the words tumbled out of his mouth. "Twenty thousand pounds."

"Twenty-five." Rathbone's voice cut through the room, his lifeless eyes daring Lucien to outbid him.

Undeterred, Lucien glared at the other man. "Thirty."

Rathbone's mouth flattened, frustration and determination etched in every line of his face. "Thirty-two."

The idea of Rathbone winning Eliza and subjecting her to his . . .proclivities sent a cold streak of fear through Lucien. He would not allow it to happen. He'd wager his entire estate, his fortune, his *life* to prevent it.

Tossing back the rest of his drink, he slammed the glass on the table. "We all have things to do, so I will cease wasting everyone's time. Fifty thousand pounds."

CHAPTER
TWO

NO ONE SPOKE. The man with the lower bid stood up and stormed out, which meant the auction was now over.

She'd been sold.

Eliza clutched the arm of the auctioneer like a safety line, her lungs sucking in air. Was this truly happening?

"Fifty thousand pounds, it is! Lady E is sold to that gentleman there for the next seven nights."

The room broke out in applause, and Eliza's mind reeled at the staggering amount as she was led off stage.

It was . . .unthinkable. With this amount of money, she could take Fanny to a sanitarium in America with fresh air and healing waters. They could buy a nice house somewhere no one knew them and start over. She could finally attend a university.

Once upon a time, she'd hoped to study at one of the women's colleges at Oxford. Her brother laughed at this, saying an earl's daughter needn't be well educated. They'd fought over it many times, with Robert insisting aristocratic ladies should marry and reproduce, not attend college. Eliza held onto that dream, however, planning to prove him wrong.

"Good for you, dearie!" one of the women cheered in the anteroom as Eliza entered.

"I'm a virgin, too, if it could get me fifty thousand quid," another one said.

"Cor, you ain't no virgin, Jane," came a shout. "Your cunt's been ridden more than a horse."

Eliza was shown to a separate room to wait. Within seconds, the door opened and Eliza crossed her arms over her chest in an attempt at modesty. Probably pointless, but it bolstered her courage.

Two men entered. The larger man was the club's owner—and the other was the masked man who'd bought her. He was tall and fit, and younger than she'd anticipated.

The owner closed the door. "Lady E, I'd like to present you with your buyer."

The bidder reached up and untied his mask. When it fell, Eliza gasped, her body rocking as if she'd been dealt a blow.

No, impossible. Utterly impossible.

Blackwood.

More specifically, Lucien, the Duke of Blackwood. Her late brother's best friend.

And Eliza's girlhood obsession.

Oh, God. Every bit of her skin burned as if she stood too close to a fire. Lucien had bid on her. Had paid fifty thousand pounds to bed her and take her virginity. Was she dreaming right now?

Emotions fluttered in her chest, and any embarrassment over appearing half-naked in a room full of men was replaced with relief. It wasn't a stranger who would take her virginity.

Instead, it was a man she'd known as a girl—the serious and kind duke who gave her maths problems to solve at the dinner table, much to the chagrin of her older brother. The man who caused a buzzing sensation under her skin every time she looked at him.

Yes, Lucien was exactly the right man for her first time.

The owner spoke first. "You have any troubles, you come to me, miss," he said, jerking a thumb to his chest. "These gents know what happens if they misbehave."

"Leave us," Blackwood said to the other man, his eyes never leaving Eliza's face. "And I'll have a word with you later about some of the *gents* you allow to participate in these proceedings."

After a frown in the duke's direction, the owner left them alone, and Eliza could feel her heart pounding in her chest as she regarded him. He was so . . .much. Still handsome, with his same windswept black hair and intense brown-green eyes, but his features had sharpened in the last five years. His shoulders had widened, too. Blimey, he was attractive.

"Thank goodness it's you," Eliza blurted. "I was worried about who would buy me."

"I'm certainly surprised, as well. Care to explain?"

He spoke to her as if she were a child who needed reprimanding, which she didn't like, nor did she understand. "What needs explaining, Your Grace? It's a fairly straightforward exchange. I have something to offer and Your Grace has purchased it."

Lucien cocked a brow. "Straightforward? Tonight was anything but, Lady Eliza."

"Please don't call me that." No one used her honorific any longer.

"Why? You are a lady."

"I *was* a lady. That was a long time ago, Your Grace."

"I'll stop calling you a lady if you stop calling me Your Grace. Now, where is your family?"

"Dead, except for my sister."

He winced. "I meant your brother's successor. The new earl."

"Haven't a clue. He turned Fanny and I out five years ago."

Lucien's jaw fell open. "He . . .turned you out? Without providing for you at all?"

This was old news, so Eliza lifted a shoulder. "Apparently Robert hadn't altered his will to include us. Everything went to William, his second cousin."

"Your cousin let it be known you'd gone to live with an aunt in Scotland."

"I have no aunt in Scotland."

"Dash it," he muttered, pinching the bridge of his nose between a thumb and forefinger. "Why not hire a solicitor to look into the matter, then?"

"With what funds, Your Grace?"

"Then why not come to me? Or to Jasper? We gladly would have helped you."

It hadn't occurred to Eliza to beg from Robert's friends, not while she was focused on finding food and shelter. Besides, no one had reached out after the funeral. Every friend and acquaintance forgot about her and Fanny, just two more young girls who were someone else's problem.

Which meant they were no one's problem.

Regardless, she had no choice but to cope with their situation and do it quickly. And, Eliza didn't mind bragging, she'd done a damn decent job of providing for the two of them. If not for Fanny's illness, they would gladly have lived out their days in their rented one-room apartment in Shoreditch. The aristocracy, Eliza discovered, weren't as essential as they believed. Happiness could be found outside of Mayfair.

In fact, being common was generally a relief. The life she'd once lived, with its restrictions and excess and expectations, had been entirely at a man's whim—first her father, then her brother. And even that had all been taken away by another man, her cousin.

She and Fanny lived simpler lives now, but lives of their own choosing, with no one controlling them. Eliza would never allow a man to dictate her future again.

Which was why she would make good on this transaction. An even exchange: her virginity for fifty thousand pounds. Her decision, her control.

Lucien stood, shrugged out of his coat, then came to drape it over her shoulders. The fine wool caressed her bare skin, while the smell of cigar and sandalwood filled her head. She could still feel the warmth from his body on the material, and it sank into her bones. "Thank you," she said gratefully.

"Eliza, honestly. Why didn't you come to me? You look malnourished. I fear a strong wind will blow you over."

That stung. She frowned up at him. "We're doing fine for ourselves. If not for Fanny's—" She snapped her jaw closed. Her sister's illness was not anyone's business.

"Fanny's what?"

"Nothing."

Simple transaction, even exchange. Then she and Fanny would start over in America.

She lifted her chin and gave him what she hoped was an eager smile. "So, when do our seven nights begin?"

———

Lucien frowned, irritated she'd even ask. "Never."

She gaped, her eyes revealing her surprise and confusion, so he held up a hand and said, "However, I will give you the fifty thousand pounds."

"Why on earth would you do that?"

"Because your brother was a friend of mine." His best friend, actually. *And I'm responsible for his death.*

The furrow between her brows deepened. "You cannot give me the money outright."

The words hung there, but he couldn't make sense of them. She was *protesting?* Why wasn't she relieved? She couldn't *want* to sleep with him; she'd sold her innocence for coin. "Why not?"

"Because I would feel beholden to you."

Beholden? She deserved this money. Had Robert known, he would've enlisted Lucien's promise to take care of his sisters. Then she never would've ended up in this predicament—too thin and selling her body like a common streetwalker.

"You won't take my money, but it's fine to sell your virginity to the highest bidder? To a stranger? Come, Eliza. Be sensible. Let's put this ugliness behind us, and I'll ensure that you and Fanny have all the money you ever need."

"Why?"

"Because your brother was my closest friend."

"Still, that is no reason to give me a huge sum of money for nothing."

"It's what your brother would have wanted."

"I don't understand. You didn't bid on me because you wanted to sleep with me? You don't wish to take my virginity?"

Did she sound disappointed, or was he imagining it? A whisper of heat snaked along his spine, but shame quickly followed. While he was a dissolute bastard, he hadn't ever taken advantage of a woman—and he wouldn't start with the little sister of his dead best friend. "Absolutely not. Your brother would be horrified."

"My brother is dead. I no longer have the luxury of wondering over his feelings—not when there are far more pressing matters at hand."

"Regardless, I won't f—" He stopped himself from using the crude word, which was definitely not appropriate to say in front of a lady. "I won't sleep with you."

"Why did you bid on me, then, if you didn't fancy sleeping with me?"

"To save you from the jackals out there. I know those men, and none of them are worthy of you." *Including me.*

"If you won't sleep with me, I'll just arrange for another auction."

The back of his neck grew hot. "Absolutely not. You'll take my money and go live your life."

"No, I won't. I won't take money for nothing. Never does a woman any good."

He could hear a hint of the East End in her speech, and his guilt doubled, sharpening his tone. "I'll not allow you to enter another auction. The owner wouldn't dare risk my ire."

"This is ridiculous. Am I so hideous, then?"

Guilt slashed his insides at her words. "That isn't it at all. You're quite lovely, if I am being honest."

An understatement, actually. Eliza was glorious, even more so up close, with lush blonde hair barely contained by pins, and blue eyes that were almost aqua, like the Mediterranean Sea in the morning. Her body was too thin, but she had womanly curves that any man would appreciate—and soon those curves would fill out.

Lucien would personally see to it. From now on, Robert's sisters would want for nothing. By next week, they'd be nibbling on tea cakes and petit fours in a drawing room somewhere, doted on by a collection of servants. Everything would be set to rights.

He couldn't bring Robert back, but he could see to Eliza's future.

Her nose wrinkled adorably as she studied him. "Then why not take my virginity? If there's a woman in your bed at the moment, I'm certain she'll understand."

"It's *women*, actually, and that hardly matters. I won't bed you."

"Even when you've paid for it?"

"When she is the little sister of my best friend, the answer remains no."

She wrapped his coat tighter around her body as she stood. "My brother is gone. You cannot continue to use him as a reason. It's illogical."

"You'll accept the money, Eliza. Save your innocence for a husband."

"No. I won't accept the money until you've had your seven nights. It's a fair exchange, and I'd rather have you than some other titled lord who won't care if he hurts me or not."

I'd rather have you.

Oh, Christ. He couldn't. It was wrong to even consider it, despite the dark thrill those words gave him.

Ready to put an end to the discussion, he stalked forward until he loomed over her. "You'll take the money, Eliza. No bedding and no seven nights. Stop being childish. Now, come. I'll see you home."

Her eyes flashed fire as she took a step back. "I'm not a child, and I'm able to see myself home."

"In this city? At this hour? Dressed like that? Absolutely not."

"I have clothes here. I'm used to doing for myself, Your Grace."

"Stop calling me that—and I will see you home if I have to tie your hands and feet and carry you out of here like a rolled-up carpet. Believe me, no one would stop me."

"Fine," she said, taking off his coat and shoving it at him. "At the very least it'll save me the fare."

Relieved, he requested her clothing, then waited outside the door while Eliza dressed. When she emerged, she was wearing a shabby brown garment hanging loose on her too-thin frame. He took her hand, not giving her a chance to escape. "My carriage is out front."

They didn't speak on the way. He could sense her unhappiness, but he didn't care. She would learn how this was going to go. He would give her the money and a house, a new life for her and Fanny, and she would accept it.

Then perhaps his guilt would ease a tiny fraction and he'd be able to sleep at night.

When he jerked open the carriage door, movement inside startled him. Oh, bollocks. How had he forgotten about Mollie and Ginny?

"Your Grace," Mollie said, wide-eyed as she took in the young girl at his side. "You said you weren't buying one tonight."

"I didn't. Move over, loves."

Mollie and Ginny slid to the far side of the carriage, sitting across from each other. From their swollen lips and disheveled clothes, it was clear his mistresses had been busy whilst he'd been away, but he was too worried about Robert's sister to regret missing the fun. He assisted Eliza inside then followed. The four of them barely fit, their knees bumping into one another, but it couldn't be helped.

"Where to, Eliza?"

"Kingsland Road in Shoreditch, please."

After he relayed the direction to his driver an awkward silence fell inside the carriage. He was about to make introductions when Eliza turned to the girls and blurted, "Hello, I'm Eliza. The duke bought my virginity tonight. We're going to spend the next seven nights together."

Before Lucien could correct that statement, Mollie dropped her hand on Lucien's thigh, close to his groin. "Is that what you want, darling? A little bit of blood and trepidation? Ginny and I can accommodate you."

"I'm not taking her virginity. Eliza is the sister of a friend of mine. We are seeing her home."

Eliza waved her hand. "He's still a bit overwhelmed at the prospect. Never fear, I'll bring him around. Actually, perhaps you ladies can help me. What are the duke's preferences in bed?"

Ginny and Mollie grinned, eyes sparkling like they'd made a new friend, while Lucien scowled. Just as Ginny opened her mouth to speak, Lucien pointed at her. "Do not answer that." Then he pinned Eliza with a hard stare, one he rarely used anymore. "Eliza, stop it this instant. We will not sleep together."

She turned to the street, ignoring him. Something told him she hadn't quite agreed, but he would convince her. He was quite in control of his cock, thank you very much, and it had no chance of meeting Eliza's quim. Ever.

Eventually they pulled up to a sad-looking East End building, and Lucien's blood turned cold. Fucking hell, it was terrible. Garbage littered the street and there was clearly a stable close by. Drunken men loitered on the stoop two houses down.

Robert's sisters lived here?

"Absolutely not," he snapped, watching a rat scurry into an alley. "Pack your things, Eliza. I'm taking you and Fanny back to Mayfair."

The girl had the audacity to reach for the handle like he hadn't spoken. "You cannot order me around, Your Grace."

"My fifty thousand pounds says I can, actually. Hurry up. We'll wait."

Her eyes narrowed as she jabbed a finger in his direction. "I *knew* it. I knew you would use that money to try to lord over my life—which is why this must remain a simple business transaction. You are not buying *me*; you are buying my body for seven nights. There is a difference."

Frustrated, he adjusted his tone to plead with her. "I cannot in good conscience leave you here in this neighborhood one second longer. My God, Eliza. You had such big plans when you were younger—you even talked of going to university. This is not the life you wanted. Go, pack your things. You're coming to stay with me in Grosvenor Square."

Mouths agape, Ginny and Mollie were following the conversation, heads swiveling as if they were at a lawn tennis match. He remained focused on Robert's maddening sister, who was currently staring at him like he was muck under her shoe.

"No," she said, her voice brittle and angry. "I've built a life here. It may not meet with Your Grace's approval, but it's ours—and no man will ever take it away from us. I'll see you tomorrow night."

She threw open the door and slipped out of the carriage before he could stop her. Damn it.

Once on the ground, she hurried away, but Lucien unfolded from the vehicle and gave chase. Unfortunately, he lost her in the dark, crooked streets almost immediately. "Christ!" he yelled, kicking an empty jar with his boot as he trudged back to his carriage.

Tomorrow, he would find Eliza and her sister, even if he had to tear the whole city apart to do it.

HIS BED WAS ENORMOUS.

Eliza stood in Lucien's empty bedroom with just the silvery light of the moon to guide her. She and Fanny discussed this plan many times today. They decided the quickest way to get the money was for Eliza to show up and seduce him. Then their seven nights would commence, and he would have no choice but to see it through.

A monetary gift, even from Lucien, was too risky. As she'd seen many times, gifts from men always came with strings. Like when a former landlord agreed to give them a few more days on their rent—if Eliza showed him her quim. She'd refused and moved them out the next day.

Then there was the first doctor to see Fanny, who offered free treatment if Eliza rubbed her stocking feet on his crotch after every visit. Most recently was the owner of a garment factory who agreed to help Eliza move up to a better paying position, but only if she became his mistress.

Did anyone honestly believe Lucien would give her that much money, wish her well, and disappear from her life? She snorted in the darkness. Even last night he'd tried ordering her about—using just the *promise* of the money as leverage. Eliza wouldn't let another man control her or her sister again.

This time was *her* choice. She wanted to earn this money, fair and square.

Her gaze drifted back to the bed, and her corset suddenly felt too tight, her clothes too itchy. The pulse between her legs was distracting, an insistent ache that began whenever she thought of him. Blooming hell, she was looking forward to this.

As a girl, she'd experienced a giddiness in Lucien's presence, like her chest was full of butterflies and bees. She stared at him during his visits, obsessed with his soft smile and biting sense of humor. They both liked maths and playing croquet, and what more had a young girl needed to know other than that? He was utterly perfect to her mind.

So, where was he? Would he stay out the entire night? Pleasuring two mistresses was double the work, after all. Would he have the verve to relieve Eliza of her innocence tonight?

His exhaustion would definitely add a wrinkle to her plan, but it wouldn't dissuade her. She could wait and return tomorrow night. And the night after that. As many nights as it took to convince him to take her virginity. It had to work eventually.

Footsteps in the corridor caught her attention. She slipped into the shadows, held her breath, and waited. It could be Lucien—or a servant. And Eliza hadn't crossed the city in the dead of night, crawled through an unlocked window, and crept through his house . . .only to be thrown out by a snooty valet.

The latch turned and a large shape filled the doorway.

Lucien.

She bit her lip, her body vibrating with . . .nerves. Excitement. Fear. More excitement. Surely there were other emotions, but she couldn't pinpoint them.

He closed the door and draped the room in darkness once more. Her eyes had already adjusted, so she could see him rip off his top coat, then toe off his shoes. "Fuck me," he growled.

Why was he angry?

Stomping to the bed, he flopped down onto his back. "Bugger it." His broad chest rose and fell with the force of his breath.

When he didn't move, she stepped out of the darkness. "May I help, Your Grace?"

Blinking, he came up on his elbows. "Eliza?"

"Hello, duke."

His brow creased, the lines too numerous to count. "They looked for you all bloody day. Turned Shoreditch upside down. I've been going out of my mind with worry ever since last night."

He'd tried to find her? She didn't know whether to be flattered or horrified. "I told you I would come tonight."

"Excellent. I'll write you a bank draft and send you back home."

"Let me undress first. How would you like to take my virginity? With me on my back, or on my hands and knees? I did see a drawing once of a woman upside down—"

"Eliza," he snapped. "None of that is happening. I cannot sleep with you."

Oh. He'd already exhausted himself, then. "Have your mistresses worn you out tonight?"

"Jesus, no—and do not think for one second that I have issues with stamina. I meant I cannot sleep with you and live with myself. It isn't right."

She smothered a smile. Poor man. He had no idea who he was up against. The last five years had taught Eliza patience. She knew that with slow and steady progress, she would eventually reach any goal she set.

And her current goal was for Lucien to want her desperately enough to overlook his sense of misplaced honor toward her dead brother.

She moved closer to the bed and ran her fingers over his shin bone. "You could kiss me. That wouldn't be so terrible, would it?"

The noise that escaped his throat sounded tortured. "I know what you are doing, you clever girl. You are hoping I'll kiss you and become so overcome with lust that I end up between your thighs."

He wasn't that far off. "Actually, I was hoping you would show me what a real kiss feels like. The kisses I've experienced have—"

"Who has kissed you?" Abruptly, he sat up, his dark eyes blazing. "Were they rough with you? Did they force you? Because I swear to God . . ."

"Calm down, Lucien." She rose and moved between his legs. They were face-to-face now, her hands coming to rest on his shoulders. "They were mere boys, sloppy and inexperienced. No one forced me. I kissed them because I wanted to, just like I want to kiss you."

Seconds ticked by while he examined her face, brow wrinkled like he couldn't believe she actually wanted to kiss him. Yet she did. Badly.

She liked this serious, protective side of him, more like the Lucien she remembered, the one who had defended her intelligence to Robert and her parents. The man who made her feel valued and *seen* at a time when young girls were often ignored and dismissed. Lord, how she'd loved him once.

Finally, his mouth hitched in a way that caused her stomach to flip. "I am definitely no sloppy and inexperienced boy."

"No, you certainly are not, which is why I want to know what it's like to be kissed by you."

He leaned in, as if drawn to her, but didn't come close enough to actually kiss her. His breath ghosted over her skin as he spoke. "I would make it so good for you. I would take my time, explore every bit of you with my lips and tongue. You would feel so safe with me, angel. I'd never let anyone hurt you again."

Was he talking about kissing . . .or something more?

Her lower body clenched at his seductive words, the area between her legs growing damp and hot. It would be so easy to believe him, so easy to let herself rely on someone else to take care of her. But she would not trade her hard-fought independence for anything. Lucien could have her body for seven nights, but he would never have more.

She said none of this, however. She merely edged forward until their lips nearly touched. "Show me, Lucien. *Please.*"

———

Lucien's head swam—and the dizziness had nothing to do with the scotch he'd swallowed earlier. No, his little angel had him off-balance, sneaking into his bedroom and asking him to kiss her. God, he wanted to. More than anything else, he longed to drag her beneath him and show her how good it could be between them. Teach her how to please him.

I could be her first.

Fuck. He had to stop thinking like that.

As much as he wanted to watch as his cock speared her virgin flesh, he couldn't. This was Robert's sister, a proper lady, and she would hate him if she knew the truth behind her brother's death. That Lucien was the reason for the loss of her family home, her wealth and position.

So despite his desire for her, it was dangerous to contemplate fucking her—and she deserved better.

Moonlight bathed her in a soft glow, showing off her slightly parted lips and the flush on her cheeks. She was absolutely lovely, her face free of cosmetics and lip paint. He stared at the delicate curve of her jaw, the slim column of her throat, both begging to be explored by his mouth. Was the skin there as soft as it appeared?

No, no, no. He couldn't.

Could he?

Her fingers found their way into his hair, their bodies nearly flush, with her lower half appallingly close to his. He wanted to touch her so badly, his hands shook with it. Why wasn't she afraid? Weren't most virgins supposed to be terrified, wilting creatures?

Eliza appeared almost . . .aroused.

Was that possible?

"Why aren't you scared?" he whispered, their breath mingling.

"Because it's you."

Swallowing, he came to a decision right then. As long as he didn't fuck her, he could show her everything her curious little heart desired —and in the meantime convince her to stay here until he could get her into better lodgings.

He was not above using pleasure to achieve what he wanted, and he wanted Robert's sisters safe and back where they belonged in a decent neighborhood.

"I'm going to kiss you, Eliza."

Her response was instant. "All right."

"But just kissing." He could do this. Just a few minutes exploring her mouth, rubbing her sweet little tongue with his, before he made her agree to return to Mayfair. "Do you remember when we used to do maths together?"

"Yes, of course." The words came out on a soft sigh, as if the memory was a good one. He hoped so—those were pleasant memories for him, too. Clever and eager, she kept up with his complex questions, and he'd been suitably impressed.

"Kissing is like solving an equation," he told her, sliding his hands onto her hips. "You have this mystery to unravel, a puzzle, and it requires careful examination and thought. Planning and patience. The answer is there, but you cannot rush it."

"And what is the answer?"

"For me, it's discovering what makes a woman purr into my mouth and rub against me like she longs to feel me everywhere. What makes her hot and eager, wet between her legs."

He paused, half-hoping he'd shocked or scared her into leaving. It was best for both of them if this never went any further.

"But I already feel that," she said, "and you haven't even kissed me yet."

His cock pulsed, a jolt of lust careening through him at her honesty, and he moved closer. "Then just relax. Let me taste you."

A willing pupil, she held perfectly still, allowing him to close the distance and cover her mouth with his. He briefly wondered how far she'd gone with those boys, whether she'd let any of them stroke her between her thighs, but he shoved those thoughts away. Tonight was just kissing.

Her lips were soft and wet, like she'd licked them in preparation for his kiss, and he moved carefully, gently, learning the shape and feel of her, while giving her the chance to do the same. He swept back and forth lightly, brushing and teasing, enjoying the anticipation building between them. Many partners complained kissing was unnecessary, but Lucien loved it. There was something about the connection, the shared breath and slick exchange of saliva, that was both dirty and beautiful. Hedonistic and necessary.

That he was kissing this particular woman, the one who used to look at him with stars in her eyes, made it all the sweeter. He suddenly remembered how her stare made him feel twenty feet tall all those years ago, like he was the only man in the room. How had he ever forgotten?

Desperate for more, he deepened the kiss, holding her face in his palms and adding more pressure. Then he nipped her lips, and was rewarded when her mouth parted to allow him inside.

It was worth the wait.

Her tongue was wet and hot, and he suddenly couldn't get enough. She was thorough, her mouth mimicking his movements, and he lost himself in the flicks and swirls, the moans and gasps as the kiss wore on. Part of him worried this might be a mistake, because he liked it *too much*, but the other part—the selfish and depraved half—wanted to take everything she offered and ruin her for other men.

Ruin her, period.

This is Eliza, Robert's sister. Get a hold of yourself, man.

Somehow he managed to hold himself in check, not once losing the thin threads of his self control. When her hands gripped his shoulders, he fought the urge to move closer. When her fingers slid into his hair, he fought the urge to cup her breasts in his palms.

And when she shifted into the cradle of his thighs, he fought the urge to grind his cock into her mound.

It wasn't easy, especially when her eagerness and innocence beckoned him like a treat just out of reach. But this must remain a kiss, nothing more.

So when she shoved his shoulders, he wasn't ready for it. Actually, he had no idea what was happening until he was flat on his back on the bed. "Eliza, what—"

His jaw snapped shut when she crawled over him, her legs straddling his thighs. Oh, Christ. What was happening?

The ceiling stared down at him blankly, as if to mock him. *You fool. Your hubris knows no bounds.*

Weakly, he tried to move but it was too late. Her glorious weight came down on him and his hands clasped the back of her knees under her skirts. Before he could order her to get up, she rocked her core over his erection, and white-hot pleasure shot through him like a bolt of electricity, obliterating everything else.

Goddamn it. Need clawed inside his belly, robbing him of all good sense. Why was fate so fucking cruel?

She pulled a small tin from her dress pocket. "I brought a shield."

He stared at her hand, his cock throbbing. The idea that she'd come prepared, that she'd turned aggressive—that she *wanted* this so desperately—nearly did him in. It would be so easy to free his erection and let her slide down, pierce her virgin cunt slowly. She would undoubtedly grip him tightly, tighter than anything he'd ever—

No. This wasn't right.

Eliza was a lady, whether she admitted it or not. Gently bred and raised to expect marriage. Lucien couldn't treat her like a mistress, no matter the fever currently burning inside him to have her. She deserved better.

Carefully, he moved her off him and onto the bed. "Let's slow down, shall we? There's no rush."

"What are you talking about? Of course, there is a bleeding rush. This is only seven nights, Lucien."

"I've always loved the sound of my name coming out of your mouth." It was an idiotic thing to say, but absolutely true.

Her mouth curved in a way that almost made him nervous, as if he'd handed her a dangerous weapon. "Indeed, 'tis a nice name." She leaned over him, her hand firmly on his chest. "Will you kiss me again, Lucien?"

"No, because you and your shield are attempting to turn this into a deflowering, and I most definitely need you to stay flowered."

"That is not a word," she said with a smile.

"Perhaps, but you know what I mean. I will not bed you."

"You may use crude words with me, you know. I promise you won't offend my delicate sensibilities. I told you, I'm no longer a lady, and I've heard all manner of improper words in the last five years."

"You are a lady and you shouldn't know those words."

"Like fuck?"

"Dash it, Eliza. This has gone far enough—"

"Fine." She held the shield up where he could see it and slowly placed the tin on the small table by his bed. "There. Now we may focus on kissing and whatever else may happen."

He groaned as images of *whatever else* raced through his mind. "You don't know what you're asking for."

"Why? What are you worried might happen?"

"Any number of wicked scenarios that involve your naked body."

"Such as?"

"Things I'll never share with you."

"Because you're not attracted to me?"

"Because of *Robert*," he snapped. "Have you not been paying attention, woman?"

"Right." Her lips twitched like she was amused. "What if we focused on wicked scenarios that involved your naked body instead?"

While his cock was more than eager for this plan, Lucien wasn't fooled. She didn't know the first thing about pleasuring a man. How could she, as a virgin?

It was past time to illuminate her innocence and their incompatibility. If this was the only way to do it, so be it. Then she would see this was foolish, that she wasn't ready for seven nights of sin with a virtual stranger. That she should save herself for a husband.

Whether she wanted to admit it or not, she was a lady. No doubt she'd go running from the room the moment his cock appeared.

Indeed, this was the best way to put an end to this right now.

Stretching his arms up above his head, he spread his body out like a buffet, a feast for the taking. "If you can ask nicely for it, then maybe I'll let you."

CHAPTER
FOUR

WAS THIS A NEW GAME? If so, Eliza was ready. It was no hardship to explore him. Attractive and well proportioned, the duke was big, his clothes outlining a fit frame with a broad chest and flat stomach. A light dusting of whiskers coated his jaw, and she longed to test the roughness of that skin with her fingertips.

"May I touch you?"

One of his dark eyebrows lifted. "I'm no thirteen-year-old boy, Eliza. If you wish to touch me, you need to be explicit. Tell me where and what you plan to do."

She bit the inside of her cheek to keep from smiling. Was he being deliberately cruel to embarrass her? Probably. Lucien was very clever —probably the smartest man she'd ever met—and fixated on his loyalty to Robert. No doubt he was hoping she would blush and stammer, as any gently bred virgin would in this situation.

But Eliza was not the same gently bred girl, not anymore.

Drawing closer, she ran a fingertip over his stomach. "May I unfasten your trousers, Your Grace?"

"And why would you like to unfasten my trousers, angel?"

In for a penny, as the saying went.

"To see your cock. I want to lavish it with kisses and lick it all over."

Lucien's face paled, his lips parting ever so slightly. He seemed to be stuck, not breathing, his gaze fixated on her mouth. Was he imagining what it would feel like?

"How . . .?" His voice trailed off.

"Had you thought I was unfamiliar with the act? Or, too embarrassed to speak about it?" She shook her head. "I'm not the sheltered girl you once knew."

"Have you ever . . .done that before?"

"No, but I'd like for you to teach me how."

His eyes slammed closed, his face twisted as if he were in pain. "Jesus, Eliza. You shouldn't say such things to a man like me."

"And what type of man are you?"

"A degenerate. A selfish wastrel. A man who will ride you so hard, you'll feel it for days to come."

Gorblimey.

An inferno ignited in her belly, followed by waves of wanting that skimmed through her veins. Was he hoping to scare her? Because honestly, the idea of his big muscled body moving over hers, giving pleasure that would haunt her long after, was more than appealing. It reinforced her sense that Lucien was the perfect man to rid her of her virginity.

He would take care with her. Provide her with seven nights of fun, then she would depart for America—and he would return to his mistresses and ducal debauchery.

She gave him her best attempt at a sultry smile. "If that was intended to deter me, dear man, I'm afraid you have failed."

He groaned, his hands scrubbing his face. "Has anyone ever told you that you are stubborn?"

"Many times." Fanny mentioned it quite often. But Eliza preferred *determined*, a trait that had helped her and her sister survive after being tossed out like trash. "Which means your resistance is futile."

He pinned her with his brownish-green stare. "Let's make a bargain."

She never agreed to anything without hearing all the details. Being cheated once in the Covent Garden market had taught her that. "Tell me the terms first."

"You let me pleasure you tonight. My trousers stay on. Then you and Fanny move in here tomorrow, and we discuss setting up a new life for you both."

"No. Here are my terms: you teach me how to pleasure you tonight, then I will return tomorrow night for more lessons."

"Damn it, Eliza."

He started to sit up—probably to throw her out or yell at her—and she panicked. Moving swiftly, she threw her leg over his hips and moved on top of him. Again. But this time her core landed on his erection, which was thick and hard under her center. They both froze.

This was his cock. Directly between her legs. Good God. It was much larger than she'd expected.

"What are you doing?" His voice sounded strangled.

She hadn't the faintest. "I'm not certain but it feels right. Should I move off you?"

"No. Yes. Wait, no."

His hesitation was promising. Because begging worked earlier for kissing, she tried it again. "Teach me, Lucien." She splayed her fingers on his chest and rocked her hips. Sakes alive, that felt delicious. "Please."

When she did it once more, they both groaned.

"Christ," he murmured as he fell back onto the bed. "I'm definitely going to Hell for even considering this."

"Is that a yes?"

"Eliza, let me lick you—"

She rolled her hips along the large ridge again and shivered as pleasure coursed through her. Leaning forward, she whispered, "You bought me, Lucien. You may do whatever you like with me tonight."

His cock jerked against her. Oh, he *liked* that.

She kept going. "Wouldn't you like to be my first?"

"Oh, God," he said on a rough exhale. "Why are you torturing me?"

"Do you want me to stop . . .or do you want to show me what it feels like to have your cock between my legs?"

"Jesus Christ!" He arched, every muscle pulled taut, with his expression twisted in what appeared like agony. Without warning, his hands shot out to clasp her hips. His eyes were wild, a man pushed to the edge of his sanity. "Roll your hips, darling," he rasped. "Make us both come."

"What about your trousers?"

"They remain on. Trust me, you'll like it. Rub your sex over the cloth and along my shaft." He guided her. "Just keep going. Yes, exactly like that."

Tingles raced along the back of her thighs as she dragged her body over his. Why was this so amazing? The friction had her seeing stars. The strength of her reaction surprised her, but she wasn't worried.

Lucien will take care of me.

She knew it in her bones. He'd been so kind to her all those years ago, telling Robert to mind his own business when her brother tried to belittle her. Lucien had made her feel special, and she hadn't forgotten it.

His fingertips tightened on her hips. "How badly do you want to please me, angel?"

She peeked at him through her lashes. "Very, very badly, Your Grace."

"Then we do this once. One time and no more. No seven nights, just this. Our clothes stay on. Say you understand."

He didn't ask if she agreed, only that she understood. Hiding a smile, she kept churning her hips, grinding on top of him. "I understand."

He grunted and let his eyelids fall briefly, his long eyelashes kissing his cheeks. "You will thank me someday."

Doubtful, but there was no arguing with him, not now.

"Does it feel good for you?" Her palms rested on his stomach as she moved, again and again, in a steady rhythm. "Because I think it feels incredible."

"God, yes, it feels good. I'm so hard for you."

The more she rocked, the more the heat built inside her. The pleasure made her dizzy, like she was drunk on sensation, chasing a high slightly out of reach. She dug her nails into his skin, the ache drawing tighter, her body on fire. "Oh, Lucien."

"Yes, keep going." His chest heaved and his lips parted on a ragged breath. "Lift your skirts with one hand. Let me see you drag your pussy over my cock and make yourself come. I need to see it."

Her thighs trembled as she gathered her skirts in her fingers and lifted them out of the way. "You're the first man to ever see it," she whispered. "You could also be the first man to touch it."

"Fuck, fuck, fuck," he chanted, his stare locked on the bare skin revealed by the slit in her drawers. "I want that so badly. I want to finger you and lick you and fuck you."

"I see couples doing those things in the alleys," she told him, closing her eyes and imagining her and Lucien in the open air, where anyone could walk by and watch him taking her from behind. The sparks doubled, quadrupled in her blood, and she moved faster, her hips becoming uncoordinated as the pleasure dragged her under.

A searing swell rushed up from her toes, flooding her, and her core contracted as she quivered and shook. It was better than anything she had imagined. The waves caused her to shudder, the man beneath her the only tether to the ground.

"I can see how wet you are," he growled when she floated back to earth. "May I taste it? Please? Run your finger through your slickness and give me one small taste."

It never occurred to her to refuse. He appeared desperate for her, feverish, like he might be close to his own climax, and she wanted to drive him wild. Dipping her finger into her sex, she coated the digit in her arousal and lifted it to his mouth. "Here."

He sucked her finger past his lips and into his mouth, his tongue swirling over her skin greedily. A groan rumbled in his throat and his eyes nearly rolled back in his head. Did he truly like the taste so much as that?

She leaned in and whispered, "Have you ever tasted a virgin before?"

His hips began bucking, nearly unseating her. "Oh, fuck. I'm—" He stiffened and his back bowed, air heaving in and out of his chest, and his shout filled the room to echo off the walls. The erection beneath her pulsed, the cloth of his trousers growing warm and wet on her skin. His *seed*. Pride filled her at his completion. She'd made him do that. Her, a virgin.

He'd never be able to resist her now.

———

Lucien may have underestimated her.

His sweet little virgin had a wicked mouth and was eager to please. His new favorite qualities in bed, apparently. That this was Robert's sister was a worry for tomorrow. Right now, she was merely Eliza, the woman who caused him to come in his trousers like a schoolboy.

He hadn't expected her to be so . . .filthy. Or competent. She rode him like a thoroughbred at Ascot, and he'd loved every second of it. The proof was now cooling and sticking to his skin.

When she'd lifted her skirts to her waist, the slit in her drawers revealed her cunt and he'd nearly climaxed right then. Christ, she was gorgeous. Downy hair covered her mound, while the pink lips of her sex glistened with arousal. For him. And the taste? Ambrosia. He wanted to bury his face there, breathe her in, taste her and lick her, and have her come on his tongue over and over until they were exhausted.

Grinning, she slid off him. "That was fun. We should do that again. Tomorrow night, say ten o'clock?"

"No. Now, what time may I expect you and Fanny in the morning?"

Her expression cleared, a wariness returning to her gaze. "I beg your pardon?"

"You and Fanny. Moving in tomorrow. What time?"

"We're not moving in with you. I told you this already."

He exhaled heavily. "Eliza, you agreed."

"No, I certainly did not."

"Let me put this plainly. If you and Fanny are not here by nine o'clock tomorrow morning, baggage in hand, there will be no fifty thousand pounds."

"Stop trying to control me with money. And!" She pointed to his crotch. "At the very least you owe me seven thousand one-hundred and forty-two quid."

"And eighty-six pence." Yes, he could do maths, too. "That amount was for your virginity, Eliza, which you still possess."

"This is ridiculous."

"No, ridiculous is you insisting on living in a hovel when I have offered to put you up here."

Her lip curled in distaste, eyes turning cold, but he had no idea how he'd offended her. Every word was the truth.

He kept going, playing his only card. "You may say farewell to the fifty thousand pounds if you do not bring your sister here in the morning."

They stared at one another for a long moment. He could see her mind working, as it had all those years ago at the dinner table when she examined a problem from every side. Logically, as he would. There was no way out of this, though, because he would not bend. She would leave that rat-infested neighborhood and come stay with him, where he would look after her like a ward.

A ward who had once ridden his cock and made them both come.

His chest ached, perhaps with regret. Or perhaps with the knowledge this evening could never be repeated. It didn't matter. He would not take advantage of her whilst she was living under his roof. She needed to feel safe here, well provided for. Exactly as her brother would have expected.

When she didn't speak, he added, "I am merely looking out for you. It's what your brother would have wanted." *And what my guilt demands.*

She gestured to the bed. "Do you sincerely believe if I moved in that *this* would not happen again?"

He felt a real flash of fear in his belly. Eliza dressing and undressing under his roof. Seeing her smile every place he turned. Watching her eat and laugh over dinner. Thinking about her lying in bed, perhaps touching herself at the memories . . . .

Could he stand it?

He bolted off the bed. Damn it, his trousers were a bloody mess. "I will behave myself," he said with more certainty than he felt. "I trust you can do the same whilst here. Now, I will clean up and see you home. Wait here a few moments."

"That isn't necessary."

"Of course, it is. I'll not have you running pell-mell through the streets of London at this hour."

She studied him, then leaned back and relaxed on the bed. "Whatever Your Grace wants," she murmured with a small smile twisting the edges of her mouth.

The words nearly caused him to trip as he headed to the washroom. God almighty, he liked her compliance. Too much, actually.

You bought me, Lucien. You may do whatever you like with me tonight.

The dark thrill at that shamed him to his soul. He'd bedded his fair share of women in the last ten years, but never had he experienced such mindless lust at a couple of sentences strung together. Yes, he wanted to own her, to be her first. To teach her and ruin her for all others.

But it was dangerous—not to mention wrong.

He spent a few minutes in the washroom cleaning up as best he could, stripping out of his soiled undergarment and putting his trousers back on. The scent of her soaked the cloth, and if it were up to him the garment would never be sent to the laundry. He'd keep them dirty and stained as a reminder of their night together, of the one time his little virgin vixen teased and tormented him.

Finally, he finished putting himself to rights and returned to his bedroom, ready to see Eliza home.

Except the bed was empty. Nor could he find her anywhere inside the townhouse.

She had disappeared.

CHAPTER
FIVE

ELIZA LEFT her flat the next morning at eight o'clock, as usual. She was due at Mrs. O'Toole's, where she would spend the day mending clothes. It didn't pay much, but it was easy work.

The task would keep her hands and mind occupied, which was a relief after last night. Upon returning home from Lucien's, she'd tossed and turned, both angry and relieved. Sated and frustrated. The dratted man should claim her virginity, give her the money, then let her go on her merry way. Why was he insisting on complicating everything?

Fanny agreed with Eliza that accepting the money from Lucien without services rendered was a mistake. Then her sister minimized her illness, saying they didn't need the money quite as badly as that. Eliza knew better.

They did need the money. Eliza hated hearing his sister cough and struggle to breathe at night, and Fanny couldn't work because employers and coworkers were terrified she had consumption. According to Dr. Humphries, the doctor who treated Fanny, it wasn't consumption and a lengthy stay at a sanitarium should help her completely recover. But such facilities were expensive, and their savings wouldn't begin to touch the cost.

"Eliza," a deep voice suddenly said from close behind her. Too close.

She whirled and drew to a stop. The Marquess of Rathbone stood on the walk, looming over her like a gargoyle. Taking a step back, she shivered and rubbed her arms despite the heat outside. "My lord. Good morning."

Three months ago she apprenticed in Rathbone's garment factory. After recognizing her, he made a point to talk to her each time he visited the floor. She was polite, even though the reminder of her brother and her family stung, while doing her best to deter him. Still, Rathbone lingered more and more, distracting her from the work.

When she requested a sewing machine of her own, the manager said Rathbone made those decisions—even though the marquess hadn't promoted any other apprentice. Eliza suspected his involvement was special to her, which should have sent her packing straight away.

Instead, she foolishly approached him and requested a machine. The marquess turned it into an opportunity to proposition her, during which he asked her to become his mistress. Eliza quit that very day, never even collecting her last paycheck.

"There you go, always so busy," he said. "May I offer you a ride?"

A slick black brougham waited at the curb. The idea of sitting in such a confined space with him turned her stomach. "Thank you, my lord, but I'm fine to walk. It's not far."

"Then allow me to walk with you. It would be a shame if you were set upon. These streets are not safe for a young girl like yourself."

"Your lordship is very kind, but that's unnecessary. Good day, sir."

When she started to turn away, he took her arm. He wasn't hurting her, and to a passerby it would appear he was assisting her, but he hadn't asked permission to touch her. If he had, she certainly would not have granted it.

He began leading her along the walk. "See, isn't that better?"

"Please, my lord. Let me go."

"Nonsense. I'm happy to help." He leaned in, his hot breath hitting her skin. "In fact, I know just the sort of help you need. Do not be too proud to accept it from me, girl."

"Rathbone." The word cut through the noise on the street like the crack of a whip.

Lucien was there, the brim of his bowler doing little to hide the absolute fury in his gaze. "I believe the lady asked you to let her go."

Rathbone frowned, but otherwise didn't move. "This doesn't concern you, Blackwood."

"It does, actually. The lady is due with me this morning."

Eliza couldn't believe this. What was Lucien doing here at this hour? How had he found her?

Lucien stared at Rathbone, as if daring him to argue. Tension strung between the two men like a wire, taut and dangerous, and she wondered if they would come to blows.

Using the distraction to her advantage, she pulled free of Rathbone and shifted closer to Lucien. "It's true. His Grace requested my presence today."

A flash of something dark, something terrifying, crossed Rathbone's face before he cleared it. "We will speak later, then." He tipped his bowler and walked in the direction of his carriage.

Lucien took Eliza's arm and began leading her in the opposite direction. She didn't fight him, but she had questions. "What are you doing here? How did you find—"

"Quiet," he snapped.

"Oh, you think to order me about, too?"

"He's watching. Follow me and I'll explain in my carriage."

Glancing over her shoulder, she saw that Rathbone was, in fact, lingering near the street, his hollow eyes tracking her and Lucien as they walked away. A chill slithered over her skin. Unnerved, she pressed her lips together and remained silent.

A block over, a closed black carriage awaited. The conveyance looked totally out of place here, with its shiny lacquered sides and matching horses, and Eliza remembered rides in carriages such as this. She hadn't thought twice about it then, and hadn't realized her privilege until it was taken away by a system and society governed by men.

The reminder annoyed her, so she dug in her heels before Lucien could drag her any closer. "While I'm grateful for your assistance with Rathbone, I'm perilously close to being late for work. So, if you'll excuse me." She tried to tug out of his grasp, but he didn't let go.

"Get in my carriage, Eliza," he growled. "Right now."

Her jaw fell open. "You're angry with me? The bloody nerve! I've done nothing wrong."

He stepped closer and lowered his voice. "Other than sneaking out of my home last night after I told you to wait? Did it ever occur to you that I might be worried sick? That I might have stayed up half the night picturing you eviscerated in some alley?"

She bit the inside of her cheek and shoved aside the guilt. "And I told you I was perfectly fine seeing myself home. As you can see, I was right."

Closing his eyelids tightly like he was struggling for patience, he bit out, "Get in the carriage. You are embarrassing us both, arguing with me like a fishwife on the street."

Anger suffused her entire body. Embarrassing him? This was her neighborhood, not his, and she wouldn't be put back in that restrictive, proper aristocratic box ever again.

She would show him true embarrassment.

Angling back, she shouted, "Corblimey, guv! That's one right big tallywag you 'ave for a toff. Let me get me muff ready and you can roger it proper."

A passerby snickered, and Lucien turned an alarming shade of red. He spoke through clenched teeth. "If you want to see my solicitor, then I suggest you get moving."

She blinked. "Your solicitor? Why?"

"Because I asked him to look into the situation with Robert's estate. Now, do you want to get in on your own, or would you rather I throw you over my shoulder and toss you in myself?"

His solicitor? Hope flared in her chest and she considered whether to go with him. Mrs. O'Toole would understand Eliza's absence, but it meant Eliza wouldn't earn her sixpence for the day.

Perhaps I could earn another seven thousand one-hundred and forty-two quid instead.

Yes, that sounded like a more reasonable financial decision.

Patting Lucien's chest, she smiled. "Whatever Your Grace wishes."

Suspicion crossed his features and his eyes narrowed, yet he said nothing as she climbed inside the fancy carriage. The inside smelled of him—leather and fancy spices—which was a far cry from the ripe horse and refuse odor on the street. She settled into the plush seat and decided to enjoy the day with him.

Soon they set off, the wheels clattering along the uneven Shoreditch streets. They hadn't even gone a block when Lucien growled, "How do you know Rathbone?"

She glanced over at him, wondering at his sharp tone. Was Lucien jealous? No, that was ridiculous. "I worked at his factory for four months."

"He owns a factory?"

"Yes, a garment factory. They make coats and shirts."

"What did you do there?"

"I was an apprentice. Fetched bobbins and learned how to cut and make clothing. I tried to get my own machine, but Rathbone wouldn't allow it unless I granted him certain privileges."

Lucien tensed next to her, his muscles stiff. "That bastard."

"It's not an original story, I'm afraid. Though his offer was better than most. It included a townhouse and a staff of my own."

"I hope you punched him in the jaw."

She lifted a shoulder. "It's not much different from what you offered."

He swung to glare at her, a tinge of red on his high cheekbones. "It's hardly the same. I want to give you fifty thousand pounds and your own home."

"I don't want it, not until the end of our agreement. We have a simple business transaction, Lucien. Nothing more. You cannot order me about or use that money to control me. I am not your ward or your mistress. I am the woman you bought for seven nights."

"My God!" He tossed his bowler onto the opposite seat. "I have never seen such foolishness in all my life. You're wearing threadbare clothing and are clearly in need of a hot meal. You could be wearing diamonds and Worth gowns, woman. Drinking champagne and eating the finest foods, while being waited on by a bevy of servants. Why are you so insistent on clinging to your poverty?"

The words slashed through her, cutting deep. Did he really think so little of her, judging her because she was no longer a spoiled Mayfair princess? Couldn't he see she was something better? She'd been cast out with a sister to take care of, no money, no one to turn to, and had carved out a life for them with her bare hands. With her blood, sweat and tears, and no help from anyone, thank you very much.

And while they might not have a lot, Eliza was proud of every bit of it.

"Nothing comes for free in this life, Your Grace. Not for women. If the past five years have taught me a single thing, it's precisely that."

"You're wrong. I only want to help you as repayment for Robert."

"Repayment? For what?"

He shifted toward the window and fiddled with his cuff. "For ignoring you all this time. For believing that story about Scotland and your aunt and not checking on you myself."

Something about his words didn't ring true. He was lying, but why?

Before she could contemplate what Lucien might be hiding, he lifted her arm and held it. "Did Rathbone hurt you?" he asked quietly, then pressed his warm lips to the sensitive skin inside her wrist.

The shifts in his mood were boggling. Has she ever met a more confusing man? His touch distracted her, though, with his gentle kisses sending goosebumps up and down her arm. "No," she whispered.

"Are you certain?" He lingered there, his warm breath and wet mouth worshipping her skin, and her muscles grew heavy, limbs sinking into the leather. He murmured, "Because I will destroy him and everything he cares about if he ever hurts you."

"Why?"

"Because you're mine, Eliza."

———

He hadn't meant to say it.

But once the words were out, Lucien wouldn't take them back. She was his. She'd belonged to him ever since those dinners when they discussed maths and her studies, and when she'd asked him questions about university and his classes. When her insatiable thirst for knowledge had her hanging on his every word, making him feel like the smartest man in the room.

The thought of truly claiming this woman, of being the first to slide inside her body and spill his seed there, had tortured him all night. It had been so long since he felt worthy of such a gift, and he didn't deserve it, especially from Eliza.

She'd hate him if she knew what happened. Only Jasper knew the truth, that Lucien's selfishness had caused Robert's death, and that if Lucien had been there instead . . .

In the end Lucien lost a friend and gained a mountain of guilt.

So, no. He wouldn't fuck her, and he certainly couldn't keep her.

But he could kiss her.

Removing his gloves, he unbuttoned the cuff of her shirtwaist and slid the fabric out of his way. Her skin was soft and supple, and he lavished kisses all the way up her forearm, loving the way she trembled in his grasp. He could still hear her moans in his ears from last night, the sounds of pleasure when she rode his body.

He wanted to hear them again.

She's only allowing this because you bought her.

The lust roaring in his blood cooled. What was he doing? Eliza wasn't his lover or his mistress. Both of them grew carried away last night, lost in the moment, but said moment had passed.

He lowered her arm, rebuttoned her cuff, then set her hand on her lap.

"You are the most confusing man," she said. "For a reprobate, you are surprisingly hard to seduce."

"Is that what you are doing? Trying to seduce me?"

"Yes, you daft man. I still have nearly forty-three thousand quid to earn."

He scoffed. "Rounding numbers? For shame, Eliza."

"Forty-two thousand eight hundred and fifty-eight."

"Always forgetting the pence. Do you need a piece of paper? An abacus, perhaps?"

She shoved at his shoulder. "Stop—or I'll climb in your lap right here and earn another night's payment."

Jesus. His groin tightened at the idea, cock thickening in his trousers. He shifted, hoping to ease the sudden ache, and tried to sound stern. "You'll do nothing of the sort, young lady."

He heard her breath hitch a second before she moved even closer, dash her. "Or what? Will you punish me, Lucien? I've heard about what teachers do to naughty young boys." Her fingers danced along his thigh, toward his groin. "Will you make me stand in the corner or paddle my bottom with a ruler?"

"Fuck, Eliza." He snatched her wrist before she could go higher. "Stop it."

"I can see you're hard. You want me."

"I want you, yes, but I won't act on it. Perhaps I'll visit Mollie and Ginny today instead." Even saying the words caused his cock to deflate, but Eliza needn't know that. Better she believed him a worthless degenerate than to hold out hope that he would take her virginity.

"No, I don't think you will," she said. "I think you want someone more innocent. More . . .inexperienced. A young girl who needs you to teach her what to do—"

Fire licked through his veins, and he snapped, "Cease speaking this instant."

Eliza laughed, a musical sound that felt like a caress over his bollocks, and crossed her arms. Thankfully, they rode the rest of the way in silence, Lucien holding onto his sanity by a thread.

By the time they arrived at his solicitor's place of business, he'd regained his equilibrium. He held her hand politely and helped her down to the walk. And if his touch lingered a shade too long as he assisted her inside, she didn't comment on it.

The secretary looked up as they entered. "May I help you?"

"The Duke of Blackwood and Lady Eliza Hawthorne to see Mr. Turner."

"Your Grace, my lady," the secretary said. "Good morning. Please, have a seat and I shall see if Mr. Turner is ready."

"Look," Eliza whispered when they were alone. "Is that a *ruler* on the desk? Shall we save it for later?"

God, he wanted that, but he couldn't. He *couldn't*. He was responsible for what happened to Robert, for what happened to her. She would hate him if she knew.

No matter her words, no matter how tempting the package, Lucien had to resist her. "Behave."

She chuckled and walked around the room, examining the art on the walls. "These look expensive. How much are you paying this solicitor?"

"I haven't the foggiest, actually." He had a business manager and secretary for those sorts of things.

Lucien hadn't troubled himself with the estate and businesses since Robert's death, more than happy to let others shoulder the burdens for a while. He'd failed at his responsibilities, had proven unworthy of anyone depending on him for anything, so it seemed best to step aside and let others do it.

"Your Grace," an older man said from the office doorway. "My lady. Won't you both come in?"

"Hello, Mr. Turner," Lucien said. "Thank you for seeing us."

"Of course, of course. Have a seat, if you please."

Lucien helped Eliza into a chair, then took his own. "Have you an answer for her ladyship on the late earl's estate?"

"I'm afraid there's not much good news. The will left by your ladyship's brother transferred all the assets to the next earl. No portion or entailment was set aside for you or your sister."

"Well, this was a waste of time." Slapping her hands on the armrests, Eliza started to get up out of the chair.

Lucien put his arm out to stay her. "Turner, there's nothing through her mother's family or distant relatives? Her mother's or father's will? Nothing at all?"

"No, I'm afraid not, Your Grace."

"Is there anything to be done about the current earl? Undoubtedly, Lady Eliza had possessions in the house at the time of her brother's death. Is she not entitled to get those possessions out?"

"I suppose, if we could prove they belonged to her and not the estate."

"He's likely thrown it all out," Eliza said with a frown. "Why would he keep anything five years later?"

"We won't know until we try," Lucien said. "And I'd like to have a little chat with his lordship anyway."

Turner cleared his throat to gain their attention. "Your Grace, I did learn that the current earl is having some financial difficulties. Perhaps if you offered him the right price . . . ."

"Good work, Turner."

Lucien started to rise as Turner reached for a stack of papers on his desk. "Wait, if you please. Whilst Your Grace is here, may I return the final paperwork for the land sale?"

He dropped back into his seat. "Land sale?"

"Yes, it came through Your Grace's secretary. It's the property in Hampstead." When Lucien didn't say anything, the solicitor cleared his throat. "I . . .That is, I assumed you knew. It has the ducal signature on it."

Lucien held out his hand. Turner placed the papers in Lucien's grasp, then withdrew a handkerchief to blot his forehead. Looking down, Lucien quickly read the legalese, which authorized a sale of some land his grandfather had purchased up in Hampstead. If he recalled correctly, it was mainly used for sheep grazing.

He flipped to the last page and saw his signature and seal.

What in the bloody hell?

"I didn't authorize this. Is it too late to stop it?"

"Of course, Your Grace. The papers come to me to finalize and file. I can misplace that one."

"Papers?" Lucien snapped. "Plural?"

Turner pulled at his collar. "I thought you knew. That is, there have been more of them as of late, but I assumed Your Grace was offloading some assets. Paring down the estate."

Lucien couldn't speak. He was stunned. Paring down the estate?

"Mr. Turner," Eliza spoke up. "May we see all the papers to which you are referring? I believe His Grace would like to review any business you've conducted on his behalf for the last few years."

"Yes," Lucien said, numbly. "Quite."

ELIZA COULDN'T BELIEVE her eyes. "Lucien, your accounts are a mess."

After they left his solicitor, they went straight to his business manager's office. Then, after taking every book, ledger, and piece of paper associated with the Blackwood estate, he fired both his business manager and his secretary, telling them legal proceedings were to follow if he found anything amiss.

Now back at his townhouse, they were inside his study, reviewing his ledgers.

"This is unbelievable," he shouted, throwing one of the thick books against the wall. "Those miserable parasites! Selling off my land and assets to put the money in their own pockets. I'll have them strung up!"

"You most definitely should press charges," she said, reviewing the lines again. "Because they've stolen quite a bit of money from you."

"Damn it!" he yelled, tearing at his hair as if trying to rip the strands out of his head. "I should have paid better attention."

"Why didn't you?"

When he didn't immediately answer, she looked up. He was staring at the fire, his chin set at a stubborn angle. She frowned at him. "Well? Why not?"

"Because I was busy elsewhere, Eliza. I didn't want to review boring reports and add up numbers all day."

That wasn't like the Lucien she remembered. What had caused such a drastic change in him? "Busy with parties and women and such? That sort of busy?"

"You try being a reasonably attractive, wealthy duke under the age of thirty and see how easy it is to resist temptation."

His words rang false. Something else happened all those years ago. But if he wanted to lie, then she couldn't stop him. They weren't friends, and he owed her nothing more than six nights of mindless pleasure and fifty thousand pounds.

She returned to the ledger, staying quiet as he continued to brood. After a bit, he stood and went to the sideboard. "Drink?" he called.

"Yes, please. Whisky, if you have it."

A crystal tumbler containing a splash of amber liquid appeared before her eyes. "I wouldn't have taken you for a whisky girl," he said.

"No? What type of girl do I seem like?"

He dropped into the seat next to her. "I don't know. I never imagined you drinking spirits."

"I like almost everything except gin."

He shuddered. "Can't stand the stuff. Tastes like perfume."

"Exactly."

They drank in silence, while the fire crackled. It was cozy, a scene her thirteen-year-old self would've killed to experience. But so much has changed since then. She was no longer that wide-eyed girl, and this was not a romance.

She hoped Fanny was faring all right at home alone. Eliza didn't feel good about leaving her sister for too long. Nights, when Fanny slept, were different. But during the day, when Eliza returned from work, there were meals to prepare, clothes to launder. The apartment needed tidying, too. Fanny did what she could, but Dr. Humphries said her sister shouldn't tax herself, and Eliza didn't mind looking after them both.

"What are you thinking about?" he asked, shifting toward her slightly.

"My sister. She'll soon wonder where I am."

"My driver can take you home. Thank you for trying to help me untangle this mess." He gestured toward the desk and the mound of paperwork, his expression angry and dejected.

She didn't like seeing him hurt. She wanted to ease those worry lines on his brow and kiss away the frown he wore. Wanted to make him smile and laugh, hear him growl into her ear and call her angel, and feel the rough press of his fingertips in her skin.

Eliza didn't want to leave him.

She finished the rest of her drink, disgusted with herself. No matter what else, she couldn't become attached to him.

Setting the empty glass on the desk, she stood up. Then she began slipping the tiny buttons of her shirtwaist through the holes, undoing them. She'd managed five before Lucien realized what was happening.

He jerked in his seat. "Eliza, what are you playing at?"

Moving swiftly, she worked her way down her sternum, revealing more and more skin and undergarments along the way. It helped to serve as one's own lady's maid—she'd dressed and undressed herself every day for five years.

Lucien's gaze bounced around the room nervously, as if he were searching for an escape. The hand holding his drink trembled slightly. "There are servants in the house. It's not yet nighttime. What about your sister?" He swallowed hard. "This is wrong. You needn't do this. I will give you the money. Christ, Eliza. Please, I'm begging you. Fasten all those buttons at once."

Never had he said he didn't desire her.

Which meant she kept going, of course.

Her body felt feverish, her heart racing as she disrobed in front of him. With every garment that hit the floor, her blood ran hotter. Her sex grew embarrassingly damp. Was he able to tell?

His expression darkened as she popped open her corset and let it fall. The bulge behind his trousers made her mouth water, and she wondered if he would finally let her see his cock.

"This is wrong," he rasped through harsh breaths as she lifted her chemise over her head. Then he reclined in his armchair, limbs loose and sprawled, like he'd given up the fight. "But oh, fuck. Keep going. God help me, don't stop."

After untying her drawers, she removed everything below her waist in one go, leaving her bare. Lucien studied her with a hot hooded gaze, eliminating any hint of shyness she might've felt.

"Bloody hell, you're beautiful." He downed the rest of his whisky and plunked his glass down, hard. "Get on the sofa, angel."

Excitement raced through her as she went to the long sofa against the wall. Lucien stood slowly and removed his coat, then his waistcoat and cravat. Now in shirtsleeves and trousers, he approached her, a devious glint in his eye. "Spread your legs."

Her thighs parted at his command, her body ready to do whatever he said. She felt giddy and drunk, though it wasn't from whisky. It was from this gorgeous and charming man she'd adored when she was a girl.

Instead of mounting her, as she expected, he knelt on the carpet and grasped her hips. "You keep trying to seduce me. I think you need to be punished."

"Are you going to paddle me with a ruler?"

His lips twitched but he shook his head. "No, not yet. Right now I plan to lick your pussy until you cry, begging me to stop because you cannot possibly come again."

Without giving her a chance to respond, he lowered his head and ran his tongue through her slit. She sucked in a breath, while Lucien let out a long groan. "You are so wet. You truly want me, don't you, little virgin?"

"Yes," she whispered. "Please, Lucien."

Humming in his throat, he licked her again, the flat of his tongue scraping across her most sensitive area. He lapped at her, exploring, never touching the place she craved him most, that little button atop her sex that throbbed with wanting. She rocked her hips, seeking, but he held her down.

"You tortured me last night," he said, flicking the tip of his tongue around her entrance. "It's my turn to torture you. Be still."

There was no more air for talking because Lucien began using his lips and tongue on her, swirling and caressing her clitoris, and everything else disappeared. There was just his mouth and the incessant tingles racing down her spine, along her legs. Bleeding hell, this felt good.

The tension built inside her, her insides pulling taut, as he drove her higher, those warm licks and kisses like nothing she'd imagined. When he sucked her bud into his mouth, scraping it with his teeth, she exploded, the bliss overcoming her in a rush. "Oh, my God," she gasped as her walls pulsed in sheer happiness.

When it ebbed, Lucien gentled but didn't stop. Even when she grew sensitive and squirmed, he held her down and continued to lap at her. She considered protesting, but then she felt his finger probing at her entrance.

"You're soaking," he murmured. "Absolutely drenched. It's like heaven."

"Lucien," she panted. "Please."

She wasn't altogether certain what she was begging for, only that she needed more. Her body felt empty, needy, even in the aftermath of the best orgasm of her life. Was he planning to take her virginity here?

Suddenly, she wanted that more than anything else in the world.

"I'll take care of you, angel," he said, the tip of his finger sliding inside her pussy. His tongue painted her clitoris, which was swollen from earlier, and her back arched from the sensations battering her system.

"Yes, Lucien. It's so good."

The stretch of her inner tissues was strange and forbidden, a wicked touch that had her panting and rocking, trying to get him deeper. He was gentle, however, so very gentle, slowly filling her for the first time. When his finger was finally seated inside her, he rubbed a spot that made her see stars. "Blast!" she cried. "What was that?"

"Magic. Do you like it?"

He repeated the motion, and she reacted instantly, grabbing his hair and rocking her hips into his mouth, unable to help herself. It was like he'd shocked her with electric current, and her body could only react. The muscles of her stomach contracted, and he doubled his efforts, his tongue stroking quickly, and she nearly came off the sofa as another orgasm swept up and over her. Stronger than the first one, it seemed to go on and on, a never-ending cascade of ecstasy that she was powerless to stop.

When the peak ebbed, she sagged into the couch, boneless. Her throat ached from her cries. Lucien kept nibbling her folds and the crease of her thigh, his finger still embedded in her channel, and he pumped his hand lazily, mimicking what his cock would do. God, she couldn't wait.

"Please," she said, her hands scrabbling at him, trying to bring him closer.

"One more, I think." He began giving her those drugging, open-mouthed deep kisses again and her eyes rolled back in her head.

"No, Lucien. It's too much."

"You can take it, my clever girl."

He didn't let up, and she could only whine, too far gone to form words as he gave her one more orgasm. When it was over, she couldn't open her eyes, her body sore and heavy, and he finally released her. She winced as his finger withdrew, but there was a strange emptiness now, a sense that part of her was missing.

"Sleep, my darling," he said, his lips brushing her forehead.

He never found his release, was her last thought before the blackness tugged her down.

CHAPTER
SEVEN

ELIZA AWOKE WRAPPED in a warm and soft cocoon, not a stitch of clothing on her body. How long had she been asleep? Dying afternoon light streamed through large bay windows she didn't recognize. An unfamiliar painted ceiling stared down, while strange furniture surrounded her.

Lucien. Ledger books. Sofa.

Ah, yes. Relaxing, she pulled the blanket tighter around her nakedness. That had been remarkable, though not quite what he'd paid for. Interesting that during his thorough ministrations, he hadn't lost control. He hadn't been overcome with need, like last night.

He hadn't come close to taking her virginity.

Was this her fate? To have the one man she'd been obsessed with for years pleasure her beyond reason, but never claim her?

He was at his desk, and she watched through her lashes as he reviewed the ducal accounting books, his hair mussed and sleeves rolled high on his forearms. He'd discarded his collar, revealing the thick column of his throat, and on his face sat a pair of thin eyeglasses. Her sex quivered. He was absolutely gorgeous, concentrating so intently that a crease had formed between his brows. She wanted to smooth it away with her thumb.

When she thought of Lucien, this was what she imagined, a serious and clever man. Dedicated and responsible, not the reprobate with two mistresses and a devil-may-care attitude. She far preferred this version.

I could love this version.

No, no, no. This was not a romance. As much as the thirteen-year-old inside her longed to fall at his feet and worship him, that was just a fantasy. Real life had taken them in different directions and she would not become his mistress. Fanny was her responsibility now.

She sat up, the blanket wrapped tight around her nakedness, and his gaze flicked toward her. Removing his eyeglasses, he said, "There you are. I was wondering how long you would sleep."

She rose and went around the desk to stand by his chair. "Your mouth should be outlawed."

The side of his mouth hitched as he leaned back in his chair. "I know."

Unable to keep from reaching out, she swept a lock of dark hair off his forehead. "Arrogant man."

He edged away and cleared his throat. "Eliza, we should talk."

"Excellent idea. Let's go up to your bedroom and talk in bed."

"Absolutely not." He pushed his chair back and stood, as if he needed to put space between them. "I have an idea."

"A naughty idea?"

"Dash it, no. Will you let me finish?" He sighed and pointed to the books on his desk. "This is a disaster. I need help sorting out the estate and you've already started working on the books with me. I'd like to hire you."

"I don't understand. You've already 'hired' me for six more nights."

"No, I haven't—and not for this. I want to offer you legitimate work. Here, for me. With the accounts."

"Oh." She looked at the desk, her mind turning this over.

"This way, we needn't do any more of *that*." He waved his hand in the direction of the sofa.

Her stomach dropped. He wasn't going to bed her. She'd thrown herself at him twice and Lucien had resisted. Now he'd found a way to pay her to *not* take her virginity.

She should've been thrilled.

She should've been grateful.

Instead, she was disappointed.

"I see."

"I . . ." He dragged a hand through his hair, mussing it even more. "I thought you'd be relieved. This way, you needn't lose your virginity. You can still marry a decent man and have a family. You needn't sleep with me for money."

But I want to sleep with you, Lucien. Badly.

It wasn't one sided, either. He admitted to wanting her. Had climaxed last night, and pounced on her when she removed her clothes earlier.

You're mine, Eliza.

Had he meant it? If so, why the sudden and annoying nobility? The man had *two* mistresses! Seducing him should not prove this damn difficult.

She considered his proposition. Working on his accounts would keep her here in the house. With him. Alone. That was a plus, unless he was determined to leave her chaste, which was a colossal minus.

Admittedly, it would be nice to put her maths skills to use. Balancing her and Fanny's meager budget each month wasn't exactly taxing her brain box. But agreeing felt like giving up on something monumental. Something she'd dreamed of for *years*.

"May I be honest with you?" she asked.

His expression wary, he folded his arms across his chest. "Of course."

"I was looking forward to more of that." She hooked a thumb at the sofa. "I was looking forward to sleeping with you."

Lips parting in surprise, he stood, frozen. "I . . .don't understand. Why? You'd be ruined."

She could only throw her head back and laugh. "Lucien, I don't care about my maidenhead or my reputation. Those things matter in Mayfair, not in the real world. And in case you haven't noticed, I like doing these things with you. I . . . " God, was she really going to confess this? "I had a crush on you as a girl. This is actually fulfilling some of my fantasies."

He dragged both hands through his hair, appearing aggravated at her revelation. "Do not tell me these things. Your brother would cut off my bollocks with a rusty knife, Eliza."

"He's not here, but I am. I'll help you with your accounts, but I want to do the rest, too."

"Why are you insisting on this? I thought you would be grateful."

"Do you desire me, Lucien?"

"I shouldn't answer that."

Which was an answer unto itself. Still, she had to push. One thing Eliza had learned in the last five years was to take charge of her life, not to let an obstacle in her path deter her.

And right now, that obstacle was Lucien's nobility.

She dropped the blanket. "Do you want to fuck me, Lucien?"

The air in the room turned heavy and thick, making it impossible to breathe. He hardly moved, and the hunger in his expression sent a torrent of heat along her veins, causing her core to pulse with desire.

"You know I do," he growled.

"Then prove it."

———

Robert would punch Lucien in the face were he still alive.

Lucien tried to resist, but he inhaled and caught the scent of Eliza's arousal, and he was lost, drowning in a sea of longing. He hadn't washed his face from earlier, either, and the taste of her lingered on his tongue, on his skin. Christ, he wanted her.

She stood there patiently, as bare as the day she was born, waiting for him to make up his mind. The curve of her hip beckoned, the perfect place to hold onto whilst he explored her body. Then he studied the slope of her breast, the swell of her belly. His cock throbbed in his trousers, insistent and annoying, and the temptation was more than he could bear.

This was terrible. *He* was terrible—spoiled and selfish, used to getting what he wanted—and his body hated to be denied. After all, he'd paid for her innocence. The idea of feeling her virgin cunt strangle his cock . . .

He closed his eyes briefly. Why wouldn't she take the fifty thousand pounds, buy a house in Mayfair, and everything could return to the way it was before? The last five years would disappear. Why did she insist on torturing him like this?

Why must she insist on giving him her virginity?

His body didn't care about the reasons at present. She was naked and asking him to fuck her, and he didn't think he was capable of refusing her a damn thing. His fingers curled into fists.

I shouldn't.

She deserves better.

She will hate me when she learns what happened to her brother.

The devil in him, however, began rationalizing.

One night. Afterwards, she would help him with his accounts. He would give her the money and ease his conscience. She would restart her life like nothing ever happened.

"You'll help me with the accounts? After we sleep together once?"

"Yes."

"And you'll accept the money?"

"In exchange for my virginity and five days of accounting, yes."

"Five days! This will take longer than that."

"I agreed to only seven nights, Lucien. You'll get no more." She stretched her arms toward the ceiling, her perfect apple-shaped breasts rising. Her nipples were hard little points begging for his mouth.

Distracted, he lost his train of thought. "Wait, why?"

"Because I have a life and responsibilities outside of you. Shocking, I know."

"But . . . ."

"But, nothing. You already have two mistresses. You don't require a third."

He hadn't seen those two mistresses in days, had lost interest in them because of Eliza, who at the moment was moving toward him, her hips swaying and breasts bouncing. The urge to bite all that perfect skin, to mark her as his own, had his hands shaking.

When she reached him, she trailed her finger down his throat, between his collarbones. "You claim my virginity tonight, then we move on to business tomorrow. Everyone wins."

"No taking it back once it's done," he warned.

"I won't regret it. Deep down, I always wanted it to be you."

Jesus Christ.

Hesitation evaporated like morning dew in the hot sun. Spinning, he found his topcoat on the chair. In a flash, he wrapped her in it, then lifted her in his arms. She clutched at his shoulders, laughing. "Where are we going?"

"Upstairs."

Then they were in the corridor, his leather shoes slapping the marble floor on their way to the staircase. The footman in the front hall quickly averted his eyes, expression unchanging, as if his employer held a naked woman in his arms every day. Despite his reputation, though, this was a first. Lucien never fucked women here.

Just Eliza, apparently.

She'd grown bolder these last few years, nothing like the young girl who used to blush when he stared at her a few seconds too long from across a dining table. Yet she was still so innocent.

A combination that hardened his cock beyond reason.

Once in his bedroom, he strode to the bed and tossed her on top. She bounced, chuckling, and he began tearing off his clothing, desperate to feel her bare skin against his own. Coming to her knees, she shuffled forward to help, her eager fingers starting with his trousers.

They worked together until he was naked, then he let her look her fill. His erection stood out proudly, eagerly, and he half-expected her to change her mind. "Are you sure, Eliza?"

She looked at his cock and reached a tentative hand toward it, all wide-eyed curiosity and fascination. "Very."

Oh, God. If she touched him, he wouldn't last.

He pointed to the bed. "On your back. Spread your legs."

She hurried to comply, limbs scrambling in her haste. Now it was his turn to look his fill, never wishing to forget the way she appeared in his bed. No lover had ever visited his home before, and he anticipated smelling her on his sheets afterward.

One night. That was all.

He crawled onto the mattress, up between her thighs, which he shoved wider to make room for himself. Her pussy gleamed in the firelight, her slickness like a sweet treat just waiting to be devoured. "I'm going to prepare you, so relax. Understand?"

"Yes," she said on an exhale of breath.

Without waiting another second, he lowered his head and nuzzled her. This couldn't be rushed. He teased the edges of her sex with his nose and lips. When she shifted impatiently, he gave a gentle lick through her seam, stopping just below her clitoris.

Then he applied himself to the task, using his tongue in creative ways—back and forth, circling, pressing—until she was panting. Her fingers found their way into his hair and she held on, her hips rocking, churning, seeking . . .and it took everything he had not to surge up and ram his cock inside her. He had to go gently.

A mewling sound escaped her throat, while her nails dug into his scalp. "Now, Lucien. Please."

The need in his body doubled, tripled, and he had to close his eyes before he began humping the bed in desperation. He sucked her clitoris between his lips and flicked it with his tongue. Gasping, she tensed and let out a moan, the sweetest sound he'd ever heard.

"It's not enough, Lucien. I need you."

Moving a finger toward her channel, he pushed gently inside, the walls sucking him in greedily. Fuck, she was tight. Hot. Slick. He growled into her flesh, every muscle clenched in agony as he tried to stem the hunger clawing inside him. Sweet Eliza, with her spine of steel and mind for numbers. He could get used to her taste, the way she swelled on his tongue. How she gripped his hair in her fist to keep his mouth where she wanted.

He could do this for the rest of his life and die a happy man.

"More, Lucien. Please."

He rose up over her as he slid another finger inside her. "Yes, my lovely girl. You're so very tight, but I'm going to fill you up."

Remembering her reaction on the sofa, he crooked his fingers inside her, and she jolted, letting out a loud moan. "There we go, angel," he crooned. "That's my favorite spot."

Soon, he wedged a third finger in her channel. This was a tighter squeeze, so he distracted her with a deep kiss, until he had the digits seated inside her. Damn, she was snug. He imagined all that heat strangling his shaft and nearly came right then.

"Oh, God. Please, now. Lucien, I'm ready." Her hands pulled at him. "Please."

He reached for the drawer next to the bed and found the package containing a shield. It took only a second or two to roll the thick rubber onto his shaft. Then he took a vial out of the drawer.

"What is that?" she panted.

"Oil. It will help me slide inside you."

He poured a small amount into his hands, set the vial down, then smeared the oil on his rubber-covered shaft, trembling at the sensation. He wasn't certain how long he could last.

Clenching his jaw to keep from spending, he lined up at her entrance and pushed forward, making certain to watch the slow invasion. His hands held her hips steady as her entrance gave way and sucked the crown inside. "That's it, darling. Take me in. Be my very good girl and take my cock inside you."

When she tensed, his gaze darted to hers. "Easy," he said, stroking her thigh. "I'm going to take care of you."

Using his thumb, he drew circles over her clitoris and her muscles eased, relaxed, which allowed Lucien to sink deeper into her sex. They both groaned. This gentle advance went on for several minutes as he invaded and conquered, stroked and petted. Wet heat surrounded him, strangled his shaft, and his brain struggled to keep up.

"More, please," she whispered and tilted her hips higher. "I need you deep inside me, where I ache."

Gritting his teeth against the need to ram inside her, he said, "I don't want to hurt you."

She wrapped her arms around his waist, then slid them lower, grabbing his buttocks. Then she sunk her nails into his backside, hard.

He hissed at the exquisite pain and his hips snapped, driving her into the mattress, their bodies fully joined. She squeaked, almost recoiling, and guilt slammed through him. "Goddamn it, Eliza. I'm sorry." He held perfectly still, his lids squeezed tightly against the absolute bliss of being fully sheathed. "I didn't mean to enter you so quickly. Are you all right?"

"I'm fine. Stop worrying." She wriggled slightly beneath him. "It was a pinch but now it's done."

"I should pull out." He started to shove up off the mattress, but she clutched him harder, digging those nails into his skin once more. He shivered.

"Don't you dare. Teach me, Lucien. Tell me what you like, what makes you come."

Groaning, he shoved his face into the soft skin of her throat. "No, no, no. Stop talking." His hips began rocking, pleasure coursing down his spine. "Fuck, Eliza. I need to make this last. I need to make this good for you."

"This isn't about me," she whispered, the vixen. "You bought me, paid for my virginity. I'm yours to do with whatever you please."

Goddamn it. Lust shot through his groin and along his cock. This was wrong. All of this was so bloody wrong.

He began thrusting then, sweat gathering on his skin, and the bed rocked with the force of his movements. "It's so good . . .you feel so good. Tight. Oh, God, so bloody tight."

"*Yes*," she moaned near his ear. "Keep going. I'm yours, Lucien. Only yours."

Whatever restraint he'd been clinging to deserted him. Pushing up, he grabbed her hands and pinned them to the mattress, holding her down as he continued to pound into her. He felt like an animal, a beast mindlessly rutting. "Do you like it? Do you like the way a cock feels inside you?"

Her walls clenched around his length, giving him her answer. "Yes, yes, yes," she chanted, her face awash in pleasure, making him feel like the most powerful man on earth. "Just yours, Lucien."

Satisfaction filled him. He was the first man to fuck this glorious creature, the first to see her expression twist in euphoria as he thrust inside her. He made certain to brush her clitoris with his pelvic bone on every stroke. His hands kept her where he wanted, but she didn't try to pull free, as if she liked being at his mercy.

A million pricks of fire exploded in his veins. "You're mine now," he said, his voice thick. "Mine to fuck whenever I want. Perhaps I'll tie you to my bed, naked, spread open so you'll always be ready for me. Ready to take my cock."

She must've liked that because her core spasmed around his length, as if she were trying to pull him deeper inside. Her shout filled the room as she came.

"Goddamn it." He couldn't hold out any longer. His hips stuttered, grew uncoordinated, and he threw his head back to roar at the ceiling. Jets of spend filled the rubber and every muscle twitched in blissful agony. When his thoughts realigned moments later, he stared down at her gorgeous face and saw her satisfied expression. His stomach instantly sank.

Oh, shit. What had he done?

EIGHT

ELIZA FLOATED FOR A BIT AFTER, contentment rippling throughout her limbs as they lay there, still joined. Lucien panted, his face relaxed, making him appear younger, more like the man she once knew. The man she'd once dreamt about marrying. Her heart quivered, then turned over in her chest. She had the sudden urge to wrap around him and never let go.

Sharing his bed had been so much more than she imagined, like he'd taken her apart and rearranged her, an equation that no longer made sense. One only he could solve. And, she craved more of him and their intimacies.

Damnation. This was a fiasco.

She pushed his shoulder and he obliged, falling to his back on the mattress with a thud. The shield still covered his softening erection, and his spend was making a mess of him and the bedclothes. Apt, considering how the afternoon had gone. She'd made a mess of everything.

Worse, she'd agreed to return tomorrow.

She had to resist the temptation, because this affection, this blooming emotion towards him would only grow worse. What happened at the end of the seven days? Would she fall in love with him? Agree to be his mistress, anything for another crumb of his attention?

She absolutely couldn't risk it. Yes, he'd taken her virginity, which was the fulfillment of so many of her girlhood dreams. Now she would straighten out the ducal accounts and help him set things to rights. Then, she would disappear from his life with her heart intact.

"I should go," she blurted and shoved up off the bed.

"Wait." He reached for her. "Let me take care of you. Clean you up and make sure you're not hurt."

Dread clogged her throat. Any hint of tenderness would do her in right now. The walls between this man and her heart had taken a beating moments ago, nearly crumbling, and she needed time and space to rebuild and reinforce them.

"I'm right as rain, duke." She removed her arm from his grasp and lunged for his silk dressing gown on the chair. "You needn't fuss over me."

"Eliza, goddamn it." He sat up and dealt with the shield. "Don't rush out of here again. I want to talk about this."

Lord, that was almost a worse idea than the bloody tenderness.

Besides, she had to get home to her sister.

Throwing her arms into the oversized sleeves, she started babbling on her way to the door. "Lovely time, must run. You were amazing. The stuff of poetry, really. Talk more later. Sweet dreams. Good night."

"Do not dare—"

She closed the door behind her and hurried toward the stairs. Humiliating that her clothing was in his study, but there was no help for it now. She had to quickly dress and find a hack. Fanny would be worried sick if Eliza wasn't home before dark.

Lucien had collected her things into a pile, bless him, so she began dragging the pieces on. Just as she fastened her corset, the door opened and the duke stormed in, his face a picture of unhappiness. He wore trousers, a shirt and waistcoat, and carried a pair of shoes and a topcoat in his hands. "So you were planning on sneaking out again? Is that it?"

"I said goodbye. I was hardly sneaking."

"I know someone desperate for escape when I see it, Eliza." He dragged on his coat. "Shall I tie you to my bed, or are you going to answer me honestly right here?"

Her mouth went dry and she had to drag in a deep breath, the words appealing to her in ways she would never have guessed two hours ago. "I must return home to my sister." It was true, after all.

He studied her face as if searching for a lie. "I called for my carriage already, so I will take you."

"No, I'd rather—"

"You'd rather take a hack or a tram. I know, but I won't allow it. So short of poisoning or stabbing me, that won't happen."

"You should return to your books. They need your help far worse than I do."

"The books may wait. I will ensure you get home safely first."

And I must put distance between us before I fall in love with you.

She tried to reason with him as she fastened her skirts. "I'll allow your driver to see me home if you stay here."

"Absolutely not. I'm not letting you go all the way to Shoreditch alone. End of discussion."

"You're being absurd."

"And you're being stubborn." Once he shoved his feet into his shoes, he folded his arms, blocking her only path to escape with his body. "I'll gladly carry you to the carriage. Your choice."

She glared at him as she buttoned her shirtwaist. "Are you like this with all your lovers, or merely me?"

"Just you, it appears. Ready?"

There was no getting out of it that she could see, so she followed him to the large fancy carriage and piled in. He sat across from her, their knees touching, and heat curled in her belly. Every bounce of the springs reminded her that Lucien had just taken her virginity.

She must've winced, because he asked, "Are you sore?"

Her chest expanded, like her heart was swelling. The urge to crawl into his lap and let him hold her roared inside her. "I'm fine. Just a bit tired. Mind if I sleep?"

His gaze narrowed as if he didn't believe her. "You wouldn't be trying to ignore me, would you?"

"No," she lied. "I'm exhausted. You've worn me out."

"Then sleep. I'll wake you once we're there.'

She thought to close her eyes for a few moments, but she must've truly fallen asleep because Lucien was suddenly shaking her awake. The carriage had stopped.

"We've arrived," his deep voice said, the expression in his eyes so soft and adoring that she nearly kissed him.

Pushing up, she straightened. He'd ordered the carriage directly to her lodgings, which meant . . . "You discovered where I live. How?"

"I've been waiting for you to ask me that all day. I had a man waiting outside my home last night, just in case someone visited me to collect on one of her evenings."

Dash it. She'd led Lucien right to her. "Bully for you, then." She reached over him to push the latch on the carriage door. "I'll see you in the morning."

He stepped down and held out his hand. Confusion furrowed her brows. "What are you doing?"

"Escorting you inside."

She barely stifled her gasp. She couldn't imagine his reaction to her humble apartment. It would mortify her beyond belief. "Absolutely not."

"If you want to make it inside, it will be with me at your side. Come, Eliza."

"You needn't worry over my virtue. You've taken care of that already, duke."

"This has nothing to do with your virtue or reputation. This is about your safety. Now, must I carry you?"

"Stop threatening to carry me," she snapped. "It's tiresome."

In a flash, he grabbed her forearms, yanked her forward, and hauled her over his shoulder. "I'll return shortly," he called to his driver.

She was draped over him like a carpet, her legs dangling while he cradled the backs of her thighs. "You obnoxious toff. Put me down this bloody instant."

He had the nerve to smack her bottom. "Quiet, impudent baggage."

"That's the way, guv!" a female voice shouted out from a window above them.

"You're welcome to slap my bottom anytime, sir," another woman called.

Thankfully, they were soon inside her building. "Which floor?" he asked, his voice clipped.

"Four—and there's no elevator, so have a jolly time carrying me up all those steps."

"I've carried pillows that are heavier than you."

Lucien proved his excellent physical condition by taking the four flights easily, not even sounding winded. "Which one?"

"Second on the right."

After he stomped over, jostling her, he knocked on the door.

"This is humiliating," she muttered.

"I told you I wanted to take care of you," he said. "I saw your wince in the carriage."

Her skin heated, partly embarrassment but mostly pleasure. This caring and possessive side of him was nearly irresistible.

The door opened.

"Is that . . . ." Fanny sounded confused. "Is that my sister over your shoulder?"

"Lady Fanny," Lucien said. "If you'll allow me in, I'll drop off this parcel and be on my way."

Parcel? Eliza huffed. So much for the caring and possessive Lucien. "Put me down, you oaf."

"Your Grace," Fanny said, a hint of disapproval in her voice. "Come in."

"Thank you." He strode in, bent down, and put Eliza on her feet.

"Was that necessary?" she asked him.

"I think so, yes."

Fanny's worried gaze looked the duke over first, then Eliza, and Eliza could see the wheels turning in her sister's head, putting the pieces in place. Of course, with Lucien half-dressed, higher level reasoning wasn't exactly required.

"Is Your Grace planning to stay for dinner?" Fanny asked. "We have soup."

Eliza didn't give him a chance to answer. "No, he's leaving. Good night, Lucien. I will see you in the morning."

"Ladies," he said with a perfectly executed bow. "I'll leave you to your evening."

Then he departed and the silence in the apartment was deafening. The sisters stared at one another for so long, they heard Lucien's carriage pull away.

"You have feelings for him," Fanny finally said.

"That's absurd." Though Eliza suspected it wasn't.

"We should rethink this plan, because I will never forgive myself if my illness forces you to become some toff's mistress."

"I'm not going to become his mistress. It's only five days and I'm only helping him with some accounting matters. No intimacy required. Furthermore, we agreed on this. It's the best way to get the money and then sail to America."

Before that happened, Eliza had to earn her fifty thousand pounds.

Fanny narrowed her eyes and opened her mouth—to continue arguing, no doubt—but she coughed instead. Deep wracking coughs that crackled in her chest. Even though it was warm in the apartment, Eliza closed the window, trying to keep the dirty London air out for the moment. Fanny needed clean air, which was scarce in the city.

When Fanny caught her breath, she continued their conversation as if the coughing fit never happened. "Just promise me you won't fall in love with him."

"I promise."

For the rest of the night, Eliza feared she'd already broken that promise.

———

The ducal books were even worse off than Eliza first believed. That Lucien allowed things to get this bad was absolutely appalling.

And quite unlike the man she remembered from all those years ago.

What happened to him?

She hadn't seen the duke in three and a half days. Instead, she came to his home, sat in his office, and poured through the accounting ledgers. The books hadn't been updated in some time, and there were strange entries she didn't understand. Those she noted on a separate piece of paper to ask him about.

She tried not to think about him, but it was hard when she was surrounded by reminders of him all day long.

You're mine now. Mine to fuck whenever I want.

Heat suffused her, as it did every time she considered Lucien's words. She dared not tell Fanny any of the details. Hearing how gloriously rough and filthy Lucien was in bed wouldn't reassure Fanny that Eliza would keep her vow never to become his mistress.

And honestly, Eliza wasn't certain she wanted to tell anyone. Not right now, at least. There were lonely years ahead of her in which she could try to make sense of him and the last few days.

In the meantime, she'd enjoy the work, the challenge to her brain, while sitting in a fine Mayfair home again, where it was warm and smelled nice. She wasn't on her knees scrubbing, or leaning over to sew in candlelight. Perhaps Lucien could write her a letter of recommendation, too, one that would allow her to find employment in an American accounting firm.

Where was he anyway? Was he intending not to see her at all before the end of the five days?

The possibility sent a pang through her chest. She hadn't expected that. When she agreed to help him with the books, she assumed they would be side-by-side, laughing and talking as they worked. Not with her cooped up alone while he did whatever it was he did all day.

Was he with his mistresses?

The pang sounded again, the pressure on her sternum like a boulder had been dropped there. She tried to remind herself that she held no claim over him. *I cannot be jealous. He is not mine.*

Besides, tomorrow was her last day here.

Afterwards, they'd both return to their lives, and Eliza would focus on Fanny's recovery. They would find an American sanitarium to accept Fanny and heal her. Then they would buy a house and settle somewhere with plenty of fresh air and sunshine.

So it shouldn't bother her if Lucien wished to ignore her. The more time they spent together would make it harder to separate tomorrow.

And yet, she couldn't stop glancing at the door every few minutes, waiting for it to pop open and reveal his handsome face.

Then the door did open. Eliza straightened, a hopeful smile twisting her lips . . .which dimmed when a footman appeared with a tray. She swallowed her disappointment.

"Your lunch, my lady."

"Michael, as I told you yesterday and the day before, you may call me Eliza. Or Miss Hartsford."

He shook his head. "His Grace's orders. We address you properly, as befitting your station."

Oh, that dratted annoying man.

"Can you tell me, is His Grace here today?"

"Yes, miss."

"I see."

He was here, yet he hadn't stopped in to say hello. Were they no longer friends now that he'd taken her virginity? Was her hymen all he'd wanted, like some sort of trophy or prize? Hurt and anger swirled in her belly, twisting and turning, until the urge to yell at him rose to a fever pitch. "Where is he?"

The skin above the footman's collar turned a deep red. "I probably shouldn't say, my lady. His Grace asked to be left alone."

"I understand. I wouldn't like for you to lose your position." Finding work was a miserable endeavor, and as much as she wished to see Lucien, she wouldn't do it at an employee's expense. "Thank you for the tray."

"Your ladyship is most welcome."

When the footman left, Eliza waited a few minutes, then set off exploring. It shouldn't be terribly hard to find Lucien. The townhouse was large, but it wasn't a labyrinth. She would conduct a systematic search of every floor, avoiding the areas reserved for the staff.

She decided to start on the ground floor, then work her way up. Moving quickly and quietly, she explored but found only empty rooms. On the first floor, his bedroom was quiet and still. Same for the other bedrooms. As she passed the ballroom, however, a thumping sound caught her notice.

Carefully, she cracked the door and peered inside. Her lips parted on a surprised exhale. A bare-chested Lucien was pummeling a large canvas bag, his hands wrapped in cloth. Sweat rolled down his skin, his muscles popping with his rapid movements.

Sweet heavens. She couldn't tear her gaze away. He was stunning, a Greek god come to life to make mortal men appear like flabby, inconsequential fools. Arousal tightened her nipples into points, the area between her legs tingling as she watched. The minutes dragged on and she began to worry she'd melt into a puddle on the floor. All that would be left was some threadbare clothing and hair pins.

She desired him. Right now.

It wasn't easy to admit, but Eliza knew when she'd been beaten. Her resistance crumbled like grains of sand. What was one more time when her heart already belonged to him?

She closed the door behind her, which caused him to pause mid-punch and glance over. His chest heaved as he panted. "What are you doing here?"

"Coming to find you."

"Why?" He wiped his forehead with the back of his hand. "Is there a problem downstairs?"

There was a problem all right, and it had to do with the ache inside her that only he could satisfy.

"Are you avoiding me?" As she approached, he went over to pick up a cloth from the floor. "Because I haven't seen you in three and a half days."

"I'm busy, Eliza." He wiped his face with the cloth. "You've been making excellent progress, though."

"You've been looking at the books after I leave, then."

"Yes."

"Why not look at them with me? Then we may discuss any questions I have."

His hands rested on his hips, making his bare chest appear impossibly wide. "Just leave the questions and I'll get to them when I can."

Why was he being so cagey?

Ignoring his deep frown, she closed the distance between them. The heat from his body was like a furnace, and she longed to touch all that sweat and strength. "I was thinking . . ." She licked her lips as a bead of sweat trickled down the center of his chest. "Tomorrow is our last day together."

"And?"

"And it would be a shame to waste it, hiding in the ballroom."

"I'm not hiding," he said, his voice sounding strangled as she caught a bead of his sweat on her fingertip before it could reach his stomach. "And you shouldn't be in here."

"Am I still yours, Lucien?"

The whispered question echoed in the empty room, and a muscle worked in his jaw as they stared at one another. *Say yes,* she thought. *Please say yes.*

"Eliza—"

"It's a simple question. Am I still yours?"

"It doesn't matter. I cannot keep you. It's best if we maintain our distance until you finish tomorrow."

"It does matter. It matters at this moment."

"Why? Because you're trying to torture me?"

She placed her palm on his jaw and stroked the heavy whiskers he hadn't shaved off today. "Because I want you to take me to your bed one more time."

CHAPTER
NINE

SURPRISINGLY, Lucien didn't put up a fight. He merely grabbed her hand and tugged her through his house as if they'd done this a hundred times. She didn't bother hiding in embarrassment. What was the point? He'd taken her virginity already and her body was burning alive, desperate for him. Let the servants talk. She'd never see them again after tomorrow anyway.

You're mine now.

How she wished it were true. To wake up with him every day, roll over into his arms and find his warm hard body. To laugh with him and discuss maths at the dinner table. To have days and months and years together, their memories and hearts intertwined.

But those were just fantasies.

Lucien wasn't for her. Dukes married girls from the very best families, not girls who once scrubbed privies and mopped vomit off the floor. Certainly not a girl who sold her virginity in a club full of aristocratic gentlemen.

Do not fall in love with him, Fanny had warned.

Too late. It felt like Eliza had loved Lucien for so long that it was hard to remember a time when she hadn't. Sharing his bed had caused those feelings to multiply exponentially. Leaving him was going to kill her.

When his bedchamber door closed, she threw herself at him, wasting no time in sealing her mouth to his. He met her kiss eagerly, and her hands skated over his bare torso. He felt divine, big and hot.

"I have to fuck you." He began walking her toward the wall while gathering her skirts in his hand. "It will be fast and hard, so please tell me you aren't too sore."

"Not sore. Please, Lucien. Hurry."

He growled and lunged for her mouth again, his tongue thrusting inside to flick and rub against hers as cool air hit her stocking-covered legs. "Put your legs around my waist," he said and lifted under her buttocks until her thighs were splayed, her knees hugging his hips.

"That's it," he crooned and, after some maneuvering with his clothing, the head of his cock nudged her entrance. "Let me in, my darling girl. I'm going to take such good care of you."

Oh, heavens. The temptation of those words. She couldn't let herself believe them.

This was all, right here. Today and tomorrow. Then they'd go their separate ways—Lucien back to his two mistresses and Eliza to America.

Even if she couldn't keep him, she'd ensure he remembered her long after she'd gone.

"I like when you take care of me," she whispered. "I like when you teach me, too. Will you spank me and put me in the corner if I'm a naughty student?"

"Goddamn it," he gritted out from between clenched teeth and shoved halfway inside her, as if he couldn't help himself. "You drive me out of my bloody mind."

It was not an easy fit, and she was impatient to lose herself in him. "More," she begged. "I need all of you."

With a grunt, he flexed his hips and drove up until he was fully seated. She gasped, her nails digging into his shoulders, as her body adjusted. "Good lord, Lucien."

"Shh, you can take me." He held still, his big body pinning her to the wall, hands under her thighs. "You were made for my cock, Eliza."

She doubted it. At the moment, it felt as if he would snap her in two. Still, she loved the feeling of having Lucien inside her, his thick shaft filling her and stealing her breath. A small bite of pain chased by immense pleasure.

So much pleasure.

"Please," she whispered into his throat. "Please, you have to move. I am dying to feel you."

"Is that so?" His voice was low and tight, like she wasn't the only one suffering. "Is your pussy greedy for me?"

Her lids fell as her head dropped onto his shoulder. Did all dukes speak in such a filthy manner, or just hers?

"Yes," she answered, wriggling her hips. "So greedy. I need you."

He gave a small thrust, and tiny sparkles raced along her spine. Her walls gripped him, unwilling to let him go, but he withdrew and pushed forward, rocking back and forth, until they built a steady rhythm. His mouth hovered over hers, his hot breath warming her skin, and she could feel him everywhere, inside and out, drowning her, and she never wanted to breathe air again. "Oh, God," she said on a moan as he ground into her, bliss echoing in every cell, every muscle.

"Would you like to learn something new?"

"Yes, please."

He carried her to the bed. "Roll over, then get up on your hands and knees."

Keeping her skirts above her waist, she did as he asked. "Like this?" She glanced over her shoulder.

With his stare locked on the slit of her drawers, he tucked his hard cock into his trousers, but didn't touch her. Instead, he went to the small secretary against the wall and opened a drawer. When she saw what he took out, her whole body quivered.

A ruler.

"You've been very bad." As he approached the bed, he smacked the hard wooden stick against his palm. "Teasing me and making me want to fuck you."

Sweet Jesus, was he truly going to spank her? She'd mentioned this in jest, but now she wasn't so sure. "What are you doing?"

His smile was sinister as he stepped just off to the side. "Giving you your punishment. Aren't you curious to know what it will feel like to have this hard ruler strike your bottom, my naughty girl?"

She hesitated. Yes, she was a bit curious, but she also wasn't keen on pain. "Will it hurt?"

"For only a second." He dragged his palm over one of her buttocks, then drew his fingers along her seam, making her squirm. "But the burn will turn into something bright and pleasurable, like your skin is shimmering. Glowing. Will you let me teach you? I think you're going to like it."

She likely would have agreed to anything in that moment, as long as he kept using that deep seductive voice. "All right."

Before she could even brace for it, he struck her backside with the wooden ruler. Fire roared across her skin. That smarted, her thin undergarment doing seemingly nothing to protect her.

He put a hand on her back, holding her still. "Good girl, there's one. Only nine more to go."

"Nine!" She tried to turn toward him, but his grip didn't budge, and another strike landed in a different spot. She inhaled sharply.

"That's it," he said. "Let the pain warm your skin. Then I'm going to fuck you and it will feel so very good."

The place where he'd first spanked her didn't hurt any longer. Instead, it pulsed, the entire area hot. She quite liked it.

"Can you take more?" When she nodded, he gave her two brisk slaps. It was over quickly, and she moaned at the resulting buzz in her veins as moisture collected between her thighs.

"Dirty girl, you cannot help yourself, can you? Taking off your clothes and begging me to give you my cock. You're so very needy, aren't you?"

After another smack, she was panting, shifting, her arousal at a fever pitch. "I do need you, Lucien. Please."

"Mmm, I can see your pussy dripping from here. You are an eager little thing, aren't you?" Another slap of the ruler, this time across the back of her thigh. She waited out the sharp pricks of misery until they eased and bloomed into something wonderful. Instead of holding her, he was petting her spine. "If you beg me properly, I might fuck you again."

"Oh, please. Please fuck me, Your Grace."

Two spanks right together. "And you're not going to tease me any longer?"

"No, Your Grace."

He gave her another hard smack. "That is for calling me Your Grace."

Before she could say anything else, he roughly pulled her hips closer with one hand. Then the head of his cock met her entrance and he was back inside her. "Jesus fuck, you're wet."

His palms slid inside the slit of her drawers to cup the red-hot abused skin. He squeezed, causing a fresh wave of pain to roll through her, but it quickly turned to a blissful throb. Finally he started moving, driving, pounding, rattling her bones with his powerful thrusts.

Whimpering, she clawed at the bedclothes. This angle brought him deeper, rubbing a certain spot with every drive of his hips, and the sound of their slapping bodies filled the room. Her skin vibrated, a reminder of what he'd done with the ruler, and it quickly became too much. "Oh, God. Don't stop . . ." The orgasm streaked through her, fierce and bright, a flash of sparks against a night sky, and she shouted, her walls clenching around his length as she trembled.

"You're so beautiful," he gasped, holding perfectly still and panting against her back. "You've always been so goddamn beautiful." He snapped his hips once. "I love the way you make me feel. Never leave me, my clever girl."

Her toes curled in blissful happiness. It was the most he'd ever revealed of his feelings for her, and the words sank in to fill the holes in her lonely heart. If only she could stay with him. "I'm yours, Lucien."

He began riding her fast and rough then, his cock punching into her sex until he pressed tight, his fingertips digging into her hips. "Fuck, Eliza!" he shouted to the ceiling. "You're *mine*." Suddenly, he swelled inside her, his body straining as he grunted with pleasure.

When it was over, she collapsed on the bed. Lucien's forehead rested on her back, his warm pants heating her spine through her clothing. "I forgot a shield," he said.

Oh.

The image filled her mind—a small boy or girl with his eyes and a keen ability for maths—and her heart twisted. If only. Some other lucky woman would marry him and bear his children. Watch him roll around on the floor to play with his son or daughter and hear their laughter.

She moved, sliding out from underneath him. "We should've been more careful."

"I'm sorry." He dragged a hand through his hair and dropped onto the mattress, disheveled and beautiful. "I don't have any diseases, if you're concerned. But Eliza, if there are consequences . . ."

She waited for him to finish. When he didn't, she knew why. There was no future between them, not in the ways that mattered.

Though it was for the best, that *hurt*.

I've survived worse. I'll survive this, too.

She willed her insides to freeze, forced her heart to toughen up. "You needn't worry about consequences," she promised, suddenly grateful for Helen's advice the night of the auction. Having a duke's bastard would add another burden onto her and Fanny's future they could scant afford, even with fifty thousand pounds in their pockets.

"You can't know that." He grimaced. "Even with a shield, it's possible. And your brother would not have wanted that for you."

It was telling that his only concern was in disappointing her long-dead brother. Why was Lucien so focused on the past when the present was what mattered?

She decided to tell him the truth. Perhaps then he would see her as an adult woman, not Robert's little sister. "There are places where a woman can procure a tonic to prevent conception. I plan to buy one after tomorrow."

A flash of surprise crossed his face before he masked it. "I see."

"I should return downstairs."

Just as she took a step toward the door, he grabbed her hand. "Why not stay and let me fuck you again?" He pressed a kiss to the inside of her wrist. "I'll remove your clothing and do it properly this time."

She shouldn't.

There were the ledgers and Fanny and the miles between Shore-ditch and Mayfair . . .but bloody hell, Eliza wanted more of him. Enough to last the rest of her life.

Once more could not make things worse. She already loved him.

After tomorrow, she'd never see him again, so better to gather all these memories while she could.

Stepping back, she began unfastening her bodice, giving her best attempt at a sultry smile. "Whatever Your Grace wishes."

———

Early the next morning, Lucien lifted the brass knocker and rapped it several times. It took longer than expected, but the door finally opened to reveal a maid. "Yes?"

"The Duke of Blackwood to see his lordship."

"His lordship is not receiving callers at the moment."

"He will see me." Lucien presented a card. "Tell him to come down or I will pull him out of bed myself."

The maid begrudgingly opened the door. "Wait in there," she said, gesturing to a front room.

Lucien entered, removed his gloves, and glanced about. Robert's former home was a pitiful sight. The once vibrant townhouse was dour, with bare walls and dirty floors. Lucien remembered flowers and laughter, family portraits and the smell of lemons. Those things were gone now.

The current earl, Lucien had learned, was a gambler and an idiot. He'd used the title to borrow funds on credit, and hadn't yet been able to pay any of it back. There were rumors of more loans through unscrupulous means, which meant serious consequences—the deadly kind—if they weren't paid back.

After what the new earl had done to Eliza and Fanny, Lucien couldn't bring himself to care. His only interest was in discovering if anything was still here for the two sisters.

Heavy feet on the front stairs caught his attention. Seconds later a bleary-eyed man entered, his necktie an absolute disgrace. "Blackwood," he said, as if they'd been introduced before. Which they hadn't. "What's this about?"

Lucien put a fair deal of menace in his voice as he said, "Justice."

"I beg your pardon?"

"By a twist of fate, you inherited this house, this title—neither of which you deserved—but you made a grave error when you turned your cousins out into the streets."

Barnett's lip curled. "You mean those two girls? They weren't my problem. Let one of the other relatives take care of them."

"Only a bloody monster would cast two young women into the streets of London without seeing them provided for, while telling everyone they went to an aunt in Scotland."

Possibly sensing Lucien's rage, Barnett edged around the back of the sofa, out of arm's reach. "Those two weren't my concern. For all I knew there was an aunt in Scotland. Besides, all they had to do was marry or find some rich man to keep them as a mistress—"

Lucien lunged. In one swift motion, he snatched Barnett's throat in his fist and pinned the earl against the wall. "You miserable piece of filth. They were mere girls—and your cousins. I am going to ruin you." He shook the other man. "You'll be left with nothing when I am through."

Barnett had the audacity to appear affronted. "Are you mad? Release me at once, Blackwood."

"Not until we have a little chat." He tightened his grip, satisfied when the earl's face turned red. "I want to know what possessions remain from the former earl's family, what you haven't yet sold off to cover your debts, you miserable worm."

"Everything here belongs to me," he rasped.

Lucien leaned in. "While that may be true in a legal sense, I find it difficult to believe there isn't one painting, one knick-knack, one *piece of lint* left over from the former family. I suggest you think hard about it, because I'm not letting you go until I get an answer."

"You have no right—"

"The best part of being a duke is that I have every right to do as I wish with absolute impunity. That includes making men disappear. There's no one to stop me from squeezing the life out of you and dropping your body into the Thames."

Real fear seeped into Barnett's dark eyes as he clawed at Lucien's unforgiving grip on his throat. "Wait, please."

"Have you thought of something?"

"Yes," the earl squeaked. "There's a painting."

Lucien eased his grip, then cast the other man away in disgust. "Then I suggest you go retrieve it for me."

Barnett darted from the room and up the stairs. In case the earl was lying, Lucien decided to give him ten minutes, no more. If Barnet hadn't returned by then, Lucien would follow.

With two minutes to spare the earl hurried down the stairs, a canvas in hand. "Here. Take the damned thing and get out."

Lucien accepted the framed portrait. It was of a young Eliza, Fanny, Robert and their parents. Robert's unhappy expression seemed to stare out at Lucien, a judgmental glare full of resentment.

I'm sorry, Robert. I couldn't resist her.

"Satisfied now, Blackwood?"

Lucien quirked a brow at the insolent earl. "No, not in the least. I won't be satisfied until you are living on scraps, cast out of this home . . .as your cousins were forced to do five years ago. Be forewarned, Barnett. Your debts are coming due." He'd personally see to it that the moneylenders came calling as soon as possible.

Gripping the painting in his fist, Lucien stalked out of the townhouse and found his carriage. During the ride, he braced himself for the sight of Eliza again. Today was their last day together, and he had to find a way to let her go.

It was why he'd avoided her for three and a half days. The more time he spent with her, the more he wanted to keep her—and that was out of the question. Someday she'd learn what happened to her brother and she would hate Lucien for it. The best course of action would be to pay her and let her start over, return her life to some normalcy. Then they could all forget the last five years ever happened.

The ride to his townhouse took hardly any time at this early hour, which was why he was surprised to see people gathered on his stoop.

It was Eliza . . .and Rathbone. The marquess stood a bit too close to Eliza, as if he was using his body to intimidate her.

Lucien was out of the carriage before the wheels even stopped rolling. "Rathbone," he barked. "Move away from her."

Eliza appeared relieved to see him, which meant Rathbone had been harassing her again.

"Duke, you're just in time," Rathbone drawled.

Lucien headed straight for the pair, painting in hand. "To pulverize you into a jelly? Excellent. Been looking forward to it."

"No, to hear me inform her ladyship about her brother."

A sinking feeling bloomed in Lucien's gut, but he shoved it aside. Only a few people knew what happened that night, and none would betray him by discussing it. Rathbone was clearly referring to something else.

"My brother?" Eliza's brows arched. "What about him?"

Rathbone's voice was sharp, like a blade, cutting and clipped. "Hasn't His Grace informed you what happened the night your brother was killed?"

"Shut your mouth," Lucien snapped as panic lit up his insides. He didn't want anyone to hear this, especially Eliza. She'd never think of him the same way again. "There's no need to dredge up those old memories for her."

"No, wait," Eliza said. "I want to hear it. Please, my lord. What about my brother?"

"Eliza, go inside," Lucien ordered. "Allow me to speak with Rathbone alone."

She never even looked at him, her attention remaining on the marquess.

Malice glittered in Rathbone's dark eyes, his lips curled into a gleeful smirk. "She deserves to know, Blackwood, especially since you were determined to win her from me the other night and make me look like a fool. Or were you planning on keeping the part you played in Robert's death a secret from her forever?"

CHAPTER
TEN

ELIZA STUDIED BOTH MEN. She didn't trust Rathbone, but Lucien appeared on edge, his body trembling as if he might strike the marquess at any minute.

Which made her wonder—again—if he had something to hide.

Had Lucien something to do with Robert's death?

Rathbone had appeared this morning outside Lucien's house when she arrived, clearly having followed her. Without preamble, he asked how well she knew Lucien. When she tried to escape inside, Rathbone carried on, insisting on speaking with her. That was when Lucien had arrived.

So, what was really going on?

"Your Grace?" she prompted when Lucien didn't say anything. "Care to explain?"

Instead, Lucien glared at Rathbone. "Get off my property."

"Interesting what I was able to learn by digging into your life, Blackwood. Your former mistresses do like to talk."

Lucien took a threatening step forward, but the marquess held up his hands and bowed to her. "My lady, when you leave him—and you definitely will—please know you have an admirer in me. I would be more than willing to step into his shoes and set you up in a fine house—"

Bile rose in her throat at the offer, but she was spared the need to respond because Lucien shoved Rathbone toward his carriage. "Get the bloody hell out of here!"

Rathbone smiled slyly and departed, his carriage soon rolling away from Lucien's, but she didn't move. She couldn't. Her feet were rooted to the walk. "Please tell me what he's talking about."

"Come inside and we'll talk."

"Lucien, now."

He rubbed his eyes and sighed. "Eliza, please. I don't wish to do this on the street."

Because he knew it would upset her?

A knot tightened between her shoulder blades, but she marched up the walk, climbed the steps, and went inside. Lucien followed, a painting in his hands. She didn't care much about art at the moment. She'd rather hear what Lucien knew regarding Robert's death.

"We'll talk in my office." Lucien led the way, the house eerily quiet.

Once there, he set the painting on the floor, leaning against his desk. The lines on his face had deepened, making him appear older than his years, and a strange ringing started in her ears. Almost as if her body was warning her of oncoming doom.

"Tell me it isn't true," she said. "Tell me you had nothing to do with my brother's death."

"Eliza . . . ."

"I want the truth. The police were never able to give us much information. I have no idea what happened to him, other than he was robbed and dumped in an alley."

He gestured to the armchairs. "Shall we sit?"

"No, Lucien. Open your gob and speak, man. What happened to Robert?"

He dragged in a deep breath, then let it out slowly. "I was having an affair with an actress. I didn't know it, but this actress was also seeing another man, a dangerous thug who ran one of the waterfront gangs. He found out about her relationship with me and decided to kill me—a fact I was unaware of."

He stared at the wall, his tone even. Like he was reciting a lesson in class. "One night, Robert begged me to attend some dinner party with him, but I cancelled at the last minute. The men from the gang were waiting for Robert when he left the dinner party. They . . .thought he was me. He was shoved into a carriage, beaten, and killed near the docks."

Disbelief and horror washed through her, the news worse than she'd imagined. Still, it didn't make sense. "They thought he was you? Why?"

He cleared his throat as he clasped his hands. "Back then, the three of us . . . We played tricks on one another, especially with women. We would sometimes assume another's identity and misbehave."

A boulder-sized lump settled in her throat. She whispered, "So, this particular woman. You told her . . .?"

"I told her my name was Robert Hartsford, Earl of Barnett."

Eliza doubled over, a hand to her stomach as she nearly crumpled to the floor. He rushed toward her, but she backed away, her palms out as if to ward off an evil spirit. "Do not touch me. God, Lucien! How could you do such a terrible thing? To your best friend? What is *wrong* with you?"

"We did it all the time, Jasper and Robert too. We laughed about it, considered it a big joke."

"I cannot believe this." The backs of her lids burned, the betrayal slashing deep through her heart. Lucien, her kind and serious hero, was no hero at all. He didn't deserve her love, not by a long shot. "I cannot believe you kept this from me, that you would let Fanny and I struggle for years knowing you were responsible. Never once did you try to find us. He died and you went back to your two mistresses and your perfect life on Grosvenor Square."

"I've regretted Robert's death every single second, Eliza. The guilt has weighed on me for five years. But you must believe me, I had no idea you and Fanny had been turned out on the street. I thought you were in Scotland! I would have helped you, I swear."

She scrubbed her face with her hands. "There were nights we ate garbage, slept in alleys. I cleaned privies and shoveled horse shit. Washed clothes and—" She bit off the words and shook her head. "Why am I bothering? You have no idea what it's like to worry, to live without all this." She waved her hand to indicate his home. "You've never had to struggle a day in your life."

"I'm terribly, terribly sorry, Eliza. I would give anything to go back and change things. I never thought any of this would happen. I never wanted anyone to suffer."

"And yet we have." A tear escaped her lids and rolled down her cheek. "We all have, my entire family. You destroyed us." Her voice broke. God, she had *loved* this man, admired and worshipped him. She let him inside her body. All the while he'd known this terrible secret and hadn't shared it.

"That's why I want you to take the money. Please, you needn't clean privies or shovel shit any longer. You can buy a house in Mayfair and forget all of this ever happened."

Was he serious? "I can't do that."

"Why not? You'll be independently wealthy, with a home of your own. Everything you've ever wanted."

I wanted you.

No, she'd wanted the version of Lucien that existed in her head. The real man was cruel and selfish. No wonder he'd been so eager to pay her off and have her disappear! It was the easiest way to reduce his guilt. He thought money would fix this, would give her and Fanny the means to go back in time. To the way things were five years ago.

But life didn't work that way.

"This cannot be fixed with money. You merely want to ease your guilt—but nothing can bring my brother back or erase the last five years."

"I know it won't bring him back, but I'd like to take care of you. I want to get you out of Shoreditch and back where you belong."

And he thought she belonged in Mayfair? "Lucien, I haven't belonged here in a very long time, even when Robert was alive. When I told him my plans to attend university, he ridiculed me. Women are not supposed to be clever here. They're supposed to marry young and fade into the background of their husbands' lives. A forgotten footnote in the sands of time. I don't want that. I've never wanted that."

"Then what do you want? Why did you need the money so desperately if not to change your circumstances?"

He appeared confused, absolutely befuddled that she didn't wish to rejoin his fragile and restrictive world. Frustrated, she snapped, "Because my sister is sick. I need money to take her to a sanitarium in America and help her get better."

"America! You cannot go there. It's . . . ."

"It's, what? Too uncivilized for Your Grace? Too progressive? Too modern?"

"No, it's too far," he shouted, then he immediately closed his eyes as if he regretted the outburst. "I cannot stand the thought of you so far away from me."

"I see." Nodding in understanding, she folded her arms across her chest. "You'd prefer me in a house in Mayfair, where you'll stop by and visit. A few times a week, perhaps? And I'll give you a key to make it easier? Just admit you hoped to turn me into your third mistress, Lucien."

"No, absolutely not. I never planned to sleep with you. I wanted you to retain your virginity, if you recall."

"But then I seduced you, right? Poor Lucien, always fighting off my advances."

"I didn't say that. Stop twisting what I'm saying." He dragged his hands through his hair. "Eliza, I care about you a great deal. I want—I *need* to make things better for you."

But he didn't love her. He didn't even care for her as a woman, only as a cause. A way to alleviate his suffering and assuage his guilt. She would never be more than a bad reminder to him of the past he'd destroyed.

And while taking his money would help Fanny and her in countless ways, it would also ease his conscience. He didn't deserve that relief.

No, he deserved to suffer, to live with the knowledge of how he'd hurt Eliza and her sister. Forever.

As if he sensed the direction of her thoughts, he jerked open a desk drawer and held up a bank draft. "Here. It's already made out to you. Fifty thousand pounds."

Her chest squeezed at the sight of it, but her anger outweighed everything else. *I will not make this easy for him.*

"Keep your money. I don't want it." She turned and started for the door, the backs of her lids burning with oncoming tears.

"Eliza, don't be ridiculous. You need this money. Moreover, you earned it."

"I don't need a bloody thing from you, Lucien. Not now, not ever."

"Wait!"

Reluctantly, she paused at the door. Escape was close at hand, and she desperately longed for space from him. "What is it?"

"Please, take the check—and take this." He came toward her carrying the painting he'd brought in earlier. "I got it this morning from your old home."

Hadn't he understood her a second ago? "I don't want anything from you."

"But it's yours." He flipped to painting to face her. "It's your family's portrait."

The breath left her chest at the sight of those people, so young and so happy. With no idea of the tragedy about to befall them. She didn't even recognize herself, a pampered Mayfair princess who'd believed anything was possible if one only wanted it badly enough.

Lucien held out the frame like he expected her to take it. She shook her head sadly. "You keep it. I don't care to remember the past. I can't afford to. Goodbye, Lucien."

———

Two Weeks Later

Lucien sat by the fountain, a basket of walnuts on his lap and a cigar clamped between his teeth. The day stretched out in front of him like all the rest—a gauntlet of misery to endure until he could start drinking. Scotch was the only way to sleep, the only way to forget the past. In the meantime, he stayed mostly outside, away from the memories.

He tossed a nut into the fountain, strangely satisfied by the plunking sound as it hit the water. It sounded like a heartbeat, not that he would know as his heart had stopped beating two weeks ago.

God's teeth, he missed her.

I don't need a bloody thing from you, Lucien. Not now, not ever.

She hated him, and rightfully so. He hated himself, too.

It should've been Lucien beaten, kidnapped, and murdered that night, not Robert. No one would have missed Lucien. He had no family, no siblings. Some distant cousin would've lucked into a dukedom and that would have been that.

Instead, his best friend had died, and Eliza and Fanny had suffered.

There were nights we ate garbage, slept in alleys. I cleaned privies and shoveled shit.

Another nut landed in the water. Everything hurt. He couldn't focus, not even on the accounting she'd started for him. Nearly every room of the house reminded him of her. He was fucking miserable.

A scratch on stone caught his attention but he didn't turn around. Likely his valet come to chastise him for not shaving and bathing. Again. "Go away."

"You'll see me—or at least listen to me."

He jolted, the cigar nearly falling from his mouth. Fanny?

Eliza's sister slid onto the stone bench next to him and tilted her chin toward the basket on his lap. "This seems like a fun game. Is there a point?"

"Why are you here?"

"I cannot talk any sense into my sister, so I thought I would try with you. By the looks of it, however, I'm probably wasting my time."

He threw another nut into the water. No doubt she'd come to hear an apology in person, something he damn well owed her. "I must beg your pardon, Lady Fanny. You have every right to hate me as much as your sister does, but please believe me. I never knew the two of you weren't being looked after."

"Just Fanny will do, and thank you for the apology." They sat in silence for a few minutes before she said, "I suppose it's difficult for you to understand why we didn't seek help after our cousin kicked us out, but young women in our world are conditioned to believe no one gives a damn about them. We're hidden away until it's time to marry, kept ignorant of things that really matter. Perhaps we could've found a distant relative to take us in or gone to an orphanage, but Eliza didn't want us separated. It was easier to stay together and find work to support ourselves. Unfortunately, I grew sick and the burden soon fell on Eliza's shoulders alone."

A sharp pain lanced his chest. "I would have given a damn. I *do* give a damn."

"Then why did you let her go?"

"What do you mean? She left."

"And you let that stop you?" She scoffed. "Your Grace, you give up far too easily. Your best friend dies, and you shirk your responsibilities to the estate. Eliza leaves you and you just let her go, willing to watch the best woman you'll ever meet move away and start a life on another continent without you. Do you never fight for anything?"

"I . . ."

The protest died on his tongue. Had he?

Life had come easily to him before Robert's death. Women, friends, the title and wealth—all of it had fallen into Lucien's lap. When the worst had happened to Robert, Lucien had retreated, horrified and embarrassed. He wasn't strong, like Eliza. He was a terrible person, selfish. A reprobate with two mistresses and money he didn't deserve.

He shook his head and threw another walnut in the water. This self-reflection was giving him a headache. "She made it very clear when she left. She doesn't care to see me again."

"Her feelings are hurt. She's angry. Surely you can understand why."

"Of course, I understand. I don't expect her to forgive me."

"So, you won't even try?"

He wouldn't even begin to know how. Hell, he couldn't forgive himself, so how could he expect Eliza to? "She's better off."

"If you could see her, you wouldn't say so."

"Why? What's wrong?" He sat straighter, angling to see Fanny's face. "Is she all right?"

"No, you idiot. She's heartbroken. She's in love with you."

In love with him? The idea was laughable. They hadn't even been reunited for a full week, and nearly all that time he'd been withholding a terrible secret. "No, she's not."

"For a smart man, you are truly thick-headed, Your Grace. *Yes*, she is in love with you. Otherwise, she wouldn't be walking around looking like a creature from a Mary Shelley novel—"

Fanny began coughing then, deep racking coughs that made his own lungs hurt in sympathy. When she quieted, he said, "Shall I fetch you water or tea?"

"No, I'm fine."

"Is it consumption?"

"No. It's some mysterious lung ailment, worsened by the dirty air." She lifted a shoulder. "But everyone fears I'm consumptive, so I try to stay at home."

"This is why she plans to take you to America."

"Yes, to a sanitarium there."

"There are places like that here, you know."

"I think Eliza prefers the idea of a fresh start. No doubt you could convince her otherwise, if you gave a damn."

Of course he gave a damn. He loved her, for God's sake. Which is why he had to let her go. She was better off without him, building her independent life without memories and judgment. He threw another walnut. "What makes you think I don't?"

"Because you're brooding here instead of telling her how you feel and trying to win her back."

"I've hurt her enough."

"Therefore your guilt is more important than a future with her?"

"Are you saying I shouldn't feel guilty?"

"You most definitely should feel guilty. You should feel awful for being a foolish young man who thought he was impervious to the consequences of his selfishness."

The next nut landed in the water with more vigor, splashing them. "Then you may sleep well at night, because I do."

"We cannot change the past, Your Grace. The present is for the living, the future for our penance. What is your penance?"

"Liver disease and insomnia, if I had to guess."

"Be serious. Free of all that transpired with Robert, do you want her?"

If he hadn't ruined Eliza's life? If Robert were still alive? The answer came instantly. "Yes."

"Then fix it."

She made it sound so easy. "How?"

"That is for you to figure out. You're clever."

The nape of his neck tightened in annoyance. He chucked another nut into the fountain. "Lovely chat. Thank you for dropping by."

She merely chuckled. "I realize it's not the answer you're hoping for, but it's for you to figure out."

"Do you . . . ?" He forced himself to ask it, even if he sounded like a fool. "Do you think she can forgive me after I ruined your lives?"

"You didn't ruin our lives. Robert's death gave us a different life, but we aren't unhappy. We have freedom, while women in Mayfair do not. I think Eliza learned how strong she was, how much we love each other. We wouldn't trade the last five years for anything."

A glimmer of light took root in his dark soul, a seed of hope that Eliza might one day forgive him. That they could live in the present and not the past. "Truly?"

Waving her hand, Fanny said, "Of course, I wish my brother was still alive—I miss him terribly—and I wish I wasn't sick. Our lives, though, have vastly improved since leaving Mayfair. Had Robert lived, we each would've been married off to a man we hardly knew and started having children. Our possessions and our bodies would've belonged to our husbands. Now, though we are poor, everything we have is ours."

Eliza's fierce independence made more sense now. Why on earth would she ever come back to Mayfair, back to him? "When you put it like that, I'm not certain I stand a chance in winning her."

She rose and shook out her skirts. "I have faith in you, Your Grace."

CHAPTER
ELEVEN

At first, Eliza stared at Lucien's seal, wary. If they were love notes, she wasn't certain she cared to read them. Two and a half weeks had passed since she saw him last, and she still felt a gnawing anger in her belly when she thought of him.

And an ache in her heart.

So she let the letters collect on the kitchen table. Each night, Fanny would ask, "Are you going to open them today?" To which Eliza would respond, "No."

Finally, when there were more than ten, Fanny apparently decided to take matters into her own hands. After dinner, she reached for one and opened it.

"What are you doing?" Eliza screeched as she dried her hands on a towel. "Leave those alone."

"I will not. I'm dying of curiosity." Fanny unfolded the paper. "Blimey. That's disappointing."

"This is an invasion of my privacy—and don't tell me what's inside. I don't want to know."

"It's not a letter. It's a maths problem."

Surprise had Eliza taking the paper out of her sister's hands. Sure enough, Lucien hadn't written a word. He'd sent her a complicated equation to solve.

How . . .clever. A smile tugged at her lips before she could hide it.

"Aha!" Fanny playfully smacked the table with her palm. "I saw that reaction—and it's the first time you've smiled in more than two weeks."

"Stop." Eliza set the paper down and returned to the dishes. "It's interesting, is all. I hadn't expected it."

As she washed their plates and cutlery, her mind turned over the problem, working it out in her head. By the time everything was dry, she'd solved it. Her impulse was to share the solution with him, but that was silly. That would require mailing the letter back, and she didn't care to start any epistolary dialogue with him, even of the mathematical kind.

I love the way you make me feel. Never leave me, my clever girl.

Damn him. Why had he said things such as that, sweet things that caused her to fall in love with him again, while hiding information about Robert's death?

The paper on the table beckoned, her hand itching to write the solution down. Of course, she could write the answer but never mail the letter back to him. Yes, that's what she'd do. She would do this for *her*, not for him.

Taking a pencil, she sat at the table and scribbled. Fanny said nothing, just watched, until Eliza finished. "Quite impressive," her sister said. "Are you going to send it to him?"

"No."

Eliza reached to open another letter. As she suspected, it contained a different problem. This one was simpler, and she was reaching for a third letter in no time.

At some point Fanny drifted away, but Eliza kept at it. When she opened and solved all ten letters, it was quite late. A familiar sense of accomplishment fluttered in her chest. It felt nice. She hadn't done that in quite awhile.

"Are you going to forgive him?" Fanny, dressed in her nightgown, strolled over and sat at the table. "Because he obviously misses you."

"I'm not certain that's true. It's not as if he poured his heart out in the letters."

"Yes, he did." Fanny rolled her eyes toward the ceiling. "Eliza, he thought up these problems, wrote them down, and sent them to you. Maths is your thing."

"Our thing?"

"Your poetry. Your flowers and valentines. Come on. Can you not see it? The man is wildly in love with you."

Eliza shook her head. "You're wrong, and I don't wish to discuss it."

"Do you hate him for the role he played in Robert's death?"

Did she? Certainly, it had been selfish on Lucien's part to pose as another, but he admitted the three friends had laughed about it. Robert and Jasper had used other names, as well.

Still, Lucien hadn't told her, not even after sleeping with her. If it weren't for Rathbone, she never would've learned what happened.

But did she hate Lucien?

No. God, no. It would be far easier if she did, if these feelings lingering inside her disappeared. Loving him was terrible, painful and awful, like a rotten tooth she wished she could extract. Instead, the ache remained, twisting her up into knots.

"I don't hate him, but he hurt me. It's unforgivable."

"Unforgivable? Really, Eliza? That seems harsh, considering."

"Considering, what? That he was responsible for Robert's death and never told me? I trusted him with my body and my heart, and he has proven unworthy of that trust."

"Yes, he should've told you before taking you to bed, but can you honestly say you gave him a chance? You said you seduced him each time."

"Believe it or not, we did have conversations outside of bed, too."

Fanny coughed, then took a moment to catch her breath. Eliza waited patiently, hating that her sister struggled. *Maybe I should've taken Lucien's money.*

No, they would find another way. They always did.

When Fanny spoke, it was quieter. "You cannot fault him for what came after Robert's death or for my illness."

"I know." Eliza rolled the pencil on the table, not wanting to meet Fanny's eye. "I shouldn't have made Lucien think I blamed him for our financial straits."

"No, you shouldn't have. You know we're happier now, together and poor, than we ever would've been as separated, married, and rich ladies."

"Yes, but your illness," Eliza said. "That's because of where we live, these conditions."

"Dr. Humphries isn't certain about that. He said I might have caught it somewhere, or I might've been born with it and it took this long to present. The truth is, we don't know."

"I suppose. Why are you pushing me to give Lucien another chance, anyway?"

"Because I want to see you happy—and you were happy during that one week. It was clearly Lucien's doing."

"I won't be his mistress, and there aren't other options for a girl like me."

"Why not? You'd make a fine duchess."

"Sure. Can't you see me in Mayfair, telling all those fine ladies about my various jobs over the years? Not to mention auctioning off my virginity. I'd fit right in over petit fours."

"You're embarrassed of how you've earned a living for us."

"No, I'm not," she snapped. "I worked my bloody tail off to support us, and neither one of us had to—"

"Sell our bodies?" Fanny finished when Eliza fell silent.

Eliza grimaced. Yes, that was what she'd been about to say.

Fanny yawned and stretched her arms. "Who cares about what people say? You never have up until now."

"You merely wish for me to end up with Lucien, like I'm Cinderella or some such nonsense. You're making it sound so easy when we both know it's not."

"It won't be easy, but you're the strongest, most determined person I know. If you want something bad enough, you'll bring it about come hell or high water. The question is, what do you want?"

Eliza considered it, but her emotions were too jumbled, too scattered to come up with an answer about Lucien. She focused on the two of them, instead. "I want you to get better. I want to take you to America so you can recover."

"At some point, you need to live for yourself. I'll be fine. Don't ruin your chance at happiness for me."

"I love you. I'm not ruining anything by taking care of you. You're my family."

Fanny reached forward to clutch Eliza's hand. "We'll always be family. But I also know we need more than just each other. You might not want them, but I do want a husband and children."

This was the first they'd ever discussed it. "So, what are you saying? You want me to send you to America by yourself?"

"Perhaps. I don't know."

It was only fair, but the prospect caused sorrow to scald the back of Eliza's throat. She couldn't imagine a life without Fanny in it.

Exhaustion weighed her down. Lord, it was after one o'clock, and such a conversation was too heavy for this hour. She stood. "I have an early morning, so I'll go to bed. Are you coming?"

"In a bit. I want to get some water first."

"All right. Good night."

Once she was in bed, Eliza told herself not to think about Lucien. Not to miss him or to wonder what he was doing.

Her resolve quickly crumbled in the darkness, however, and she fell asleep to memories of his filthy words and possessive touch.

———

"A letter arrived for you today," Fanny said as soon as Eliza walked in the door from work. Fanny grinned. "Several letters, actually."

Eliza didn't want to admit it, but her heart leapt at the news. The letters from Lucien had continued, even a week later, and she looked forward to them. One might even have said they were the highlight of her day.

She strove for nonchalance. "Oh?"

"And they're not all from Lucien."

That got Eliza's attention. "Please don't tell me it's from a bill collector."

"Don't be absurd. We're current on all of our payments." Fanny held up a very fancy looking letter. "This is from Somerville College."

"At Oxford?" Eliza's brows climbed as high as they could go. "Who is it for?"

"You, silly." Fanny rushed over and handed Eliza the letter. "I didn't open it. I wanted to, very, very badly, but I didn't."

"Thanks, Fan," Eliza drawled. There was no privacy between two sisters who lived together.

"Open it!"

Eliza opened the letter and then gaped. "It's from Mrs. Maitland, the principal."

"Cor," Fanny whispered. "What does she say?"

Eliza read quickly. Apparently, Mrs. Maitland had reviewed the maths solutions Eliza had sent and invited her to sit for Somerville's entrance exam next term.

"Oh, my God," Eliza breathed. "I've been invited to sit for the entrance exam at Somerville College."

"You're going to Oxford?" Fanny screamed.

Eliza looked at Mrs. Maitland's words again. Wait, what maths solutions? And she'd never written to Somerville. "This doesn't make any sense."

A guilty look crossed Fanny's face as she twined her fingers together. A sure sign of nerves. "What have you done?" Eliza asked her sister.

"Nothing! I returned those solutions to Blackwood. After that, I never saw them again. You'll have to ask him what he did with them."

Eliza pinched the bridge of her nose between her thumb and forefinger. "Lucien. I should've known."

The man couldn't help himself.

Even though she'd refused his money and assistance, he'd gone and done *this*. He must've sent those sheets of paper to Mrs. Maitland and begged the principal to take Eliza on. How embarrassing.

"Wait, why are you frowning? This is exciting, Liza."

"I suppose, but I can't go." She folded the principal's letter and set it on the table.

"Whyever not?"

"First, no doubt Lucien has paid the woman to make the offer to me. Second, we cannot afford it. Third, I cannot leave you to fend for yourself."

"Lucien wouldn't do that, and there are charity societies who could cover your costs. And if you're concerned about me, you needn't worry any longer." Fanny held out another letter, this one addressed to her.

"What's this?"

"Read it," Fanny urged.

Eliza took the paper. Her breath caught at the name on the outside. "The Royal National Hospital for Chest Diseases?"

Fanny's grin took up almost her entire face. "They've accepted me. I'm leaving for the Isle of Wight tomorrow."

"Tomorrow!" To mask her rioting emotions, Eliza quickly read the letter. Sure enough, Fanny had been given a treatment bed there and they would send someone to escort her to the hospital tomorrow. "I can't believe this."

"It's a bleedin' miracle. They only take thirty or so patients a year. And my fees have been paid."

"It's not a miracle. It's the Duke of Blackwood."

"I don't care. I'm not stupid enough to turn down an opportunity like this."

The comment dug under Eliza's ribs like a sharp knife. "And you think I am? Stupid enough to turn down Oxford, that is?"

Fanny sighed. "I don't think you're stupid. I think you're proud and stubborn, and in the past I've always agreed with you. Someone without your best interests at heart will try to take advantage, but that isn't the case here. Lucien has your best interests at heart. Can't you see? He's in love with you. He's trying to make things better for you without gaining anything in return."

In love with her? The idea was ludicrous. "Wrong. No doubt he expects me to . . . ."

"To what? Go to Oxford and study until your brain melts? He's not even trying to keep you in London, Liza. He's giving you a life without him in it. How is that possibly serving his own interests?"

"He's doing this because he feels guilty."

"And? Why do you think rich nobs give to charities? To ease their guilt." Fanny shook her head, clearly frustrated. "Do you think for one second I am going to turn down the opportunity to recuperate at this prestigious hospital because I'm worried about easing Lucien's guilt?"

"No, and I wouldn't let you. This is a tremendous opportunity for you."

Fanny gestured to the letter from Mrs. Maitland. "This is no different."

"Wrong. Going to study at Oxford isn't life or death."

"Isn't it? If you stay here, you'll work yourself to the bone for the rest of your days. If you go off to school, everything will change for the better. This will change the course of your life."

"For which I will owe him."

"Who solved those maths problems every night? Who will have to pass the entrance exams?"

"That is hardly—"

"Who?" Fanny repeated.

"Me, but—"

"There is no but. You proved your worth on those pieces of paper. You deserve this. You deserve to go. You owe no one for your intelligence. He merely helped you illustrate it to the right people."

Ever so slowly, the heaviness sitting on her chest began to lift. Was Fanny right? Did Eliza deserve this? Biting her lip to contain her hopeful smile, she stared at Mrs. Maitland's letter. Could she really sit for the entrance exams?

It seemed almost too good to be true.

Was it more than guilt on Lucien's part? Fanny thought the duke was in love with Eliza, but he'd barely hinted at deeper feelings whilst they were together.

I cannot stand the thought of you so far away from me.

Yet he was helping her leave London to study in Oxford.

She couldn't think about this right now. Apparently, Fanny was departing in the morning and Eliza needed to help her sister prepare. There would be time to contemplate her own life later.

TWELVE

"I DON'T CARE what it costs," Lucien snapped at Mr. Paulson, the architect. "We cannot throw these people out on the streets. Offer them twice the fair market value and do not bully them."

"Your Grace," Paulson started. "With all due respect, this sets a terrible precedent for other—"

"That is not my problem. If these families won't sell, we'll find another property."

"Very well. I'll see to it personally." He started to collect the plans, but Lucien held out a hand.

"I'd like to review those drawings. Leave them with me and I'll see them returned tomorrow."

The architect blinked several times behind his spectacles. "You wish to review the plans?" At Lucien's nod, Paulson said, "Shall I explain them to you first? They can be rather complicated to the untrained eye."

"I'll manage." Lucien struggled to keep his tone polite in the face of the architect's condescension. "My man will see you out."

Lucien's new secretary rose from where he'd been taking notes and escorted Paulson out of the office. Standing, Lucien spread the plans for the settlement house on his desk. Hartsford Hall would be a place to offer food, shelter, and education to poor women and girls. They were searching for the right location, though he was leaning toward the Old Nichol, a notorious slum situated between Shoreditch and Bethnal Greene.

"Your Grace, a visitor."

Lucien glanced up to tell his butler to refuse any caller—and the words died in his throat.

Eliza.

She was there, standing tall and beautiful, a vision straight out of one of his dreams. His mouth dried out and he couldn't think of a thing to say, lest he scare her off somehow. Was she truly here?

He drank in her fine features and golden hair. The lithe curves barely visible under her garments. Her cheeks held a slight flush, her lips plump and red, as if she had been biting them. Goddamn, he missed her.

She nodded at his butler and came closer, her skirts rustling, and his butler pulled the door shut. "Hello, Your Grace."

He hated the formality, loathed the distance between them, but he had no one to blame but himself. Though he ached to take her into his arms and kiss the living hell out of her, he forced a smile and folded his hands behind his back. "Lady Eliza. To what do I owe the pleasure?"

"May I sit?"

"Of course." He came forward to help assist her, but she waved him away. He would accept her independence or be damned.

His chest twisted, his insides raw and tattered. He'd screwed everything up from the start, and he deserved the misery now permanently lodged in his heart.

Clearing his throat, he lowered himself into his chair. "You look well."

"I've come to thank you."

Straight and to the point, as always. He wanted to grin, but his face hadn't attempted one in six weeks. He wasn't certain he was capable of it any longer.

Besides, she was only here to thank him for Fanny and the Royal Hospital. A small sliver of disappointment dug under his skin, but he pushed it aside. What had he expected? That she'd missed him, as he'd missed her?

He held her gaze. "That wasn't necessary."

"Indeed, it is. You've given Fanny the very best hope for recovery. I'm entirely grateful."

"She's left already?"

"Yes, yesterday."

He nodded once. Good. The hospital was the best in Europe and if anyone could heal Eliza's sister, it was those doctors. "I'm happy to hear it."

"I admit, it wasn't easy to let her go." She gave a small laugh, as if she knew it was silly. "We haven't been apart for five years. I felt like a mama bird watching her baby leave the nest."

"They'll take very good care of her."

"I know. Whatever your reasons for helping us, I cannot begin to thank you enough."

He didn't want her gratitude. He wanted her laughter and kisses. The touch of her hand across his bare skin. He wanted to roll over every morning and see her face beside him, then finish the day by solving problems together before taking her to bed.

I love you, he almost said. *I would do anything for you.*

But she would never believe his motives were pure. She would always think he was trying to rid himself of his guilt or control her through privilege and money.

He nodded once, unable to think of anything more brilliant to say other than, "You're welcome."

"I leave for Oxford next month. I thought you'd like to know."

Straightening, he blurted, "Oxford?"

"Come now. Surely you were aware."

"Aware of what, exactly?"

"I've heard from Mrs. Maitland. About sitting for the entrance exams."

"At Somerville College? Eliza, that's tremendous. Congratulations."

"I have you to thank for that, as well."

"Why? Because I sent her the problems you solved?"

"Yes, and asked her to take me on as a student."

"I did no such thing." When her expression didn't change, he leaned forward. "Eliza, I didn't bribe her or pay her to offer you a spot, if that's what you mean. I merely sent her the problems along with your address. I didn't even affix my seal to the letter."

Her mouth parted. "You didn't wield your ducal influence?"

"Not with Mrs. Maitland. I admit I did so with the Royal Hospital, however."

"You mean . . . ."

"You did that all on your own, Eliza. Because you're brilliant and tenacious. I couldn't be prouder."

"I can't believe it," she murmured, rubbing her forehead. "I thought for certain it was because of you."

Remaining silent, the truth began to sink in. Hope and happiness were pushed aside as his own thoughts turned darker. Even if she forgave him, she would go away to study and live apart from him. Build a life free from the horrors of her past, including him. It was what he'd always wanted for her, except he hadn't expected it to hurt this badly.

When she finally looked up, her eyes were moist. "I don't know what to say."

"It's very happy news." For her, anyway. "You're allowed to be overwhelmed."

"No, that's not what I meant." She exhaled slowly. "To you. I don't know what to say to you."

"Oh." He lifted his shoulders and let them fall. "I don't quite know what to say to you, either, other than I'm dashed proud of you and I wish you all the very best. You're going to have a marvelous time."

"Part of me doesn't want to go."

"Why on earth not? You no longer have Fanny to look after. You may do anything you like now."

"I don't want to go because . . .well, because you won't be there."

His muscles jolted, the words hitting him square in the chest. Had she missed him? Was she entertaining the idea of a future with him? "What are you saying?"

"I can't stop thinking about you. About us. I miss you."

"God, Eliza." He closed his eyes briefly. "I miss you so much. I'm miserable without you."

"Then why haven't you told me?"

"I did. With the letters. I thought . . . ." He thought she'd understand what he was doing.

"I knew you were thinking of me and trying to get my attention, but I want to hear what's in your heart. I need the words, Lucien."

Do you never fight for anything?

Remembering Fanny's words, Lucien swallowed his nerves and stood. In a few steps, he reached Eliza's chair, where he took her arm, pulled her to her feet, and cupped her face in his hands. "I love you madly, Eliza. I love everything about you, from your clever brain to your stubborn will. I want you here with me, by my side, until I draw my last breath."

A tear slipped free from the corner of her eye. "Even after everything I've done for the last five years? After offering up my virginity to a room full of strangers?"

He gently brushed the tear away with his fingers. "Do you still want me after everything I've done to you, to your family? I kept a terrible secret from you, and let you suffer on the streets."

"Yes, I do. We can't change the past, and my brother deserves his fair share of the blame for not providing for Fanny and me. But you need to be sure about how you feel, because the whispers will dog me for the rest of my life if I stay in London."

"Let them whisper. It's because of all you've done that I love you. There's no one stronger than you, no one who needs rescuing less than you. You don't need me, but I hope like hell that you want me, because I need you so desperately, angel."

"I love you. And I do want you, but I'm not certain this world is one in which I fit any longer."

He shook his head. "You'll fit in wherever you go. And besides, I thought we were moving to Oxford."

"You would move to Oxford for me?"

"You make that sound like a hardship. I wasn't jesting, Eliza. I need you by my side, day in and day out. I don't care where."

"Even if we never come back to Mayfair?"

"I don't give a fuck about Mayfair."

A spark flashed through her blue gaze at his profanity. Then she rose up on her toes and sealed her lips to his. He wasted no time in kissing her deeply, the sensation washing over him like rain on a barren desert. He'd missed the feel of her mouth, the soft stroke of her tongue. He would never get enough.

When they broke for air, she whispered, "There's that filthy mouth I like so much."

"You may have it whenever you desire."

"What about now?"

A blast of heat bored through his system, filling every pore and cell with lust for her. "Sit on my desk and lift your skirts so I may lick you and make you come on my tongue. Then you'll agree to marry me."

Her hooded gaze darkened. "Yes, Your Grace."

Edging around his desk, she looked down and paused. "What's this?" She was staring at the plans for the settlement house. "Hartsford Hall?"

He removed his topcoat and tossed it onto an armchair. "A settlement house I'm building in Shoreditch."

"You . . .what?" Head lowered, she trailed her fingers over the plans. "This is amazing, Lucien."

"It's nothing. The very least I can do." After removing his cufflinks, he began unbuttoning his vest. "On the desk, my sweet girl."

The edge of her mouth lifted as she took him in. "Sit down, Your Grace."

"What?"

She pointed to his chair. "Right now."

He liked this bossy side of her. Crossing to his heavy leather armchair, he asked, "Why?"

After he sat, she lowered herself to her knees. Lucien's lungs seized as she reached for the fastenings on his trousers, her fingers skimming his hard cock. "I feel like I need another lesson. And I promise to be a very diligent student for you."

"Oh, Jesus," he gasped, her palm pressing hard on the ridge of his shaft and sending a jolt of pleasure down to his toes. "You're sure?"

"Very." She bit her lip and stared up at him through her lashes.

"And you know what studying at Somerville College means, don't you?"

He swallowed. "No, what?"

"I will have access to many, many rulers."

The End.

THE GANGSTER'S PRIZE

From a good upstanding family, Isabelle Kelly is dedicated to righting the city's wrongs. But when her father goes missing, Isabelle knows who is responsible . . . and she will get answers from the devil one way or another.

As the leader of the Hell's Kitchen Gang, Billy Baxter always gets what he wants. And he's had his eye on the beautiful Miss Kelly for months. She doesn't know it yet, but she's fallen into his world now.

And he has no intention of ever letting her go.

CHAPTER
ONE

New York City, 1890
Tenth Avenue Athletic Club

Isabelle

I CAME DRESSED LIKE DEATH.

Wearing my aunt's old widow's weeds, I slipped inside the club and began threading through the raucous crowd. My stomach was cramped with nerves, but I pressed on. The devil was here somewhere. Billy Baxter, leader of the Hell's Kitchen Gang.

The entire city lived in terror of this man. But I hadn't the luxury of terror, not any longer. My father was missing and I had to find him.

My father had recently finished an eight-year term as New York City's comptroller, where he cracked down on corruption and graft. He was a hero in this city. The newspapers had even dubbed him "Honest" Dan Kelly.

Not everyone appreciated his crusade, however. Some viewed my father as an enemy and threatened his life. Now he was missing . . . and all evidence pointed to Mr. Baxter as the responsible party.

So I needed to find the notorious gang leader tonight and force him to talk to me.

Unfortunately, Mr. Baxter was never alone in public. He went everywhere with a bevy of women at his side, along with several members of his gang. No stranger drew within ten feet of the man, not if they wished to live. So I searched while keeping the black veil over my face, a harmless widow in the crowd.

The place was packed with loud men and scantily clad women. They were laughing and cheering, drinking and kissing. It was a world unlike anything I'd imagined. Free and exciting, and without the rules and expectations that weighted down my life. Here, no one paid me any attention.

My eyes drifted to the front row. A man sat there with four well-dressed women draped over him like fine silk. Men nodded in deference as they passed, as if paying homage to a king.

Was this Mr. Baxter?

I tugged on the sleeve of the older fellow next to me. "Pardon me, sir. That man over there with the women. Who is he?"

His brow creased in concern. "Oh, you don't want nothing to do with Billy Baxter, ma'am. Stay far, far away from the likes of him."

So, it was Mr. Baxter. Based on the rumors about him, I'd expected scars and menace. A rough and hulking figure in bloodstained clothes.

He was nothing of the sort.

He was handsome, with a chiseled jaw and lean patrician features. Rather a large nose, but it suited him. His dark hair was swept back to reveal the hint of a widow's peak. His appearance reminded me of the statues of Roman emperors in the history museum. Strong, fearsome. A warrior of old.

He wore a fine navy suit, his keen gaze on the ring. Occasionally he whispered to the woman directly on his right as she stroked his thigh affectionately. Though he was relaxed, danger crackled in the air around him.

Well, dangerous or not, he needed to answer my questions. I had to find my father.

Papa was the only relative I had left. Without him I had no one. And there was no time to lose. Each minute he was gone meant more danger, more risk.

Suddenly, the contest in the ring took a turn and the crowd swelled, growing excited as people yelled and jeered at the fighters. The melee gave me the opportunity to weave unnoticed through the sweaty bodies and move closer to Mr. Baxter.

I edged around the spectators and reached the corner of the ring. The path to him was clear, as if no one dared get too close. Taking a deep breath for courage, I threw my shoulders back and marched forward.

As if he sensed my arrival, his head snapped toward me. His face revealed nothing, however, as he tracked my progress with a cool, dispassionate expression. My heart raced, every instinct screaming for me to turn and run away, yet I soldiered on. Had I any other choice?

When I was a short distance away, I withdrew a pistol from my skirts. I pointed it directly at Mr. Baxter's face.

My hand trembled slightly, but I didn't move. A hush rippled over the crowd until the entire space became quieter than a tomb. Mr. Baxter held my stare, his dark gaze flat and curious, but remained silent.

The men behind him withdrew their pistols and cocked the hammers, but Mr. Baxter held up a hand to wave them off. "Everyone out. Now."

The command was quiet, laced with the rough edges of downtown. The crowd reacted as if he'd shouted. People scattered and chairs overturned. Shouts of "Hurry! Go! Move it!" echoed in the large space.

Mr. Baxter's women hung back until he added, "I said everyone."

The women shot wary glances my way, but I hardly noticed. My focus remained fixed on the man in front of me. He leaned over and whispered to the woman on his right. Nodding, she rose and led the rest of the females away.

Then we were alone.

Mr. Baxter gestured to the empty room. "You have my attention, widow. I assume you're not here to kill me, else you'd already have pulled the trigger. Why don't you show me your face, yeah?"

Reaching with one hand, I shoved the heavy netting up until it fell down my back like a lace waterfall. My unobstructed gaze met his—and I suddenly couldn't breathe. The intense weight of his dark stare went through me, my lungs squeezing tight. I lifted my chin and tried to remain calm. Something told me this man fed on fear.

The edges of his mouth curled. "Well, well. The fancy daughter of a politician at a Tenth Avenue boxing match."

I nearly dropped the gun. "You know who I am."

"You are Miss Isabelle Kelly, the only child of Honest Dan Kelly, current mayoral candidate and former city comptroller."

I clasped the gun with both hands, steadying my aim. "Now perhaps you'll explain why you kidnapped him."

Mr. Baxter rose and straightened his cuffs. "Not many would dare to accuse me of such a deed to my face, let alone hold me at gunpoint." He approached with slow, measured steps, and sweat broke out between my shoulder blades. He looked me up and down. "Lucky for you, I don't offend easily—at least when the offense comes from a beautiful woman."

Up close, Mr. Baxter was even more intriguing. Indeed, more handsome. The navy wool suit fit him perfectly, the simple cloth well-tailored and clean. His dark eyes swirled with intelligence and gleamed with perspicacity, as if the game had already been waged and won in his mind. He was clean shaven, but the hint of whiskers kissed his square jaw.

I wouldn't be fooled, though. This man was dangerous, a criminal, and had probably kidnapped my father.

Despite my trembling hands, I kept the barrel of the gun pointed at him. "Do you claim ignorance, Mr. Baxter?"

"Call me Bax." He leaned a hip against the ring's platform and folded his arms. "And kidnapped, you say? Tell me why I'm responsible."

"Three days ago, my father disappeared from our home, the latch on a downstairs window pried open with a metal tool, his office in shambles. The only clue was a piece of paper from the American Ice Company—your ice company."

"You believe this implicates me."

"Yes, I do."

"It could mean your father purchased ice from my company."

"I review all the household bills. We have never purchased ice—or anything else—from you. That piece of paper was dropped by the kidnappers."

"What do the coppers say? I assume you talked to them."

His smug attitude scraped across my nerves like the tines of a fork. "They lost interest when they saw the name of your company on that piece of paper."

Bax lifted his hands and shrugged. "No one ever claimed the Metropolitan Police were efficient—unless we're talking about accepting bribes. Then there are none more expeditious. What do you want from me, Miss Kelly?"

"Did you kidnap my father?"

"No."

The response came quickly. Almost too quickly. "Why should I believe you?"

"If I kidnapped him, there'd be no reason to hide it. Do you honestly think anyone in this city would lift a finger to stop me from doing whatever I wanted?"

No, I didn't. "Perhaps one of your men kidnapped him without your knowledge."

"My men don't eat, shit or fuck without my permission, let alone kidnap someone, widow. And why would I bother kidnapping your father?"

"My father is running for mayor this autumn on a reform platform. No doubt your livelihood would have suffered under such reforms."

"You think I'm scared of your father?" He snorted and lifted his chin. "I'm above the law, Miss Kelly. Untouchable. A king below Fiftieth Street. I see these so-called reforms for what they are: hot air from men who like to hear themselves talk. Now, get that gun out of my face so we can have a real conversation, yeah?"

I believed him. There was no artifice, no hesitation in his voice. My shoulders sagged and I lowered the gun. Blast it all. I honestly thought Billy Baxter held the key to my father's whereabouts. Without that lead, what did I have?

Absolutely nothing.

This was a waste of time. I needed to return to police headquarters and press them to investigate. Perhaps if I told them of Mr. Baxter's denial, they would reconsider. I shoved the gun back in my pocket and turned for the door. "Thank you for your time, sir. I'm truly sorry to have bothered you."

"Wait."

The single word was laced with command and I immediately stopped. Bax came to stand in front of me, the lines of his face sharper. More determined. "Do you honestly believe you can stroll in here, hold a gun on me in front of a crowd, then turn around and walk out?"

My throat nearly closed in terror, but I tried to brave it out. "I already apologized."

"We have a different way of settling things around here."

"And what is your way of settling things?"

He rubbed a hand along his jaw as he stared down at me. I couldn't tell what he was thinking. "What're you planning to do about your father?"

"I haven't any idea." Hopelessness, hollow and painful, twisted in my belly. "Hire Pinkertons, I suppose. I know he's alive. If they wanted him dead, they would've killed him in his study. Why bother to take him from his home?"

"Pinkertons are a waste of time and money."

"I haven't any other choice. The police won't help."

"I'll help you."

I blinked at him, certain I'd heard incorrectly. "You would help me?"

"I might be convinced to do so, yeah."

"Meaning?"

"Meaning I won't involve myself out of the kindness of my heart."

This I believed. It was rumored he had no kindness. "I can't pay you, not right away. But my father—"

"It's not money I'm after, widow."

The words bounced off the walls. I froze as the room narrowed down to only the two of us. His expression turned positively predatory, and I prayed my instincts were wrong, that he didn't want the one thing girls were warned about. "What are you after, sir?"

"That's the wrong question to ask."

"Then what is the right question?"

"What're you willing to do for me, Miss Kelly? How far are you willing to go to find out what happened to your father?"

CHAPTER
TWO

Baxter

WELL, well. The night was certainly looking up.

I returned to my chair and let her absorb the words. Once there I busied myself with a cigarette, but it was damn hard to employ patience.

Did she remember me? While it had been a long time ago, I hadn't forgotten her face. How could I, when she was the most beautiful thing a sixteen-year-old boy had ever clapped eyes on in his miserable life?

When we were still rising in the ranks, the boys and I used to go to the Seventh Avenue Mission for the occasional meal. We'd take the food outside, where we could eat in peace.

One night a man was there, giving a speech about the scourge of gangs and violence. He was Daniel Kelly, New York City's new comptroller, and he promised to help crack down on crime in the city. It pissed me and the boys off, especially when he pointed and called us "vermin."

"We ain't fucking vermin," Timmy said on my right. "He's the fucking vermin."

"Fuck him," Jack added from my other side.

There was a dead rat not even two feet away. "Maybe he don't know what vermin is," I said. "Maybe we should put that rat in his carriage. That'd show him."

"Do it." Jack elbowed me. "He'll piss his proper pants."

I found a flat piece of metal and scooped up the rat. Edging around the crowd, I approached the fancy carriage. I started to lean in the window—and found her sitting inside. The prettiest girl I'd ever come across.

I couldn't move, awestruck by her delicate features and dazzling smile.

"Hello," she said to me.

I dropped the dead rodent. My mouth wouldn't work, so I stood there. Staring. I hadn't seen that color hair before. It looked like spun gold in the gaslight. Her skin glowed with health and happiness. She was an angel.

The crowd began clapping. The girl nodded toward the street. "You better go. My father's coming."

My legs carried me back to the boys. When I sat, they clapped me on the shoulder. Timmy said, "I can't wait to hear him scream when he spots that rat!"

"I didn't do it." I couldn't defile the carriage, not with an angel sitting in it. "Don't worry. We'll come up with another way to get back at Daniel Kelly."

I had watched that night as Kelly climbed into the carriage. The girl gazed at him like a diamond necklace and slice of roast beef rolled into one. But he spared not a single glance for her. Instead, he'd shoved her aside to wave out of the carriage window, his smile slick.

Some do-gooder. Treating his own daughter like dirt so he could soak up the attention and praise of strangers.

In a snap, I hated Daniel Kelly.

As I smoked, I regarded Isabelle. I hadn't thought of her much after that night. After all, she was the unattainable princess, too good for a rotten man like me.

But all these years later, the angel was here in my club. And she was even more beautiful, with all the curves I loved on a woman.

Better, she needed help.

I really was a bastard, because I couldn't resist turning the situation to my advantage. It was what I did best, after all.

"What will I do? How far will I go?" The edges of her mouth turned down. "What does that mean?"

"Exactly what I said. Tell me what you're offering."

"What do you want? Money?"

Now we were getting somewhere. I blew out a stream of smoke. "Perhaps it's to merely spend time with you."

"Doing what?"

I threw my head back and laughed. Was she truly this innocent? If so, it hardly made this fun. I had no interest in taking a woman against her will. And seducing a sheltered uptown princess—even the daughter of a man I hated—sounded boring as fuck.

I liked my women eager. Experienced. Filthy.

Not that I'd had time for any recently. Being king of the underworld consumed my every minute. There truly was no rest for the wicked.

"Forget it," I said, pushing to my feet and putting out my cigarette. "Run along, Miss Kelly. Good luck with your Pinkertons. They'll never find your father."

I shoved my hands in my trouser pockets and started for the exit. There was a meeting in a few minutes down at the docks and I needed—

"Wait!"

Miss Kelly's hand landed on my arm, and I swore I could feel the heat from her body through layers of cloth. Awareness crawled over my skin. It caused my voice to come out sharper than I intended when I asked, "What is it, Miss Kelly?"

"Please, wait. I really do need your help."

"Yeah? So what are you willing to give me? And before you answer, let me warn you. It had better be worth it. I'm a busy man, yeah?"

Seconds dragged and she hesitated. I took pity on her. "You're too innocent for the likes of these games, Miss Kelly. Go back uptown, where you and your precious hymen belong. Leave the dirty business to men like me."

Her lips pressed flat and something flashed in her expression. Determination? Anger? "I'm not as innocent as I appear."

It took everything I had not to laugh. Instead, I dropped back a step and folded my arms. "Yeah? Prove it."

Would she tell me a tedious tale about sharing sloppy kisses with the groom's son? Or how she'd once read a racy novel? I resisted the urge to check my pocket watch for the time. I didn't want to be late for this meeting.

She stared at the floor. Just when I lost all hope, she reached for her skirts. With shaking hands, she began lifting them.

I froze. What the hell?

A better man would've stopped her, but I was not about to interrupt whatever was happening. Was she about to flash me her quim?

No, impossible. Honest Dan Kelly's daughter would never—

Then I saw a flash of red silk and white lace. My mouth went dry. Those were her drawers? I would've expected burlap or the thickest cotton known to man. Padlocked and sewn shut.

But this . . . ? Jesus fuck.

Her calves were wrapped in white silk stockings. Red silk clung to her thighs, and a delicate edge of white lace peeked out below her knees. I sucked in a breath. Heat blasted through me like a furnace, settling low in my belly.

They were the most erotic drawers I'd ever seen.

And they were on an uptown virgin?

"How . . .?" It was the best I could manage, considering.

"I have a collection. They make me feel confident. Pretty."

She started to drop her skirts, so I had to intervene. "No, wait. Just a few more seconds, now that I've recovered from the shock."

"I feel silly," she whispered, but kept her lower half exposed to my greedy gaze.

Her thighs were thick and perfect, exactly the kind a man liked to sink between to lose himself. I couldn't see her pussy, but I wondered if this little show was turning her on. Was she wet? My cock twitched at the idea. I would love nothing more than to drop to this hard floor, shove my face in her folds, and tongue her until she screamed. "You little vixen."

Her fingers opened and the skirts fell to her toes. "So you see, you were wrong about me. Now, will you help me find my father?"

I stroked my jaw and considered this. My dick had a clear opinion on the matter, but I hadn't let him run me around since I was a lad. No, I had to think about this logically.

Not many people surprised me, and the little widow had gone and done it twice tonight. Maybe I was wrong about her being boring and sheltered. Maybe she had a naughty streak just waiting to be fanned like the spark of a flame.

And her father would fucking hate her being associated with the likes of me.

I ran my tongue over my teeth. "Does the corset match?"

"Of course—but I'm not showing you."

I could demand it, but I really did need to leave for my meeting. I went with my gut, which was never wrong, and made a decision.

I started for her. She tracked my approach, her big eyes shining up at me. Frightened or excited? Maybe both? *Christ*, I couldn't wait to find out.

She began backing up, but the ring prevented her escape. Instead of going for her gun again, she lifted her chin and stood her ground. *Good girl.*

Closer now, I could see the bluish veins under her pale skin, the beat of her pulse along her throat. Leaning in, I dragged a knuckle over her smooth jaw. It felt like the purest silk. I longed to run my lips over that soft expanse, then scrape it with my teeth. "You agree to do whatever I want, widow, whenever I want it."

Her breath hitched. "No," she whispered. "I couldn't possibly."

I let that statement linger as my finger trailed down the heavy fabric covering her throat. Her pulse fluttered under my touch, but I didn't stop. Instead, I moved lower, along the fine arch of her collarbone, then across to her shoulder. She was dainty and feminine, but strong. The perfect combination in a woman.

"Do you want help with finding your father?" I asked softly.

"Yes, but I won't sleep with you."

I caressed her arm, my fingertips grazing her elbow, and she shivered. "You will—and you'll beg me for it."

"You're delusional."

I stepped back, smothering a smile. "So what will it be? Am I saving Honest Dan Kelly for you?"

"Do you agree with me that he's still alive?"

"Yes, because it would be stupid to kill such a high-profile figure and think to get away with it. They are clearly waiting to ransom him off."

She seemed to mull this over. "Can you get him released quickly?"

"Hard to say. It will take time." Days and days, if it meant keeping her by my side. Weeks, maybe. Hell, I might wait until next year.

"I don't want him suffering in some damp warehouse or musty opium den until you do."

"I'll see that he's well cared for by his kidnappers—if you play nice."

"So you know his whereabouts."

"My reach in this city is vast and pervasive. I have the ability to ensure his well being, if I choose to involve myself. Am I involving myself?"

I didn't miss the way her gaze flicked over my body, then traveled up to my mouth. Lust raced through me, my skin prickling with awareness. She was curious, I could tell. Wondering how it would be between us.

I'd make it so good for you, angel.

She closed her eyes. "Fine. I'll let you kiss me."

"Such a sacrifice," I murmured. "And you have it backwards, yeah? It's whatever *I* want, not whatever *you* want."

"Too vague. I won't agree to a deal without knowing the terms first. Nor, I suspect, would you."

She was so cute. Did she honestly think to negotiate with me? "The clock is ticking, widow."

"What you are suggesting will ruin my reputation."

"A woman with drawers like yours?" I smirked. "I'd wager she isn't worried about her reputation."

She bit her bottom lip, and I watched the plump flesh disappear between her teeth. Envy crawled through my veins. I wanted to bite her, then have her bite me in return. This was going to be fun.

"For how long?" she asked, her voice thin.

"As long as it takes."

"To get him released?"

"Among other things," I said cryptically.

"I don't really have a choice, do I?"

"You're asking a lot of questions for a woman who very nearly showed me her quim two minutes ago. I told you what I want. Are you in or out?"

"I'm in."

A dark thrill unfurled in my stomach, moving lower to my groin. "Good. Follow me."

CHAPTER
THREE

Isabelle

THIS WAS MADNESS.

I was letting Billy Baxter lead me outside of the club toward the street. I had no idea where we were going and my father was still missing.

So why was my heart beating so fast in my chest?

Now Bax knew my secret obsession with fancy French undergarments, the delicate, racy sort unavailable in America. This happened to be one of my favorite sets, red silk with white lace on each leg. Tiny beads in the lace shimmered in the light. I felt powerful and bold in these garments, which was precisely why I'd worn them this evening.

"You little vixen."

I knew the ensemble was pretty, but Baxter's reaction made me feel like the most gorgeous woman in the city. No one had ever regarded me so carefully and with such admiration. My father usually ignored me or treated me like I was an annoyance.

As if Bax could read my mind, he asked, "Does your father know you own such undergarments?"

"Good heavens, of course not." Papa didn't pay much attention to anything when it came to me. He was more concerned with his career and speeches.

"I am busy at the moment, Isabelle."

"I haven't any time for this, Isabelle."

"You couldn't possibly understand, Isabelle."

But he was all I had. My only family, my rock. Yes, his causes came first, but I couldn't complain. His hard work was making a difference for the people of New York.

I used to grow angry when he insisted that I refuse my invitations and stay home. But now that all my friends from finishing school had married, what would I do? They were much too busy with their own lives to spare me any time.

So the undergarments became my naughty secret. I got a thrill every time I put on one of the pieces. I felt less bored and pathetic in them. And in addition to what I owned, I had pages and pages of designs that I'd drawn. Patterns I dreamed of one day seeing produced for women to wear.

It was silly. My father would never allow such a scandalous enterprise, nor would a husband. No, my existence would continue to be dictated by the men in my life, while I waited at home, over and over until I died.

A depressing thought, but then women in my world weren't bred for exciting lives. We were praised for our chastity and the ability to keep a man's home. Which most days felt dashed unfair.

"What about the staff?" Bax asked.

"My maid is the only one who knows and she would never betray my trust. What I wear under my clothing is no one's concern but my own."

"And mine."

"For now."

A big hand wrapped around my upper arm and pulled me to a stop. Bax's body was right there, pressed close to mine, and his heat sank under my skin. He put his mouth near my ear. "As long as you're with me, I'm the only man to see those undergarments. If you show them to anyone else, he won't live to draw another breath."

The violence should have repelled me. This man was a hooligan, a killer. I should run far, far away from him.

Yet the rough threat excited me, and I swayed closer to his large frame. He smelled of tobacco, leather and gunpowder, and I had the strangest desire to press my lips to his.

Goodness, what was I doing? I could already hear my father's disappointment. *"People will only take advantage of you. You're better off staying at home, Isabelle."*

I needed to keep my wits about me. This was to save my father. Nothing more.

"I have no intention of showing my undergarments to anyone," I said.

Bax nodded. "Good girl. Let's get in the carriage. I have a meeting a few blocks away, but it won't take long."

"A meeting?"

"Yeah, a meeting. I told you I was busy. Have patience."

Patience? Was he serious?

My father was missing. God only knew what the kidnappers were doing to him. And Bax wanted me to have patience? The tips of my ears grew hot and I pressed my lips together to keep from screeching at him.

We approached a black closed carriage with matching curtains. If it were a tad longer, the conveyance could have passed for a funeral carriage.

Death. It looks like death.

Appropriate considering how I was dressed. Still, apprehension crawled over the nape of my neck like tiny spiders. Was I really going along with him? And where would he go after the meeting, a robbery? A saloon? A *brothel*?

Any sane woman would have refused this bargain. But I was desperate. I needed my only family to safely return home.

For that, I could put up with the devil and his underworld kingdom for a few nights.

A young boy jumped down to open the door. He was likely only nine or ten. He offered no word in greeting, just stood as still as a statue.

"The docks, Pete," Bax said he handed me up.

Bax sat next to me, his large frame overwhelming in such a cramped space. I hadn't been this close to a strange man before. I tried to edge away, but there wasn't anywhere to go.

"You best get used to it," he said. "We'll be getting very close, Belle."

A nickname? No one had given me one before, not even the girls at finishing school. I wanted to protest, but I liked it. It felt special, a thing just between us.

"What is this meeting about?" I asked, desperate for anything that would take my mind off the heavy weight of his thigh against mine.

"Are you genuinely interested? Or filling the silence?"

The truth spilled out of my mouth. "The latter, I suppose."

He chuckled. "I like when you're honest."

"Why?"

"Because you lie to everyone all day long, pretending to be one thing when you're really not. I'm much more interested in a woman who goes after what she wants, rather than one who plays it safe."

He couldn't possibly understand my life. "I haven't a choice. There are certain expectations that go along with being the daughter of Honest Dan Kelly."

"Such as?"

"Maintaining my reputation and avoiding scandal. We always had to worry about re-election."

Bax's hand shifted to rest on his big thigh, and his pinky finger was dangerously close to my leg. I couldn't stop staring at the digit, wondering if he would touch me. What would it feel like, rough or soft?

"What other expectations are there?"

Glancing away from his hand, I exhaled shakily. "Let's see. Since I returned from finishing school, he prefers me to stay home. He chooses my suitors. And he works long hours, so it's my responsibility to run the house."

"That's no way to live, Belle."

How could I make him understand? This man could do what he liked, go where he liked. There was no more powerful criminal in

Manhattan. My life was the complete opposite in every way. "I can't complain when I've been given so much. It wouldn't be fair."

"Fair?" He shifted toward me slightly. There was an edge to his voice, one I hadn't heard yet tonight. "No one gives a fuck about fair in this city. Do you think police care about what's fair? What about the residents of those mansions on Fifth Avenue? Or your father? He certainly doesn't care about what's fair."

I studied his face. "How do you know what my father does and does not care about?"

He flicked his fingers. "All politicians are the same."

A sweeping generalization, but I didn't feel like arguing over it. "They say you grew up on the streets."

I nearly winced. Why had I asked such a personal question? This man's life was no concern of mine.

The long pinky finger drifted ever closer. It tapped against his leg, as if impatient to get to me, and I wanted to crawl out of my skin. He had nice hands, strong with veins running along them. Hands that had committed unspeakable violence, no doubt. How would they feel on my body?

"I left home at the age of eight." His deep voice filled the carriage. "Not a unique story, I'm afraid."

"That must've been difficult," I said as his fingers curled into a fist.

"You keep staring at my hand. Is there something you want, widow?"

I jerked my head up and stared straight ahead. "Absolutely not."

"Do you want me to touch you?"

The place between my legs heated and I could feel myself growing wet. "Don't be ridiculous."

"Hmm. Perhaps you'd rather touch me instead?"

Oh, I hadn't considered that. My mouth dried out as I imagined running my hands over his chest and thighs. His groin. The growing bulge in his trousers.

"I'd be so patient with you," he said softly. "I'd teach you how to please me. Show you how good it could be between us."

My eyes drifted to his hand once again. His fingers were slowly trailing up his thick wool-covered thigh toward the center of his legs. I couldn't speak. I couldn't *breathe*.

The placket of his trousers tightened and I could see the stiff column under the cloth. My heart thumped, the pulse echoing between my legs. I wished that was my hand. I wanted to know what a man's erection felt like.

Abruptly, the carriage drew to a halt, interrupting us. I grabbed onto the side to keep myself from pitching forward, both relieved and disappointed the moment was over.

Leaning closer, he murmured, "To be continued."

CHAPTER
FOUR

Baxter

WILLING MY COCK TO deflate quickly, I jumped out of the carriage and closed the door. "Stay here until I get back."

Belle stared at me with wide eyes. "Wait, you're leaving me?"

"Yeah. Pete'll keep watch. You'll be fine."

While I wanted her with me, I didn't care to truly frighten her. The meeting tonight was not a friendly one. There was every possibility it could turn violent.

I wouldn't risk her safety.

I started toward the warehouse. Matty and the other women trailed me as usual, fingers on their weapons.

Most people assumed my female companions were my lovers. I never corrected the assumption. Why would I, when it kept me safer? Any one of these four women was more deadly than a Bowery street tough crossed with a river pirate. They'd saved my life and protected me for years, and I compensated them handsomely for it.

Charlie, my right-hand man, waited to open the front door. "Evening, Bax."

"Everyone here?"

"Yeah. And no weapons, just as you said." Charlie tipped his cap at someone behind me. "Evening, miss."

What in fucking hell?

I spun and found Belle there, trying to push her way through my guards. "I told you to wait in the carriage."

"I want to come with you." She lifted her chin.

Everything in me recoiled at the idea. I locked eyes with Matty, my friend and head guard. I trusted her opinion the most, but she shrugged. Damn it.

I didn't want to delay this meeting any longer. If Belle wished to see what I did, then who was I to stop her? "Come on, then." With a gentle push, I guided her inside.

"What is this meeting about?" she whispered.

"Not undergarments," I answered dryly. She elbowed me in response and I had to smother a smile. Feisty widow.

Walsh was already here, sitting at a wooden table in the middle of the empty floor. Three of his men stood behind him. "I don't like to be kept waiting," he called as Belle and I approached.

Irritation slid along my skin like hot wax. Walsh was the leader of the Mudlarks, a river gang in New Jersey. We occasionally partnered on jobs, depending on my mood. These days I was tired of Walsh's incessant demands for a bigger piece of the North River pie. This meeting would settle all that.

Eager to get this over with, I led Belle to the other side of the table. Without giving her a chance to argue, I sat and brought her down onto my lap.

I casually rested a hand on her thigh. I liked the weight of her on me. Was she enjoying the feel of the silk drawers pressed to her skin while in this position? "I hear you have complaints."

Walsh jabbed a finger at the tabletop. "The way I see it, things ain't exactly fair."

"Yeah? You think you deserve more?"

"That river belongs to us," Walsh snapped. "The Mudlarks have always worked it alongside your boys. You're making a fortune while we're scrounging for scraps."

My hand itched for a pistol. I'd love to put a bullet through Walsh's heart. "You're lucky that I'm dealing you in at all. It's pure charity; I don't need your help."

"That's horse shit. I ain't no newcomer, Bax. You can't shove me aside."

Wrong. I could do whatever the hell I wanted. Not many had my muscle in Manhattan, and certainly no one in New Jersey could touch me. "Stop making a nuisance of yourself, or consider it a declaration of war."

"You would go to war instead of giving us our rightful percentage?"

I glared down my considerable nose at him, letting him see the truth of my words. "In a fucking heartbeat. So go back to Jersey and keep the fuck quiet."

"This isn't over, Baxter."

"You've wasted my time." I helped Belle to her feet, then rose. "Worse, you've wasted Miss Kelly's time."

"Do not leave, not until we settle this."

I gestured to where my guards had his men surrounded. "There is nothing to be settled, Walsh. You see who holds all the power here. Stay out of my way."

With a firm grip on Belle's hand, I started for the exit. Once outside, we headed toward my carriage.

"I thought my father was inside," she whispered. "That's why I followed you."

Ah. So she hadn't trusted me.

Smart of her.

"I told you I would deal with your problems after this meeting. You need to start believing me."

I handed her into the carriage and waited as Charlie caught up. "No one goes back to New Jersey alive," I told him quietly.

"No problem, Bax."

"Wait!" Belle leaned out of the open door, her face pale. "Bax, no. You cannot have those men killed."

I regarded her carefully, the moment heavy with expectation. Charlie was probably choking on his tongue that someone questioned one of my orders. Normally I wouldn't tolerate it, but Belle was special. "Why not?"

"You can't fault him for trying to do better by his men."

Yes, I certainly fucking could.

I braced an arm on the side of the carriage. "That meeting was an insult. I can't tolerate insults."

"But it doesn't mean you have to kill them."

Oh, my sweet, sweet girl. Better she learned now the type of man I was. "I'm a bad man who does bad things, sweetheart. This ain't no surprise, yeah?"

"Yes, but is it necessary to do this particular bad thing?"

Charlie muttered, "Bax, we need to know what to do."

I kept my eyes locked on Belle. "Why should I spare their miserable lives?"

"Because it's the decent thing to do. Please, Bax."

Begging. I liked it. Just how far would my naughty widow go to save these men? As far as she'd go to save her father?

"Bax," Charlie said impatiently. "They're trying to leave."

I stared directly at her as I ordered, "Lock them in and burn it down."

She gasped. "No, don't! Please. I'll show you the other thing. From earlier. The matching piece."

Her red corset.

My heart thumped hard as I considered it. I wanted to see her slowly disrobe, willingly remove every item of clothing for me until she reached her corset and chemise. Fuck, that was a performance I could savor for hours. But was it worth leaving Walsh alive?

The answer was obvious.

"Let them go," I said.

Charlie knew better than to question me, so he merely nodded. Just for him, I added under my breath, "The package I have stashed? I need you to fetch it and bring it to Lisette's."

"Now?"

"Yeah. I'll meet you there when I'm finished."

Charlie saluted and hurried off, taking a few of the men with him. I glanced at Matty and the other guards waiting nearby. "I need to see Miss Kelly home."

Matty nodded once, her eyes flat and serious. "We'll follow in a second carriage."

I climbed inside my carriage and shut the door. The dim lighting did nothing to hide Belle's flushed skin.

When I settled on the opposite seat, I gestured to her bodice. "If you think I am too gentlemanly to collect, think again. I want what you promised and I want it now."

She licked her lips. The pulse in her throat pounded beneath her skin, and I longed to put my tongue there, feel that throbbing heat with my mouth. But there was time enough for that later. This was something else entirely.

"I don't have enough room here." She folded her hands in her lap. "It'll have to wait."

"No, no, no. I've paid for my ticket, widow. Therefore, I demand the show. Take off your clothes—and do it slowly."

"But . . ."

"The corset, Belle. No stalling." I stretched my legs, settling in.

Seconds crawled by but neither of us moved. I was more than happy to wait her out. Promises were promises where I came from.

And I knew that, deep down, she really wanted to show me.

The anticipation was goddamn killing me. Honest Dan Kelly's daughter, in my carriage, about to show me her corset. It was almost too good to be true.

Looking down, she removed her gloves one at a time. Then her fingers danced near her neckline, hovering. Nerves, or was the vixen actually teasing me? My muscles tightened, like an animal ready to pounce at a moment's notice. "Are you trying to drive me out of my skull?"

Her eyes sparkled. "Just ensuring you're paying attention, William."

William? My body went hot and cold, a bolt of white-hot lust filling every vein and cell. No one called me William, ever. I was Bax or Billy, occasionally "Monk."

Jesus fuck, this woman.

While I was still reeling, she plucked at the hooks of her black bodice, unfastening them one by one. I stayed quiet, barely blinking, as she worked.

Lower and lower, her fingers kept going, tantalizing me, and my heart thumped louder than the carriage wheels bouncing over cobblestones. The entire city could have burned down and I wouldn't have been able to tear my eyes away from her delicate hands.

When the bodice was undone, she held out her arm. "You'll have to pull."

Isabelle

WHY WASN'T I NERVOUS? I was removing my clothing in front of a man. Yet the way Bax looked at me made me feel powerful. Beautiful and in control.

He reached for my sleeve and gently pulled to help me slip my arm from the fitted fabric. Cool air washed over my newly revealed skin as I angled to give him my other arm. "Now this one."

He complied silently, acting like the most handsome and dangerous ladies' maid I'd ever encountered. When I was free, I let the bodice fall behind my back and squared my shoulders. Though my arms were now bare, I still wore a thin black cover over my corset for protection.

We turned a corner and the streets grew smoother. Broadway, probably. I was grateful for the heavy curtains that covered the windows. At least no one would ever know I had disrobed in front of the notorious Billy Baxter.

The buttons on the corset cover were tiny and my hands were trembling, so it was slow going. I tried to keep the sides closed as I opened the garment, just to prolong his torture—and mine. The intense way his eyes tracked my movements caused a slick heat to bloom between my thighs. Did he find this arousing, too? Would the sight of me in such dishabille produce another erection in his trousers? Oh, how I hoped so.

Finally, I peeled off one side and then the other. I let him look his fill at the red corset edged with white satin.

He took his time with his examination. My chest rose and fell quickly with the force of my breaths, and the carriage closed in on us, like we were our own little island. The sweep of his intense gaze caused goose bumps all along my skin.

"My God, Belle," he rasped. "You are stunning."

"Do you like it?"

"If you were anyone else, I'd be fucking you already."

I almost asked why I didn't qualify, but immediately thought better of it. There was no use in provoking him, not when I had no intention of handing over my virtue to him. "You are quite fond of that word."

"Because it has so many practical uses. If you ask nicely, I'll show you my favorite one."

I didn't dare ask. I feared I would like the answer too much.

Reaching for the corset cover, I started to shrug it on. He put up a hand. "Wait. Don't."

"Why?"

"Come here."

The rough order was laced with quiet authority, an undeniable command. I considered refusing but, in truth, I didn't *want* to. Whatever was happening between us pulled at a deep part of me, one I hadn't even known existed. It was the place inside me yearning to be noticed, to be desired. To *matter* to someone else.

And Bax noticed me.

This man, one who commanded half the island of Manhattan, noticed me. Wanted me, even. It seemed unreal, but the truth was plain in the lust stamped across his flushed features.

Still, I hesitated. What did he plan to do?

"Anything I want, whenever I want it." He jerked his chin and patted his thigh. "That's our bargain, widow."

My enthusiasm dimmed considerably. This was a bargain, nothing more. I couldn't forget it. I was doing this to save my father and Bax was doing this to . . . humiliate me? Humiliate my father? Either way, this wasn't a romance, and I was Bax's willing strumpet for however long it took to rescue my father.

I had to remain brave. Sliding across the carriage, I gingerly placed my bottom on Bax's knees. *It's no different than sitting on his lap during the meeting.*

Except the upper half of my body was nearly naked.

His palms swept up my back and across my ribs, shaping and testing me. Feeling how the garment supported my breasts. My nipples tightened inside the whalebone, silk and cotton, pushing out and begging for his attention. *Yes, definitely a strumpet.*

His hands drifted over my middle. "Look at all the beauty you've been hiding under that hideous crepe gown."

"That is generally where undergarments are worn. Under gowns." I was nearly panting, my voice thin from lack of air.

"I wasn't referring to the undergarments."

My belly clenched at the compliment. No one had ever said something so thrilling about me before. "Thank you."

"Is it comfortable?"

"Yes, actually. It's very well constructed. The silk is imported from —" Dash it. Billy Baxter didn't care about the stitching of my expensive undergarment.

"Don't stop," he urged, his fingers gliding perilously close to the mounds of my breasts.

I wanted him to touch me there. Desperately. I arched my back ever so slightly.

"Belle. Keep talking."

"Hmm? Oh, the silk. You don't really wish to hear all that, I'm sure."

"Wrong. I want to hear every thought going on in that gorgeous brain of yours."

He really needed to stop with these compliments. They weren't necessary. "The silk is woven in Lyon by a group of nuns. They've used the same process for hundreds of years, taught to them by the

Italians when they first moved into the area. Then the silk is shipped to Maison Joubert in Paris. Monsieur Joubert designs these corsets."

"Yeah? All I know is I fucking like the feel of it."

"I have seven others," I said.

He groaned and dropped his head back onto the seat. "You're killing me, widow."

"I don't care if people think it's extravagant or wasteful. Some Fifth Avenue princess wasting her father's money—"

"Whoa." He slid me closer. "I didn't say any of that. If you want to spend your pin money on pretty undergarments, who am I to complain? I love the way you look in them."

"You don't think they make me look loose?"

"No one could ever accuse you of being loose." He dragged a fingertip along the satin edging, and I shivered. "If they do, they will answer to me—and I will cut their tongues out for disrespecting you."

My heart swelled like a lovesick schoolgirl. Why was that the most romantic thing I'd heard? Goodness, I was being foolish.

I inhaled and reminded myself who I was and who I was with. This was a means to save my father, nothing more. "It doesn't matter, because I can't buy them any longer."

"Why not?"

"The tariffs on luxury fabrics. The customs house charges almost double the cost of garments like this."

His head shot up, eyebrows lowered in curiosity. "What?"

"The law started earlier this year. It's the McKinley Tariff Act. Haven't you heard of it?"

"No. We play by our own rules over in Hell's Kitchen. Besides, laws were made to be broken, Belle."

"Not for me," I rushed to say. "I'm Honest Dan Kelly's daughter."

He opened his mouth then closed it, like he'd thought better of whatever popped into his head. I couldn't leave it alone, so I asked, "What were you going to say?"

"Nothing. No doubt the stupid law will be repealed soon. The Fifth Avenue ladies won't like paying more for their gowns."

I snorted. "Mrs. Astor already went to war with them and gave up.

The customs house confiscated two of her Parisian gowns, charging her double the price. So she let them keep the garments."

"Good for her." He ran a finger down the middle of the corset, right over the fastenings. I could feel his hardness growing beneath my bottom. It felt larger than it had looked earlier. Without thinking, I shifted on his lap.

He hissed through his teeth. "Are you trying to get me to unload in my trousers?"

"No." I instantly stiffened. "Though I don't know what that means."

His chest rose and fell. "Have you never seen a man's cock before?"

"Of course not." My skin was on fire, like I was standing in front of a furnace.

"Would you like to? Because you've got my balls aching right now, widow. I'd love to show you what that means."

I bit my lip. I admit, I was curious. As soon as my father was released, my life would go back to lonely hours in the house by myself. Right now, I had the chance for excitement and danger. A way to make memories for cold winter nights ahead.

Bax and I were alone, in the middle of the night. Lost somewhere in a carriage in Manhattan. No one would ever know . . . .

"Yes," I whispered.

Bax lifted me and placed my bottom on the seat beside him. "Fuck, I've never been so happy to hear that one word before." His fingers went to his waist and he quickly began unfastening his trousers. "I can't wait to look at you in that corset while I stroke myself off."

Heart thumping, I watched as the buttons fell open. He wore a thin union suit, but I could see the length of his erection behind it. I couldn't look away.

He popped the undergarment and then I saw it. Smooth skin, wide and long. A flushed cap on the end. He gripped the base to pull it free of his clothing. Heavens, was it supposed to be so big?

"What do you think? Do you like it?" He moved his hand up the thick length until he reached the crown. His body twitched and he groaned. "I'm so hard for you, Belle."

"Does it hurt?" I couldn't imagine having this . . . thing grow between my legs.

"No, it feels fucking amazing."

He pumped his hand up and down a few times, his thighs spreading wider. I could feel his gaze on my breasts, which were pushed high under my corset and chemise. But I continued to watch his hand, mesmerized by how he pulled and twisted, manipulating his own flesh. I clenched my thighs, unbelievably aroused. A steady rhythm throbbed in the button atop my swollen sex, insistent and relentless.

"See how much I want you?" He was breathing hard now. "You've had me worked up since you lifted your skirts earlier."

"Yeah?" I whispered.

His hand picked up speed. "Say my name like that, in that throaty whisper."

"Bax."

It was hardly a sound, but he heard me, letting out a moan as he stroked. Raising his free hand, he held one finger up to me. "Suck my finger into your mouth."

I didn't question why. He was my guide, and I was more than eager to follow him down a sinful path tonight.

I parted my lips. Instead of shoving inside roughly, he dragged his fingertip along the edges of my mouth, tracing me. Then he fed his finger gently onto my tongue. My toes curled at his taste and texture, so different from my own finger.

I liked it. I had a part of this man inside my body.

His nostrils flared. "Suck, Belle."

I drew him deeper, tightening my lips. His dark gaze never left my mouth, and his hand moved faster over his shaft. "Tight and wet, just like I imagine your pussy to be."

I was burning up, lust pounding in my veins. The carriage bounced and rocked, but I hardly noticed. I only wished to please him, to see where all this feverish desire led.

A pearl of moisture beaded from the slit on his crown. He used it, smearing the liquid on his shaft. What did that fluid taste like?

When I flicked his finger with my tongue, he groaned. "Oh, shit.

It's too much." His chest heaved. "Get the handkerchief out of my inside coat pocket."

Keeping his finger in my mouth, I reached for the pocket and found the soft handkerchief. I held it up for him, but he shook his head. "I'm going to come. Put that cloth over the crown. Catch my spend in it."

The words were tight, rushed. As if there was no time to lose.

I held the handkerchief atop his shaft. He snarled as his hips jerked, and jets of white fluid shot from his body and into the cloth. It went on and on, pulses of hot liquid, and I tried to catch what I could. There was quite a lot of it, and he wasn't exactly remaining still.

When he finally slumped against the seat, his face was relaxed. Almost happy. The hard edge that accompanied him wherever he went had melted away in those few seconds of pleasure. Goodness, he was beautiful.

I looked down. His appendage had deflated. The skin was red, and it glistened with his fluids. Remarkable.

"Less impressive now," he said with a chuckle.

"Less intimidating, as well."

He took the handkerchief from me and wiped his hands off. Then he dropped the used cloth onto the carriage floor. As he refastened his clothing, he asked, "Are you shocked?"

"No."

His head came up and he smirked. "Aroused?"

I couldn't answer. I was aroused, of course, but it wasn't the sort of thing a lady admitted out loud.

"I see. Your pussy making a lot of cream for me?"

The filthy words were unlike anything I'd heard before tonight. I wasn't used to it. "I suppose my drawers are ruined."

The edge of his mouth hitched as he finished with his trousers. "You tell me how to replace them, and I'll have five new pairs delivered as quickly as I can."

"You can't get them."

He leaned over and tucked a strand of hair behind my ear. "I can get anything you want. When you're with me, the world is yours, sweetheart."

The carriage wheels slowed and Bax's brow furrowed. "Damn it."

I took the opportunity to scramble to the other seat. With shaking hands, I started putting myself back to rights.

"Here. Let me help." Bax knelt on the carriage floor and pushed my hands away. He maneuvered the tiny buttons of the corset cover easily.

Then he helped me pull on the bodice and secured each hook, one by one. Occasionally, the back of his hand brushed the mounds of my breasts and my belly tightened with need. I wanted to feel his big hands on me, shaping and molding the sensitive flesh, pinching my nipples . . . all the things I did to myself in the dark.

I whimpered.

Bax's head shot up and his coffee-colored gaze pierced into mine. I bit my lip, mortified.

"Fuck, Belle," he whispered. "The filthy things I want to do to you."

I didn't know what to say. I wanted things as well, but they were much too vague to put into words. My body had demands I didn't understand, needs I barely recognized.

I knew Bax was the key, though. This gang leader had unlocked some secret part of me, and I wasn't certain I wanted to close it back up just yet.

He threw open the carriage door and helped me down. We were parked directly in front of my home on East Sixty-Eighth Street.

Bax started up the walk and I instantly dug in my heels. I couldn't have the neighbors see Billy Baxter escorting me to my door, especially at night. One never knew who could be peeking out their window. "This isn't necessary. It's perfectly safe here."

He slipped on his derby and tugged me toward the stoop. "You're mine for the foreseeable future, Belle. I take care of what is mine."

The possessive words sent a riot of flutters through my belly. I lost my will to fight him and went along to the door.

Once there, he held out a hand. "Key."

I dug into my small bag and retrieved the house key. I held it, not handing it over. "Do you think I'm safe here? After they took my father, I mean."

He lifted the heavy metal piece from my fingers. "I can have a few of the boys come and watch your house at night, if you're worried."

"Bax, you don't need—"

"Belle," he said, his voice tight with impatience. "If it helps you rest easier, then I'll do whatever it takes."

The flutters expanded behind my breastbone. From dressing me in the carriage and now sending his men to stand guard, Bax was certainly looking out for me. "Thank you."

"You're welcome. But fair warning—if I think you're at risk here, I won't hesitate to make you stay elsewhere. Understand?"

I plucked the key back from his hand and swiftly unlocked the door. "I'm sure that won't be necessary. You're going to help me get my father back."

"As long as you keep doing what I want, yeah?"

"I already gave you what you wanted."

"Hardly. In fact, I've now thought of something else I want." He crowded closer. "Do you touch yourself? Between your legs, I mean."

"That is a very personal question." The words came out breathy and surprised rather than annoyed.

"Yeah, it is. What's the answer?"

I considered stalling, but there was no point. I'd agreed to play his game in exchange for my father's rescue. "Yes. Happy that you've embarrassed me?"

He closed his eyes, as if in pain. "Jesus, I'm getting hard again just imagining it." He looked at me intensely. "Listen carefully. Once inside, I want you to go to your room, remove all your clothing and slide into bed completely naked—"

I inhaled sharply. "I couldn't possibly—"

"I'm not finished." He set his hands on my shoulders, keeping me in place. "Once in bed, put your hand between your legs. Pet your pussy with your fingers. Tweak your nipples and cup your breasts. Rub your clit. I want you to imagine it's me the entire time, that it's my hand giving you pleasure. Keep at it until you climax. Can you do that for me?"

I should've been scandalized by such an order. How could he discuss these things so openly, so frankly? What if someone overhead him?

But part of me liked it. No one spoke to me like this. Yet Bax did.

Bax talked to me as if I were a real person, with thoughts and opinions of my own. Could I do what he was asking?

If it meant pleasing him, then I knew the answer. "Yes."

"Good girl. I'll see you tomorrow afternoon." He jerked his chin in the direction of the door.

"Wait, what about tomorrow? Where am I meeting you?"

"Don't worry. I'll find you." With that, Bax opened my door and guided me inside. "Sweet dreams, widow."

When I was finally inside, I didn't hesitate to hurry upstairs and follow his instructions to the letter.

––––––

Baxter

After giving Pete directions, I climbed back into my carriage. Matty was waiting inside. She said, "It smells like sex in here."

Ignoring her, I dug into my coat pocket and pulled out my cigarette case.

That resulted in a sigh. "I hope you know what you're doing."

Matty and I grew up on the streets together, our lives intertwined for what felt like forever now. Lovers once, but not for a long time. Instead, she watched my back along with the other guards, and I trusted her opinion. She was fierce and loyal, and one of the smartest people I knew.

She was also one of the few people to whom I ever explained myself.

"I do." I knocked on the roof and called out, "To Lisette's."

Matty snatched the cigarette out of my fingers and brought it to her lips. "Your little bird put you in the mood for more pussy tonight?"

As if I'd want another woman with the image of Belle sucking my finger still tattooed on my brain. "No. I asked Charlie to bring that package over to Lisette's bordello for safe keeping."

Her eyes rounded. "You're joking." When I lifted an irritated eyebrow, she started laughing. "She really has a hold on you, doesn't she?"

"Fuck off, Matilda." She hated when I used her given name. "I made a promise and I mean to see it through."

"If you want to fuck her, then do it already. There's no reason to drag it out."

"It doesn't work that way," I said. "She's innocent. Well bred. She's only interested in saving her dear old dad."

"Too bad she doesn't know he isn't worth saving."

We were in agreement on that. "I want eyes on her house."

"Why the fuck would we bother?"

"Because I want her kept safe."

"She's in no danger, Bax. Unless it's from you."

I struck a match and held it up to my fresh cigarette. "I would never hurt her."

"You sure about that?"

I blew out a stream of white smoke. "Walsh saw us together. He might try to get to me through her."

"Which is why I already put Sad Pete and Timmy on watch at her place."

Damn, Matty was efficient. "Thank you."

"Just as long as we're clear on how this ends. I know you never apologize, but—"

"I have no intention of apologizing." Apologies were for weaker men. I was the leader. I had to make decisions and stand by them.

"She's not yours to keep."

"I know," I barked. "Leave it, yeah?"

We rode south in silence. I closed my eyes and continued to smoke. Was Belle following my instructions right now? Was she strumming those delicate fingers over her clit? Fuck, I'd give anything to see her pleasure herself. To hear her gasps and sighs as she climaxed.

God knew I didn't deserve her, but New York wasn't about what you deserved. It was about what you could *take*.

I'd risen from nothing to sit atop an empire of violence and corruption. Never had any kind of formal education. All my knowledge came from the streets and from whatever books I could find. I wouldn't live long, not with enemies around every corner, but I had no regrets.

So if Isabelle Kelly wanted my help, then I would help. For a price.

Minutes later the carriage rolled to a stop and I threw open the door. Years ago I gave Lisette, a former lover, the cash to start this bordello and she'd done well for herself. The girls were here willingly, well taken care of, and everyone shared in the profits. They wouldn't mind having an extended guest as a favor to me.

Charlie and Lisette were waiting in the entry when I went inside, Matty on my heels. Lisette came over first. "Bonsoir, mon ami," she said in her fake French accent. "I see you sent over a gift?"

I kissed her cheek. "Yeah. I need you to look after my guest for a little while."

"Bien sûr, monsieur. We have given him the Versailles room."

"You're too good to me. I appreciate it."

"Anything for you, Baxter." Drawing closer, Lisette brushed a lock of hair off my forehead. Her voice lost its French accent as she spoke quietly. "You look tired. Are you going to stay a while? I could find you some company."

It wasn't an unusual request, and the answer would've been different last night. Before Belle arrived at the fights with a pistol. "Thanks, Lizzy, but I've got more to do and it's already late. Take good care of my guest, though. Whatever he wants, yeah? I'll cover the cost."

She nodded. "Will you tell me who he is?"

"No, and it's gotta stay quiet. Make sure the girls know."

"Of course. They won't talk."

"Good. Do me a favor? Bring me a pencil and paper up there. I need him to write something down for me."

"His last will and testament?"

I chuckled. "Not quite, but close."

She trailed her fingers over my jaw. "You sure you won't stay? I have some time."

I shook my head and kissed her temple. "Can't, not even for you. If there's a problem, let me know right away."

"I will," she said with a sigh and drifted toward her office.

I approached Charlie. "Any problems?"

"He got a little rough, but the boys handled it. No idea why anyone would fight an extended stay at Lisette's."

"He won't resist for long. A flea on a dog has more restraint. I give it a week before he's fucked his way through the house."

Charlie chuckled and held out the room key. "You going up now?"

"Yeah. Thought I'd welcome him to his new temporary home."

"Want me to come with you?"

I took the key and clapped his shoulder. "Not necessary. Go home and get some sleep."

"Thanks, Bax." Starting for the door, he nodded at Matty as he walked past. "Night, Matilda."

Her expression didn't change. "Fuck off, Charlie."

I took the stairs to the second floor, Matty close behind. I didn't bother knocking. Instead, I threw open the door and strode inside. My prisoner was stretched out on the bed, his hair and clothing disheveled. He sat up slowly when I entered.

"Hello, Kelly."

CHAPTER
SIX

Baxter

HONEST DAN KELLY glared back at me. "I trust you've seen the error of your flagitious ways and are ready to release me."

I stared down at my prisoner. Kelly was a blowhard. A corrupt liar, just like the rest of the politicians. I generally left them alone unless I needed something in particular. So when Kelly finished his term as comptroller, I thought I'd heard the last of him.

Then he announced he was running for mayor a month ago.

That was too far. The man who once called me vermin would not ascend to the highest seat in City Hall. No fucking way would I allow it. I ran this city, not the mayor. And certainly not Dan Kelly.

So I'd taken matters into my own hands.

I folded my arms over my chest. "Are you complaining about your upgrade in accommodations? Because I'm happy to take you back to the warehouse."

Instead of answering, he asked, "Why am I here?"

"Perhaps I'm feeling benevolent."

"Men like you don't have a benevolent bone in your body."

"You better hope I do, if you want to continue breathing." I stepped closer and put a great deal of menace in my expression. "And you should be fucking grateful. When the city learns what you've done, you're finished here."

"I don't appreciate blackmail, Baxter."

"Get used to it. Until I get what I want, I own you."

"And what is it you want?"

Looking down my nose at him, I answered, "I want you ruined. Destroyed. Humiliated."

"Then why hold me here? Why haven't you played your cards yet, Baxter?"

Did he think I was bluffing? "Anxious to lose everything so soon?"

"I'm skeptical you possess any proof whatsoever. I think you are stalling while having someone fabricate the evidence."

"I have what I need, Kelly. Though I suspect those boxes of paper we found in your home office will give me more." I went to the mirror and smoothed my hair. I was tired, but that orgasm had given me a burst of vigor. "Don't worry. Just as soon as the boys finish sorting it all, I'll call a few reporters and tell them everything I know."

"Let me go." His voice was an entitled snarl, a man unaccustomed to ceding his power to another.

But I was a man used to *taking* power. I would grasp and claw for whatever I could gain in this city—and I would not lose my leverage when I was so close. "Rescind your candidacy for mayor and I will."

"Absolutely not. I'm the front-runner."

A knock sounded and I went for the door. "Then I suggest you get comfortable and enjoy Lisette's hospitality."

"You'd like that, I suppose."

"Sit and stare at the wall, if you want. Though you should know Lisette's girls are the best in the city. No one would judge you for having some fun."

I jerked open the door and Lisette was there. She handed me a pencil and paper. "Here, mon chou."

"Thanks." I tossed the items onto Kelly's bed. "Write a letter to your daughter. Tell her you're alive."

Kelly's gaze grew suspicious. "Why?"

So she doesn't worry herself into an early grave over you, you bastard.

"I'll see that it's delivered to her."

"Again, why?"

I wanted to punch him in the face. He hadn't given one thought to Belle's well being since his kidnapping. I forced myself to shrug. "If you don't care about her, then I'll go see her myself. Put her mind at ease."

He frowned, clearly not liking the prospect of his precious daughter with me. Good. He would really hate knowing she showed me her undergarments, then sucked my finger as I tugged my cock.

Too bad I couldn't rub it in his face. But I wouldn't do that Belle. Never mind why. For now, everything we did was our little secret.

He dashed off some words on the paper. I read it to make sure he hadn't given her any incriminating information about me. He hadn't.

Instead, the letter was dry, like a list for the market. All it said was that she should stay home and not worry about him.

I shook my head and put the letter in my pocket. "Touching," I drawled. "Enjoy your stay."

Kelly didn't respond as I left. Matty closed the door and I turned the key, locking Kelly in. We left the key with Lisette and headed back out to my waiting carriage.

I climbed inside and closed my eyes, more exhausted than I thought. But the idea of my empty bed sounded as appealing as a trip to Police Headquarters. Maybe I should've stayed with Lizzy . . . .

No, I didn't want another woman. I wanted to curl up next to Belle and breathe in her sweet scent all night.

Whatever I want, whenever I want it.

"Where to?" Matty asked when I didn't speak.

Before I could think better of it, I made the decision swiftly. "Take me to the widow's house."

———

Isabelle

I woke slowly, the bed warmer than usual.

I'd never felt more comfortable, more secure. I was wrapped tightly, like a butterfly in a cocoon.

My dreams . . . . Goodness, I would never repeat them to a single soul. A familiar gangster featured prominently in all of them, his eyes devouring me as I showed him more of my special undergarments. I didn't ever want to wake up.

"Easy, Belle," a man's voice whispered. "Go back to sleep."

I was instantly alert. Bax was in my bed. Wrapped around me. And I was naked. Oh my goodness, had we . . .?

No, I wasn't sore and Bax was on top of the covers. Thank heavens.

Wait, how did he get in? I needed him to leave before my maid arrived.

"What are you doing here?" I hissed.

"Sleeping. And I'd prefer to continue, if you don't mind."

"I do mind!" I tried to shove him off. "This was not part of our deal."

He put his face in my hair and growled in his throat. It tugged something deep in my core. I sucked in a breath, and instantly became aware of my bare skin rubbing against the soft bedclothes, sensation everywhere.

Now I remembered. I'd followed Bax's orders last night, slipping into bed naked and pleasuring myself before falling asleep. Subsequently, my dreams had been filled with the dark-eyed gangster.

It was as if I'd summoned him from the underworld, the devil.

While confusion, outrage and desire battled inside me, Bax's hands slid atop the coverlet to rest on my hip. Goose bumps trailed in his wake, and he threw one of his big legs over both of mine, trapping me. "Are you naked under there?"

I didn't want to answer. I couldn't. It was far too embarrassing.

"You can tell me, sweetheart," he purred, the words silky and smooth, like satin over bare skin. "The possibility has been driving me out of my skull all night."

He'd been here all night?

Bare shoulders filled my vision as he loomed over me. Oh, my. Bax had shed his clothing before getting in my bed. Had he shed *all* of his clothing? I tried to raise up and look. All I saw was golden skin stretched over glorious muscle.

"I kept my trousers on," he murmured into the sensitive skin of my throat. "I didn't wish to frighten your delicate sensibilities."

I shivered at the scrape of his morning whiskers, so delicious and unexpected. For some reason, I didn't want him to think of me as a boring, sheltered innocent. Even though the description was mostly true.

"My sensibilities aren't so delicate, as I proved last night."

"You're so goddamn pretty with your hair down." His lips brushed the underside of my jaw. "You should never pin it up."

Closing my eyes, I sank into the mattress. My body vibrated with the need to touch him, to satisfy my curiosity about his lean frame. Did he feel as hard and rough as he looked?

He kissed along my collarbone. "Mmm, this is my new favorite way to wake up."

I had to admit, it wasn't terrible. Wildly inappropriate, but not terrible.

A knock sounded on my door. I froze, cold terror sliding through my veins. Bax continued to kiss my skin, clearly unconcerned.

"Miss, are you awake?" It was my maid, Mary.

"Give me a few minutes, please!" I called back.

"Very good, miss." I heard the breakfast tray rattling as my maid departed down the hall.

I shoved Bax's shoulder. "Get out of here. You had no right to come into my bedroom."

He rolled onto his back and stretched, showing off his long half-naked body. "I said anything I want, yeah?"

"That does not include sleeping."

"It does if I say so."

"You cannot sleep in my bed. It is unseemly and improper."

The side of his mouth lifted ever so slightly. "I love the prim and proper way you talk. But you aren't a good girl, are you, Belle?"

"You hardly know anything about me."

He chuckled. "Sweetheat, you wear undergarments that would make a Tenderloin floozy blush. You sneak out with your father's pistol and shove it in my face at the fights. Best of all, you fingered your clitoris last night because a gangster asked you to."

Humiliation scalded my skin. I didn't like that he saw me so clearly. "You need to leave."

He moved a hand to his chest and slowly dragged it toward his belly. "Are you sure? I might be persuaded to stay." The sight of his long fingers brushing over his big body sent ripples of excitement along my spine to war with my anger. I could still picture his big hand wrapped around his male appendage, stroking.

"Get out, Bax." Was my voice unsteady? Why was my heart beating so fast?

Rolling toward me, his eyelids swept open. We stared at one another, the air crackling with danger and possibility, but I couldn't predict what he was planning to do. Still, I didn't waver. He could not walk all over me, no matter our agreement.

Fighting my nerves, I put as much bravado as possible in my expression. Slowly, he unfolded and raised off the bed. He found his shirt on the floor, tugged it over his head and shoved it into his trousers. Then he pulled up his suspenders and sat on the bed to put on his shoes.

Once he was dressed, he started around toward my side of the bed. His hair tousled from sleep, he was more attractive than any man had a right to be at this time of morning. I clutched the bedclothes like a shield, more terrified of the excitement rioting inside me than of Bax.

He neared and I held my breath. What was he going to do? My bare toes curled into the bedclothes, my mind racing through possibilities. He placed his hand above my head. There was a strange light in his eyes, and it caused the place between my legs to grow damp.

He leaned down, his voice quiet. "You need to come to terms with our agreement. That is, if you still wish to find your father."

"I do."

"I'm glad to hear it." He bent and dragged his nose over my cheek. "Sundown. Be ready. I'm coming for you."

The contact sent little shocks of pleasure over my skin, and I marveled at how such a simple touch could turn me inside out. There was hidden meaning in his words, but I couldn't decipher it at the moment, not with him so near, making my pulse race.

He needed to leave before I did something rash. Like kissing him.

Without another word, he pushed off the bed. "By the way, there's a letter for you on the nightstand. Have a good day, widow."

He walked out. I sagged, the air leaving my lungs in a rush. Mercy, that man. He had some nerve. We would have a serious discussion later regarding his sleeping arrangements. He was not allowed to visit my bedchamber whenever he wished.

My gaze drifted toward the bed. His side was rumpled, exactly like mine. Pillow indented, exactly like mine. We'd cuddled, for heaven's sake.

And if I were being honest? I liked it.

A folded piece of paper rested on the nightstand. What was this? I crawled over and quickly opened it. It was my father's handwriting!

Isabelle,

Do not worry about me. Stay at home, where you're safe.

D. Kelly

I chewed my lip. Papa wasn't much of a letter writer, so the terse brevity shouldn't have bothered me.

Yet it did.

Perhaps he was too injured to write? Or maybe he knew the kidnappers would read the letter and didn't wish to be too mushy?

Whatever the reason, I should be grateful to hear from him. My father was alive, which was what mattered. Not my silly feelings.

How had Bax managed to get this letter? Had he learned the identity of the kidnappers?

I would force him to tell me everything tonight.

Just the thought of seeing him again had my stomach dancing with anticipation. What undergarments should I wear?

A knock sounded, startling me. Mary, no doubt, had returned with breakfast.

I lunged for my wrapper, covered myself, then tried to relax on my pillows. "Come in."

Mary entered and held up the tray. "Would you like your breakfast in bed? Or shall I set it on the table?"

I glanced at the bed as if it were the scene of a heinous crime. Bax's scent was undoubtedly all over the bedclothes. I was caught between wanting to never leave the bed and running far away from it.

I said, "The table, please. Thank you, Mary."

"Very good, miss."

When I sat at the table, I noticed a sealed note by my tea cup. "What's this?"

"Arrived for you this morning. Do you require anything else at the moment?"

I was already unfolding the heavy paper. "No, that's all. I'll ring when I'm ready to get dressed."

Mary closed the door softly and I smoothed out the note in my hands. Was this another letter from my father?

We have information about your father. 550 West 37th Street at 3:00 p.m. today. Come alone.

This was not from Papa. Nor was it from Bax. No, this had to be from the kidnapper. Or someone who knew the kidnapper.

Hope fluttered in my chest like tiny butterflies. Could I find my father on my own?

Finding Papa meant putting an end to all of this. No Bax, no ruined reputation. My life could return to normal. Daniel Kelly would save the city again, and I would go back to rambling about in this big house by myself. We would occasionally see one another. Perhaps he might even be grateful and praise my bravery and intelligence.

Still, I wasn't a fool. This was dangerous. I had no idea who wrote the note. It could be from someone with information . . . or it could be someone looking to hurt me.

I had to try. Relying on Bax to help me was problematic for many reasons. My eyes drifted to the bed, still rumpled from where he slept.

"I'm so hard for you, Belle."

Watching him perform the act of self-pleasure had aroused me, far more than I ever dreamed. But I couldn't let this go further.

Resisting him was growing more and more difficult. I had no protection against his particular brand of danger, one that came with slick smiles and racing heartbeats. One that had me contemplating my own ruin.

"Anything I want, whenever I want it."

I needed to get that man out of my life.

Indeed, decision made. I'd take my gun and go to that address on Thirty-Seventh Street today. And I'd leave a note here at the house in case I didn't return. If disaster struck, the police could use it to look for me.

And if all went to plan, then I would never see Billy Baxter again.

CHAPTER
SEVEN

Isabelle

THE BUILDING LOOKED DESERTED.

I tried to remain calm. The pistol sat heavy in my coat pocket, my nerves stretched tight as I approached the door. Whoever wrote the note wasn't expecting me for another forty-five minutes. Arriving early would give me the element of surprise.

My mouth was dry, but I forced my feet to move forward. I slipped through the unlocked front door and entered what turned out to be an empty room. As quietly as possible I started across the worn wooden floor. I retrieved the pistol from my pocket and held it in front of me. Was someone here?

Dust tickled my nose, the musty air uncomfortable in my lungs. The place clearly hadn't been used in some time. I went up a set of stairs in the back, my shoes nearly silent on the treads.

A door stood open at the top. No one was in there, just a desk, a few chairs and cabinets. Excellent. I could hide under that desk.

Moving into the room, I heard a squeak behind me. I started to spin, but I wasn't fast enough. Thick arms grabbed me from behind and pinned my hands to my sides. My pistol clattered uselessly to the floor. *Dash it!* I couldn't pull free, so I began to struggle.

"Caught you," a deep voice said before strong fingers wrapped around my throat, squeezing.

I tried to suck in air but couldn't. Chest burning, I began to panic. Was this stranger intending to kill me? I couldn't die, not without finding my father first.

Not without seeing Bax again.

"I wonder how much he'll pay to get you back," the man sneered and started dragging me across the floor. "No guarantee on what condition you'll be in by that time, of course. We're all eager for a turn."

Oh, God. Icy terror slid down my spine. I had to get to my gun.

I went boneless. His grip slipped and I fell to the floor at his feet. I didn't waste a second. As quickly as I could, I scrambled for my pistol. My fingers clenched on the cool metal, but he pounced on me, an angry snarl filling the air. His fist tightened in my hair, pulling hard until tears sprang to my eyes. I screamed as loudly as I could manage.

"You bitch!" The side of my head slammed into the floor. Pain exploded in my skull and I grew dizzy. No, no, no! I had to keep fighting.

He was on top of me, his heavy bulk preventing me from drawing in a full breath. I gripped the gun, but couldn't maneuver my arm to shoot him. He lifted my head again, probably to slam it onto the floor once more, so I acted on pure instinct.

I tilted my hand and aimed toward us both, then pulled the trigger.

His body jerked, then he slammed my head onto the ground once more.

The edges of the room dimmed. Distantly, I heard a shout. Was someone downstairs? Thankfully, my attacker let me go and rolled off. I immediately sucked in air to fill my lungs as the room wavered. Feet pounded on the wooden floor.

Then the blackness rose to swallow me.

———

Baxter

"Where the fuck is she?" I charged into the building, my chest tight with fury and panic.

"Upstairs," Sad Pete replied, pointing me toward the back. "I'm sorry, Bax. It all happened so fast. One minute she went inside, the next a gun was going off."

I took the stairs three at a time. "And you didn't think to get in here and put a stop to it?"

"Wasn't time, I swear! When we stopped, I followed her while Timmy went to fetch you."

"She never should've been allowed inside here. I thought you were watching her house!"

"We were. She gave us the slip and caught a hack. We caught up as soon as we could."

"I will deal with you later," I snarled and pushed into the room upstairs.

Christ almighty. There she was, my Belle. Crumpled and hurt on the floor.

Fuck, fuck, fuck.

I was at her side in a flash, checking for blood and injuries. Her eyes were closed, her limbs lax. There were bruises forming on the sensitive skin of her throat. A wicked knot was forming on the side of her head. But she was breathing.

She was alive.

"Blood on the floor belongs to whoever had her," Timmy said. "I think she shot him."

Under the heavy fabric of her skirts, I located her pistol. *Good girl.*

"She fought him, that's for sure," Matty murmured behind me. I wasn't surprised she was here. No doubt she followed the second I went running from the saloon.

"Where is the bastard who did this to her?" I glared at Sad Pete as I hoisted Belle up in my arms.

He paled. "Lost him in the alley two streets over."

I wanted to strangle both of my men for this, but I didn't have the time. "Both of you out of my sight. Go and find him. No doubt he works for Walsh. Bring him to me alive. Matty, with me."

I carried Belle down the stairs and out of the building. Matty's carriage was at the curb, so I climbed up and settled, still cradling Belle in my lap. Matty followed, yelling, "As fast as you can!" to Robbie up in the box.

When we started moving she said, "You know how I feel about you leaving the saloon unguarded."

I frowned. This was not the time for one of her lectures regarding my safety. Not when Belle had almost been killed. "There wasn't a choice."

"You plan to keep her with you, I assume?"

"Yes, until further notice."

"She won't like it. She—"

"She will stay until I say otherwise."

"You could let her father go."

I glared at my longtime friend. "No."

Matty pursed her lips. "Whoever hurt her was trying to hurt *you*. This isn't about her father. And keeping Kelly hostage will only make things worse."

Logically, I knew this. But I wasn't capable of thinking straight when it came to Belle. "She's safest in my care."

"Billy," Matty said on a disapproving sigh.

"Not another word, Matilda." I didn't want to hear it. I was in charge, and they'd all pledged their loyalty to me. That meant not questioning my every goddamn decision.

Belle began to stir when we pulled up to the saloon. The Devil's Hand was my domain in Hell's Kitchen. The saloon and back rooms offered a safe meeting place, while the second floor was my office and some living quarters. The third floor was where I stayed. No one was ever allowed up there, except for Matty. And now Belle.

"Bax?" Belle's fingers curled into my vest as she stirred.

I continued up the stairs, ignoring the looks from my men. "It's me, widow. Just relax."

Matty followed, and I was grateful for the help in getting my door unlocked. Before she left, Matty said, "I'll go see what I can find out."

"Good. Send the doc up." I had one nearby for emergencies. "Also deal with Timmy and Sad Pete."

Matty nodded and disappeared, leaving me alone with Belle. Striding into my bedroom, I placed her on my bed. Her eyelids fluttered open, finally showing me her gorgeous eyes, and it was such a goddamn relief that my knees went weak. I sat heavily on the mattress.

She licked her lips. "Where are we?" Her voice was rough, like pebbles were stuck in her throat. It had to hurt like a son of a bitch to speak.

Guilt pricked at the nape of my neck. Belle had been hurt because of me. I got up and poured her a glass of water from the stand. "Don't talk. Rest your throat."

"Then . . . answer."

Returning with a full glass, I helped her sit upright enough to drink. "You're in my apartment, atop my saloon."

She finished half the water, then relaxed. "Home."

Walsh—or any of my other enemies—could find her there. It was too much of a risk. "It's not safe."

She turned her head to the side and closed her eyes. A single tear slipped from the corner onto my pillow. I wiped the wetness from her skin with a fingertip. Then I bent to press my lips to her temple. "Someone tried to hurt you. Until I find out who, I'm not letting you out of my sight."

"Why . . . you care?"

I wasn't sure.

I just knew I couldn't let anyone hurt her. Ever.

"Until we find your father, you're mine," I whispered into her skin, a promise sworn into flesh and bone. "And I will burn down this entire city to keep you safe."

She turned her head and kissed me.

I nearly fell off the bed. Jesus, I hadn't expected this. But her lips were on mine, our noses rubbing, and I kissed her back. Her mouth was soft and sweet, and I soaked in the reassurance that she was still here. Still alive.

Before it turned into something more, I eased away. "I'll let you sleep, sweetheart."

"No, stay." Her fingers clutched my arm. "I don't want to be alone."

I understood. She'd almost died. It could rattle a person.

Standing, I removed my coat and boots. Then I went to the other side of the bed and stretched out next to her. She rolled toward me and curled into my side, as sweet and trusting as a kitten. I didn't know a damn thing about heaven, but I had to imagine it was this right here. Belle in my bed, in my arms.

My cock was growing stiff, but I ignored it. "Try to sleep."

"Talk to me. Tell me . . . a story."

"I'm no good at talking." Ask me to win a fight or fire a pistol, cheat the coppers or rob a bank. But spin a yarn full of fantasy?

My life was about hard truths and cold realities. About staying alive long enough to see another day. Fairy tales were for the privileged.

"Please, Bax?" she asked through a yawn.

Christ. How could I refuse such a sweet request?

I decided to go with the partial truth. My voice low, I said, "There once was a powerful man, one the entire city feared. His every waking moment was consumed by thoughts of money and power."

She remained quiet, her soft exhales warming my skin.

I stroked her back with my palm. "This man had been raised with nothing, a forgotten soul in a city of forgotten souls. Vermin, they called him. As a boy he vowed to conquer the island, to make every single person bow and scrape at his feet. To get revenge on those who wronged him. And he succeeded. He'd never let anyone hurt him or make him vulnerable again."

Belle's breath was even and steady, so I peeked at her face. Her eyes were closed, lips parted slightly. She'd fallen asleep.

"Then he met a woman. A fierce angel who was so much more than she seemed. And his world turned upside down."

A sense of contentment washed over me, a sense of rightness. I always trusted my gut, and it told me this was exactly where I was supposed to be. With this woman, here in my saloon.

I stared at the ceiling, feeling no desire to move whatsoever. "What the hell are you doing to me, widow?"

CHAPTER
EIGHT

Isabelle

I CAME AWAKE SLOWLY, every bit of me sore. Especially my head. In a flash it came rushing back—the building, the attack, firing the pistol—and panic bubbled up to rob me of air.

"Calm down," a feminine voice said. "You're safe. You're at Bax's place."

Oh, thank goodness. I was *alive*. I hadn't died on the dirty floor of that empty building.

Wait, I was at Bax's place? As in, Bax's *bed*? I vaguely remembered him lying here with me, talking to me as I tried to rest. It seemed like a far-off dream, one I knew I needed to recall but couldn't.

Matty, Bax's guard, was sitting in a chair beside the bed. I blinked at her. "Why?"

"Why did he bring you here, or why does your skull hurt like hell?"

I struggled to sit up, then reached for the water glass by the bed. Matty merely watched, her flat, emotionless stare making me slightly nervous.

After I drank, I set the glass back down with a shaky hand. "Why am I here?"

"Haven't you figured it out yet?"

"No."

Matty folded her hands and leaned back in the chair. "Why were you in that building?"

"A note was delivered, saying they had information regarding my father's whereabouts."

"And the man who attacked you? Did he say anything?"

I searched my memories. Snippets of those terrifying moments came back to me like flashes. Being grabbed, the smothering feeling of going without air for so long. His deep voice. *Caught you.* I took a deep breath and fought the wave of dizziness that came over me. "He said 'I wonder how much he'll pay to get you back.'"

"Any idea who 'he' is?"

"No."

"Anything else?"

"Not that I can recall."

Matty slapped her palms on her thighs and pushed to her feet. "I'll let Bax know you're awake. He's been a fucking bear downstairs."

"How long have I been sleeping?"

"About twenty-two hours."

Almost an entire day! Goodness. How was that possible?

Matty looked me up and down. "You need help getting to the toilet?" The expression she wore made it clear that assisting me was the last thing she wanted to do.

"No, I can manage. Thank you."

She started toward the door, her boots thudding on the carpets. Then she paused. "I've been looking after Baxter for a long time. Don't hurt him, Miss Kelly. If you do, you'll have to answer to me—and I won't go easy on you."

Without waiting on a response, Matty disappeared into the other room. The outer door opened and closed, and I blew out a long breath of relief. Matty was intimidating and slightly terrifying.

Shoving off the bedclothes, I pushed to my feet. Once my knees were steady, I slowly made my way toward the washroom, which I found behind one of the closed doors in the outer room.

There was a rain bath inside, too, so I decided to soak my sore muscles under the hot spray. It was heavenly.

When I finished, I wrapped myself in Bax's silk dressing gown and emerged from the washroom. A figure was propped against the wall, frowning at me.

Bax stepped forward and scooped me up in one smooth motion. I wrapped my arms around his neck, not ashamed to admit that I liked his display of strength.

"You should've called for help." He strode toward the bedroom. "Don't get on your feet again until I know you won't collapse, yeah?"

I didn't hate his concern, even though it was misplaced. "I'm fine, Bax."

"I'll decide when you're well enough, widow."

I pushed my face into the warmth of his throat, not wanting him to see my pleased grin. There was so much upheaval and chaos in my life, but he was here, solid and sure. He was like the bedrock under Manhattan or the steel used to construct the Brooklyn Bridge. I knew we'd just met, but I felt cared for, protected. Like I mattered to him.

"You aren't a good girl, are you, Belle?"

His earlier words flitted through my mind. He was right. I wasn't proper and I was tired of pretending otherwise. I almost *died* yesterday. And what did I have to show for my life? Some fancy undergarments that no one ever saw?

Instead, I was waiting around in my big home. Waiting for Papa to notice me and treat me like I was more important than his causes. Waiting for a suitor to take me on boring drives in the park and tedious walks along the avenue. Waiting, waiting, waiting . . . .

But I had the chance to live at this very moment with the most exciting man I'd ever met. Yes, it was temporary, but shouldn't I grasp every opportunity when it came?

I didn't want to fight this any longer. I wanted *more*. More naughty undergarments, more cuddling. More of Bax's attention and filthy words. Until we found my father, perhaps I could view this as an adventure.

I wanted, even for a short time, to belong to Billy Baxter.

He bent and placed me on the mattress, but I wasn't ready to let go. I held onto his neck. "Don't go." The word fell easily from my mouth. "Stay with me."

He unwound my arms from his neck, his face stern as he put distance between himself and the bed. "I'll sit in the chair."

"No, please. Lay here with me on the mattress."

He stared down at me, his gaze piercing my soul. "Why?"

"It's after sundown."

"And?"

Was he truly going to make me say it? "You said you were coming for me."

Something dark flashed in his gaze, like he found the reminder arousing, and my toes curled. Still, he didn't budge. "You're hurt. You should rest."

"I feel excellent. I slept for almost a day and stood in a hot rain bath. Please?" I could sense his indecision, so I pressed. "I need you."

"Yeah? You want me to hold you?"

"And other things." I must've been the color of a tomato, if the heat I felt under my skin was any indication.

"Yeah? What other things?"

"Kissing me, touching me."

"I see." Dropping on the mattress next to me, he leaned in to lick the lobe of my ear. "Is your pussy wet?"

Goodness, the manner in which this man talked. I nodded.

"*Fuck.*" He began kissing my jaw, my throat. "I can help with that."

Sparks ignited deep inside me, every part of my body hyper aware of this complicated man. Everything about him appealed to me, from the way he smelled—like tobacco and leather—to the shape of his muscles under his clothing. The long sweep of his lashes and the rough rasp of his voice. A knot of craving formed between my legs, an ache that was bone deep.

"I like the way you look in my dressing gown," he murmured against my throat. His hand slid over my hip and along my ribs, and I shuddered.

He pulled on the ties and the sides fell apart, revealing my bare skin. I started to cover myself out of habit, but he held my hands. "There's no reason to hide. You're the most beautiful thing I've ever seen."

"You can't truly mean that."

He rocked his erection into my hip. "I mean it, sweetheart. Feel that?"

"Oh." I couldn't contain a small smile, which he noticed, of course.

"You like that I'm always hard around you? That my cock and balls ache all the time?"

"Yes."

He leaned over, chuckling softly. "There's my naughty girl."

Then he kissed me, but this was nothing like our earlier kiss. This was deep and thorough, aggressive. I could taste his hunger and possession, the fierce need, and I fed it right back to him in equal measure.

Pleasure raced through me as my heart pounded in my ears, and I held on as his tongue slipped past my lips to find mine. It was so intimate, almost shocking, but I loved the way he surrounded me, his tongue flicking and swirling. Heat jumped between us in a perfect circuit and I arched closer, needing more.

He broke off and trailed his lips along my jaw, then down my throat. Goose bumps followed in his wake and I panted for air. My back bowed as he kissed the tops of my breasts, a delicious torture that wasn't quite enough. "Bax," I whined.

His mouth met my nipple and drew me inside, sucking. The answering tug in my core caused me to gasp, and desire pooled between my thighs. He didn't let up and I squirmed beneath him, desperate. By the time he moved to the other nipple, I was mindlessly begging. "Oh, please."

Leaving my breast, he descended the length of my body until his shoulders were pressing my thighs wide. Instinctively I tried to close my legs.

"Relax," he breathed and pressed a kiss to my folds. "I'll take care of you."

The first swipe of his tongue sent shocks through me, like I was electrified. "What . . .?"

Bax growled and did it again. "Your pussy is soaking. Just fucking dripping." He licked my entrance, then hummed. "So damn delicious."

Was this a thing people did in the bedroom? I hadn't imagined it, never even considered it a possibility. Yet Bax proceeded as if this was perfectly normal, something we would both enjoy.

The button of nerves atop my sex seemed in perfect agreement. It was throbbing, pulsing, as if trying to work its way inside Bax's mouth.

He shifted his attention there, and my brain lit up with bright colors. I moaned as he dragged his tongue over me, painting the flesh, drawing on my body. The pleasure was intense, nothing I'd ever experienced before, and I was soon thrashing beneath him, a mindless mess. My fingers curled into the bedclothes as every muscle strained toward the peak.

His lips and tongue kept at it, and then I felt him probing my entrance. A finger slipped inside and the resulting fullness came as both a surprise and a relief. I hadn't realized how empty I was there until he entered me, and now I never wanted him to leave. "Oh, God," I said on a long delirious moan, my hand drifting to the top of his head.

When he sucked on that tiny bud, my brain left my body. I became a quivering mass of nerves and sensation, climbing higher and higher, racing toward the finish as his finger worked in and out.

"You call out my name when it happens, Belle," he growled into my flesh. "No one else's."

I rocked my hips, greedy, well past all reason and propriety. I only knew I had to reach the peak or I'd die. This was so much better than anything I'd ever felt before.

The climax rushed over me with the power of a locomotive. "Bax!" I shouted, the bliss flinging me into the ether, and my body trembled uncontrollably. I clutched at him, riding out the waves, chanting his name like a prayer.

When the pleasure ebbed, he continued licking me, rubbing his nose and chin on my skin, until I twitched with sensitivity. Then he dropped onto his back beside me, his chest heaving.

I couldn't speak, not yet. My mind was a jumble of fragments, scattered thoughts just out of reach. I felt dazed and disoriented in the very best manner.

"Fuck, that was good," he said.

My sentiments exactly. There was so much that I had yet to experience in this world—and there was no time to lose. When my father returned I would go back to lonely nights and boring days.

I curled toward Bax, my fingers playing with the buttons on his vest. "How soon can you do that again?"

———

Baxter

The delicious flavor of her filled my head. I licked my lips and smiled. "I'd happily tongue you day and night, if you allowed it."

"Why on earth would anyone ever prevent you?"

Goddamn, this woman. I needed a minute to calm down. My cock was impossibly hard, my balls aching and heavy. Closing my eyes, I took a few deep breaths and resisted the urge to hump the mattress like an animal.

I felt her shift closer, the scent of her pussy filling the air like the sweetest perfume. I wanted to bathe in it.

Her hand swept over my chest and ribs. "Are you unwell?"

"I'm fine. Merely need to—"

Her palm brushed over the ridge of my cock through my trousers. I nearly jumped off the bed, hissing through my teeth.

She snatched her hand away. "I'm sorry. I thought since you had touched me . . . ." She bit her lip.

I hated the hurt and confusion in her gaze. Placing my hand on her jaw, I moved in close. "I want your hand on my cock—you have no idea how much—but there's no reason to rush. We have plenty of time."

"I feel as though I've been waiting forever," she whispered. "And do you know what I thought about when I almost died in that abandoned building?"

Every muscle in my body clenched, my anger returning full force. I didn't want to think about her in that place, hurt and almost dying. We needed to have a serious conversation about the irresponsibility of going there in the first place, but now was not the time.

I forced myself to relax. "What did you think about, gorgeous?"

"You."

She tried to duck her head, but I wouldn't let her. Not after saying something like that. I held tight so I could see her expression. "What about me?"

"I didn't want to die without seeing you again. I don't want to waste more time before doing this." Her eyes were unclouded, bright with reason and awareness. Lust and determination.

"This, meaning letting me lick your pussy."

"Yes—and letting me do things to you in exchange." She leaned in to press her lips to my jaw, and sparks raced down my legs. "May I touch you?"

Shit. Was I truly contemplating this? Every thump of my heart echoed along my erection, but I didn't want her to regret anything that happened.

"You've had a scare," I said. "And you're hurt. Let's wait until you start thinking clearly again."

"I am thinking clearly. I'm tired of not living my life." She dragged her fingertips over my thigh, trailing higher toward my groin.

My willpower crumbled. If she wanted it, she could have it. Chest heaving, I rolled to my back and ripped open the fastenings to my trousers. I freed my cock as quickly as I could manage. Cool air washed over my skin as I stroked myself.

Then I released my shaft and waited. She would need to do the rest, provided she really wanted to. "There you go."

She nibbled the inside of her cheek and stared at my cock, almost as if deciding on how best to proceed. "I should just do what you did in the carriage?"

"Yeah. Show it who's boss, sweetheart."

I held my breath and waited. I craved the feel of her hands and mouth, needed it like air. So what would she do?

"It's so pretty," she whispered, scooting closer to my belly. "I hadn't expected that."

Fuuuck. My little virgin widow. I longed to shove inside her pussy and claim her. Thrust into her until she screamed. Teach her how good it was going to be between us.

Her brows shot up. "It just moved! Why did it move?"

Because it was thinking of splitting you in two, filling you up with come.

"It does that sometimes," I said, my voice threaded with lust.

Her look of eager fascination had me gritting my back teeth. One delicate fingertip reached to stroke along the shaft, the touch light and brief. "It moved again," she said.

I groaned and wrapped a fist around the base, unable to stand it any longer. I needed friction. "Belle."

"No, let me." She shoved my hand away. "Please. I want to, Bax."

Then she dragged her fingers around me lightly, like she was petting my dick. My thigh muscles clenched in frustration. "Harder. Grip me around the base and pull like you're angry at it."

"Oh. Won't that hurt?"

I nearly laughed as I stretched my arms over my head. "Sweetheart, I've been shot, stabbed and hit over the head with a brickbat. You can't hurt me. Now, lick your palm and make me come."

Never breaking my stare, she brought her hand to her mouth. When her pink tongue emerged to slowly wet her skin, I thought I might spend right then. It was the most erotic thing I'd ever seen in my life. "Yeah, that's it," I whispered. "Get it nice and slick."

She licked once more, then reached for my cock. She worked me good this time, her grip tight and rough, just as I preferred. Between the glide of her spit-coated skin and the determined glint in her eyes, I figured it wouldn't take long. I could already feel my balls tightening in readiness. "Goddamn, the things I want to do to you."

"Like?" Her hand kept pumping, her wrist twisting over my crown. Just as I'd done in the carriage.

It was so good. So perfect. Sweet little naughty widow. My brain couldn't function, every nerve and cell focused on the movement of her hand. Words started tumbling from my mouth. "I want to feed my cock between your legs, but I'd go slow, yeah? I'd rub the head all through your pussy, get your cream all over it, have you panting and begging. Then I'd push inside your cunt—but not too fast. I want you to feel every bit of it, stretch you wide, while I suck on your nipples. I want to give you so much pleasure, Belle. So much that you pass out on me."

She shifted on her knees but kept stroking with her hand. So I didn't understand what was happening until it was too late.

Suddenly she was straddling my hips, her pussy hovering close to my cock. Lust shot through my groin as I fought the urge to thrust up and claim her. "*Belle.*"

Her voice dropped to a husky whisper. "Problem, William?"

God, I loved when she called me by my given name. No one but her had ever used it. "Not if you're ready to fuck."

I thought it would scare her, but it had the opposite effect. Her eyes went hooded as her tongue darted out to lick her lips. "I'm prepared for such an event to transpire."

"Yeah?" I didn't believe her, but I was fixated on the sight of her bare glistening folds hovering above my shaft. So close . . . .

Suddenly, she shrugged out of my silk dressing gown, letting it fall behind her. Naked. She was *naked*.

Jesus fuck.

I studied her face, waiting for the trick. Was this a dream? Isabelle Kelly, naked in my bed? It was too good to be true.

But this was real—and it was too soon. I knew in my bones that she would regret it later on. Better to wait and seduce her properly.

Most of all, I didn't want to do this before she knew about her father.

Billy Baxter, owner of a fucking conscience. Who would've guessed? Too bad the timing was utter shit.

But even I knew lying to her while sleeping with her was wrong.

Putting a hand on her hip, I said, "Belle, stop. Wait a minute."

She reached for the buttons on my vest. "You're right. You're still wearing clothes."

"No, wait. You aren't ready." *And I kidnapped your father.*

"You don't want me?"

The doubt in her voice nearly destroyed me. I cupped her jaw with one palm and rubbed the soft skin with my fingers. "You, Isabelle Kelly, are all I've ever wanted. But you're too good for a man like me. Your first time should be soft and sweet, with a husband who plans to—"

Before I could prevent it, she lowered her pussy onto the underside of my bare shaft, grinding down with her wet heat, and my back arched. "Shit!" I hissed, white-hot sparks punching through me. "Have mercy, widow."

Then she rocked her hips a few times, tempting me, teasing me, and the tip of my dick caught the edge of her entrance. We both froze. My nostrils flared as I dragged air into my lungs, and I prayed for a sliver of control. "Isabelle, no. There are things you don't know."

"Do you have a disease?"

My fingertips dug into the skin of her hips, where I held on like a man about to drown. "No, I mean about me. Things I've done."

"Bax," she whispered, leaning down to press a light kiss to my lips. "I know what kind of man you are, and I know how you feel about me. This feels right, here and now. With you."

"*Christ.*" I couldn't take it. In all my years, I'd never felt more on the edge. She was killing me, with her naked body atop mine, giving me all her sweetness. I was selfish. I needed this, needed her.

But I didn't want her to hate me for doing this now. It was better to wait until after the news of her father's misdeeds went public.

She must've taken my silence as agreement because she adjusted her body, widened her thighs and tilted her pelvis. My crown breached her entrance.

My muscles clenched and she moved again, bringing me in deeper. Her walls gripped my cock, sucking me in, and I lost the battle. Belle had shattered my self-control.

Except I hadn't fucked a virgin before, so we had to go slow. I closed my eyes tightly. "I don't want to hurt you."

"You're not. It feels strange, but it doesn't hurt."

I used my thumb to make tiny circles over her clitoris. I wanted to keep her nice and wet, so I could slide in easier. "Go at your pace. Let your body stretch around me."

Her lips parted on a moan and she began rocking, sinking lower, tiny movements that drove me to the edge of sanity. But I held still, letting her do this. Rumor was a virgin never found the first time pleasurable, but I was determined to disprove it. I cared about her and I'd be damned if she didn't enjoy this.

"That's it." I kept rubbing her clitoris. "My cock is yours, sweetheart. It's yours to use whenever you want it. Whenever your pussy feels empty inside."

"Oh, God. Bax." She threw her head back and braced her hands on my stomach. "I do. I do feel so empty inside."

"Then use it, good girl. Fill yourself with me until I'm all you can feel."

"I like when you call me that."

"Yeah? Then be my good girl and fuck yourself on my cock."

CHAPTER NINE

Isabelle

IT WAS ALL SO STRANGE, but I knew this was right. My heart told me it was exactly the moment, exactly the man. He'd proven it time and time again since we'd met.

"I will burn down this entire city to keep you safe."

Was it possible for me to fall in love in such a short amount of time?

He was so sweet and tender like this, quite unlike the hardened criminal he presented to the world. The angles of his face were taut with desire, but the softness in his eyes undid me, melting my insides like hot wax. He was being so careful with me, ensuring I enjoyed it.

"Oh, goodness," I breathed as he continued to brush his thumb over my clitoris. I could feel every swipe deep in my core and along my legs. Pressing down, I took more of him this time, until my body couldn't easily fit any more.

His gaze locked on where we were joined. "Have you ever put your fingers inside yourself?"

"That night you told me to imagine it was you? I slipped two fingers inside."

I wanted him naked. I began unbuttoning his vest, but he held my hands. "Belle, I'm dying to get inside you. Deep inside, like where your fingers went that night."

I frowned and looked at the size of him between my legs. "I don't understand. You are inside, at least as far as you can go."

His chuckle sounded pained. "No, sweetheart. I'm not. I'm only halfway."

"What?" The rest of him was thicker. No way would we fit. "Bax, I don't think I can take any more."

"You can." He pinched my bundle of nerves and a mixture of pleasure and pain exploded in every part of me. With his free hand, he tugged on my nipple, squeezing my breast until I moaned again. I sank lower, and he said, "See?"

He was all around me, taking up all the room inside my body. "It's too much."

"We still have more to go."

"Then you'll have to do it. I can't."

Holding my hips steady, he pressed up slowly and I tried not to whimper. I appreciated his consideration, but I just wanted it done. "Please."

He smoothed my hair off my face. "Belle, we can stop. This doesn't need to happen right now."

Yes, it did. I was tired of waiting for my life to happen, of letting others make decisions for me. Bax was allowing me to choose—and I chose this. "Now, Bax. Do it now."

"Isabelle, no. Let's go slow."

I could hear the hesitation in his voice. He wasn't going to finish it.

Taking a deep breath, I lifted up on my knees slightly then drove down as hard as possible. Pain stole through me as our hips met, a pinch between my legs that didn't let up. I hissed and held perfectly still.

"Fuck, Belle!" He arched his back, the tendons in his throat standing out in sharp relief. "I didn't want you to get hurt."

"I know." I panted and prayed the burn would subside. "But it's done now."

"You are killing me. What am I going to do with you?"

I wriggled a bit, the feeling morphing into an intense stretch now. "And you did promise to show me your favorite use of your favorite word."

He paused, his mouth curling into a grin. "So I did. How are you feeling?"

"Better. Full. Like I need to move."

"You're not in pain?"

I shifted, making certain. "No, and you don't need to be careful with me."

"Good." In a flash, he rolled us over. Keeping his erection buried inside me, he growled, "Because I need to fuck you hard."

He pressed me into the mattress, but I liked it. "Then take your clothes off and do it properly."

"No time." He eased out and gave a thrust that rattled my teeth. "When we start up again I'll get naked for you."

Then he started moving, the length of him dragging across the sensitive tissues inside me, and I was lost in a sea of sensation. My body surrendered to his, accommodating his thick shaft, welcoming him, and pleasure coiled inside me like a spring. With me naked and him fully clothed, it felt debauched. Secret and naughty.

Just like my undergarments.

The silk of his vest swiped across my swollen nipples, and he hit a spot in my channel each time that caused me to see stars. "Oh God, Bax."

"Yeah? You feeling it, widow?"

Long dark hair fell over his brow and his gaze was hooded with lust. He looked like the devil himself and I clutched at him, never wanting this to end. It was a high I had never imagined, so much better than when I touched myself.

"I feel it." I lifted slightly and pressed my lips to the skin of his throat, needing more of him. Needing to connect with him in every possible place. "God, yes. I feel it."

"You're so fucking tight. I need you to come."

I dragged my teeth down his neck, across the tendons. I could almost taste his strength and power. "I'm so close."

Pushing up on his arms, he said, "Touch yourself while I fuck you. Do it now, and do it fast. I can't hold out much longer."

Without an ounce of shame, I followed his instructions. The second I started rubbing my clitoris, I could feel the pressure building inside, a huge wave coming toward me. The intimate touch, combined with Bax's fullness, was too much. I didn't have a hope of withstanding it.

He was watching me, his keen eyes on my face. As he pounded into me, he practically snarled, more animal than man.

I loved it.

His voice was pure wickedness. "That's it. You're my good girl, aren't you, Belle? You're letting me in, so deep inside you. Just me. No other man will ever have you." He started riding me faster, his hips churning. "You're *mine.*"

The words took me right over the edge and into the heavens, cast up into the stars and light. A shout ripped from my throat to echo in the room. I held on tight, Bax anchoring me as the muscles in my body convulsed, my walls grasping, pulling him in.

As I started to float down to earth, Bax's hips stuttered, his mouth stretched into a grimace. "Shit, goddamn it. I shouldn't—"

Roaring, he kept pressing and rocking, his eyelids slammed tight. The harsh lines of his face eased in his climax and I loved watching the transformation. This powerful and dangerous man was losing himself in my body, his shaft swelling and pulsing.

It was perfect.

When he slowed, he shook his head. "Just this once. I swear it, Belle."

I pulled him down for a very thorough kiss. "Just once, what?"

"I won't spend inside you again," he said against my mouth. "I couldn't control it this time, but I'll do better next time."

Oh, right. This was how men and women procreated.

My skin heated. I was so foolish. I knew babies resulted from when a man and a woman were in bed together, but I hadn't known exactly how until now. It had taken seeing him spend last night in the hand-kerchief to having him inside me right now. "You must think I'm silly for not knowing this."

"I could never think you're silly. I blame your father, the women in your life—your entire uptown world—for not teaching you." He kissed me long and hard, our rough exhales mingling as our bodies cooled.

Then he shoved up on his arms and his softened shaft slid from my channel. He moved toward my toes and settled between my legs. I didn't understand what he was doing when he pushed my thighs wider. "Oh, fuck," he whispered as he used one finger to trace my entrance. "There we are. Look at my come mixed with your blood and cream."

After swirling his finger just inside my channel, he lifted it to his mouth and licked the mixture off. His lids fell as his face slackened with pleasure. "Christ almighty."

Then he reached to gather more and held his finger up to my mouth. I didn't hesitate. I opened my lips and let him feed it to me, and the combined taste of us exploded on my tongue. Copper and salt. It was strange, but not bad.

And I liked the idea that it was from the two of us.

A deep groan rumbled out of his chest. "I won't come in you again, I promise."

Then he stood, his thick member hanging down between his legs, and began removing his clothing. No doubt he was trying to distract me from the conversation . . . and it worked. The more he removed, the more fascinated I became with his body. Rough skin stretched over wide shoulders and a broad chest, showing sleek muscles that were not honed in a boxing ring or on the back of a horse. He was pure New York street tough, wiry and strong. A god in silk and wool.

My heart flipped, giddiness filling my lungs—and I froze. What was happening to me? Was I developing feelings for him?

The possibility caused my mouth to dry out. I couldn't. He was Billy Baxter, violent criminal and gang leader. I was . . . the opposite, part of a family who crusaded to bring down the gangs. My father had been trying to rid the city of such ne'er-do-wells for years. There was no future for Bax and me.

"I don't like the expression on your face, widow." Bax shucked off his union suit, leaving him completely bare.

All thoughts in my brain disappeared except for one: *Good heavens, he is gorgeous.* I drank him in slowly. It was my first look at a naked man and I was not going to waste the opportunity. "Turn around."

With a smirk, he spun to show me his backside.

I bit my lip and admired the view. Tall and muscular, he was even more magnificent from this angle. There were scars, signs of the life he'd lived, the fortitude he'd shown to get to the top of the New York City underworld. Perhaps I should've been scared . . . but I wasn't.

Quite the opposite.

He crawled onto the mattress, stretching out his long frame at my side, then cupped my cheek in his palm. His fingers stroked my skin almost reverently. "Thank you for trusting me."

The adoration in his gaze melted my insides, and I couldn't prevent the rush of affection in my chest. "It was perfect, Bax."

"Good." He settled at my side and held me close. "I have an idea."

"Oh?"

"I've been thinking about your undergarments. And the tariffs you talked about."

I studied the far wall and stroked the flat planes of his chest. "Meaning?"

"I can help you skirt the tariffs. If you want to buy more undergarments, that is."

Easing back, I smirked at him. "Why, Bax. Are you encouraging this for my benefit . . . or yours?"

His grin was positively wicked. "Both?"

"So I buy more fancy undergarments and you see me in them, is that it?"

"I call that a win for both sides."

I chuckled. "Rascal." Then I decided to be honest with him. "I once thought of opening a store, where I could sell them publicly. I also have some designs of my own."

"I can help you with that."

"Unfortunately, it's impossible. The daughter of Honest Dan Kelly could never."

"Because you're embarrassed?"

"Because everyone would know I like those undergarments. That I *wear* those undergarments. And besides the tariff problems, Mr.

Comstock would probably shut me down over indecency. It's impossible."

"Sweetheart, you can't live your life for other people. If you want to open a store selling racy unmentionables to help women feel pretty and make men want to fuck them, then do it."

He didn't understand. Rules and conventions didn't apply to Bax. "Easy for you to say. You do whatever you like and to hell with the consequences."

"Yes, but I've learned to listen to the only person whose opinion matters: mine."

"Women are not so fortunate. I have to work within the bounds of both society and the law."

"No, you don't. You have me now. I can twist the entire city to suit my whims—and yours. Whatever you want, Belle. You only need to ask."

It was so very tempting. He was offering up my dreams on a silver tray like a glass of champagne. But at what price? What would I need to give up to claim them? My father would never approve. He would rather I stayed inside the house and didn't cause trouble.

I was caught between fantasy and reality, where nothing was quite real.

Bax kissed my forehead. "Think about it."

"I will." Very likely I'd do nothing else. Was it a mistake to turn him down?

Then my breath caught when he began nibbling on my earlobe. "Rest up, yeah? You have five minutes before I make you come again."

CHAPTER
TEN

Baxter

I WAITED until she fell asleep before I got up and dressed.

My mind raced over the events of the last few hours. Belle in my bed, Belle begging me to take her virginity. Belle's sweet pussy wrapped around my cock. Jesus fuck, I was a lucky man.

A long-buried part of me had roared to life the second my cock slipped inside her. It had been primal and instinctual, turning me into a snarling beast who would be sated by only one thing: her.

And everything changed in that moment.

I felt the shift deep in my corrupted, jaded soul. She breathed new life into me, like waking me up from a long lonely nap. She was sweetness and joy and unexpected delights, my reward for scrabbling and scratching all these years to survive. I decided right then to keep her.

Belle was mine. I wasn't letting her go, and I'd kill anyone who tried to take her from me.

We could make this work. She was miserable in her uptown prison, and I could help her spread her wings and fly. More undergarments, her own shop . . . whatever she wanted. I'd give her the fucking world on a gold plate.

Unfortunately, there was the problem of her father. She deserved to know what I did—and why. She needed to learn the truth about Honest Dan Kelly.

I didn't regret kidnapping Kelly. I wouldn't allow the hypocritical blowhard to become mayor. While lining his pockets off blackmail and graft, he campaigned that men like me ruined the city.

Which was ridiculous. Men like me kept Manhattan organized and neat. Without me, crime and lawlessness would run amok here.

Belle would understand. She was a logical, brave woman. I'd explain and show her the proof. She'd soon realize that her father was undeserving of any sympathy or compassion. She would see my side.

And from now on, I would only give her the truth. Her father had lied to her enough.

First, though, I had to deal with her attacker. The piece of shit was found in a Hell's Kitchen alley earlier, shot in the hip. Matty dragged him into the saloon's cellar to stew in fear and misery until I was ready.

After one last look at the woman tucked in my bed, I dragged on my boots and rose. Belle stirred as I crossed the floor. "Bax?"

Her voice was low and thick with sleep, and I longed for nothing more than to crawl back into bed with her. But I needed confirmation about who tried to kidnap her and why. There would be no rest until I killed every last man involved.

"Go back to sleep, sweetheart."

"But where are you going?"

"I have some business I need to handle. I won't be long."

"Promise?"

My chest ballooned at the sweetly-spoken question.

I have to tell her. Soon.

"I promise, widow."

Her sleepy gaze studied my face intently. "Be careful, William."

Before I lost the will to leave, I forced myself out the door. When I entered the cellar, Matty was there, cleaning her nails with a knife, while Charlie stood against the wall with his arms folded. A man lay crumpled on the floor, wheezing. I knew the sound of that wheeze. Belle's attacker wouldn't live much longer.

Using my foot, I rolled him onto his back and waited until pain-filled eyes stared up at me. "Do you know who I am?"

The man's lips moved but no sound emerged. I nudged the bullet wound with the tip of my boot, causing him to howl. When the screams quieted, I snapped, "Answer me."

"Billy . . . Baxter."

"Good. I'm going to ask you some questions and you have two choices. One, you can answer them to my satisfaction and I'll kill you quickly." I bent near the man's face. "Or two, you can refuse to tell me what I want to know and I will peel the skin from your bones. It's your choice.."

The man's eyes were clouded with pain but coherent. He understood the offer. "Don't kill me. I'll tell you anything you want to know."

I dragged over a chair. Then I sat, took out my long knife, and held it loosely in one hand to serve as a reminder. "Who paid you to wait in that building and kidnap her?"

"I-I don't know."

"Wrong answer."

I leaned down, ready to slice, when the man shouted, "Wait!"

I paused and snarled, "Start fucking talking."

"I didn't get his name." Grimacing, he closed his eyes and panted. "But I know he w-works for Walsh."

Exactly as I'd thought. "You said, 'I wonder how much he'll pay to get you back.' Who is 'he'?"

"Ransom her . . . to you."

I nodded. "Where were you supposed to take her?"

"Bank Street."

"The address?"

"Thirty-one."

I glanced at Charlie, who turned on his heel and went up the stairs. We would find Walsh and this building, and I would have vengeance on every single person involved.

"Is there anything else you can tell me? About the plan, about what Walsh intended?"

"No, sir. I told you all I know."

I rose, removed my coat, and rolled my sleeves high on his forearms while the man on the ground watched, his expression twisted in pain and uncertainty. Then I lifted the chair and placed it against the wall. "You put your hands on her. You scared her. Worst of all, you nearly killed her. For that, I have no mercy. No forgiveness. So I've changed my mind. I won't kill you quickly."

Crouching, I put the tip of the knife directly against the man's balls. "This will be slow. And it will be fucking painful."

For the next hour, the only sounds coming from inside the room were screams.

By the time I finished, I was covered in blood and my body hummed with dark energy. "Dispose of him," I told Matty. "I have to clean up and get back upstairs."

"Have you told her about her father yet?"

I didn't answer. There was a spigot in the cellar with running water, so I used it to wash off. Once I bathed, I put on a clean shirt and trousers, not bothering with a vest and coat in my haste to return to Belle.

As I climbed the stairs, I heard a commotion in the saloon. Damn it. Was there a fight going on? Exhausted and annoyed, I stomped into the main room—and halted.

Belle was there, sitting on top of the wooden bar, laughing with my men, a queen holding court. She was dressed in her gown, her hair piled neatly atop her head, every inch a lady.

My lady.

I grew hot, jealousy building like a frenzy in my blood. I wanted to rip her away from their appreciative gazes and take her back upstairs, keep her just to myself.

"Bax!" She grinned when she saw me. "Come have a drink with us!"

As if they could sense my mood, my men sank lower, hunching, as they slowly turned toward me. My expression had them scurrying off to other parts of the building, leaving Belle alone.

Christ, she was gorgeous, looking at home here in my domain. She fit in perfectly. Unafraid and with no airs whatsoever.

Belle pouted when I reached her. "You made them all leave. We were having fun."

"I bet." Moving in, I touched her jaw, letting my fingers linger on her silky skin. "What are you doing out of bed, widow?"

"I was awake and bored, so I decided to come down. Everyone was very nice to me. I was asking them about you."

No doubt this was true. The men were probably falling all over themselves for her attention by telling stories about me. "Yeah? So what do you think?"

She glanced around, taking in the saloon. "It's nice. Nothing like the rumors."

"The rumors?"

"Things people say. You know, about you. About the gangs. My father—" She sighed and shook her head. "My father tells these stories in his speeches about the gangs and the destruction they cause. Snatching children off the streets to sell to brothels, forcing opium onto unsuspecting women. Murder and violence everywhere they go. But this is nothing like those tales. All the men are . . . sweet."

Sweet, sure. I'd just sliced a man to ribbons one floor below us. But I was glad Belle liked it here. I wanted her by my side for as long as I could keep her.

"You changed your clothes." She ran her hand over my shoulder. "Why?"

I gestured to Asher behind the bar. A half glass of bourbon appeared in front of me, and I downed the liquid in one swallow. *Only the truth from now on.* "We found the man who attacked you and I made him pay. In the process my clothes were soiled."

"Oh."

Our eyes met and I braced myself. I expected to see horror or condemnation.

What I didn't expect to see was *admiration*.

She stared at me like I could do anything, a hero to slay her dragons. I wanted to rip my beating heart out of my chest and place it at her feet. At that moment, there wasn't anything I wouldn't do for her.

And she was beginning to see the truth, how her father had lied about men like me. Now she needed to know everything. It was time.

I jerked my head and Asher disappeared, leaving Belle and me alone at the bar. "There's something we need to discuss."

She trailed her fingers over my chest and down to my stomach. "Does it have to do with returning upstairs?"

I grabbed her hand before she could distract me. "Not yet."

"That's a shame, because I'm not sore any longer."

My cock twitched, pleased at the news, but I ignored it. "It's about what you said. About your father and the stories he tells in his speeches."

She straightened, her eyebrows drawing together. "What about him?"

I paused. I wished I had more time before starting this. My stomach clenched as I searched for the words. "Some crusaders, they don't really believe what they say. But they like the attention it brings, the notoriety that accompanies their words. Often it brings money, as well."

"This doesn't have anything to do with my father, though."

"Yeah, it does, sweetheart. Turns out Honest Dan Kelly ain't so honest after all."

"That's nonsense." She pulled her hand from mine. "The whole city knows of all the good he's achieved in the last seven or eight years."

I plunged ahead. "And there's some of us who know the truth. That he blackmails criminals and lines his pockets through graft and bribery—"

She sucked in a breath, her expression wild with panic. "You're lying. Why would you say these horrible things about my father?"

"I'm not lying, Belle. I have the evidence upstairs. Come with me and I'll show you."

CHAPTER
ELEVEN

Isabelle

I STARED AT HIM, my ears ringing with disbelief. "No, you must be mistaken."

Bax's gaze didn't waver. "He embezzled money from the city. I have the proof."

"Embezzled! He would never do that."

"He did. I can show you the documents up in my office."

This could not be happening. My stomach was churning, squeezing, and I needed Bax to take the words back. "Someone is lying to you, then."

"It's the truth, Belle."

I stared at him, this man who I'd let into my body and my heart. Why was he doing this?

Questions and denials spun like hoops in my brain. "If you have proof of his crimes, why not make it public?"

"I have what I need to ruin him, but we were investigating the boxes of documents we found in his office. We thought there might be more."

His *office*?

I shoved past him and jumped to the floor. Whirling, I put my hands on my hips. "What do you mean, found in his office? Did you have something to do with my father's disappearance?" It hit me like a pile of bricks. "Oh, my God. You lied to me about kidnapping him."

A muscle jumped in his jaw. "Yes, I did. But it was for your own good."

The words fell between us like a stone. Bax had kidnapped my father. I should have known. I never should have believed a criminal over my instincts.

My knees buckled, so I grabbed the smooth wooden bar with one hand to steady myself. "My own good? Tell me, Bax? Why would any of this be good for me?"

"Because he is the worst kind of hypocrite," he snarled. "He's a criminal, like me, but worse because he hides behind fake words and speeches. At least I don't pretend to be anything other than what I am."

"You're trying to *justify* this to me?" I stepped forward and poked his chest. "Where is he? I want him released *right now.*"

His shoulders swelled as his chest expanded. He cast a glance over his shoulder, but I didn't look away. My mind was spinning with fury and disbelief, humiliation and hurt. I wanted to undo this. I wanted to turn back the clock.

I wished I'd never met this man.

Leaning in, I hissed, "I should have shot you when I had the chance."

Without warning, Bax put his shoulder in my belly and lifted me clean off the ground. I pounded his back. "Put me down this instant, Billy Baxter!"

He ignored me. Swiftly, he carried me up the stairs and strode to his apartment. When we were inside, he set me on the floor—and I promptly scrambled away from him. "I want to leave. And I want you to release my father. *Now.*"

He gripped the back of a chair with both hands, his knuckles turning white. "That's not how this works. I decide when your father is released—and I decide when you leave here."

I sucked in a shocked breath. "Is this another kidnapping? Is that what you're doing?"

"I'm not kidnapping you. I'm trying to keep you *safe*. Someone hurt you and tried to kidnap you, Isabelle."

"You already caught and killed that man."

"Which doesn't mean the danger has passed. There's still the man who hired your attacker, yeah?"

"Who is no longer a threat to me after I cease my association with you."

His upper lip curled. "You think ending our *association* will keep you safe? Don't be so naive, widow."

"I know it will! You are the only danger to me in this city, Billy Baxter."

The temperature in the room seemed to drop. His expression turned menacing. Scary. No longer my lover, but the man who ruled the underworld of the city.

He spoke quietly, every word enunciated. "I will lock you up if it keeps you safe, Belle. Even if you hate me for it."

"Oh, so now I am in the wrong? I won't forgive you for this, Baxter. No matter what you do or say. *You kidnapped my father*!"

"He deserves to be ruined, not sit in the mayor's office."

"Then why haven't you ruined him? If that is what you're after, then why not release your proof and sabotage his campaign?"

"I will, when I'm good and ready."

"What's stopping you?" Suddenly, my gaze flicked to the bed. Oh, God. No, no, no. Not that. I put my hand on my stomach, nauseous. "Was this about getting me into your bed? It was, wasn't it? And I fell right into your trap."

"Stop it. I kidnapped your father, but it wasn't like that between you and me."

"Every word out of your mouth has been a lie. I don't believe anything you say anymore."

His expression went blank, his eyes turning hard and flat. "I haven't lied about anything, other than your father's whereabouts."

"Oh, my God. I'm a fool. You were trying to hurt my father by ruining me—and I let you!"

"You have it all wrong, Isabelle."

My laugh was full of bitterness. "No, I'm seeing things clearly for the first time. You are truly horrible. I can't believe I ever had feelings for you."

"We'll discuss this later, after you've sat with it awhile."

"It doesn't matter how long I *sit* with this. I won't forgive you. I'm leaving and I never want to see you again."

His jaw tight, he pointed at me. "I'm not letting you leave until I know you're safe. So wrap your pretty little head around that, while I go and kill every single person involved in hurting you yesterday." He stormed from the room, slammed the door shut, and locked it.

I stared at the door, unable to believe his gall. Bax wasn't letting me go and had *locked me in.* How dare he! Oh, this would not do.

I had to get out of here. I wouldn't meekly await his return, then beg for his attention. No, I'd done enough of that in my lifetime. I was done letting others control me.

I ran to the window. It overlooked the front of the saloon on Forty-Fourth Street. I was too high up to jump and there was no fire escape.

But there was a drain pipe.

A small group appeared on the walk below, with Bax in the lead. He was shouting orders to his men, though his exact words were lost in the wind. I didn't care where he was going or what he was doing. I would never forgive him.

Bax and his guards climbed into a carriage and the wheels started off, while a smaller group loaded into a second vehicle. Betrayal sat in my stomach like a rock, my chest burning with anguish and fury. I should've known better than to trust a man like Billy Baxter.

There would be time for recriminations and regrets later. Right now I needed to escape and find my father.

I opened the window and leaned out. The drain pipe ran the entire length of the building. It was thin, but it should hold. Besides, what choice did I have?

I threw one leg out and adjusted my skirts, trying not to get tangled in the layers of cloth. I reached for the pipe and held on tight, moving slowly out the window until I was completely outside. The metal was wet and slippery, so I dug in, clasping it as hard as I could, using my feet for support. I tried not to look down.

I went slowly, one inch at a time. When my arms began burning, shaking with the effort, I risked a peek at the ground.

It seemed miles away.

Swallowing my fear, I kept going. Finally, I was close enough to jump. My feet landed on the ground with a thud, and I bent over as far as my corset allowed to drag in a deep breath. *God, I hope I never have to do that again.*

I was free.

Now I had to find a hack—

"Going somewhere?"

I whirled around. Matty leaned against the building, one foot propped up on the brick. My stomach plummeted and I began backing away. "W-what are you doing out here?"

"I knew you'd run."

I lowered my chin and raised my fists. "I won't go back inside. You cannot force me."

"You think to fight me?" Matty threw her head back and laughed. "You wouldn't stand a chance, princess."

"I'm tougher than I look."

"I don't doubt it, not if you've hooked Bax."

I hadn't *hooked* Bax—and even if I had, I was throwing him back. "I'm leaving. You can't stop me."

"I don't want to stop you. I want to help you."

This sounded like a trick. "Why?"

Matty pushed off the wall and came closer. "He should've told you about your father. He was a bastard for keeping that from you, which I made perfectly clear many times."

"So, you're going to just let me leave?"

"Yes—and I'm going to tell you where to locate your father." She held out a piece of paper. "There you go."

I snatched the note, but didn't read it. Matty put her fingers in her mouth and let out a piercing whistle. A second later, a hack rounded the corner and stopped in front of us. I stared at the other woman, trying to make sense of it. "I don't understand."

"Then you've never met another woman in dire straits. How nice for you. Not all of us have led a life of such privilege."

I was confused, but I'd never encountered anyone like her. Matty was fascinating and competent. Unafraid and strong. I doubted she'd let a man ever get the best of her.

But I didn't want her to risk herself on my account. "Won't he be angry with you?"

"He'll be spitting mad. But in time he'll come to see I was right. Take this pistol." She held out a gun.

"Thank you."

"I don't need your gratitude. Just promise to help someone else when the time comes." Matty headed toward the saloon doors. "Go in through the rear kitchen. The door's usually unlocked. Go up to the second floor, third door on the right."

I wanted to say thanks again, but Matty disappeared inside the saloon. So I hurried into the hack and gave the driver the address on the piece of paper.

Sadly, it wasn't far, which was both a relief and completely frustrating. This whole time my father had been mere blocks away.

———

The front of the brick townhouse appeared well kept. What was this place? I paid the driver, climbed down and shook out my skirts. Then I moved quickly to the path that ran between the buildings.

Was that laughter I heard inside?

I clasped the butt of my pistol tight in my palm. Were they having a grand time while they tortured my father? I had to hurry.

As Matty predicted, the rear door was unlocked. I slipped inside and found an empty kitchen that smelled of herbs and lemon. Dishes were stacked by the washbasin, waiting to be washed, so I hurried through lest someone come in to begin the task.

A set of servants' stairs led up from the kitchen, so I began to climb. When I reached the second floor I could hear more feminine giggling and the sound of a rhythmic slapping. Wait, was this . . .?

My God. Bax had imprisoned my father in a *bordello*? I ground my back teeth together. My father must be appalled at these conditions. It was exactly the sort of vice and impropriety he railed against in his speeches.

I hurried to the third door on the right. I tried the knob, expecting it to be locked. To my surprise, the door flew open.

I came to an abrupt halt. Naked bodies were sprawled every which way on the bed. Bare limbs filled my vision, and I couldn't piece together what was happening. It was . . . shocking. Confusing. Scandalous.

Then I recognized a face.

My *father's* face.

I couldn't believe it. Dan Kelly was in the midst of it, his hands and mouth quite busy between two women. He didn't appear to be held against his will *at all*.

Heads swiveled toward the door and the coverlet was quickly dragged up to shield the lower half of their bodies. Three surprised faces stared back at me.

Slowly, the coverlet moved and a fourth participant crawled out to peek at me. It was another woman, her big eyes round and wary.

What on *earth*? How did this even work? The silence stretched as I tried to make sense of this *orgy* in front of me.

"Isabelle!" My father scowled as he started to disentangle himself from the bodies. "What are you doing here?"

"Coming to rescue you," I snapped. "But you're clearly in no need of rescuing."

Spinning on my heel, I hurried to the stairs. I was so stupid. I'd climbed out of Bax's saloon and hurried here to rescue my father, anxious to save him from pain and torture.

Except he wasn't suffering at all. He was enjoying himself.

"He is the worst kind of hypocrite. He hides behind fake words and speeches . . . ."

Bax was right. I didn't know my father at all.

"Isabelle," my father called urgently from behind me. "Stop right there."

Taking a deep breath, I whirled on him. Thank heavens he'd put on a dressing gown. "Why? So you can tell me the importance of your work? How you're trying to save the city from corruption and vice? Spare your breath, Papa. I've seen the truth."

"Don't be ridiculous. I am here under duress, yes. But I still have the same needs as other men."

"That was not duress—and this is exactly the sort of thing you've always publicly shamed in your speeches. Houses of sin, you called them. And you've encouraged Comstock and the police to shut them down for years."

"You wouldn't understand, being a sheltered young girl. Someday you'll be married and your husband will teach you about these things." He gave me the same patronizing look he always did when I questioned him. It used to make me feel small; now it made me furious.

I fisted my hands. "Sheltered because you *forced* me to stay home. You said people would use me to get to you. That it was to protect me." I gave a bitter laugh and gestured to the room he'd departed. "Now it's clear you didn't wish for me to discover that you're a hypocrite."

His eyes rounded. "How dare you say such things to me? I am not a hypocrite."

I hadn't ever fought with my father. In all my years I did everything he asked without complaint, thinking he was working toward the greater good. Some greater good, indeed.

Everything Bax had said was true—which I did not find reassuring in the least. No, I felt even more foolish for believing my father for so many years.

But I was done playing the good daughter. I was done pretending like my life didn't matter.

I straightened my spine. "Not a hypocrite, you say? Then I suppose you won't mind when I spread the word of today's orgy, *Honest* Dan Kelly."

"What has come over you?"

Stepping closer, I gave him the truth. "I searched for you for *days*. I went to the police, I went to—" I bit it off, unwilling to say his name. "You have no idea how difficult this has been for me."

"Well, that was foolish. You should have waited at home, as I've taught you. This city is far too dangerous and immoral for the likes of you."

"But just the right sort of immoral for you, apparently."

"Young lady," he growled. "This lack of disrespect will not be tolerated."

"That door wasn't even locked! You could have left at any time. Why didn't you?"

He rolled his shoulders and didn't meet my eye. "I hadn't realized it was unlocked. Obviously I would've left had I known."

Lies. I didn't believe him for one second. I would never believe him —or any other man—as long as I lived. I shook my head. "He tried to tell me what kind of person you are, but I didn't want to hear it. I almost died because of you! What a fool I am."

"Who?" My father grabbed my arm. "Who has filled your head with lies?"

"Let me go," I tried to pull away, but he held tight. "And they weren't lies, it turns out. You are everything he said—and worse."

A deep angry voice reverberated off the walls. "Get your goddamn hands off her, Kelly."

Baxter

I CHARGED UP THE STAIRS, a red mist coating my vision. All I could see was Kelly's hand on Belle's arm, and how she was trying to pull away from him.

Kelly sneered at me. "This is none of your concern, Baxter."

"Let Isabelle go immediately," I snarled. "Or I'll rip your arms off, then throw you and your bloody stumps into the East River."

Kelly released her, but didn't move away. "How do you know my daughter's given name?"

Fists clenched, I headed straight for him. "I know more about her than you do, apparently. I know she's under the misguided notion that you're a decent person, that you actually believe the shit you say during those speeches of yours."

Belle shoved past me on her way to the stairs.

"And where are you going?" I asked.

"Go away, Bax."

"Keep Kelly here," I barked at my men as I followed her.

"Leave my daughter alone, you hooligan!" Kelly shouted, leaning over the railing as my men held him back.

I hurried down the stairs. "Fuck off, Kelly."

When I reached the bottom, I caught up to her at the front door. "Widow, wait."

She shook off my hand and whirled toward me. Her face was flushed, her eyes wild. "I'm not a goddamn widow! And I don't want to hear anything you have to say. Ever."

Panic clawed in my throat. I couldn't lose her. I gestured toward the empty drawing room. "I need to talk to you."

"You kidnapped my father, Bax, and you locked me in!"

She tried to edge past me, but I darted into her path. I put my palms up. "I'm not letting you leave until you hear me out. Please, Belle."

I suspected it was the *please* that won her over. She nodded once and marched into the drawing room. "Talk, Bax."

I shoved my hands in my trouser pockets to keep from reaching for her. "I've handled this all wrong."

"Illuminating," she drawled flatly. "And correct."

"Belle, I didn't hurt him. And I wasn't planning to keep him much longer. I just wanted a little more time."

"To dig for more evidence."

"Yes, but also for more time with you."

Her eyes narrowed, like she didn't believe me. "And you feel this justifies lying to me and hurting my family?"

"Does he look hurt?" I pointed to the ceiling. "Let me guess? He's disheveled because he was availing himself of Lisette's hospitality. How many women were there with him?"

"Three—and that is not the point!"

I pressed my palms together, pleading with her. "I know I lied, but I never thought I would develop feelings for you. When I saw you again at the fights, I couldn't help but take advantage of the opportunity."

"What do you mean, when you saw me again?"

Only the truth.

I dragged in a deep breath. "I saw you once outside the mission on

Fifty-Second Street. About seven years ago, I suppose. Your father was giving a speech and you were watching him."

She cocked her head. "Seven years ago?"

"Yeah. He called me and some of the other boys vermin. You were with him. I was going to slip a dead rat into his carriage, but then I found you inside."

"I don't recall that."

I wasn't surprised. I would've been another dirty street kid, one of thousands in this city. "I hadn't thought of it in a long time, not until you walked into the fights."

She appeared unimpressed, her mouth flat. I kept talking. "You deserve to escape that big house, Belle. To wear your scandalous undergarments and live the life you want, not the one your father wants. You deserve the truth—and all he did was lie to you."

She wrapped her arms around her waist, as if protecting herself. "Did you think I would fall to your feet in gratitude after you've ruined my father's life? Ruined *my* life? You lied and deceived me."

"No, but I thought you would be reasonable. Don't you see? I want you to stay with me. I want to give you everything."

She gaped at me. "You're from a completely different world than mine. One with kidnappings and lies."

Shame scalded the back of my neck. "There are no different worlds in this city, not like that. The only thing that separates the criminals uptown is their address. Trust me, they're criminals just the same, Belle."

"I'm not a criminal," she hissed. "And my father doesn't *kill* people."

"Oh, so there are some sins you're willing to accept. Just not mine."

"Your flippancy is misplaced. You are perfectly aware of what I mean."

"I hear you making excuses for that bastard upstairs, a man who has ignored you his entire life." I thumped a fist against my chest. "I would lay the entire world at your fucking feet, but you can't forgive me because my sins are somehow greater than Honest Dan Kelly's?"

"If you expect gratitude from me, you'll be waiting until Hell freezes over. I barely know you—and what I do know, I don't like."

I was losing her. She was slipping through my fingers like sand. My voice tightened, fear turning my blood cold. "Horse shit. You know me, almost better than anyone else. And you were happy in the saloon with me and my men. Tell me you didn't love every minute we spent together until you learned about your father's kidnapping."

She blinked several times, her eyes glassy, and I grabbed her hand. "Please, Belle. I will make it up to you."

"You can't. You just want to corrupt me. The perfect uptown princess you can set free and drag downtown into your world. But you don't have the faintest idea of who I am or what I want."

"Wrong. I know you—"

"No you don't, Bax. I'm more than what you *see*. I also have thoughts and feelings. We met *three* days ago, for goodness sake!"

"Then stick around. Give us a chance to get to know each other."

"I'd rather not. I used to trust you. Not anymore, however."

My face fell, the words like a dull knife between the ribs. "Let me change your mind."

"Why must I do all the accommodating when *you* have hurt *me*?"

"I'll make this up to you, I promise."

"It's not enough. My God, you haven't even apologized to me."

"I don't apologize," I said. "Never. Not to anyone."

"Do you hear yourself? You hurt me. You have upended my life, only thinking of yourself. And you won't even apologize for it!"

"Actions are what matter, Belle, not words." After everything with her father, I'd think this was obvious.

She gave a brittle laugh. "The fact that you're not even willing to say it tells me all I need to know."

"Which is?"

"That your pride means more to you than I do."

"Nothing means more to me than you do."

"Except admitting you're sorry, apparently."

I didn't speak. I couldn't. I wasn't sorry. Dan Kelly didn't deserve to be mayor. I would do anything to prevent it.

And I didn't regret a single second of the time Belle and I spent together.

She went around me and headed toward the front entry. "Goodbye, Bax."

I wanted to stop her, take her back to the Devil's Hand and keep her with me forever. But I couldn't kidnap her. I called, "This isn't over."

"I'm terribly *sorry*," she drawled with a heavy dose of mockery. "But this is most definitely over."

"Someone could still try to hurt you."

She paused with her hand on the doorknob. "Did you handle the man responsible for my kidnapping attempt?"

"Yes, Walsh is dead." We'd found Walsh in New Jersey. I'd killed him quickly, eager to get back to Manhattan. "But—"

"Then we needn't worry. Besides, no one on earth could possibly hurt me more than you have, Billy Baxter." She yanked open the door and disappeared outside.

Sucking in a ragged breath, I stared at the wood floor. The walls closed in as my stomach sank to my toes.

Shit. I'd lost her.

CHAPTER
THIRTEEN

Baxter

ONCE AGAIN, I broke into Daniel Kelly's office after dark.

While the breaking in part felt familiar, everything else was different.

It all changed after Belle's departure, from the way I looked at myself to the way I saw the world.

And I didn't like what I discovered. She was right. I'd let my pride and feelings for her father cloud my judgment. I took away her choices and backed her into an impossible corner.

I deserved to lose her.

And so, for the first time in my life, I was doing the right thing. The decent thing. It wouldn't get her back, but not doing it would hurt her. And I would do everything in my power to keep Belle from hurting ever again.

Easing the window open, I threw a leg over the sill and climbed inside.

Daniel Kelly was at his desk, a lamp turned low in the corner. The soft glow illuminated the pistol in his hand.

"I ought to shoot you," he snarled. "How dare you come here, Baxter?"

Four days ago I released him. Four days since Isabelle walked out of my life. She hated me—and I didn't blame her.

I waved my hand at Kelly's gun. "Put that down and hear me out."

"You'd like that, wouldn't you?" His lips twisted into a sneer. "So you can kidnap me again. Go to hell!"

Already there.

I dropped into the arm chair across from his desk. "You're going to want to hear what I have to say."

"What I want is to shoot you right between the eyes." He leaned in, the gun never wavering. "You seduced *my daughter*, you filthy piece of—"

"Stop." I held up my hand. "Calling me names got you into this mess in the first place. I suggest you keep a civil tongue in your head."

"Are you denying you seduced her?"

I thought of Belle, throwing her leg over my hips and begging me to fuck her. *"I know what kind of man you are, and I know how you feel about me. This feels right to me, here and now."*

But she hadn't really known me or what I was capable of.

And the hatred and disappointment in her eyes when she finally did learn?

It haunted me. I couldn't breathe, couldn't *think* without her. I'd hurt her—and I hated myself for it.

"I seduced her," I admitted. "And you can shoot me for it, if you want. But I'd suggest waiting to hear me out first."

"Why? So you can attempt to justify it?" He gave a bitter laugh. "I know the reason. You did it to hurt and humiliate me!"

I shook my head. "Wrong. It was about her. And I'd do it all over again if I had the chance."

He hadn't expected that, if his bewildered expression was anything to go by. "You're full of shit."

"You don't know a damn thing about your daughter, do you? She's . . . ." I swallowed the lump in my throat. "Perfect. She's brave and kind, loyal and caring. She would've gone to the ends of the earth to save your corrupt ass."

"Yes, she told me about holding a gun on you at the fights. If only she'd shot you then, it would have saved us all a great deal of aggravation."

"No doubt. But then the evidence I had would have reached the newspapers."

"Had? Don't tell me you've destroyed it, because I won't believe you."

"No, I gave it to your daughter."

I left the papers proving Kelly's misdeeds in Belle's bedchamber just before crawling in to the office. She'd been downstairs at supper, ignoring her father while she ate.

"You gave it all to Isabelle? Why on earth would you do that?"

"Because she deserves to know the real Honest Dan Kelly."

"Jesus Christ," he muttered before his jaw hardened. "So this is where you blackmail me, I suppose? It's exactly what I'd expect from someone like you."

"Vermin, you mean?" I fisted my hands but tried to remain calm. "I'm not here to blackmail you."

"Why not?"

"Because exposing you would hurt her."

He cocked his head, like he was trying to hear better. "Let me understand. You were willing to do anything to prevent me from becoming mayor—even kidnapping me—but you're giving up because you believe it will upset my daughter?"

"I *know* it will upset your daughter. She stupidly loves you. And don't pretend like you didn't fuck your way through that bordello. I asked Lisette."

He didn't say anything, not that I expected him to.

Slapping my hands on my thighs, I pushed to my feet. "Well, that's that. Best of luck in robbing the fine citizens of this city."

He also stood, not lowering the gun for an instant. "It's no different than what you do, Baxter."

"True. But I've never claimed otherwise. I'm a villain, through and through. You pretend to be a savior, but you're just as bad, yeah?"

His nostrils flared, but he didn't comment on that. Instead, he said, "I won't let you have her, even if I have to kill you to prevent it."

A bitter bark of laughter escaped my throat. "You keep her locked in this house, isolated and alone. But you can't control her. She has her own mind, her own goals. A word of advice? Don't try to get in her way. Because she'll only hate you for it."

"I don't need tips from you on how to raise my daughter. And a word of advice from *me*? Stay away from her. If I catch you near her again, I will shoot you, Baxter."

"You can try, Kelly, but I love her. I'm not giving up, not until she hears me out."

The other man sneered. "Is she worth dying over?"

"Yes."

The door flew open. I turned—and found Belle there. My body jolted, and I couldn't look away. I drank in the sight of her, mesmerizing every detail. Her hair was pulled into a simple braid, and bare feet peeked out from under her dressing gown.

Christ, she was lovely. My fierce widow.

My chest felt hollow, like a fist was squeezing my heart. I needed to say something. I needed to beg for her forgiveness, pledge my undying love. Let her hear how goddamn sorry I was.

Just as I opened my mouth, the gun went off. All the air left my lungs as pain exploded in my body. My legs went out from under me and I was on the ground, staring at the ceiling. The last thing I saw was Belle's panicked face. I had so much I wanted to tell her . . . then everything went black.

CHAPTER
FOURTEEN

Isabelle

BAX WOULDN'T WAKE UP.

I hovered near his bedside, unwilling to leave. The doctor had removed the bullet two days ago, but Bax developed a fever shortly after. He'd thrashed and muttered, tortured by what sounded like childhood memories of torment and pain. My heart had ached for him as I struggled to keep him alive.

I forced water and broth down his throat. Bathed him in a cool cloth when the fever spiked, covered him when he shivered. Matty helped, but I did most of it by myself.

I would not let this man die.

Seeing my father shoot Bax in the back had been the most terrifying moment of my life. My scream brought Matty and two of Bax's men charging into my home. My father's face was deathly pale, like he couldn't believe he'd actually pulled the trigger, but no one paid him any attention. Not with Bax unconscious and bleeding on the floor.

We loaded Bax into his carriage, while one of the men raced to fetch the doctor. I held Bax's head in my lap as Matty pressed on his wound with a cloth, trying to stem the blood.

Bax's life dangled by a thread in those next few hours, and I vowed not to leave until he was better.

Finally the fever broke, and there was nothing to do but wait. I kept myself busy by listing my grievances toward him. Even though he couldn't hear me, it helped. I was still furious with him.

I must've fallen asleep because the softest brush of a fingertip across my cheek startled me awake. Where was I?

I straightened, memory rushing back. My eyes flew to his face—and I found him staring up at me. "Bax," I breathed, my chest expanding with relief. It was so good to see his sharp gaze once more.

"I'm sorry," he croaked.

An apology? I never thought to hear those words out of his mouth. Was he delirious? I felt his forehead. He was cool to the touch. "Please rest. You needn't talk right now."

He frowned and weakly gripped my hand. "I'm sorry, Belle."

"Bax, you nearly died. Do not overexert yourself."

"I'm sorry."

I bit my lip, torn between amusement and frustration. Then I reached for the water glass I had by his bed and helped him take a sip.

"I'm sorry," he repeated as I replaced the glass.

"You plan on continuing, I assume, until I acknowledge your apology."

"I'm—"

"Baxter!" I threw my hands up and let them fall in my lap. "Stop it. I hear you. Let me check your bandages."

I rose and leaned over the bed. Just as I peeled back his bandages to ensure the wound wasn't infected, he said, "Forgive me."

The hole was healing nicely, packed with some medicinal herbs that Matty swore worked on almost any injury. I replaced the bandage and sat down. "I appreciate the apology."

"Wanted to tell you . . . at your house. Before I was shot."

Two days, but it felt like a lifetime. "I heard you tell my father you love me." And that I was worth dying for, which couldn't be true. Yet he'd turned his back on his enemy, knowing there was a loaded pistol trained on him. "You also gave me the evidence you collected. I cannot believe you relented after all this time."

"I would . . . do anything for you."

"Just because you didn't ruin him doesn't mean you are absolved of wrong-doing."

"I'm sorry."

"Oh, sakes alive." I pushed off the chair and started pacing. "Don't say it again. It won't make any difference. I can't forgive you."

He struggled to sit up and winced. I rushed over and helped him back down to the mattress. "Stay still or else you'll reopen that wound."

"Have to . . . make you listen." Sweat dotted his forehead, his breath labored. "Please."

"I'm listening." I wiped his brow with a cool cloth. "I heard almost every word you said to my father."

"Belle, I need you."

Was he in pain? Uncomfortable? Hungry? I swept a lock of his hair off his face with my fingertips. "What is it? Do you need laudanum? Broth?"

"No, I need *you*. Here. Always."

My chest ached. Hurt and confusion battled with happiness over his declaration. And a big part of me wanted to stay. I loved this man, and nearly losing him showed me how precious our time was here on this Earth.

But I couldn't.

I had to decide what I wanted in life. Not what my father wanted or what Bax wanted. This was about *me*.

Nearly my whole existence had been spent alone, locked away. And both of the men I'd trusted had let me down. I couldn't rely on my judgment, clearly. I had to stand on my own, gain life experience, before attempting to trust anyone ever again.

"I can't." I choked out the words and stepped away from the bed.

His fingers fisted the coverlet, his body tensing. "Don't go. Please."

My heart squeezed. The agony in his expression shredded my insides, but I knew I was doing the right thing. I couldn't stay. And it was probably better to leave now, while he was still too weak to stop me.

A cowardly move, but Bax had a habit of kidnapping people.

I drank in his rough, beautiful features for the last time. No man would ever mean more to me. And though I was angry with him, I was also grateful. He'd shown me so much in our short time together.

Stepping closer, I bent and pressed my lips to his forehead. "Thank you. Because of you I want more for myself. Now I just need to figure out what *more* means."

He tried to grab my arm but didn't have the strength. "No, Belle. I can help."

"I don't want your help." Perhaps a tad harsh, but the words were true. "I have to do this on my own."

I could see the moment he shut me out. It was like a curtain descended over his expression. One second he was staring at me eagerly, desperately. Then his gaze became impersonal, with no hint of emotion. As if I were an inanimate object, like a piece of dust or a plant.

Then he shifted his head, looking away.

My hands shook with the need to touch him, but I kept perfectly still. This was for the best. Bax was going to live. He would continue his reign here in Hell's Kitchen, while I figured out the rest of my life. Perhaps our paths would cross again one day.

If only it didn't hurt so much.

Tongue thick, I whispered, "Be well, William."

He didn't acknowledge me, didn't even blink.

So I left.

On my way down the steps, I passed Matty. Whatever she saw in my face had her straightening off the wall. I licked my lips to moisten them. "He's awake. Fever's gone."

"You coming back?"

The backs of my eyelids burned as I shook my head. "Take care of him for me."

She squeezed my shoulder briefly before letting her hand drop. "I always do. You need anything, you know how to find me. And it can stay quiet."

I never expected such kindness from her, and I nearly started crying right then. "Thank you."

She went up the stairs toward the man I loved and I walked in the opposite direction. Toward the street.

Toward my uncertain future.

CHAPTER
FIFTEEN

Isabelle

Three months later

IT WAS strange to be on my own. Strange, but also exhilarating. My father and I hadn't spoken since I moved out of our Upper East Side home. I lived above my shop these days, and I loved it.

My shop.

Hard to believe, but the place was really mine. After fencing my jewelry, I had enough money to buy a small storefront and adjoining apartment. Then I put both parts of my plan into motion.

First, I approached a few modistes and asked them to let me sell some of their undergarments on consignment. As dresses were their true money items, most of them readily agreed to supply me with corsets, drawers, silk stockings, and the like. This gave me the inventory to open up the doors.

The second part of my plan would take a bit longer. When I had extra money, I would take my own designs back to the modistes and pay to have them made. These pieces would have a label under the store's own name: *Belle's.*

We were an instant success. I chose a space near both Ladies' Mile and the Tenderloin district, which gave me a wide clientele. Curious and daring uptown ladies shopped here, as well as flocks of dancers and actresses. And the working girls of the bordellos were some of our best customers.

Though I was busy, I still had time to think about Bax.

Had he moved on without me? Of course he had. Did I honestly think Billy Baxter was pining away for me? I didn't dare ask Matty when she occasionally stopped by to visit.

Regardless, it felt as if something was missing from my life. Or rather, someone. I just wasn't sure what to do about it.

Could I forgive him? I didn't know. As time went on, I wasn't as angry. Just hurt.

"No, I need you. Here. Always."

My lungs constricted and I pressed a hand to my chest. Sakes alive, I ached for him.

The bell above the door chimed and I left my office in the back to come out front. Matty was there, her expression flat and angry.

"Hello, Matty," I called.

She didn't greet me. Instead, she slapped a piece of paper on the counter. "You broke him."

My jaw fell, but I quickly recovered. "What are you talking about?"

"You fucking broke him, Belle. And I need you to fix him." She pushed the paper over. "Look at that."

I looked down and almost swallowed my tongue. "This can't be real."

"Oh, it's real. He's out on the campaign trail already."

I studied the advertisement, which was a very gentlemanly portrait of one William Baxter, candidate for the position of mayor. Of New York City.

I couldn't help it—I laughed. "This is absurd. He'll never get elected."

"You know who he's running against, yeah?"

My amusement died. Dan Kelly was the current front-runner in the mayoral election. I still possessed the evidence against my father, but I hadn't released it on the condition that he left the gangs alone. "Why is Bax doing this?"

"To win you back. To be worthy of you."

I locked eyes with her. Matty was deadly serious, unhappiness etched in the lines of her face. "That doesn't make any sense."

"He hasn't said as much, but I know what's going through his thick head. Belle, this"—she pointed to the paper—"is going to ruin everything and likely get us all killed."

I knew the gangs were territorial. Any sign of weakness was seen as an invitation for enemies to attack. "Is there a chance you're exaggerating?"

"No. The other gangs won't allow Bax to ascend to fucking royalty. It's one thing to have a politician or two in your pocket. It's another to have all the pockets and all the politicians at your disposal."

It would be unprecedented power in the city. Bax would control not only the underworld, but the political world, as well.

"Shit," I muttered.

That got her lips to twitch. "You've really taken to cursing in these last few months. I approve."

I shoved the paper toward her. "I don't know what you expect me to do."

"You have to talk to him. Convince him this is a bad idea. Take him back. Kiss and make up." She lifted the paper and shook it. "Because he will die if he pursues this."

"You say take him back as if that's an easy decision."

Bending, Matty rested her elbows on the counter. "Please. You named the place Belle's, after all. Those dark circles under your eyes haven't let up, even when the store started to turn a profit. You've lost at least fifteen pounds. Maybe more, the way your dresses hang off you. When will you admit you miss him, for Christ's sake?"

Damn. Why must this woman be so perceptive?

I lifted my shoulders. "If he won't listen to you, then he certainly won't listen to me."

"Wrong. You're the only person who convince him he's worthy exactly as he is."

"I don't see how—"

"He's miserable and he loves you," she repeated softly. "This is a last-ditch effort to win you back. Even if it's just to tell him it won't work, go and talk to him, please."

Was I ready to see him? A strange flutter erupted behind my sternum. I was still angry with him, of course, but the idea of losing Bax was intolerable. It would destroy me if something bad happened to him.

Because I'm still in love with him.

I ignored that inner voice, the one getting louder and louder by the day. But this wasn't about a future with Bax. This was about keeping him from making a huge mistake.

And I had to find a way to make him listen.

An idea came to me then. A very wicked idea. I grinned at Matty, the first real smile I'd given in months. "I need your help."

———

Baxter

I came awake slowly, my mind filled with cotton. Had I been shot again? I remembered leaving the campaign office last night—

Shit! I'd been jumped from behind by four or five men and forced into a carriage. They must've drugged me, because everything else was a fog.

I tried to move, but my arms and legs were held tight. I was trapped, tied to a chair. I tried to stay calm. Panicking never solved a damn thing. Where the fuck was I?

The room was dark, with no windows to offer light of any kind. I squinted, trying to see if someone was there. When I got loose I would beat every one of these sons of bitches to death.

Twisting my wrists, I tried to get free. I gritted my teeth as the rope dug into my skin. Goddamn it. These were tied with no give whatsoever. Matty was the only person I knew who could tie ropes so well.

The door opened and the light switched on. I blinked, unable to see. "I'm gonna to get free and slice you into little pieces," I growled at the shadowy figure by the door.

"I certainly hope not."

I froze, my heart leaping into my throat. That voice. It couldn't be.

My eyes finally adjusted. It was her. *Isabelle.*

God almighty, she was gorgeous. A navy dress hugged her curves, soft wisps of blond hair framing her face. My tongue dried out as her gaze locked with mine. I felt the impact of those blue eyes down to my toes.

"Hello, Bax."

The sound of her voice hollowed out my stomach. "Isabelle."

She folded her arms across her chest and cocked her head. "Tell me why."

"Why what?"

"Why you're running for mayor."

I hadn't seen her in months and this was what she wished to discuss? "As soon as you tell me why you've kidnapped me and tied me to a chair."

"I want to know why, Bax."

"Why not?" I shrugged as best as I could, being tied to a chair and all. "If your father can do it, anyone certainly can."

"He's been a city employee for years. And as far as Manhattan is concerned, he has a sterling reputation."

"You think I won't win."

"I think you're trying to prove something."

"Sure." I huffed a dry laugh. "That I have enough money for campaign bribes."

"Bax," she sighed and closed the distance between us. "We both know you're trying to prove you're good enough."

My back stiffened. "I don't need to prove a damn thing." A lie, but I'd never admit it.

Now she was before me, and it was the worst kind of torture to have her this close and not be able to touch her. "Are you going to untie me now?"

"No, not until you come to your senses."

I didn't wish to discuss politics with her. I'd missed her so fucking much. I studied the delicate features of her face. I knew every freckle, every curve. She looked thinner, but still beautiful.

"There's no reason to run for mayor," she continued. "You don't need to prove anything to the world. Look at how far you've come."

And it still wasn't enough to keep her.

"There's always higher to climb," I said.

"Running for mayor will get you killed."

I inhaled, trying to catch a hint of her sweet scent. "Probably."

"I can't let you do that."

"Why?"

I waited for her to say more, but the silence stretched. My heart fell.

It wasn't enough. She didn't love me or want to stay with me. And why would she? Our past could never be undone—and that was my fault.

Clenching my jaw, I struggled uselessly against the bindings. *Matty and her fucking knots.* "I appreciate your concern. I'll be fine. Now, untie me."

"Do not dare get angry with me, William. You have no right whatsoever."

I could feel my protective walls crumbling, all the built-up anger and misery leaking out. "I confessed my love and apologized. I begged you to stay. And you left!"

She pointed her finger at me. "You know why I left. You kidnapped my father. You lied to me." She drew in a deep breath and let it out. "You hurt me."

"And I'm fucking sorry for that, Isabelle. So damn much. I know you'll never be able to forgive me—and it rips my heart out, woman."

"Oh, Bax." She sighed heavily. "In some ways, I'm grateful."

I wasn't sure I heard right. "Grateful?"

"I was living a lie. I thought my father was a paragon, a crusader who would change the city. It made his ignoring me easier to tolerate. I accepted it, did whatever he said. I was the perfect daughter."

"You're still perfect," I pointed out.

Her expression softened. "There was once a princess, locked in a tower. She lived a lonely life until a brave knight came to set her free. He gave her the gift of independence."

Her skirts brushed the tips of my shoes as she leaned in and placed her palms on my bound chest. What was happening? I licked my lips, the need for her swelling, clawing inside me. "The knight didn't do that. The princess did it all on her own."

"Well, he helped. And do not disparage the man I fell in love with."

My heart tripped over itself. "Love?"

"Love," she confirmed with a nod of her head. "I fell in love with a gangster. But he's more than just a thug. He's loyal and smart, so very brave. And he would do anything for me."

"Absolutely anything. Just fucking ask, sweetheart."

"Drop out of this silly mayoral race."

"Done. Now, untie me." I needed to touch her in the worst way.

Instead, she bit her lip and slid onto my lap. My body instantly responded to the feel of her soft curves.

Her fingers tangled in my hair. "That was easy. And here I thought you wouldn't listen. I was worried that you'd moved on."

Was she cracked? The words tumbled from my mouth. "There is no moving on from you, widow. I'm drowning without you, but I can't feel it. I can't feel anything."

"I miss you, too. Very much."

I forced the words out, though I feared I might be wrong. "Does this mean you're giving me another chance?"

She rested her forehead against my jaw. "Are your kidnapping days behind you?"

"When it comes to you and your family, yes."

She threw her head back and laughed. "You're impossible."

"If you're hoping to redeem me, I will disappoint you."

"I don't want to redeem you, William. I want to love you."

Jesus, those were the sweetest words I'd ever heard. I kissed her temple. "Oh sweetheart. I'm going to spend the rest of my life making you happy. Every day. You'll never regret it."

She hummed and shifted on my lap. The friction sent fresh waves of sparks through my blood. She said, "I wish you had been honest with me from the start."

"From now on, I will be."

"You'd best mind that promise, Bax. Because I really will shoot you this time if you don't."

I couldn't help but grin. My bloodthirsty girl. "I hope you do."

She patted my chest. "Then this means I'm yours and you're mine."

"And you'll come live with me in Hell's Kitchen, yeah?"

"Eventually." She ran a finger along my jaw. I shivered, the light touch driving me out of my skull.

"Untie me, widow. Right the fuck now."

"I don't think so. I like having you at my mercy."

"I need to get my hands on you. Please, Belle."

"I'd much rather show you the undergarments I wore just for you."

More blood rushed between my legs, and my cock went rigid. I couldn't move, and yet I liked this game we were playing.

I put my lips close to her ear. "You gonna be a good girl for me and put on a show?"

"Let's call it research for the store, shall we?" Climbing off my lap, she moved to stand in front of me. "Would you like to see the drawers or the corset first?"

"The drawers," I instantly answered.

"Then I think I'll start with the corset."

I groaned and closed my eyes. "You brought me here to torture me."

"Indeed, I did. It's nothing less than you deserve. Watch carefully, darling."

The endearment caught me by surprise, the result like an electric charge to my blood. "Goddamn it. Hurry, woman."

She unfastened her bodice slowly, methodically, and I clenched my teeth to keep from snarling at her to go faster. I was dying for her. Starving. I didn't know how much more I could take. By the time her bare arms emerged, I was breathing hard.

The corset cover was pale pink, a delicate scrap of nearly transparent fabric. She removed it like she had all the time in the world, the vixen.

"Belle," I snarled.

"Patience, William."

She placed the cover on the chair, where the bodice rested. When she stood, I got a look at the corset. Black silk edged in pink, the dark fabric a perfect contrast to her milky skin. Her tits were pressed high and tight, begging for my mouth.

"*Fuuuck.*" I groaned and tried to free myself once more.

Her lips twisted with a secret smile as her fingers started on the ties of her skirts. I wasn't going to last through all the layers. It was awful, sitting here watching when I could be touching her.

I could torture her, too.

"I love you so much, sweetheart," I said in a low, seductive tone. "I'm going to make you so goddamn happy. Every morning I'll wake you up with my mouth between your legs, feasting on your pussy. You like that, don't you? When I tongue your cunt?"

She exhaled shakily and the ties in her fingers knotted. She quickly got them undone. "Stop distracting me."

I didn't miss how fast she was breathing, the flush to her skin. "Then, after you come, I'll slide my cock inside you a little at a time. So you can really feel it, yeah?"

The outer skirt fell to the floor. She moved faster on the petticoat. *Good.*

I kept up a stream of erotic conversation until she was down to her drawers. Black, just like the corset. Just like my soul. Yeah, she would fit in fine with me in Hell's Kitchen.

"Get over here," I growled.

"Do you like them?"

"I fucking love them. They're perfect, just like you." I rolled my wrists again, trying to get free. "Now, come straddle my lap and take out my cock, Belle. I want to show you how much I missed you."

She bit her lip and came toward me, her tops of breasts bouncing above the corset. "You are quite bossy for a man who broke my heart."

Guilt lanced through me. "I'm sorry, sweetheart. You can torture me as long as you want."

"That's better." Now standing before me, she slipped her fingers into the slit of her drawers.

Then she rubbed herself and moaned.

My mouth fell open. *Christ.* She really was going to torture me.

Her lids fell closed. "Every time I did this I thought of you."

I couldn't do this. I wasn't strong enough. Writhing against the ropes, I begged, "Have mercy on me, widow. I'm dying here. For God's sake, please."

"You'll never lie to me again?"

"No, I swear it."

She kept circling her clit. "And you won't get shot again?"

"I'll do my best, sweetheart."

"Good, because I have no wish to become a true widow."

I froze. Was she saying . . .?

I licked my lips. "I want to marry you. I want you at my side every second of every day. You are the air I breathe and the blood in my veins. I'll spend my life giving you the fucking world, if you let me."

Expression softening, she came over to stand mere inches away. She slipped her fingers into my mouth, the same fingers that had been stroking her clit. The musky flavor of her pussy flooded my senses and I moaned, sucking on her skin. My God, this woman.

"I don't need the world," she whispered, taking her fingers away. "I just need you." She threw one leg over my lap.

"You have me, sweetheart. Now fuck me and put me out of my misery, yeah?"

The End.

ALSO BY JOANNA SHUPE

Fifth Avenue Rebels:

The Heiress Hunt

The Lady Gets Lucky

The Bride Goes Rogue

The Duke Gets Even

The Uptown Girls:

The Rogue of Fifth Avenue

The Prince of Broadway

The Devil of Downtown

The Four Hundred Series:

A Daring Arrangement

A Scandalous Deal

A Notorious Vow

The Knickerbocker Club:

Tycoon

Magnate

Baron

Mogul

Wicked Deceptions:

The Courtesan Duchess

The Harlot Countess

The Lady Hellion

Novellas:

ABOUT THE AUTHOR

USA Today bestselling author **Joanna Shupe** has always loved history, ever since she saw her first Schoolhouse Rock cartoon. Since 2015, her books have appeared on numerous yearly "best of" lists, including *Publishers Weekly*, *The Washington Post*, *Kirkus Reviews*, Kobo, and BookPage.

Sign up for Joanna's <u>Gilded Lilies Newsletter</u> for book news, sneak peeks, reading recommendations, historical tidbits, and more!

www.joannashupe.com

www.ingramcontent.com/pod-product-compliance
Lightning Source LLC
Chambersburg PA
CBHW070656010826
48975CB00014B/1727